the

human

a novel

chris fenwick

New Kingstown, Pennsylvania
www.sunburypress.com

the 100ᵗʰ human

FIRST PAPERBACK EDITION
Printed in the United States of America
June 2006

Library of Congress Control Number: 2006920284

ISBN 0-9760925-5-7

Published by:

Sunbury Press, Inc.
P.O. Box 178
New Kingstown, PA 17072-0178
www.sunburypress.com

For Erin, Alex and Gralyn
my children, my teachers

ACKNOWLEDGEMENTS

This book would not exist without input and support from my life partner, best friend and editor extraordinaire, Wynne Kinder. You have helped to create an environment of love, peace and positive encouragement - the absolute best place from which to write and create. I can not thank you enough; this book is yours as much as it is mine.

I also would like to thank my daughter, Erin, for her encouragement and fresh perspective as an editor. Your life continually demonstrates your determination to understand and live the keys.

Many, many thanks go to Larry Berger-Knorr, a true friend, business partner and editor. Few opinions have I ever trusted more.

Also, a very heart-felt thanks to Christen Coscia. Your input made the book so much the better.

I want to convey a warm thank you to my family, especially to my son Alex, for never wavering in his belief in me as a writer, even when I doubted myself.

Finally, I must thank my mentors, Deepak Chopra and Wayne Dyer. I have been inspired, mesmerized, encouraged and have grown from your books and your examples. Thank you for your continual commitment to Life, Happiness and Human Enlightenment.

PREFACE

Many people are familiar with the story of The Hundredth Monkey. It has been told many times and cited in various books and magazines. Just in case this legend is new to you, I have included Ken Keyes, Jr.'s version below. Please read the "Author's Notes" for my personal ideas concerning this story and the premise as a whole.

The Hundredth Monkey

by Ken Keyes, Jr.

The Japanese monkey, Macaca fuscata, had been observed in the wild for a period of over 30 years.

In 1952, on the island of Koshima, scientists were providing monkeys with sweet potatoes dropped in the sand. The monkeys liked the taste of the raw sweet potatoes, but they found the dirt unpleasant.

An 18-month-old female named Imo found she could solve the problem by washing the potatoes in a nearby stream. She taught this trick to her mother. Her playmates also learned this new way and they taught their mothers too.

This cultural innovation was gradually picked up by various monkeys before the eyes of the scientists.

Between 1952 and 1958 all the young monkeys learned to wash the sandy sweet potatoes to make them more palatable.

Only the adults who imitated their children learned this social improvement. Other adults kept eating the dirty sweet potatoes.

Then something startling took place. In the autumn of 1958, a certain number of Koshima monkeys were washing sweet potatoes -- the exact number is not known.

Let us suppose that when the sun rose one morning there were 99 monkeys on Koshima Island who had learned to wash their sweet potatoes.

Let's further suppose that later that morning, the hundredth monkey learned to wash potatoes.

THEN IT HAPPENED!

By that evening almost everyone in the tribe was washing sweet potatoes before eating them.

The added energy of this hundredth monkey somehow created an ideological breakthrough!

But notice.

A most surprising thing observed by these scientists was that the habit of washing sweet potatoes then jumped over the sea --

Colonies of monkeys on other islands and the mainland troop of monkeys at Takasakiyama began washing their sweet potatoes.

Thus, when a certain critical number achieves an awareness, this new awareness may be communicated from mind to mind.

Although the exact number may vary, this Hundredth Monkey Phenomenon means that when only a limited number of people know of a new way, it may remain the conscious property of these people.

But there is a point at which if only one more person tunes-in to a new awareness, a field is strengthened so that this awareness is picked up by almost everyone!

(This is an excerpt from the book "The Hundredth Monkey" by Ken Keyes, Jr. The book is not copyrighted and the material may be reproduced in whole or in part. You can refer to the whole book in its entirety at http://www.wowzone.com/monkey.htm.)

Part 1

"The only reason for time is so that everything doesn't happen at once."

--Albert Einstein

Chapter 1

December 10, 2012

Apu stumbled along the rough terrain as he struggled up the hill in the dark. His lantern in one hand rocked unsteadily back and forth. This was partly due to his haste and partly due to the intermittent tremors following the earthquake. Everything was unstable; the Earth herself was rumbling and groaning as if she were wide awake and angry. Panting, Apu clawed at the stones with his free hand. As he slowly made his way up to the mouth of the cave, his mind raced imagining what he might find.

Apu knew he should not be surprised by the earthquake. This part of Mexico was squeezed by the Cocos, Caribbean and North American tectonic plates, which are both being swallowed by the North American tectonic plate. He knew these plates move very slowly, barely nudging each other. A nudge sounds gentle enough and as far as real movement, it is only miniscule, but for the inhabitants on the surface, those nudges can be cataclysmic. All in all it made for a volatile environment. There were rumbles all the time, daily in fact, but nothing compared to what Apu had just experienced. His hut had shaken so hard that the thatched roof had caved in. Fortunately, he had raced out the door just in time, as he hurried across the small clearing to check on Jack.

The maelstrom around him was deafening, made more acute by the darkness. He could not see them in the dark, but Apu knew trees were snapping and crashing into each other in the surrounding jungle. The ground beneath them was shaking and groaning at a deafening pitch. Mountain rocks and dirt fell all around, spraying the valley where they camped with small boulders, smaller stones and dirt.

Apu had thrown open the wood plank door to Jack's hut. In the dark, he could not see if Jack was there, but he knew the general vicinity of the cot. His short legs stumbled over something lying on the floor. He realized as he caught himself, it was Jack's boots. When he reached the cot, he found Jack in a deep sleep. After unsuccessfully trying to rouse him, Apu desperately grabbed the corners of the mattress and pulled it and the occupant off the cot. Jack stirred and groaned, but did not wake. Apu strained as he dragged the mattress, and Jack's large frame, out of the hut to what he felt would be relative safety. He knew Jack wouldn't wake up, and there was no time to waste. He touched Jack's shoulder in a gesture of hope. Without looking back, Apu grabbed his lantern and headed for the mountain.

Apu's thick black hair was dripping with sweat. His headway up the mountain was slowed by the now unstable terrain. Apu knew why Jack would not wake up. He had celebrated too much the night before. They had just received additional funding from The National Science Foundation. Even though their discovery of an ancient Mayan mural was not difficult to excavate, they had been running short on cash. This money would be invaluable.

Preliminary tests on the mural had placed the time of it's creation at circa 1000 AD, some time after the climax of the Maya culture, yet there was no mistaking it to be Mayan. Jack Reese, the team's leader and Professor of Anthropology at the University of Michigan specializing in Mayan culture, had taken a much deserved break to celebrate their good fortune. Apu Chohan - anthropology grad student from India and Jack's right hand, and Carlos Vejar, a Mexican national, had been up late into the night. Apu had drunk a little less than the others, preferring wine to the swills of heavy liquor that were being exchanged. His less than "party animal" approach had paid off more than once. He now hoped it would again.

What if the quake caused the cave to collapse? What if their find was now buried beneath tons of dirt and rock? How would they unearth it again? Could they get more funding for such a monumental excavation? He doubted it. Though it was in amazing shape and clarity, and the date of its creation was intriguing, money for archeological investigations had become scarcer in the current political climate. Apu knew it would be filed as just another Mayan artifact buried in the jungle. Apu's stomach flip flopped inside of him as he slipped on loose dirt, nearly letting go of the lantern in the process. The thought of losing this find made him worry in a way he could not explain. It was more than losing the last two months of hard work. No, there was something about those bizarre symbols that plagued Apu's mind, as if he knew what they meant, but couldn't remember.

To the far left of the mural, there were hieroglyphs that were unlike any he or Jack had ever seen or studied. He had been up nights trying to decipher the glyphs. Something about them made him very uncomfortable. He pushed himself harder up the unstable surface of the mountainside towards the entrance. Slipping and sliding, he ignored the cuts and bruises he knew he was getting along the way.

Trying to understand the feeling in his gut, Apu arrived at the mouth of the cave. There were rocks, large clumps of dirt and branches in the way but with some effort, Apu was certain he could clear a way into the cave. He steadied the lantern on a rock and began to push and pull aside the debris, layer upon layer. Fatigue was setting in as Apu grew more anxious. When he was finally able to crawl through a small opening, ducking his head and shoulders, he scraped his neck and back on top of the opening. He entered The Cave to the Underworld, as named by Jack. The Maya believed such caves were portals to their gods.

Inside the cave, which wasn't much larger than his hut, a relieved Apu pushed his glasses up on his nose, as he saw the mural. It appeared to be intact. The shoring braces they had placed about had helped retain the ancient walls. One had cracked and was leaning against the opposite wall, but the others were still vertical and holding. Standing just inside the opening, Apu could see, though his glasses were speckled with dust and sweat, that there were some areas where the ceiling had crumbled; rubble littering the cave's uneven floor. The odor was unchanged, old and musty, with a slight metallic tinge in the air. Trying not to step on anything of value, Apu carefully navigated over the rubble towards the cave's back wall, where the mural remained. In spite of his exertion from coming up the hill, Apu's breathing suspended in anticipation at what he might see.

At first glance, The Cave to the Underworld's prize possession seemed intact. Standing back a bit to view the whole mural while holding the lantern up high, his eyes began to scan from right side of the mural to the left. Something wasn't quite right, even in this light. Apu knew every inch and nuance of the wall. For two months Jack, Carlos and he had spent hour upon hour clearing, cleaning, exposing, photographing and documenting this mural. Apu adjusted his glasses and elevated the lantern as shadows leaped about the cave. He shivered. The odd symbols at the far left were no longer undamaged. Apu's large dark brown eyes looked down at the ground where pieces of the symbols had broken off and fallen to the floor of the cave. He could just make out the colored particles scattered on the cave floor. The remains were now not much larger than dust. Apu stepped closer to the spot, trying to avoid stepping on any of the pieces. As he got closer he noticed a faint glow coming through cracks in the mural. The

hair on the back of his neck stood on end and his increasingly shallow
breath caught in his throat. His face was now only inches from the wall,
his nose nearly touching it. Apu tried to figure out what was causing
the illumination. Just then he lost his footing. The lantern crashed into
the wall precisely where the symbols were disintegrating. Instantly,
what was left of the symbols disappeared. They simply fell away,
vanishing into powder and small crumbs further littering the cave's
floor. Horrified, he gasped as he struggled to regain his balance.

      Apu stood staring at the wall in disbelief, amazed at what he
saw. In that moment, he forgot how angry Jack would be for causing
part of the mural to crumble. He forgot how he may have forever
erased a piece of the mysterious ancient painting. He just stood there,
mouth agape, frozen for what seemed like hours, though it was merely
seconds. Then in a blink, Apu inhaled deeply, swung around, scrambled
out of the cave and shot all the way down the mountain as fast as he
could without tumbling.

Chapter 2

December 10, 2012

Apu reached the camp, huffing and puffing from combined excitement and exhaustion. He rushed over to Jack who was now sitting on his cot, his curly blond head in his hands, looking miserable and confused. Stammering, Apu tried to explain what had happened. Realizing he was getting nowhere with his explanation to the recovering drunk; he gave up. He pulled on Jack's arm and bade him to follow him up the mountain to see for himself. Jack swayed a little as his long body attempted to stand up. After regaining his balance he followed Apu's lead. The pace was much slower this time. Repeatedly, Apu had to stop and wait for Jack to catch up. He could see, upon looking into Jack's bloodshot green eyes, he was in some pain; one hell of a headache, he guessed.

Finally, Apu and Jack both stood side by side, surveying the damage. They both gazed at the glowing jade that had been hidden behind the now cracked and crumbling outer painting; the mural they had once valued so deeply.

For some time, Apu had to admit, they just stared, taking in the beauty and magnificence of what was peeking out at them. He could hardly believe their luck. If the earthquake had not occurred, they may never have found such a prize.

Apu recalled the exact moment of discovery. As he had leaned in closer, trying to discern the source of the glow, he realized it was a huge piece of jade deeply embedded in the stone behind the crumbling symbols. When the lantern had crashed into the outer mural, he could see that the large glowing green bauble was part of a much larger relief and a whole new set of symbols.

Now, it was obvious that the mural they had been studying for the last two months was only a veneer, albeit beautiful and fascinating, it paled in comparison to what they faced. As an enchanting woman undressing, the Earth had shaken off her outer garments to reveal an even more alluring and mysterious essence beneath.

After contemplation and discussion they decided that they must see more of what lay behind the entirety of the mural, the layer

Jack soon referred to as the "faux artifact". They had, after all, already sufficiently documented the external mural.

They worked with great care to remove the outer mural in large pieces, to preserve its beauty and value. No matter what its purpose or origin, it was still very old and full of stories. However, each time they attempted to excavate it in large pieces – regardless of the methods of preservation, it crumbled. It was amazing how something could survive unscathed for so many generations including the recent earthquake, and now so easily just disintegrate into dust. It was as if the mural itself knew it had fulfilled its purpose and was tired, ready to return to the earth from whence it came. At the end of a very long day, the two men had only successfully saved two pieces unbroken. One was hand-size, only 4 by 6 inches. The other was a little larger, measuring 15 by 28 inches in size.

That night as they slept outside on cots, their huts were still being repaired by Carlos, they both dreamed of the strange and fantastic jewel-studded wall-size relief that now totally took ownership of the cave and their imaginations. The whole of it was a beautiful set of pictures and glyphs, all intertwined into a grand relief etched into stone. In various places embedded into the wall there were stones of sparkling jade and obsidian. The work was so fantastic; its essence seemed other-worldly. Apu had seen and studied many ancient Mayan relics, beautiful and majestic, but he had never felt the awe that this bejeweled wall had inspired in his very soul. Many would argue that it was simply the romance of discovering it that brought him such a sensation. But Apu knew it was more than that. For one thing, not since his grandfather died two years ago, had Apu sensed his presence so profoundly as today. He felt his grandfather was trying to tell him something. He wasn't sure what it meant, but his grandfather was in his dreams that night, standing in front of what Jack had *now* named, *Pared Secreto* - Secret Wall.

* *

December 11, 2012

The next morning when Apu awoke, Jack was already up. Jack was dressed in his normal khaki bush pants, boots and one of many Exofficio shirts. He and Carlos were getting coffee and making plans to finish the repairs to the huts. Jack was going to stay behind this morning to help Carlos. Sleeping outside, even with the mosquito

netting had not spared him from a restless night and many bites. Apu
suspected it was more than the mosquitoes that kept Jack up. Apu was
tasked to begin the documentation process in the cave. He didn't mind.
He washed up, got some coffee and headed up the hill, toting his
camera and equipment. He worked in the cave all day, only taking a
short break to eat the lunch that Carlos had delivered in the early
afternoon. Jack had joined him just after lunch and the two worked
until late into the day.

  As evening approached, the sun began its slow decent into the
western sky behind the Sierra Del Norte de Chiapas casting long
shadows over the valley. As it did, their campsite seemed to grow in
size. They had both just hiked the trail down the side of the mountain
toward the camp. The late afternoon sun as it beat down on the back
of Apu's neck was a welcomed contrast to the cool, musty cave in
which he had spent the day. He had taken picture after digital picture
and meticulously mapped the dimensions and markings of their
newfound and appropriately named treasure - the Secreto Muro.

  The relief was a full twelve feet wide, while reaching five and a
half feet tall. The design was clearly Mayan, with intricate and
interlocking pictures obviously telling a complex tale, though they
didn't know what the story was yet; they were excited to find out.
There were many dates recorded in typical Mayan style. In several key
places jewels were embedded in the stone, as eyes or as part of a
headdress or payment as offerings to their gods. It truly was
magnificent and mystical. The mystical aspects included two new sets
of strange and unique symbols.

  These were most fascinating and also the most troubling. They
just didn't look like the rest of the etchings; in fact they looked quite
out of place, almost foreign. One set was much different from the
other, quite unfamiliar and odd. The other set was equally strange but
more familiar, nearly recognizable but shrouded at the same time –
pictures within pictures. Apu and Jack puzzled over both of them,
coming back to them again and again. They hoped that when they were
able to decipher the known Mayan glyphs, these unknown symbols and
their meanings would become clear. The whole of it became a beautiful
secret waiting to reveal itself to them.

  Without a word to each other, both were working on the
puzzles in their own minds, wondering what secrets to the Maya society
and their civilization would be revealed. Apu was pretty skilled at
interpreting Mayan glyphs; Jack was only moderately good. Each of

them were personalizing the hunt for the answers. Each had their own motivation and it seemed that those symbols, whether sacred or not, were having a profound effect on both men. Their brains were buzzing with thoughts and curious energy, as if a low sounding gong had been hit and the vibration continued to cause their nerves to whirl and murmur. This same vibration was being felt by others, people neither Jack nor Apu knew, at least not yet.

When they reached camp that afternoon, Carlos was preparing food in the mess tent and a fire was already roaring in the pit. Jack sat down on a chair and announced, to Apu's surprise, that he would be going into town the next day. Their new distraction had allowed them to get dangerously low on supplies. The earthquake had changed many aspects of their lives.

Chapter 3

December 11, 2012

The adrenaline of a once in a lifetime find had worn off some for Jack, now in its place – a mixture of excitement and anxiety. He didn't understand why he felt so protective. His mind kept going over the imagery of their new discovery again and again. There was so much they didn't understand, so much to work out. He sat looking into the fire, it had only been a day since the earthquake had occurred and this new mystery had entered his life. They needed help - that was for sure. The symbols were complicated, much more than he or Apu could ever decipher alone. They needed an epigrapher, a scholar who specialized in ancient inscriptions, symbols and glyphs, preferably a Mayan epigrapher. He searched his memory for the few people around the world who would qualify. He could conjure up only two. He knew one had recently died and he knew the other was in Egypt engrossed in another ancient people's hieroglyphs.

Jack thought of Max McMillan, a lingual anthropologist at Tulane University. Jack had known Max for some time and trusted him. Max would be helpful, he was sure, even if he wasn't exactly what they needed. This job required an expert. Jack was confident that Max could refer him to the right person. He'd place the call tomorrow, when he went into Ocosingo for the much-needed supplies.

As Jack continued to stare into the fire, he suddenly recalled an article in *Current Anthropology* magazine centered on Alana Borisenko. Jack jumped up and rushed to his hut, rummaged through some papers in the bottom of his trunk and found the magazine. He had met Alana Borisenko two years earlier at a conference in Southern California. She was brilliant; undoubtedly an expert in Mayan epigraphy. Her breadth of knowledge of Mayan glyphs, in addition to her fluency in a multitude of other ancient languages and writing systems, was impressive, to say the least. He had tried to steal a moment with her at the conference, but she had been flanked by colleagues and he was already scheduled to return home that afternoon. He had thought about writing to her afterwards, but never got around to it. On the first leg of his flight here to Mexico, he was milling around the airport shops, when he saw her name on the magazine's cover. He was immediately intrigued. He bought the magazine and threw it into his bag. The flight had been long but was filled with other plans and details; he had forgotten about Alana until just now.

He scanned the article by firelight looking for the details of where she was working these days. To his delight, he discovered that she was in Mexico; at least she had been when the article was written, two months prior. She was listed as working at the *Museo Nacional de Antropología*, National Museum of Anthropology in Mexico City. The article stated that she was investigating and recording similarities between stones found at the new Monte Alban site and some older Olmec stones. There was no mention about the duration of this assignment. Jack decided he'd try and call her tomorrow. If she were indeed still in Mexico, he would jump through hoops to entice her to take a look at their amazing new mystery. It seemed to be right up her alley, he thought, as he read the remainder of the article.

That night Jack dreamed of Mayas guarding the door to the cave while someone or something else hid inside; a bright glow shined out from its narrow doorway. He tried to see what was causing the glow but was unable to see anything more. Just before he woke up; he could have sworn that he heard the faint sound of an infant crying. When he was fully awake, he realized it was a dream. His emotions were swirling near the surface. He had a new, heightened sense of responsibility towards this discovery, the Secreto Muro, as he had named it. This dream was dramatically different from the dreams or nightmares that reoccurred nearly every night for Jack.

* *

December 12, 2012

The next morning Jack got up early, dressed and threw his bag into the back of the jeep. He thought of trekking up the mountain to see the relief one more time before he left for town, but knew he had to get on the road early. It was a two hour drive to Ocosingo. He lumbered over to the mess tent and got a cup of strong coffee from Carlos. Carlos had been hired as a guide and gofer, but he had quickly become a true friend. Jack grabbed some food and threw two large water bottles into the jeep as well. Somewhere during his preparations, Apu stumbled in, joining the men for coffee. Jack could tell Apu had not gotten enough sleep; he wasn't his normal chipper self. "What time did you finally give up last night?" Jack inquired.

"Not sure, sometime after 3 a.m." Apu replied.

"Any luck?"

"The part that is closer to classic Mayan hieroglyphs, I'm still working on, but the other stuff - I have no idea."

"Well, I'm off to get us some help with that," offered Jack. "You just keep working on what you can decipher."

"Okay. Hey, would you mail this letter for me?"

"You aren't advertising our find are you?" Jack didn't know why he said that. Low-level paranoia must have set in.

Apu's brow lifted at Jack's suggestion, "It's to my parents."

"Of course," Jack just shrugged it off as he took the letter, put it in his pocket and got up to go.

"When do you think you'll be back?" Apu followed him out to the jeep.

"Around dark, if everything goes well and it doesn't take too long to get Carlos' supplies." He announced the last part loud enough for Carlos to hear, as he waved the long list in the air. He was giving Carlos a hard time. Jack laughed, he knew they needed the supplies but was anxious to get back as soon as possible.

"See you tonight and be careful," Apu said as Jack climbed behind the wheel. This time it was Jack's turn to raise his eyebrows. Apu had never told him to be careful before - ever. In that moment there was an understanding that passed between the two men. Everything was different now, though neither one could conceive of how or why.

"Yep," was all Jack said in reply, as he started the engine and took off down the bumpy dirt road toward the closest town.

Chapter 4

December 12, 2012

Jack arrived in Ocosingo stiff and sore, from miles of rough
dirt roads, half washed out and half covered in new debris from the
recent earthquake. All of this had taken a toll on him. He had stopped
once to get out, stretch his legs and pop his back. After only a few
moments and a couple swigs of water, his stomach clenched with
apprehension. He jumped back into the jeep and took off again. While
driving, he ate the sandwiches Carlos had packed for him. He knew he
should be excited and he was, but there was an anticipation, an
apprehension; of what he wasn't quite sure. He just knew he needed to
hurry, and that he did, at least as well as he could on the roads.

As Jack navigated the bumpy terrain, he began to think of how
life seldom turns out the way you expect. He was raised in a middle
class working family, where his parents had taught him the value of
hard work. Jack Reese Sr. seemed to have simple aspirations and was
contented to work hard, putz around the house, watch baseball and
take care of his family. He was a computer programmer and worked for
one of the more stable companies of that time. Jack's mother, Charlotte
Reese, was a kind woman who also seemed very content in her
Midwestern middle-class life as wife, mother and part-time real estate
agent. Both of his parents had encouraged him and his older brother
Jerry, also a computer programmer, to pursue any path that inspired
them, to work hard and put family first. Jack had always tried to follow
their example. He was fascinated with ancient history and civilizations
from an early age, thanks to a wonderful 10th grade teacher at Seaholm
High School in Birmingham, Michigan. It was there that he had
discovered Anthropology. Mr. Rafferty had always wanted to be an
archaeologist, but his children had come along earlier than planned, and
he had settled quite skillfully into teaching. But he always offered an
Anthropology elective course to 10th graders in contrast to his regular
World History. Mr. Rafferty not only gave Jack an outlet and direction
for his interest in ancient peoples, but also inspired him to teach. John
Rafferty made the job look easy and had one of those rare personalities.
He didn't mind the kids teasing him about his own excitement, because
he knew they would catch it too.

After high school, Jack went on to study at the University of Michigan, in Ann Arbor. It was there that he had met the woman who was to become his wife. Mary was beautiful, smart and funny. They married while Jack was in grad school and she stuck with him through the grueling study sessions and the long periods away while he was doing field work. In the end, a relieved and exhausted Jack finally earned his doctorate. Jumping right back into work, he accepted a position as an Adjunct Assistant Professor at U. of M. and had focused his research on the religious movements in Mexico. After a little more than three years, and several publications, he was promoted to Associate Professor and later to full Professor, where he has thrived ever since.

His interest in the Maya came during his junior year at the university. Again, a teacher was responsible for affecting the direction of his life. Dr. Marcus had taught a class on early complex societies. The idea of not really knowing what had happened to such a vast civilization as the Maya was indeed a mystery, one that caught Jack's imagination then and even more intensely now. Jack was intrigued by the idea that the ancient Maya had the mathematical concept of zero. This was something rare in ancient civilizations. The Maya may have had this advanced concept long before Western civilization and perhaps even before the Arabs.

As fascinating as they were, the Maya were still second to family and when Mary became pregnant, Jack was completely filled with joy. His son, Jack Reese III, was born October 28, 2009. He was healthy and beautiful. Mary had done an amazing job. The whole adventure of pregnancy and the baby's birth had left Jack not only with the love of his life, but also with a sense of awe regarding the process of birth and true miracle of life. He was a completely happy man then, fulfilled in every way he could imagine. Of course, that was all before his life went to hell in a hand basket; before horrible tragedy struck and made him question everything.

January 14, 2010, that was the day his life would be forever altered. The details of that morning were irrevocably etched into his mind, though at some point afterward, most would become a blur. He had gotten up early - 5 am, his usual time to rise. He had put on his running clothes, his favorite gray sweats and started the coffee for when he returned. He looked in on Mary who was still sleeping. She had been up with Jacky many times during the night. They had an agreement. During the week, Mary was on duty for night feedings. On weekends, Jack got up and let Mary get some much needed sleep. This was Tuesday and he tip-toed to Jacky's room to peer in on that precious face. He never got tired of staring at those tiny pink bowed lips, touching the dark silky hair on the top of his head or stroking his puffy soft cheeks. Jack slowly pushed the door open, peering into the dimly night-light lit room, squinting to see as he approached the crib. Jacky's eyes seemed to be open, and as Jack got closer, immediately something felt wrong. He didn't expect Jacky's eyes to be open at this hour; the babe usually awoke at about 6:30 am. As he peered in the crib, Jacky wasn't moving. Time seemed to progress in slow motion now, as fear gripped his chest allowing him no air at all. When he reached out and touched Jacky's cheek it was cold and he noticed that his son's small pink lips were blue. Jack could see the subtle shades even in the nursery's dim light. He just stood there for a moment in disbelief, waiting, wanting to wake up, hoping it was all a horrible dream. But he was already awake and the nightmare that followed was his life.

As time stood still, he tenderly scooped the tiny lifeless body into his arms, his knees buckling beneath him as the father and his baby son crumbled to the floor in a heap. Jack wept then, as if grief and tears could bring his son back to life. At some point he heard Mary come in and in her confusion and then harsh realization of what was happening, she fainted hard to the floor. She did not wake for a few long moments. Jack remembered wrapping Jacky up in his blanket and laying him gently back into the crib. He also remembered looking at Mary lying motionless on the floor, wishing he didn't have to rouse her, ever. He wanted to spare her the agony that would follow. Finally, he bent down and patted her cheek. She came to quickly and when the inevitable realization again flickered across her face, she shot a questioning look at Jack, silently asking him if it was true. He hung his head and shook it as tears continued to flow down his cheeks. Mary's primal scream of deepest agony filled the room. She buried her face in his chest and sobbed long and hard.

The wails that continued through the morning were almost more than Jack could endure. The pain and loss were rocking him to the core, but watching the suffering of his wife was beyond what he could process. He went into a numbed state of efficiency. He had lifted his wife's limp body up, off the floor and carried her to their bed. He called 911 and explained to them what had happened; they said they would send an ambulance out immediately. He then called his in-laws.

They lived close by and he hoped they could help Mary the most right now. He would need as much support as possible. Jack called his own parents next. They had come down right after Jacky's birth three months ago to see their newest grandchild. Jerry had already given them two. Jack didn't remember exactly what he said to his parents when they arrived.

He did remember the ambulance coming. He had showed the paramedics into the nursery, but he could not stay to watch. After only a few moments, an attendant had come out and uttered the most dreaded of words. He said that there was nothing that could be done, and that they were very sorry for his loss. A coroner would arrive sometime later that morning. It was all very surreal. Mary's parents had arrived and tried as best they could to comfort her, considering the awful circumstances.

The funeral was brief and a non-event in Jack's memory. He knew his parents had come, his brother too. Jerry hadn't brought the family, perhaps to spare them the agony. The sight of healthy children would not be at all comforting. Mary was now on medication; her depression had become all encompassing. Jack knew that in order to survive he had to go back to work. It wasn't that he didn't want to help Mary. He had certainly tried. Jack just didn't feel that he had any of the answers. He could not give what was required of him. He knew he was barely holding onto his own sanity. He worked harder and longer hours to cope. Mary's parents took her to their house for a while, hoping that the change in scenery would help. She never came home.

Jack tried for months to persuade her to come back. She refused, sighting that she just couldn't stand the reminders. She couldn't bear to even see Jacky's room. She tried to kill herself once by taking a handful of pills, but her mother found her in time and rushed her to the hospital. After that, Mary was in therapy and closely monitored. Many months later, she was finally able to leave, but not to be with Jack. That could never be. She eventually got a job close to her parent's house, in the next town over and rented an apartment. She said she didn't know if she still loved Jack. She was not sure she could love anything or anyone again. She had lost that part of her heart. Jack understood.

That had been over two years ago. The divorce became final six months ago. It seemed the only thing to do. He needed to move on as best he could. He had thrown himself into work, trying to forget it all. Mary's leaving had helped him with that. He tried to close off that part of himself, but it visited him night after night. His dreams were filled with cold and blue lipped Jackys. He would wake himself up with his own screams, drenched in sweat and tears. The worst visions were of Jacky's eyes, open and lifeless, staring up at him. One word came from his lifeless little body, "Why?" Jack knew it was his own mind asking the question - his subconscious mind. It would not let him forget the morning of January 14, 2010. He needed to know why it had happened, why he had lost his son. So he searched.

Jack began investigating spirituality. He had never been a religious person; they had gone to his mother's Methodist church when he was a boy, usually just on holidays and special occasions. He honestly didn't remember anything he had heard or learned there. He had a general sense that most religion was just a control game. After studying religions in college, he knew there was nothing in it for him, beyond the academic intrigue. He had never felt compelled to go to church, knowing his answers weren't there. In retrospect, he realized he didn't even really have questions back then.

One day while shopping the campus bookstore, the New Release rack sported a title that caught his attention – the latest written by The Dalai Lama. He wasn't inclined toward Buddhism, but he was intrigued. He bought it, took it home and read it in two nights. The second night, the nightmares weren't as vivid. He didn't know if the book had anything to do with it but he was encouraged to continue that line of pursuit.

Over the next year, Jack read over fifty books on spirituality and mysticism. Many of the things he read didn't make any sense. Some of the ideas he was able to dismiss immediately. But there were moments; concepts that he felt brought him a little peace and a glimmer of hope again. He had felt dead himself, since that morning in January. He craved anything that offered life. Often times, he felt as if his new quest had left him with more questions than answers, but the pursuit itself felt good and he was really learning new things. These ideas made him feel hopeful for the future again.

During his search, he had stumbled upon books about the Maya and their prophecies. It seemed preposterous that he had not heard much about these ideas before. He had known of the Mayan calendars, of course. Maybe there had been some brief references to the prophecies during his schooling, but he had been so focused on discovering the economic, social and religious reasons for the Maya's demise that he had not ventured deeper into these other theories. Now, in light of his growing understanding of man's spiritual journey, he found all this prophecy stuff truly fascinating. As a scientist, he found much of the data given, as supporting evidence for the conclusions presented, flawed. He realized however, that much of the underlying basis for such books remained the same – 'Did the Maya know something we still do not? Something we so desperately need?' Jack's rational self scoffed at such a premise but that rational self had much less hold on him since unexplained tragedy had struck him so completely. He decided not to tell many of his colleagues about his new interests. Instead, he began to read every book he could find on the subject. Some were outright absurd; others contained a few ideas worth pondering. In the end, he had decided to return to Maya territory himself. He wasn't sure why, but he was drawn to Mexico. If truth be told, he didn't know if he was looking for what the Mayans may or may not have known or if he was just trying to find an answer to why Jacky was gone. There were moments when he thought he must be completely crazy. There was no rational connection between understanding the Mayans, their calendar and their prophecies and understanding why his child had died and his family disintegrated. Still, he felt there was some reason and so he continued to investigate, all in private, of course. He didn't need to ruin his career in the process; enough of his life had been sacrificed. He would at least keep his pride, if not his sanity.

     He had begun to feel as if there was a reason for everything. Isn't that what all the books were saying? As much as he hated to think that there could be a good reason for his son's death, he could not just leave it to chance or the act of a vengeful god. After the earthquake that hit and the cave had revealed a seemingly more valuable prize, he was sure. Sure that he was being led to something by clues intentionally left along the way to guide him. He wasn't certain who or what was leaving the clues and for now he was okay with leaving that part unknown. It was enough to believe in something, anything at this point. There were many moments when he questioned his own sanity. He wondered if all of the theories spinning in his head were just plain useless. Either way, he just kept reminding himself that this new life was better than the cold-hearted, mechanical life he had been living for the past three years. He would see it through, he must.

     A string of coincidences and clues began to become increasingly clear and now perhaps the best Mayan epigrapher in the world was here in Mexico, right when he so desperately needed one. At least he hoped she was. Upon seeing the majesty and mystery of Secreto Muro, he was now convinced that its answers would reveal his own. He was hoping that the writing really was on the wall. Despite his sore back he smiled at that thought.

Chapter 5

December 12, 2012

Jack pulled up outside the cantina he had frequented in prior visits. Timas greeted him smiling, as Jack walked through the old screen door. "Señor Reese, I am happy to see you. How can I help you today?" he said in his thickly accented English.

"Buenos Dios, Timas. I have several things that I need. Could Pipan get them for me?" Jack replied, looking over to Timas' oldest son, Pipan, who was sweeping up in the back. He handed Timas his list of supplies.

"Si, for sure, Señor Reese," he then spoke rapidly to Pipan in Spanish, handing him the list. "Can I get you some lunch, Señor Reese?"

"Yes, I would love some, but I have to make some calls first. Can I use your phone? Is the one in the hallway still working?"

"Sure thing, Señor Reese, shake it a little if you can't get a dial tone." Jack had used this phone after they had first arrived, calling his family to let them know he had landed safely. He had also let them know that since there was no phones at the site, that he wouldn't be able to call them again for a while.

"Gracias!" Jack said over his shoulder as he headed for the back hallway that connected the front cantina with the portion of the building that was Timas' family dwelling. About shoulder height on the wall, at the end of a dark arched hallway was an old rotary phone. It was ancient, but most of the time, it worked.

Jack pulled out his International calling card and began to dial the number to connect with an operator who would in turn be able to place the calls. When the operator came on the line, Jack read his numbers slowly and asked to be connected with Max's number at Tulane University first. Judy, Max's officemate answered the phone. "Hi, Judy, this is Jack Reese, is Max there?"

"Hey Jack, I thought you were in Mexico? Max isn't here, he is teaching a class until 2:00 pm. He should be back after that."

"Oh, okay. I *am* in Mexico, but I have an important question for him. I will try again after 2:00. Can you tell him to wait for my call, since he can't call me?"

"Sure Jack, anything wrong?" she sounded concerned.

"Nope, I just have something here I need his advice on."

"Okay, I'll have him wait for your call."

"Thanks Judy, take care." Jack pushed the button on the phone to disconnect the call. With a click, he had the operator again. He asked her to connect him with the *Museo Nacional de Antropología* in Mexico City. It was the middle of the day and if Alana Borisenko was still in the country, he hoped she would be at work. It was a long shot, he knew, but worth a try. Besides he had a feeling, a sense, about this.

"Museo Nacional de Antropología, pueda yo le ayudo?"

"Yes, hello. I am looking for Alana Borisenko. Is she there?"

"Alana Borisenko?"

"Si, Alana Borisenko, she is a Maya epigrapher, a professor, from…" Jack paused, he hesitated to say America because Alana was actually *from* Romania, but she had been teaching in Southern California. Finally, Jack decided to finish with, "the University of Southern California, in America."

"Ahh," the woman now responded in thickly accented English, "the foreign scientist. Yes, she was here, but she recently left." This confused Jack for a moment and then he realized what she was telling him.

"Left the museum or the country? Is she returning to the United States?" he asked with increasing panic in his voice.

"Si."

"Has she already left?" Jack's heart began to step up a beat. He couldn't believe she was still in Mexico and he might just miss her.

"She has just left the museum, Señor." She attempted to calm his obvious anxiety.

"Do you know when she will be returning to the United States?"

"Not until tomorrow, I think."

"Do you know where she is staying?" There was a pause on the other end of the line. Jack detected and understood the woman's reluctance to divulge another woman's residence. "Señora, por favor, my name is Jack Reese. I am also from the United States and I am a colleague of Alana's. I must speak with her before she returns." The woman must have believed him, because she trustingly offered Jack the name of Alana's hotel. "Muchas gracias Señora," he quickly hung up.

One more time Jack dialed the operator. This time he asked for The Four Seasons Hotel and after a long moment he was put through. Jack's pulse quickened with the thought of talking with Alana Borisenko about their mysterious discovery. A man answered, "Four Seasons Hotel Mexico, podría ayudarle?"

"Alana Borisenko's room please."

"One moment please," the man responded in English.

Jack couldn't believe how anxious he felt. It was more than excitement; it was the feeling of a strong connection, an attraction, to this scientist. She was a woman, beautiful and extremely intelligent. But it wasn't a sexual attraction, though she was striking, he had to admit. It was something more. Much more… he didn't have time to finish the thought; he heard the sound of a woman's voice on the other end, "Hola!?" speaking Spanish, with a strong other-world accent. It was a Romanian accent, of course, but in this moment Alana Borisenko seemed to be from another world. The world that makes dreams come true.

Chapter 6

December 12, 2012

Alana Borisenko always felt melancholy after an assignment was completed. It was a feeling that was inevitably followed by a sense of dissatisfaction and even let down. She had come to Mexico City with high hopes, only to be left with that all too familiar feeling of emptiness. Alana was on a mission, one she would not admit to anyone, not even to herself most days. But today, though the sun hovered high in the sky, Alana was gray with disappointment. Her shoulders slumped and her long brown hair fell forward as her gaze followed the sidewalk just in front of her. When she returned to the Four Seasons Hotel México, walking the two blocks from the museum for the last time, she made her way up to the front desk to check out. Barely smiling to the clerk, she paid the bill and left a forwarding address, just in case. She then went to her room to finish packing. Her flight was scheduled for departure later that night.

When Alana unlocked the front door, the phone was already ringing. 'Must be the front desk; everyone at the museum already said goodbye. Maybe I forgot to sign something.' She clumsily climbed over her bags, which were open alongside the bed, blocking her way. They were only half packed with all she had brought with her and of course the countless items she had bartered for at the local bazaar. The phone continued to ring. She finally picked up the receiver and muttered a breathless, "Hola!?"

"Alana Borisenko?" an American male voice inquired.

"Yes?" Her English was perfect, she knew, with only a slight Romanian inflection.

"My name is Jack Reese. I'm an archaeologist doing fieldwork here in Mexico in the Chiapas region. We are excavating a new site." Alana wasn't sure where this was going. She decided to just wait for Mr. Jack Reese to continue before responding.

"Uh, hello?" Jack said, not sure if the connection was lost.

"I'm here," was all Alana offered.

"Yes, well…" Jack stumbled for a moment. He took a deep breath and said, "I observed you speaking at a conference at Southern

Cal last year. I was very impressed by your work, most especially by your theories on the epigraphy of Native Americans."

"Thank you," Alana tried to sound friendlier. She was slightly intrigued but still didn't know why he was calling her. "Some of my ideas aren't very popular."

"I suppose, not yet. But I predict they will be. I wanted to speak with you after the conference, but I had to catch my plane back home. Nervous, Jack shortened his explanation, knowing he needed to get to the point of the call.

Alana appreciated the compliment and the confidence in her work, but as she leaned back on the pillow, she was getting anxious to return to her packing. She hoped this guy wasn't flattering her for personal reasons; she wasn't interested in getting involved with anyone right now. Her last romance had been a disaster and had ended just prior to this project in Mexico. She had run away and worked very hard to avoid facing her failings in relationships. Finally, Alana asked, "What can I help you with, Dr. Reese?"

"My small team has discovered a unique mural in a cave near Ocosingo, in Chiapas, with markings and hieroglyphs unlike any I have seen before. Many of the glyphs are classic Maya and at this very moment, my assistant is working on deciphering them. But there are others. These we just do not recognize at all." Jack inhaled loudly, perhaps too loudly. The mere idea of so openly sharing this information with a stranger left Jack feeling unsteady. He tried to relax his stance, knowing he needed her help. He was now holding his breath, hoping he had gotten her attention and interest.

Pulling away from the pillow, Alana quickly inquired, "What do they look like, these glyphs? I mean, can you describe them?" Nothing intrigued her more than the mention of unrecognizable ancient writings.

"Some of them look very geometric in their form, while others remind me of the Egyptian hieroglyphs. Some are simple in their design, while others are more complex. Anyway, they are familiar but unknown at the same time, if that makes any sense."

Alana was tense all over, her one arm hugging her drawn up knees, while the other clutched the phone. Her brain buzzed with thoughts, 'Could this be the one?' Then she cautioned herself, 'Don't get your hopes up, not again.'

Jack was still wondering, out loud, where he had seen similar markings, "It could have been in Samaria or India that I have seen them before, I just don't remember."

"I could come and look at them. I am not that far from you, am I?" Alana asked, not quite sure where Ocosingo was located. She wasn't looking forward to going home anyway. Besides she knew she had to try, this could be what she was looking for.

"Great! That would be great!" Jack was thrilled that she had offered. "But what about your flight? Do you have other obligations at home? You've been gone a long while, a year right?" Jack gave her an excuse to decline, not wanting her to be sorry for offering.

"No, I mean, yes." Alana fumbled. "Yes, I have been here a year, but my family lives in Romania and I am not visiting them until summer. My work in California is on hold until I return, whenever that is."

"Oh, okay, great." Jack said again. "Where? When can we meet?"

To Alana, he sounded nice, a little keyed up, but his voice seemed kind, trustworthy. "I will need to make some arrangements, can I call you back?"

"Actually, right now I am in town for the afternoon on a supply run. The dig site is about two hours from here, by jeep. Ocosingo is a long way from Mexico City by automobile. I would suggest you fly into San Cristabal or Palenque and then hire a jeep to drive you down to Ocosingo. Also, I should tell you - our living conditions onsite are not wonderful. It is not much more than a rustic campsite, not like working in a museum, I'm afraid. Also, we are in a jungle climate, with all that the jungle has to offer..." Jack warned.

"I've been on location before, Dr. Reese. I'm sure I will be fine." Alana said, though she wasn't as confident as she tried to sound. 'Jungle?' She thought to herself.

"Please, call me Jack. I will make sure you have your privacy and as many comforts as I can, given the conditions." Jack tried to ease her mind without making it sound like the Ritz. "I have to make some other telephone calls. How about I ring you back in an hour? Is that enough time?" Jack inquired.

"I think so. That should do." Alana said.

"Okay, great! Talk to you in an hour," Jack concluded and the line was dead.

"Good-bye." Alana replied to the empty silence. After she replaced the receiver she just sat there, stunned and motionless. The excitement of the hunt rang through her being once again, replacing all traces of melancholy. Her sense of purpose felt renewed, restored. She leaped off the bed smiling, picked up the phone again and dialed the front desk. She would need to cancel her flight home. She could reschedule the ticket later; it was refundable. She needed a flight to Chiapas right away and a driver to take her to Ocosingo. She also needed to repack, as suddenly she was now going camping. When the clerk came on the line, Alana began spouting off instructions in Spanish. Her tone was friendly but direct; there was absolutely no time to waste. While the right hand held the phone, the left quickly unpacked and sorted. She knew to only take what she really would need, nothing more.

* *

Alana had just hung up the phone, for the fourth time in the last hour, when it rang again - making her jump. She had spent the last hour deep in a flurry of activity. After making all the travel arrangements and changes, she went about the task of paring down her luggage. Now she had just one backpack and one small duffle bag. She wasn't sure what she would need or how long she would be there, but did her best to guess. Alana arranged for her other bags to be shipped to her house in California. She hoped her neighbor Jenn would get her phone message and put them inside for her when they arrived. Alana had emailed her Chair at the university. She didn't really want to speak with him personally. She didn't want to have to try to explain anything right now. 'After all, I don't know very much at this point, do I?' she thought to herself. After sending the email, she went online and transferred money from her savings to her checking account. She didn't want to run short. She then stowed her laptop in the over-stuffed backpack along with her water bottle and some snacks for the trip.

The ring of the telephone made her jump again, causing her to acknowledge her heightened sense of excitement. "Hello?"

"Hello, Alana? This is Jack Reese again. What's the plan?" Jack got straight to the point this time.

"I am leaving here in five minutes for the airport. I booked a flight into Palenque. A jeep and driver will be waiting to shuttle me to meet you in Ocosingo. I should be there before dark. Will you stay in town and wait for me?"

"Absolutely. I will meet you in front of the Cantina on the main street in Ocosingo. Timas is the owner of the Cantina, he knows me," Jack said, brimming with confidence born of optimism.

"Okay, see you soon." Alana assured him abruptly, hearing the jeep beeping from the street below.

"Okay, travel safe." Jack said and hung up.

"Wait…" but it was too late. Alana wanted to ask what he looked like. 'Oh, well. I hope you are the only American-looking guy with a jeep in front of the Cantina in Ocosingo this evening.' She smiled to herself and put down the receiver. Sporting the backpack over her shoulder, she grabbed her duffle. The rest of the bags had already been picked up and were on their way home. She proceeded out the door and down to the jeep balancing the weight of her heavy bags. Her depression was a distant memory now, replaced with excitement and hope. Her secret quest once more fueled with the chance of discovery. This time it felt different. Or was she always this eager? She couldn't remember. She knew that right now she was shaking inside, buzzing with energy. She felt like she was on to something, something really big. Maybe this was it. She felt goose bumps on her arms at the thought. Her private visitor, the one in her dreams, seemed to be smiling at her. This made Alana smile too. In the jeep, she thought about how comfortable she already felt with Jack over the phone. She wondered what he looked like. She shook her head, trying to put an end to this personal curiosity. Alana reminded herself that it really didn't matter; she was after answers, *her* answers, not a relationship. She stared straight ahead, her favorite direction.

Chapter 7

December 12, 2012

Jack hung up the phone with Max. He had called him right after his conversation with Alana. As he turned to leave, he bumped into Izel, one of Timas' helpers, who was pushing a broom around the floor at the back of the restaurant. Jack apologized. He had been facing the wall, so focused on the conversation that he didn't notice how close Izel had been to him. Izel mumbled something, bowed his head and shuffled away.

Jack made his way into the main dining area. He was starving. The important things were taken care of, now he only had to wait for Alana. He ordered a cerveza and some food from Timas and sat down at a table. Izel brought over the beer immediately. Jack downed it by the time the food came. The chipilin tamale dish was one of Jack's favorites. It also went down quickly and easily.

As he dined, Jack thought about Alana and Apu. He had a long wait until Alana arrived. They would get back to the camp well after dark. Apu would be worried, it couldn't be helped. There was no way to get word to him. Alana would be quite tired and sore by the time they finally arrived at the camp, of that he was sure.

Jack ordered another beer as his thoughts turned to the conversation with Max. At first Max had been excited about their new discoveries. But when Jack started to describe some of the strange markings, Max's interested murmurs went quiet. As Jack related the similarity between these and known Egyptian or Babylonian glyphs, Max seemed distracted. When Jack finally paused and inquired about Max's change in mood, he responded with incredulity, citing that the markings weren't anything that fantastic. The ideas of a common ancestry between other ancient civilizations and the Mayas were outlandish and completely unproven.

This attitude was very unlike Max. Jack had known him for nearly eight years now, and in all that time Max had always been open, inquisitive and adventuresome. Jack had never heard him dismiss or demean any idea or theory, either from a student or colleague. In fact the idea that Max was dismissing what Jack knew to be a significant archaeological find, strange markings not withstanding, caused him to feel guarded toward the find itself. To feel this protective while speaking with Max McMillian, shocked and dismayed him. Jack was going to ask for Max's help to find an epigrapher. The thought now made him cringe, especially with Alana already on her way. He was going to ask Max for guidance and to act as a back up in case they needed more help or Alana was unable to discover the translations. Instead, Jack found himself changing his tune and humoring Max, saying he was probably right. He would have an epigrapher look at them later when he returned to the States. Max agreed and in fact seemed anxious to get off the phone. Jack just stood there, puzzled for a moment after he hung up, feeling that now all-too-familiar turn in his stomach along with a nervous apprehension. He shouldn't have called Max, but how was he to have known. It was so unlike Max. Jack drank his beer and tried to figure out what had happened. Without any luck, he had to just let go, comforted that Max could not do anything from Louisiana that could hurt them or their secret anyway.

Jack turned his thoughts to the additional equipment they would need to accommodate a woman at the camp. He finished his food, paid the check and went to see how Papan had made out with getting all his supplies. He would spend the afternoon tracking down the rest of the items himself.

* *

When Max hung up the phone with Jack, he just sat at his desk staring out the window. His mind struggled with what he was about to do. In ten years as a professional archaeologist, he had only made the call twice before, each one had thankfully been a false alarm. This time he knew his luck had run out. It troubled him that it was his friend Jack Reese that drew the short straw. He picked up the phone and dialed the number that despite little use, he knew by heart. As the phone rang on the other end, Max was justifying in his mind that it was for the greater good. *They* had to preserve the balance. It was his duty, was it not? A woman's voice answered on the other end, "Veni Victus Headquarters. Can I help you?"

"Yes, Discoveries, please."

"Discoveries?" the woman sounded confused as she typed the keys on her computer keyboard.

"Yes, the Discoveries Department," Max responded confidently.

"Oh, here it is, sorry. I'm new and I haven't gotten requests for that department before." The woman transferred him.
Max heard a click, then music on the line as he waited for a connection to the correct department. This time a male voice answered, "Yes?"

"Hello, I am calling in a possible 702 in Mexico." Max stated.

"A 702? Are you sure?"

"Well, yes I …" Max stuttered. He knew this was big and the thought of his friend Jack crossed his mind again. A pang of guilt entered his heart. Then he remembered that he was protecting their way of life, everyone's. He felt renewed resolve and continued, "I haven't seen it personally, and it has not been officially verified yet or even really deciphered for that matter. I think I have put him off for a couple of weeks at least on that. By what the archaeologist on site told me a few moments ago though, I believe it is a true 702."

"Very well. Your ID?" the man said in an unimpressed tone.

"EDU21."

"Location?" The man was very matter of fact about the whole report, just taking down the details.

"I believe he is in Chiapas, Mexico."

"The archaeologist on site is?"

"Dr. Jack Reese, Professor of Anthropology at the University of Michigan."

"Are there any others on location with him?"

"I am sure there are, but he didn't mention their names to me. Probably one or two of his graduate students." Max replied.

"ETD?" the man inquired.

"ETD? Estimated time of departure? I am not sure when they will be returning to the states." Max said, puzzled.

"No, estimated time to decipherment." The man corrected him.

"Oh," Max said feeling a little silly but not really knowing why. "That shouldn't be for some time, at least not fully, until after they return to the United States. Jack was all excited, but I think I calmed him down a bit and he isn't planning to get an actual expert until he returns."

"Is he suspicious of you at all?" The man asked.

"No, no… I don't think so. We are friends and I have never given him any reason not to trust me." Max felt another quick pang of guilt.

"Very well. Please keep us apprised of any changes you become aware of, until we notify you of containment. If you call again, ask for extension 99. You will be transferred to a voicemail. Do not use your name, just leave your ID number and any details you further discover," the man instructed. "You are not to discuss this call with anyone. You will receive payment as soon as the 702 is confirmed. Is your account information the same?" the monotone voice asked.

"Yes, my information is the same as the last two reports. Thank you," Max stated and started to assure the man that he wouldn't say anything to anyone, but the line went dead. Short and sweet, well short anyway, Max thought to himself. It was actually very cold and precise and just a little scary. But it was effective and functional. Max put the down payment on his house with the first call he had made, even though it had not turned out to be as serious as he expected. The second call had afforded them a nice family vacation a couple of years ago. Again it had been down-graded, but nevertheless revealing. He hoped this one would put his kids through college. The thought eased his needled conscience. Margaret, his wife would be happy. He started searching all the creative options for another reason a new windfall of money would come their way.

Chapter 8

December 12, 2012

An aged gray-haired man sat slouched in his leather easy chair, dozing off in the afternoon sun. The light reflected dust particles that danced in the air of the plush office, filled with leather and heavy mahogany furniture. The old man startled when he heard a gentle tap at the dark French doors that led to the foyer beyond. He shifted in his chair with some difficulty and answered, "Come in," in a weak and raspy voice.

"Sir," the butler said softly in a distinctively British Windsor accent.

"Yes, Rufus?"

"Sir Charles asked me to relay news of a possible 702 in Mexico and there is a briefing at 3:00 p.m., should you wish to attend," Rufus informed his employer.

"Thank you, Rufus. I will be attending. Have Baron bring the car around in an hour." He knew Charles would have everything in hand. Still, out of habit, he would go, always keeping his hands on the wheel, if ever so loosely.

"Yes, sir. Is there anything you wish now, sir?"

"No, just be on hand when the car is ready."

"Very good, sir," Rufus said as he silently closed the door behind him.

The old man got up and walked slowly over to his desk. He knew this was coming. He hoped beyond hope that the year 2012 would end without the prophecies coming true. But the hour was upon them, these were the final days of their long battle. They had to win now, if ever they would. He touched one of the buttons on the small panel of the left side of the desktop. Without a sound, a large screen panel descended from the ceiling across the room, along the east wall. He decided to also check the news. He tapped another button and a hanging picture, which was alongside the screen, slid down the wall into the floor, with only a slight swish. This exposed another monitor mounted into the wall itself. From this room he knew he controlled the world or at least what was his part in it. This thought had always comforted him, but today it just made him feel weary. He wondered about the truth. He knew the information that he and the others had suppressed all this time, was dangerous. He knew he was a protector of the ideals that all civilized people held dear. But the price had been high. And he now questioned what the truth really was. He was tired. 'Perhaps, I should not go this afternoon. Perhaps, I should just let Charles handle it from now on.' He thought to himself. 'No.' He would go; this was the most important moment in a very long fight. All they needed to do was get past this year, get through to the end of this month, and then the prophecies would have been proven false. Gone and done. Finally, he would truly rest.

Chapter 9

December 11, 2012

The sweat poured down Eligio Cuscun's chest and belly, into the rim of the cloth that bound his loins, which was soaked through. He sat cross-legged on a now drenched woven thatch mat with colored designs woven throughout. He was chanting, his hands resting on his knees. As if the heat and humidity outside weren't enough, Eligio had a fire going in the fireplace, around which different offerings of corn bread, meats and honey wine were scattered. The atmosphere was thick with burning incense of dried healing herbs and roots.

Eligio no longer noticed any of these things, not the heat, not the sweat or the smell. He had been deep in trance for four hours. Eligio was a Maya Shaman, a Daykeeper, in Chiapas, Mexico. He was responsible for the physical and spiritual wellbeing of hundreds of Maya in the area, Chiapa de Corzo. This was his sacred ceremony. The Mayan long count calendar was approaching its end, the time of Zero, of endings and beginnings.

Eligio's words started to slow and slur some. His eyes had been shut, but they were now fluttering, half open, half closed. He began rocking forward and back, slowly at first, then quickening. His chant became a hum that increased in volume until it filled all the empty spaces left in his small hut. Then everything stopped - the humming - the movement. It seemed that even his breathing stopped. Total stillness, save for the embers slowly burning down, prevailed for many minutes. No one was there to count the minutes. Eligio was present in body only. His mind was roaming elsewhere. He witnessed visions, glimpses into secrets of the past, situations in the present, fleeting hints of the future. Eligio peered into the place where there is no time, where all things exist in a single moment. This realm is off limits to those not trained to navigate through such richness in one moment. But Eligio had been a Shaman for more than fifty years and was no stranger to this shadowy other-world. He knew how to traverse its complexities, retrieving the answers and insights he required. Today Eligio encountered something in this continuum that he had been expecting.

He saw it. The Cave of Secrets had been re-opened and its mysteries had been revealed for all to see. Foreigners - Americans were responsible. With spirit-eyes he beheld the glory of the Wall of Hunab Ku - the Great God who exists only in spirit, exposed within the cave. This ancient treasure had been hidden for well over a thousand years. Glimpsing its greatness, Eligio immediately understood many of its secrets, spelled out on the wall before him. As he peered at the wall, with his spirit-eyes he noticed unfamiliar markings but he knew their purpose. He also knew that it was time for these secrets to be revealed. Eligio was surprised and dismayed that foreigners were the ones. He expected the Maya would eventually find and expose such wonders to the world, in fact he hoped he would be the one to do it. He had waited all this time, constantly looking for the clues to where the secrets were hidden. His offended ego nearly ended the trance. This would have put him back into his body, without knowing the cave's precise location.

Eligio began chanting again in a slow monotone ramble of sounds and words that most, even Mayas, would not understand. His body began rocking back and forth in a slow rhythm. Sweat, creating streams, flowed into one another toward the mat on the floor. His physical eyes fluttered again in the mostly closed way that they had previously, while his spirit-eyes focused clearly again.

Eligio's attention drew back somewhat, from the wall, noticing the cave's surroundings and the faces of those working on it. He saw a dark haired, dark skinned man with glasses, working meticulously to copy the writings onto paper. His attention turned to the left and he saw a taller man, with blond curly hair and white skin talking to the other man. Eligio didn't understand what they were saying, but he thought it was English, though he spoke very little of it himself. Eligio drew his spirit attention out further; now he was looking at the opening of the cave. With a kind of far sight that had nothing to do with actual distance, he saw the mountain and turned to take in the surrounding area. Eligio distinguished the relationship of the mountain to where he was, inside his small hut in his own village. He now knew where the cave was. It was some distance, but he had been close to that spot twice in his life. When he began to think of these past two times, his spirit traveled to them immediately, having no boundaries in time. He was amazed at how close he had been to the Cave of Secrets.

Eligio's chanting slowed to silence as did his rocking on the mat. After several moments of quiet tranquility, he opened his eyes. A

sole tear trickled down his sweaty cheek. He had to let go of his
lifelong dream of finding the secrets himself. But he didn't have to let
go of his responsibility to protect them. He had to make sure that these
foreigners were really the fated ones. It was his duty and that of his
order. He was descended from an ancient line of exclusive
DayKeepers, tasked with the keeping of the secrets and at the time of
revelation, to authenticate and prepare the destined ones. If it could not
be him, then he must do his best to prevent imposters from finding
and exploiting these mysteries.

Eligio knew the time was upon them. It was the end of 13
Baktuns, the end of the long count calendar. He knew only the One
would be able to expose the truths to the whole world. This One was
known as Zero – the beginning and the end. There were many things
about the Zero that Eligio did not know. There were many things
about the prophecies that he remembered but did not understand.
However, understanding was no longer his concern. He would relay
them to the Zero, if indeed this foreigner was genuine. He now realized
he was the first Gatekeeper. The Gatekeepers would be on hand in the
precise moment they were required. Now he understood what that
meant.

Eligio took several deep breaths, recovering from his
disappointment and resigning himself to fulfill his duty as a Gatekeeper
to the best of his ability. This is what he had been trained to do. Only
he could make sure it was done correctly.

He raised his aging body from the drenched mat. Sitting in
trance for hours on end was not as easy as it used to be in his younger
days. He stretched his muscles and cracked his spine. Eligio opened the
door and windows allowing the fresh night air to cleanse the heaviness
of the hut. His lungs and his whole body took it in. Tomorrow he
would start the long journey. He knew the scene he had witnessed
could have been as old as a week, but he didn't think it was any longer
than that. He knew there was no time to waste. After cleaning the ritual
space, Eligio ate a little and then went into a deep restful sleep,
knowing tomorrow would begin a new and perhaps final chapter in his
life.

Chapter 10

December 12, 2012

    Alana tried to shift in her seat to get more comfortable, but it was no use. The bumpy road tossed her about in the seat constantly, making comfort impossible. In addition to the rough ride, there were dark clouds looming ahead, threatening to unleash a torrential downpour at any moment. Since there was no top on the jeep, the fear of being drenched while exhausted was discouraging.

    They had been on the road for nearly two hours. Alana initially tried conversation with Manuel, the driver, but finding things they had in common was difficult and they both fell into a fairly comfortable silence within the first few minutes. Manuel did ask her if she wanted to stop and rest once. She was relieved to allow her inner organs the chance to feel stationary for a few moments at least. She had gone off into the jungle a few steps, the opposite direction of Manuel, to pee. The stop had been brief though, the road ahead was still calling.

    Most of the trip Alana had tried to take her mind off her discomfort with excited thoughts of new discoveries. Alana thought of Jack and wondered what he would be like. He seemed nice enough on the phone. She hoped they would be able to work well together. She spent a long time trying to conjure the imagery of the wall that Jack had described. She hoped that she had enough reference material in her laptop to decipher the glyphs that puzzled them. She felt pretty confident. Alana would not quit until she had uncovered the truth multiple times before. Though none of the past mysteries she had uncovered answered her personal quest; the people she had worked with and for had always been dually impressed and grateful. Alana knew she did good work and could be relentless when necessary. For her that necessity was constant.

    While bouncing around the back roads of the Mexican jungle, on her way to meet a stranger and searching for new pieces to her own personal life's puzzle, Alana allowed herself to think about what really drove her. It had been nine years since that afternoon in the Smoky Mountain's Hilton hotel. She was attending a conference at the Department of Anthropology, University of Tennessee. Early that morning, she went out for her daily meditation run at 6:00 am, listening to her favorite Enya CD. She felt as if she were running through the very same white fluffy clouds that dotted the sky. It was spring and the weather was beautiful. When she returned to her room around 7:00 she was hot and sweaty but feeling calm and contented. She stripped off her running attire on the way to the shower. She entered the bathroom, not bothering to turn on the light. She sat in the dark for a moment on the toilet to relieve herself. She dropped her head into her hands, elbows propped on her knees, and in an instant everything changed.

As if in a dream, she felt herself flying through the clear blue sky, soaring in and out of those white puffy clouds. She was completely awake, her body still sitting on the porcelain commode, but her conscious mind, or her spirit, was no longer in the bathroom, but rather - flying through the air. She decided to just go with the sensation and feel the breeze rush past her as she rose higher and higher into the atmosphere. She felt freer than she had ever felt. She was light and full of wonder, immersed in a new appreciation for everything and everyone. A true feeling of bliss overtook her whole being as she laughed out-loud, gleefully giggling as she soared through the clouds.

After a moment, she noticed the ground below had given way to sea. She was now flying over open ocean, with no land in sight. This didn't bother her in the least, on the contrary, she loved watching the scenery of colors, blue and green and white, playing and dancing with each other as she dipped down just above the ocean's surface.

Suddenly she spied land far ahead in the form of a mountain jutting up from the ocean's depths. She felt a moment of apprehension and rose up higher in the sky to get a better look. As she drew nearer, she slowed a bit. As she approached the land, she realized it was a large island with several towering mountains and swooping valleys, surrounded by several smaller islands. From her distance, high in the sky, it looked green and lush, but there were glittery objects speckling the green landscape. She was too far up to tell what they could be. They resembled specks of glass littering a lush carpet of green. She decided to fly down closer to see what they were. As she descended, she marveled at the vision. 'Was it glass or crystals?' she asked herself, quite confused. As she drew nearer she saw that they were actually buildings, crystal buildings shaped like pyramids, scattered on all the islands. Each pyramid was connected to the next by gleaming pathways. They looked like narrow roads made of a zillion small diamonds, instead of gravel. Everything about this world was clean and fresh, bright and shiny.

She swooped down low and slowly flew about ten feet above the surface of one of the pathways, following it toward the largest of the pyramids. She was soon in awe, attempting to take in the whole amazing scene. Alana realized that she was not far behind an actual person, one who was walking along the path ahead of her. She was so startled that she felt as if she would fall out of the sky. It took her a moment to recover her balance in flight. She realized that this was a real place, not just apparition in a dream. She decided to speed up to see who or what this person was. An alien maybe? Afterall, this place didn't look like anything she had ever seen on earth. The very idea enticed her. She flew down a little lower, closer to the eye level of the one she was following. Feeling invisible and silent, she didn't worry about being detected. She still thought somewhere, deep in her mind, that this was all a dream or a vision and that she was somehow still safely sitting in a dark bathroom in Tennessee.

She came right up behind the person, and was taken aback by the fact that *she*, definitely a female figure, was very human in looks, her form and, although Alana couldn't see her face, she radiated beauty. This woman had long brown hair neatly flowing over her shoulders and down her back. She was wearing a full spandex-like bodysuit that was the color of pearl, though the color changed as the sunlight hit it from different directions. Alana flew behind this woman for a few moments, noticing she was carrying a computer panel, but it didn't look like anything she had seen before. It was white and crystal, with no keys or buttons, just a bluish-white screen, that she guessed was off, for there was nothing showing on it currently. Glancing around, Alana suddenly noticed that there were others walking along the path ahead of this woman and still others walking on different paths around the area, each going to and from similar crystal buildings. It all seemed quite remarkable and totally foreign to Alana.

Alana's attention turned back to the woman. Without warning the woman stopped. Alana had to put on the 'brakes' herself, to not run into her. She ended up hovering in mid-air behind the woman. In the next second, the woman spun around and looked right into Alana's eyes. Green eyes matched and reflected the same green eyes. In that moment, Alana's brain hit a snag. Her mind struggled to reconcile the messages those green eyes were sending hers. The woman, who was obviously looking and smiling directly at her, *was* her. It was Alana's own face, exactly, as if she were looking into a mirror. Then, as if this moment was not intense enough, the radiant woman spoke to her.

"*Why are you following me?*" she asked Alana sweetly. The woman seemed more amused than annoyed, as if she were teasing Alana. Now Alana's brain nearly turned upside down with this latest development, for not only did Alana understand the woman, but at the same time, she knew the woman was speaking a language she had never heard before. How could both be true? But before she had time to figure it out, the woman continued.

"You are very beautiful, Alana." She paused for a moment then continued more seriously. "You have an important mission to fulfill, one that will benefit the whole planet. You must follow my words and they will lead you on the correct path. My words dwell in the ancient words and ancient ways. My message, though, is of the future, your future, and all of our futures. You and I are one. I am revealing myself to you, so you will be prepared when the time comes. You will know the path by the symbols, by the words and by your own heart. Alana, find the words. Find the words." Rather than understand it, Alana felt the importance of what the woman was saying.

After she finished her brief message, Alana felt a surge of emotion overtake her whole being. It was so profound that it traveled with her all the way back in time and space, to where Alana's body patiently waited, on the toilet in Tennessee. She felt the seat under her rump, her head still in her hands. To her body and her more rational mind, it seemed as if only a couple of seconds had passed, but to the rest of her it had felt more like an hour. The overwhelming emotions that the woman had left her with, almost as a parting gift, caused Alana to sit in the dark bathroom and cry. She cried for joy, she was filled to overflowing with love and bliss. She felt she might burst; her skin could not contain such joy, she just cried out loud until totally spent. Soon, the feeling subsided, leaving a calm, wonderful glow that made her face shine and eyes glimmer. She saw the shine reflected back at her, when she was finally able to stand and look into the mirror hanging on the bathroom wall. It was an odd sensation, to look at her reflection now, as if looking through time.

The woman looked like Alana, but she knew things that Alana did not. It was her, but not her. It was hard to explain, even to herself. She allowed her mind to rest a bit and took a long hot shower. Afterwards, she went down to breakfast, but could hardly eat. The rest of her stay in Knoxville, TN was a blur. She just kept playing the woman's words over and over in her head. Each time she did this, she would hear them in the language they were spoken, but she understood them immediately. That mystery remained until today.

Since that spring morning Alana had been searching for that language. She became an epigrapher, and searched for the origins of language, for the words that she now knew by heart. She had dreamed the same words nearly every night since that vision, years ago.

The woman's message gave Alana clues that she had followed tirelessly. Alana now believed that the woman was either from her future or from an alternate reality. 'Didn't Einstein's theories suggest that all reality exists at the same time?' She could not yet prove it and might never be able to, but she believed that this same language was spoken in the lost world of Atlantis, though she still had no idea why she adhered to such a theory.

Alana had spent her life in pursuit of answers and had looked to fulfill the important mission that the woman spoke of. She felt in her heart that it was true, even if the whole story was too outlandish to tell anyone else. They would think her completely off her rocker. No, this was Alana's private quest. She had never spoken the words to anyone else, much less consulted with anyone about them.

Now here she was knocking along in a jeep, on a dirt road in the back jungle of southern Mexico, following one more lead, hoping to find the answers she still sought. Alana felt something different this time; a gut feeling. She hoped she wasn't being too optimistic.

Soon rain began to fall from the sky in heavy drops, soaking them almost immediately, as they both silently wished for a top on the jeep. Manuel had to slow down; he could hardly see the road ahead of them. They went on in the rain for about thirty minutes when Manuel said that they only had a couple miles to go. Alana asked how long he thought the rain would continue.

"It is hard to say, Señorita, it could last for a couple of hours or a couple of days."

"A couple of days? Then I think we should continue on as fast as we can, don't you?"

"Si, Señorita, we should complete the trip." They drove on a few more minutes when Alana looked up just in time to see the fallen tree ahead. Unfortunately, she was not driving. Manuel had looked down at the gas gauge for a second and when he looked up again, it took him a moment to adjust his vision in the rain. It was a moment too long. He slammed his foot into the brake pedal precisely as Alana screamed and braced herself. Manuel managed to turn the wheel at the last moment to avoid a collision with the tree. With so much rain coming down, the road was muddy and slick. The jeep swerved to the right and slid off the road and down the hill. Fortunately, it wasn't far to the bottom, but when they finally came to rest, the right front tire was punctured by a broken branch. It whistled and squealed as the air seeped out.

For a moment, they both just sat there, surprised and grateful that they were still in one piece. They climbed out to check the tire. "Do you have a spare tire?" Alana asked Manuel.

"Si, Señorita. I have a spare tire. But I do not have the tools to change it. I do not have a jack."

"What do you mean you do not have the tools, doesn't every car have the tools stowed away somewhere?" She asked desperately.

"Si, Señorita. But I took this jeep's tools out yesterday to change my brother's tire; *he* did not have a jack. I forgot to put them back this morning when I was rushing to leave." He replied defensively.

"Isn't there a way to change the tire without the jack?" Alana asked with a little more panic in her voice. Rain was still falling, it was getting dark, they were a couple of miles from their destination and they had a flat tire, not to mention she was tired and now soaked to the bone. Her voice was going up in tone.

"No, Señorita. We can not change it without a jack." Manuel said apologetically. Alana realized he was just as wet as she and decided to let up on him a bit.

"What can we do?"

"We will have to walk the rest of the way, Señorita. There is no other choice." He started to pull her bags out of the jeep.

"Walk? How can we walk? Can you find your way in the dark? How far is it?" She shot all these questions at him all at once, her voice rising to a desperately high pitch.

"Si, I can find my way. I have a flash light in the jeep. It is only about four kilometers from here. This way." He said as he casually pointed to the southeast. "We will follow the road; we can't make it through the jungle. Maybe someone else will come along and give us a ride." He tried to give Alana some hope.

She just muttered under her breath, something about having a flash light in the jeep but not a jack and not bloody likely that anyone else would be traveling in this monsoon. She gathered all of her things and started up the hill, back to the road. Thankfully Manuel lugged her heaviest bag, while she carried her backpack. When they reached the road, they trudged along in the rain. Alana was grateful it had been so warm and that they were moving at a brisk pace, otherwise she would be chilled by the rain. She hoped Jack would wait for her. There was no way to contact him and let him know that she would be late. She refused to believe that this incident was an omen, telling her that this was another wild goose chase.

Chapter 11

December 12, 2012

It was twilight as Apu reached the camp. He had been in the cave all day. He did not want to rush through even the smallest detail. His dark brown eyes were fatigued from straining to see in the dimly lit cave. Even with the battery-generated lights, he found the shadows caused him to see things that were not there and he was afraid that he didn't see things that were. After studying the wall for so many hours, it seemed to Apu that the symbols and characters moved around and changed, playing tricks on him. He knew he needed a day off, but with Jack gone, there was no one else to do the work. Apu had 40 or so sketches, along with his digital photographs, that he had downloaded onto his laptop, where he was creating a digital replica of the wall. He had also made a paper rubbing of the area of the wall that was the most unusual; the enigmatic symbols. Apu looked forward to creating a three dimensional rendering of the whole site, but he would need the computing power of his lab at home or the university to accomplish that.

He carried his thin agile frame to his hut to stow his gear, he half expected to see Jack drive up at any minute. 'He should be back soon.' Apu hoped he hadn't run into any trouble; he wasn't sure what that trouble would be, but the feeling of apprehension was more acute since Jack had left early this morning and he was eager for his return.

Apu ran his fingers through his thick dark hair, pushing it out of his eyes as he went over to the mess tent and greeted Carlos, who was fixing dinner. Carlos was amazing, tall for a Mexican, with a muscular build and strong hands. His face was kind and his smile always friendly.

"Any sign of Jack?" Apu asked knowing that they would hear him coming long before they saw him. The canyon narrowed around the road about two miles back. This generated an echo from any noise coming up from the valley below. They could hear a vehicle approaching a good ten minutes before they would see who was approaching. It was a handy early warning system, although Apu couldn't imagine that they would really need it.

"No, Señor Apu, I haven't seen or heard a thing. I hope he was able to get all of the supplies I asked for."

"I'm sure he got them, Carlos." Apu replied as he sat down to eat. The food was not as spicy as usual. Apu suspected Carlos' supply of spices was one of the items he was short on. Just then they both looked up, instinctively, to the unmistakable sound of a vehicle rolling through the canyon below. It was completely dark now, and since the cooking was done, only the battery operated lanterns were on. "Ah, that must be Jack now." Apu said. Carlos responded with a nod and subtle grunt of agreement.

"There may be something wrong with Señor Jack's jeep, it sounds different." Carlos commented.

"Maybe the rough road put a hole in the tail-pipe, that would cause it to sound rougher than usual." Apu rationalized. He too had thought the sound was lower pitched than when Jack had left, but had dismissed it as his imagination.

After fifteen minutes and no Jack, jeep or anyone else coming up the road, Apu grew concerned. They had both heard the initial noise. There had definitely been someone coming up the canyon. It could have been someone else, Apu considered, but they had not seen nor heard anyone else in the two months since they had arrived. Another fifteen minutes passed with no one driving into camp. Apu's gut was in complete upset and his mind and hearing were on high alert. They were both sitting around the fire now, waiting. Apu got up and went to his hut. He returned to the fire, a couple of minutes later with his walking stick and his notes. Carlos just looked at him with eyebrows raised, wondering if Apu was going for a walk in the dark. Apu laid the notes down beside his seat, held onto the stick, and said to Carlos, "Just in case."

They sat there and waited for Jack, or whoever had come up the canyon, to show up. It was too dark to go looking for anyone. Apu relaxed some and read through his notes, while Carlos was busy reading a book. Time passed uneventfully for a couple of hours. Apu tried not to worry. If Jack was in trouble, there was nothing he could do about it tonight. He went to bed around 11:00. He and Carlos would walk down to the canyon tomorrow morning and see if there was anyone or anything there. Apu took the walking stick with him to bed and put it beside his cot, it was the only *weapon* of defense he really had, that and his wits, he guessed.

Chapter 12

December 12, 2012

Jack sat in the cantina eating dinner while going over the list of supplies that was now all stowed high in the back of the jeep. He was glad he had a tarp to cover everything since it had started to rain. Alana should be near; he calculated and was hoping that the rain didn't ruin the whole trip for her.

He wanted to make Alana's stay in camp as comfortable as possible so he had gotten all the items needed to build her a private hut. All of the huts were pseudo tent structures, with canvas sides over wood frames and a thatched roof. This gave them a cooler inner environment than an actual tent and still kept the mosquitoes more or less at bay. Jack marked everything off Carlos's list too. He was glad to make Carlos happy, who in turn, made the rest of them happy. It was a win-win arrangement.

Jack just had to wait for Alana, everything else was set. She should be arriving at any moment. Jack finished his dinner and was sipping on a beer when a local police officer walked in from the rain, shook off his raincoat and asked in very broken English, "Pardon, Señor. You, Doctor Jack Reese?" Jack was taken aback, but answered the officer.

"Si, I'm Jack Reese." he suspected something might have happened at home, who else would know he was here?

"You to follow me, please." The officer stated confidently and turned to go, fully expecting Jack to follow.

Jack got up, but didn't immediately follow. Instead he asked, "What is the problem officer?"

"We must to ask you questions at estación de policía." He only half turned to answer, continuing slowly for the door, all the while remaining confident that Jack would follow him.

"I am waiting for someone. I can not miss them. Can you just ask me the questions here?" Jack was becoming more alarmed. He did not want to miss Alana when she arrived.

"Timas?" the officer paused and turned toward Timas, pointing to him questioningly. Timas, who had heard the conversation, realized what the officer was asking and nodded his head affirmingly.

"He will watch for your amigo. You must come." The officer demanded.

"Si. I will watch for your guest, Señor Jack." Timas offered immediately.

Jack felt trapped and worried. Something wasn't right about this police officer. 'How could he not know Timas? This is a small town; everyone knows everyone's business here.' Jack detected that this officer was not really from around here. This realization worried Jack more. He didn't want any trouble, this was Mexico and things could get ugly fast. He knew he had no choice but to follow the man to the police station.

"Thank you, Timas. There is a friend coming to visit. Her name is Alana. If she arrives before I return, please have her wait for me. Maybe she will be hungry." Jack instructed Timas. To the officer he asked, "How far is the station?"

"Not far, but you will be wet. It's raining." The officer warned. Jack grabbed a hat from beside his chair and followed the man. He was very suspicious of who this man was. His mannerisms were suspicious, perhaps he was from the city, Jack guessed. Jack had been careful not to reveal any details of who he was waiting for; in his mind he knew he had to protect the cave. He didn't want it to fall into the wrong hands and he did not want the Mexican government to step in until they were sure what they had. He felt like a mother bear needing to protect her cubs. His mind was racing to figure out what this officer from the city could want and why he had to go to the station. Jack trotted through the rain the couple of blocks to the station, following the officer.

When they entered the small adobe-style building, the dimly lit hallway led him past the front desk to an office off to the right. Inside, sitting at another desk was a Mexican official dressed in a suit. The officer, Jack never got his name, left him in the office with the man. However, Jack was keenly aware that he remained close by. The man in the suit introduced himself as Huetzin De Los Reyes, inspector for the Ministry of Antiquities, charged with monitoring archaeological digs and making sure Mexico's treasures stay in Mexico. His demeanor was pleasant but very business like.

"I am sure you are aware of our on-going problem with looters. It is my job to help diminish that problem and preserve our treasures for all to enjoy." He said pointedly but with a smile.

"I understand completely. I am more than happy to help in any way that I can." Jack replied honestly. It was to the advantage of any self-respecting scientist, to help prevent the profiteering that often happens within the world of ancient art and artifacts. "Has there been a problem in Ocosingo?" Jack asked.

"This is routine. We have you registered in the Chiapas state and Ocosingo district. This is correct?" He asked while referring to his notes.

"Yes. That is correct. I do not have the exact coordinates with me." Jack responded. He decided to wait and see if this was, in fact, routine. It seemed strange that they accosted him on the very day he was here in Ocosingo; otherwise they would have had to come out to the site. This man did not look like he was used to going into the jungle, not often, anyway.

"You are from the University of Michigan?"

"Yes, that is correct." Jack offered no more.

"And what is the nature of the find that you are investigating?"

"We are excavating a Mayan mural, created sometime during the classic period." Jack gave the official line from his visa application.

"How long have you been excavating at this particular location?" Señor De Los Reyes continued, as if following a questionnaire in front of him, to which he kept referring and making notes that Jack could not see.

"We have been here for two months." Jack answered.

"And who is with you?"

"I have a graduate student, Apu Chohan, from the University of Michigan with me. And I have hired a local man, his name is Carlos Vejar."

"Have there been any new developments since you began excavations, any new discoveries?" The first few questions may have been routine, but this last one made Jack hesitate. There was no way he was going to tell this man about the *Secreto Muro*. He would tell no one else until he knew what it was really all about. The man looked up, eyebrows raised, waiting for Jack's answer. Jack knew he couldn't stall too long without raising suspicion.

"Well, we are not sure. But some of the preliminary carbon dating tests have come back with a more recent creation date, between 1200 and 1500 AD." Jack hoped such detail would feed his curiosity but not throw up a red flag or cause much concern. Jack hurried on to explain, "But it is not uncommon for dating to be way off in the beginning. More extensive testing usually shows a time period that is recognizable and in alignment with the physical evidence."

"These dates suggest that the mural was created in the Post-Classic period, I think." The government inspector said while he wrote on his papers.

Jack had hoped that the Mexican official didn't know too much about Mayan time periods. But it was now evident that he was well studied. Jack just waited for the next question, hoping all of this would end soon. He wondered if Alana had arrived yet. She should be here by now.

"Have there been any other developments?" he asked Jack while writing on the notepad.

"No." was all that Jack said in response.

Finally, Huetzin De Los Reyes looked up and said, "We will have to come to the site and do our own date testing." This completely shocked Jack. He had been lulled some by the routine nature of the interview so far, now he was on guard again.

"You want to come out and do your own carbon dating?" Jack was incredulous.

"Yes, Professor Reese. We have many accomplished scientists and well-equipped labs to do such work." He sounded offended.

"No. I mean, I know you have experts here in Mexico. I am just surprised that you want to come all the way out to my little site." Jack tried to cover up his dismay.

"We take our treasures very seriously. Confirming that findings are recorded and dated correctly is one of my tasks for the Ministry of Antiquities. I will come myself and collect a sample, though I will bring along another scientist."

"Yes, of course, I understand you must make sure that everything is recorded and filed correctly. However, I would be more than happy to share our final results with you and the Ministry. Or if you prefer, I could bring you a sample personally, so your own labs can test it. I would be interested in another lab's findings. You should not have to make the long hot trip into the jungle. I am happy to assist." Jack tried very hard to dissuade him from coming to the site.

"Thank you very much for your offer, professor. However, it is my job to authenticate the process and record the answers. I can not entrust that job to another." He looked Jack straight in the eye. Jack knew he had lost.

"We will not be able to make it until the day after tomorrow. That is the soonest Professor Ramirez from Mexico City can be here to assist me. Will you be at the site by then?" he inquired.

"Yes, we will be there." Jack was relieved that it was two days off, but his mind was racing to come up with a solution, maybe even a diversion. He was surprised that this man didn't ask him about the friend for whom he waited. He must not have known about Alana coming. Jack knew there was no way he wanted anyone, let alone an official, to see the new wall. He wasn't sure himself why he was so adamant about this point, but he was. He only knew he had to get Alana there as soon as possible. Again he wondered if she was waiting in the Cantina for him. He was now more anxious than ever to get out of there.

"Very well, professor. I will see you en dos dias, two days. You may go. Will you be staying the night here in Ocosingo, in case I have any more questions in the morning?"

"No, I am not. They are waiting for supplies at camp." Jack had thought about staying, but now there was no time to waste.

Jack was on his feet and ready to head out the door when Huetzin De Los Reyes made his final comment. Jack swore there was a tone in his voice in that moment, as if Inspector De Los Reyes knew more and would soon catch Jack red-handed. "Okay, I think I have everything for now. I will save any more questions for when I see you at the site. Adios." He offered confidently. A gloated warning, it seemed to Jack. But when he turned to look at De Los Reyes sitting behind the desk, the man was looking down at his papers and was calmly writing again. Jack thanked him quickly and left.

Jack ran back to the cantina, stomping in mud puddles that were caused by the continued downpour. He flew in the front door of the cantina and scanned the room for a woman sitting alone waiting. But there was no one there that fit that description. Only some other patrons that Timas was serving. He excused himself and came over to Jack.

"Señor, Jack. No lady friend has come. I am sorry." Timas looked sad for him, probably due to the puzzled look on Jack's face.

"Not here?" mumbling to himself more than asking Timas.

"Si, Señor. Can I get you anything? Would you like a room, so you can wait for her?"

Jack just stood there for a moment trying to figure it all out; the events of the last hour were spiraling in his head, making any concentration difficult. He tried to focus. She couldn't be far. He would drive towards Palenque to look for her.

"No, glacias, Timas. I am going back to the camp tonight. Thank you for all your help. This is for you and Pipan. He quickly gave Timas a wad of pesos, including a nice tip, and jumped into the jeep."

"No, thank _you_, Señor Jack. If there is anything else we can do for you, please let us know. Timas called after Jack as he drove off in the dark toward the north. "Be careful on the road, Señor Jack, the rain washes out the roads sometimes."

* *

After Jack left his office, Huetzin picked up the telephone. "This is Huetzin De Los Reyes. I have interviewed Dr. Jack Reese in Ocosingo, Mexico. He did not mention any of the new discoveries at the site. He is hiding many details, that's for sure. I can not confirm the reported 702 until at least two days from now. I will go out to the site personally." He listened to his instructions on the other end. "Yes, of course. I understand. I will call and report at that time." He listened again and then hung up without saying goodbye.

* *

Jack had the top on the jeep pulled and snapped up and the high beams on. He was driving as fast as he dared on the wet, muddy roads at night in the pouring rain. There were several turns where he spun the wheels in the mud, nearly losing control. He was not sure how far he would go to look for Alana Borisenko. He wasn't thinking clearly at all, he just wanted to find her, quickly. He would figure out the rest later. Along the side of the road were two people walking. The jeep slid to a stop. It was so hard to see that he would have missed them, had they not waved and shouted at him. When they were close to the jeep, he recognized Alana immediately, even soaking wet.

"Alana? What happened?" he asked excitedly, omitting any formal introductions.

"We slid off the road in the mud and punctured one of our tires. Unfortunately, we didn't have a jack to change it."

"Well, now you do." Jack smiled at his own joke; he was so relieved to see her. "Please get in." He leaned over to open the passenger door for her.

"This is my driver, Manuel." She introduced the two men.

"Hello. Manuel. How can I help you with your vehicle?"

"Thank you. If you could just take me to town; I will get help in the morning. The weather is too bad to change it tonight." Manual was embarrassed by his need for help.

"Yes, of course. I understand. I would be happy to take you into town." Jack offered. They all piled into the already overflowing jeep. He worked to turn the jeep around and head south into Ocosingo. No one really said anything for the twenty minutes it took to pull up outside the cantina again. Alana was squished in the front seat, very close to Jack, it was a little uncomfortable since they really didn't know each other, but Jack had to admit, she smelled nice. As Manuel got out, Alana gave him the money he was due, and then some, and thanked him for getting her to Ocosingo. He almost wouldn't take it, he felt so guilty about the accident and flat tire. "You will need it to stay the night and get the jeep fixed tomorrow." She insisted.

"Tell Timas, inside, that you are a friend of Jack Reese, and to give you a good room," Jack told Manuel.

"Thank you, both." He said humbly and got out and ran inside. Jack drove off in the direction of camp. They would not get there 'till very late, but they had to hurry now.

"I know you must be very tired and you are wet and I am sure uncomfortable. But, we have trouble and we must return as soon as possible. I have some towels there on top of the supplies, help yourself. There is also some food in that container, please eat. You must be hungry." Jack tried to console.

"What kind of trouble?" was all Alana said. She was exhausted. She had hoped for a shower and a meal and a bed at least for tonight. The thought of traveling in a jeep for another two hours was almost more than she could bear. 'This had better be good,' she thought putting most of the blame on herself for getting into this situation in the first place. She got one of the towels and dried her hair and face. Then she devoured the food, all the while listening to Jack's account of what had happened with the government official in Ocosingo.

"Why are you so worried about them seeing what you have discovered?" she asked curiously, having racked up endless run-ins with nosey officials.

"You will see - soon. As soon as we can get there." Was all Jack could say. He really couldn't explain why. She had to see it for herself. Alana just nodded and rested her head. In spite of the bumpy road, soon she was asleep. Jack drove on into the night.

Chapter 13

December 13, 2012

Apu was not a light sleeper normally, but since the discovery of the Secreto Muro, he found his sleeping was often times shallow and riddled with dreams. Tonight was the worst. Sleep was an elusive memory after having heard the noise echoing up the canyon. He heard another echo and immediately got up from his cot, dressed and carried his walking stick over to the mess tent to make a quick pot of coffee. He was on alert.

He hoped that this time it was Jack. It was now 4:00 am. It would be light in a couple of hours. He was worried - worried about Jack and worried about the noise they had heard earlier. He decided to take some time for himself later. His grandfather had taught him how to meditate when he was in grade school. It had helped relieve the stress of his exams and peer problems. He continued the practice throughout high school and college. He knew he needed the clarity and peace that always seemed to follow his practice sessions.

For now, Apu would wait and see who, if anyone was coming up the road. He stirred the fire from the night before and threw on a couple of small sticks to get it going again. He sat down to watch and wait.

It only took a couple of minutes before a jeep came rolling up to the campsite. Apu stood up, leaning on his walking stick just in case. It was Jack who slowly crawled out from behind the wheel. Apu went over to greet him.

"What happened to you?"

"It's a long story. I'll tell you later. In the meantime, we need to make room for Alana Borisenko here." Jack said as he gestured to the woman getting out of the passenger side of the jeep. Apu was surprised, first by the fact that he was so focused on Jack that he didn't see his passenger. Secondly, he knew Jack was going to try and reach the epigrapher, but had no idea he would actually be returning to the camp with her.

"Hello. I am Apu Chohan. Can I help you with your things?" Apu offered.

"Yes, thank you."

With all the commotion, Carlos was up too. He exited his hut and came over to the jeep. His hair was askew and he looked only half awake.

"Señor Jack. You finally made it back and you brought company?" He asked.

"This is Carlos. He is our cook, carpenter and generally takes care of us up here" Jack said to Alana. "Carlos and Apu, this is Alana Borisenko. She is an expert Mayan epigrapher and is here to help us decipher the Secreto Muro." Jack introduced her.

Alana tried to smile. She was a little self-conscious about her disheveled look and she knew her exhaustion showed.

"Nice to meet you," was all she could manage.

"Carlos, since you are up, can you help us put up Ms. Borisenko's tent?" Jack asked.

"No, Señor Jack. It is too dark. It will not be long before it is light and I have already slept well. Why not give the Señorita my cot to rest?" This made sense to Jack. He doubted that he could get the tent up anyway as tired as he was. He gave a questioning look to Alana, who only nodded her head. Jack went to the jeep, unpacked new sleeping gear and Alana's larger bag and gave it to Carlos. Carlos nodded and asked if the Señorita would follow him. Alana grabbed her smaller bag and gratefully followed.

The hut was dark when they first entered through an opening in the mosquito netting. Carlos soon lit a lantern that easily illuminated the whole hut. He went around and stowed away a couple of items to make room for Alana's things and then rolled the sleeping gear out on the cot, over top of his own.

Alana just stood there for a moment. The hut was a crude shelter, but not terrible. She was too tired to really care. Carlos oriented her to where the el baño, bathroom was, and which one was the mess tent, then he excused himself. Alana just stood there for a few more seconds before she unzipped one of her bags, pulled out some dry clothes, changed and crawled into the bed. She was fast asleep before she had any time to think.

Around the fire, Apu told Jack about hearing the sound of another vehicle, earlier in the evening. This news put Jack on edge. He needed sleep, even though there wasn't much night left and they had much to do before the officials would arrive. He knew everything was about to change. Apu could see how tired and anxious Jack was, as much as he wanted answers; he knew Jack needed to sleep first.

"Go to bed Jack. I will keep watch and let you know if anything happens. Actually, Carlos and I will both be on watch," he said as Carlos returned from the mess tent with a cup of coffee.

"Si, Señor Jack, go to sleep, we are okay for now. I will take care of the supplies as soon as it is light."

Jack grunted his thanks and headed to his own hut. He stopped before he entered and turned. "Apu, don't let us sleep too long. We don't have much time here. Just one day in fact. We must use it wisely. Wake us in a couple of hours."

"Okay, Jack." he agreed, though puzzled by Jack's comment.

Jack went inside his hut and collapsed.

Chapter 14

December 13, 2012

At nine a.m. Apu went into Jack's hut to wake him up. It had taken a great deal of will power to wait so long, but he knew Jack would need the sleep for whatever the day brought. "Jack. Jack, it's 9 o'clock, time to wake up." Jack moved but didn't wake immediately. Apu was reminded of the night of the earthquake. He had trouble waking Jack then too, but for a different reason. Apu was amazed that it had only been three days ago. It seemed like weeks. He shook Jack until he slowly opened his eyes. "It is 9 o'clock," he said a little louder this time, hoping to cut through Jack's sleepy haze. It worked. Jack made eye contact and acknowledged with a grunt as he rose up from the cot.

"Coffee and breakfast are ready" Apu said turning to go.

"Wake Miss Borisenko too, will you?" Jack said in a raspy voice.

"I will try." Apu said as he walked out into the sunlight.

Arriving at Carlos' hut, Apu knocked on the door. There was no answer. He tried again with no luck. He figured that since she didn't answer, she was asleep. He went inside.

"Miss Borisenko? It is time to get up."

"What time is it?" she asked sleepily.

"Nine." Apu replied.

"Is there a place where I can clean up a little?" Alana hoped, not remembering Carlos' instructions just hours before.

"Yes, you can go to the back of the mess tent. We have clean water and soap. The outdoor toilet is further down the hill, a little to the south. You'll see the path." Apu informed her.

"Apu sensed that she needed a cup of coffee. "We have coffee and breakfast ready, whenever you're ready." Apu tried to cheer her.

"Thank you," she said again. 'I bet they don't have Starbucks out here," she groaned to herself as she rolled off the cot.

Apu left and went back to the campfire, threw on another log and waited again. He was impatient; eager to find out what was going on, but his meditation early in the morning had helped with his anxiety.

Soon Alana came up the hill from the outhouse and disappeared behind the mess tent to wash up. Jack was moving a little slower, but before long everyone had gathered and ate in silence.

"Yesterday, while in Ocosingo," Jack began after swallowing the last of his coffee. "I made some phone calls." Jack continued to tell the group about the events of the day before, detailing his conversation with Max McMillan and how Alana came to be with them today. He didn't go into every detail, but ran through the basics, until he got to the part that really influenced them the most.

"While I was in the local cantina last evening, waiting for Alana to arrive, a police officer came in, asked for me and took me to the station house to answer questions. I was very nervous, but tried not to show it. I could not imagine what they would need to ask me. I thought perhaps something was wrong at home. When I entered the station, there was another man, a Mr. Huetzin De Los Reyes from the Mexican Ministry of Antiquities. He asked me a lot of questions about our excavation here in Chiapas. He had our official request and visas. He said he was in charge of making sure none of Mexico's archeological treasures fell into the hands of thieves or looters. I cooperated as much as possible. Then he asked me if there were any new discoveries here at the site. I struggled with that one. I decided to tell him about the discrepancy we have discovered with the first mural's dating. I thought he would just dismiss that, giving the, oftentimes, unreliability of initial testing. But instead he fixated on this and said that he would have to come out here and test for himself. This completely surprised me. It seemed very irregular. When I offered to share our final results, he only got offended and said Mexican tests were just as good as American. There was nothing I could say. They are supposed to arrive here tomorrow to do testing on a mural that is now only dust, save for a couple of small pieces. I did not tell him anything about the new find. I can't explain why but I sensed from the beginning, when we first saw the jewels peering out at us, that we needed to protect this wall and its messages. It is strange how personally responsible I feel regarding this new find." Jack ended his speech with what the others could tell was uncertainty about his own behavior.

Apu understood Jack's actions and paranoia. He felt the same way. He wondered why Alana didn't cause the same reaction. Perhaps, because Jack obviously trusted her. He knew thought, that Alana would not understand it until perhaps when, she actually saw the mural. He too was becoming anxious to get her up there. They only had today. A mere twenty-four hours, or less, to decide what they would do next.

"We need to get Miss Borisenko up to the cave." Apu stated. Jack agreed. They both turned towards Alana, who had not really said anything yet.

"I am ready to see this wall that you both seem to think is so important. I do not understand why you both are so protective though; especially getting to the point of lying to the authorities. But I guess I'll see for myself. Let's go." With that, she rose from her chair somewhat impatiently. Jack and Apu both were happy she did not condemn their actions and were actually grateful for her willingness to go along with them until she could decide for herself. They both got up and headed in the direction of the hill.

"Do we need any gear? How far is it?" Alana asked.

"No, it is only up on the side of that hill, over there, see the rocks gathered in that one spot. You can't actually see the opening from here, but it isn't far." Jack said pointing out where they were going.

Carlos didn't say anything the whole time. He was worried about the noise they had heard last night, and now the authorities were coming too. He wasn't really worried for himself; he was more concerned for Jack and Apu and now this woman, Alana. His loyalty was to Jack and he would protect him as much as possible.

* *

The trek up the hill was not very difficult. The sun was rising in the sky, but the soon to be stifling heat had not set in yet. When they reached the outside of the cave, Jack and Apu each grabbed lanterns and turned them on. Apu went in first, then Alana. Jack, taking a quick glance over his shoulder, came in behind them. Jack was amazed at how much he missed seeing it. He felt like it was a child who he was returning home to see. This was a curious realization, considering the loss of his own child. He didn't have time to think about that though, he was too curious to watch for Alana's reaction.

Alana was holding back her own excitement and curiosity. She had been disappointed so many times and for so long. After the long ride and the crash, all she had thought about was sleep. Since she opened her eyes this morning however, this moment had been on her mind. In her dreams, just before Apu woke her, the familiar words and symbols from her vision were even more real than usual, clearer, and quite tangible. Still all her anticipation didn't prepare her for what she was now gazing upon. Open-mouthed and not wanting to blink, she stared at the wall in front of her. She could see the edges of what remained of the original mural and how it had been in front of the new amazing wall. She felt an emotional surge; it was strong but difficult to identify. The hieroglyphs pulled her in as she began to read a few of the easier and more common writings. As she was drawn from one side to the other, she began to sense the complexity of the message spelled out on the wall. It was clear to her that there were many glyphs that she would need extended time to decipher, if she could at all. She recognized words like 'god' and 'man.' She also recognized several dates carved into the stone, and there were different representations of the Mayan calendars.

Her attention shot over to the unfamiliar symbols on the left. They were familiar, but different, unreadable. 'It is a puzzle – something you know hidden in a jungle of other glyphs.' She was musing over the differences when she scanned a little further to the left. Her breath caught in her throat. Her mind reeled as she recognized a small set of symbols bunched together. Another set of strange symbols seemed to shout out to her and called her by name. "Beauty, mission, world." She whispered softly the words that screamed at her in her head, as her knees began to give way and dizziness took hold. She felt Jack's hands on her forearm and Apu grabbed her other arm to keep her from falling. They held her up as she tried to grasp what she saw etched into this ancient Mayan wall, carved thousands of years ago. '*Just for me?*' Jack and Apu let her slowly settle onto the cave floor. '*It is inconceivable. Impossible,*' she thought. But here she was staring straight at the same symbols that had haunted her dreams for years. Something happened inside her in that moment. Everything changed for Dr. Alana Borisenko; she knew her life had been irrevocably altered. Forever.

Though Jack and Apu didn't know what exactly was happening for her, they definitely related to the emotion and the lingering effect. No one spoke for what seemed like hours, but was actually about thirty minutes. Finally, the trio slowly made their way silently down the mountain and remained quiet until they sat in front of each other around the fire-pit. Then they began to discuss what they would do next.

Chapter 15

December 13, 2012

"One thing's for sure, we can't let this fall into the wrong hands." Jack began. Apu and Alana nodded. Alana was still stunned by what she saw and experienced in the cave.

"We have to figure out what it all means, what all those unusual symbols mean," Apu said.

"I can tell you what one set of symbols means. The smaller set to the far left." Alana said as she stared off into space. She didn't tell them how she knew, but she relayed just enough of her story to convince them that she knew what she was talking about. Apu and Jack were stunned, but didn't have time to really contemplate it for long. Jack knew he was staring at Alana hard. Finally, he shifted his focus and turned away.

"Well, we need time to decipher the *others*, and with the authorities coming tomorrow, who knows what will happen." Jack interrupted.

"They may be just fine with it. Why wouldn't they be?" Alana suggested.

"Well, aside from the fact that I lied about finding anything new on site; I have not had a very good response from others regarding the oddness of those other symbols." He sensed his own quickening heart-rate. "I'd be willing to bet the Mexican government, most especially this particular official, doesn't want "fringe" ideas getting out. They take all of this very seriously. Symbols that could possibly connect the ancient Maya with other ancient civilizations will not be warmly received." Jack said.

"So what are we going to do? Apu is right, I, or we, need time to study the symbols." Alana amended, not wanting to leave Apu out of the process. He had obviously already done a lot of work.

They all sat there in silence for a moment. Each one had their own reasons for wanting to decipher the wall and to protect it. But they all were thinking about how remarkable it was that a set of ancient etchings on a wall could conjure up such intense emotions. Though their reasons were different, they were united in their feelings of protectiveness.

It was Apu who broke the silence. "Many of the glyphs puzzle me. For instance, the odd ones in the foreground of the Hunab Ku symbol." Alana agreed though she wasn't as puzzled regarding the area of the wall that clarified her own personal vision and dreams. "Also there are a great many glyphs that seem to be explaining the Mayan calendar system." Apu went on. "There are the markings of the different calendars, like the front mural had, but there is more to this other group. I would venture to guess that there may be details regarding their prophecies foretelling the end of time – or of the long count calendar – their version of the end of time." Apu clarified as he referred to the most extensive of the Mayan calendars. They all knew how the Mayan were very concerned with time and mapped it with amazing precision, especially considering the rudimentary tools they had vis-à-vis today's technology.

"You both are aware that the end of the long count is the 21st of this month, right?" Apu questioned. Alana and Jack both nodded affirming agreement. It was one of the reasons they were here in Mexico, though neither Jack nor Apu, nor even Alana had admitted that particular fact to anyone else.

In a rush, Carlos came running over to the circle with a strained look on his face. He had been in the mess tent, preparing for the day, when something strange at the edge of the clearing caught his eye. The jungle was not as thick around the campsite; he could even see the surrounding hills to the north, and all of the way up the hill to the cave. "Señor Jack!" He said in an alarmed voice. They all looked up and followed Carlos' focused gaze up the side of the hill. Jack was on his feet first. Apu and Alana were not far behind.

What they saw was a short, dark-haired man making his way down the side of the hill moving away from the opening of the cave. He had a pack on his back and was carrying a flashlight. It took a moment for the scene to register in each one of their minds, but soon all four were scampering up the hill to intercept the man, the intruder. Carlos felt obligated to help the others and followed right behind.

As they drew closer, they could see that the man was dressed in what looked like traditional Mayan-styled clothing: loose white pants, matching shirt and a embroidered red sash synched around his waist. He had deep lines on his face and a full head of gray hair, aging him roughly 70 years. He sported a scraggly gray mustache and beard. In spite of his advanced years, his body language and facial expression showed determination and anger.

When Jack reached the older man, he defensively questioned the man about what he wanted here. The man said something just as brusque back to Jack, only in Ch'ol-Tzotzil, one of the local Mayan dialects. Without intervention an argument would ensue despite the language barriers.

Carlos had just reached the others as they gathered half way up the hill. He quickly asked the old man in Spanish, what he was looking for. Fortunately, the Mayan understood and replied in Spanish. Carlos' language skills proved invaluable as he smoothed over the tense situation. Alana was also fluent in Spanish and followed the conversation closely, prepared to step in if needed.

"What are you doing on our land?" The older man asked accusingly. Carlos translated for the others.

"Your land? Who are you?" Jack shot back and Carlos continued to translate with a little less emotion.

"I am Eligio Cuscun; I am the Shaman in charge of this entire region. You are on our land." Eligio stated clearly.

"We are here on official business with permission from the Mexican Archaeological Ministry." Jack shot back, just as clearly.

Eligio was not put off. He pointed up towards the cave and said, "This is a secret Mayan shamanic cave. What gives you the right to defile it?"

Jack also did not back down. "We found this site while investigating ruins further into the jungle, last year. We have full official approval to excavate this site." Jack began to see that this line of conversation was not going to get them anywhere. He decided to take a different tact. He softened his voice just a little.

"We do not intend to destroy or steal anything. We are only documenting the cave for posterity and further study."

Eligio followed Jack's lead and lightened his tone, "By what rights have you to explore this sacred space? Who are you? Why have you come and what do you intend to do with the information that you find here?"

Jack realized with Eligio's final comment that the shaman may be helpful in understanding the messages on the wall. He asked hesitantly, "What *information* are you speaking of?"

"The prophecies of course. This is a cave of prophecy. The most sacred of them all. You do not know what you have tampered with." Eligio said indignantly.

Alana felt that the fire was gone from his temper and there was more he wanted to say. She decided to join in the conversation. "Please, Señor Cuscun, come to our camp, have lunch with us so we might discuss these prophecies?" she implored.

Jack was a little surprised when she spoke to the man, but when Carlos translated her words back to him in English, he agreed with her tactics. Carlos spoke to the Mayan shaman about lunch, also imploring him. The man seemed to be calming down a little more with Alana's request and spoke with Carlos directly. However, he did not take his eyes off of Jack.

Jack looked into Eligio Cuscun's eyes and said, "We would be most honored if you would join us Señor Cuscun," he said without reservation. Jack knew this man didn't have the same agenda as the official from yesterday. After the initial scare of having someone unknown in the cave, Jack had begun to feel that there was an order to what was occurring. Eligio agreed to have lunch with the strangers. They all silently marched down the side of the hill toward camp.

Chapter 16

December 13, 2012

Carlos excused himself and went off to the mess tent to prepare the lunch. Jack offered Eligio one of the tree trunk seats around the fire pit and offered Alana another. He was about to offer Apu the third seat but Apu opted for the mat from his hut, instead. Jack took the empty spot. Since Carlos was not present it was up to Alana to bridge the language gap.

"Donde vive usted, Señor Cuscan?" she began in Spanish, and then translated both her questions and Eligio's answers for the others.

"I live in Bachajon; it is west of here." Eligio replied.

"Did you just arrive today?" Alana asked curiously, mostly just trying to make the conversation light hearted, to begin.

"I arrived last night. I camped on the other side of that hill." He said as he pointed to the north-west. That explained, for Apu at least, the vehicle noise they had heard earlier last evening. Apu felt more at ease. He half suspected that the authorities had arrived earlier than expected and were spying on them. The idea of Eligio spying on them somehow felt better to him.

Jack found Alana's translation style very appealing, but chastised himself for letting his mind wander. He knew he needed to stay focused on the present situation. He was already panicky with Señor De Los Reyes coming tomorrow, now Eligio today? He hoped no one else lurked about.

"How do you know of this cave?" Alana tried, hoping the question would not inflame the man again, since he now looked calm, though perhaps cautious. He seemed to be visually evaluating each of them, individually. There was a long pause before Eligio answered, as if he was deciding what to and what *not* to tell them.

Finally, he replied. "I am of a selected line of Maya shaman. My family has known about this cave since the beginning. It was my own ancestors who carved the message into the stone many Baktun ago. Later, when the old ways were in danger, my family decided to protect the message by constructing the outer wall to protect the original. There was a great spell of silence bestowed upon the cave and upon all those who protect it. Only the chosen shaman of my line, have passed the secrets down through the ages. I have always known that I was the last one." Eligio paused, waiting, for any reaction.

A long pause followed this last revelation. Apu was thinking about Eligio being *the last one* and what that really meant.

Internally, Jack thought about the spell of silence and protection, wondering if perhaps this was why they had all felt so protective of the cave.

Alana wondered why this man was so trusting of them, with such remarkable secrets. She pulled her shirt around her as she felt a shiver run through her body. An overwhelming sense of destiny filled her to the point of feeling another full-body shudder. None of this did she allow to show. Instead, as calmly as she was able, she asked Eligio the next natural question. "Why are you the last one?"

"I am the last one, because this is the end of the old ways." Eligio said very matter-of-factly. Then before more questions came, he continued, "This is the end of the long calendar; the end of the Age of Man." A heavy pause fell over the group.

"Do you mean that mankind will end, be destroyed?" Apu asked with an air of disbelief.

"More like we will destroy ourselves, if you ask me." Alana chimed in, half under her breath.

"It is not the end of man; it is the end of man's ways. The next time period will allow humans to be more as the gods. But you are right to worry." Eligio turned to Alana. "There is much that can go wrong. My job as a Daykeeper and a Gatekeeper is to make sure only the fated people take the secrets, and expose them to the world." This last part, he said in a manner that showed that he was still somewhat reluctant to trust them. He looked around the cold fire pit at each one of them, clearly trying to evaluate their true nature, to see into their souls. Jack, Alana and Apu returned Eligio's gaze without trepidation. They knew they were supposed to be here. That was clear to each of them, although right now, not much else was.

Carlos returned to the circle and politely announced, "el almuerzo está ya preparado." Everyone understood and rose to go to the mess tent. The silence that accompanied lunch was unnoticed. Each worked to process, in their own ways, what Eligio had told them so far.

It was Alana who finally spoke when she finished her last morsel, "I don't understand. What did you mean by, 'expose the secrets to the world'?"

Eligio chewed slowly, plainly thinking of just how to respond, "You must know the whole story. You must understand the whole prophecy."

"Will you share it with us, the whole prophecy?" she asked.

Eligio did not answer this question; instead he asked a completely different question of his own. Looking directly into Jack's eyes he spoke "Why are *you* here?" He did not look away, unmistakably challenging Jack to tell the absolute truth. The contemplative atmosphere over lunch changed immediately with Eligio's challenge. Jack wasn't sure what to say at first, taken back by both the bluntness of the questions and the reversal in attitude. He realized by the way the shaman was looking at him, that he wasn't interested in the academic or official reason. Jack recognized that Eligio was only interested in the real reason Jack was here. He felt as if he were being interviewed for an important position, possibly even tested. He didn't know why, but he wanted to pass the test. He struggled for a moment to respond. He had not spoken the words out loud to anyone before. Even Apu, who had worked with him for over a year, knew little about Jack's true motivations. Alana was more or less a stranger. To divulge such intimate details was, at first, uncomfortable. Then he realized he didn't really care. This was his chance to come clean. It felt cleansing to say it out loud.

He began slowly, "Several years ago, my wife and I had a baby. We were very excited and happy. Our son was born healthy and beautiful, as perfect as my wife. Three and a half months later, I went in to see him in his crib. It was early in the morning, just before my run. When I went over to the crib to check on him, he was dead." Jack stared away, looking at nothing anyone else could see. His voice sounded distant, farther away with each word. "Jacky just stared up at me with open lifeless eyes, his skin cold and his lips blue." Jack paused, lost for a moment in reliving that horrible morning. He trembled. He closed his eyes hard and ran his hands through his hair. It seemed to the others, in acknowledging those moments from the past, that Jack looked older and more tired. He then took a deep breath, opened his eyes and continued on, more quickly now. "My wife couldn't handle it. She had a nervous breakdown and after trying to kill herself, she never really recovered. She lived with her parents for a while, and then moved on. She couldn't stand to be with me for any period of time, too many memories of Jacky. She just wasn't strong enough. Who ever is? So I lost them both. I threw myself into my work. I all but lived for my research and I took on as many classes as they'd let me. Nights were the worst, nightmares woke me regularly."

"Finally, I started reading spiritual materials, trying to understand how and why it happened. I didn't really think about God much before. But after Jacky died, I thought about God a lot, wondering how he could do this to me or what I had done to deserve it. Soon, I came to realize that I didn't believe in that kind of reasoning. I didn't believe that there was some all-knowing, single entity that issued out consequences, some good and some bad, depending on one's merits. I shifted my understanding and beliefs of God to a more all-encompassing energy field that was neither good nor bad. Instead, it included everything and everyone. I studied middle and far eastern philosophies. I don't know what the truth really is, but I know when something feels right. I know when something helps me with the immense grief that I carry. I have had the same nightmare of walking in to see my dead child staring at me nearly every night since it happened. When those nightmares lighten up or shift from horror to calm, I feel as if I am on the right track." Jack shook his head and took another deep breath. As did the others.

"Anyway, during the course of my investigations into all things spiritual, I came across the Mayan prophecies and the knowledge of the end of the long count calendar. There seemed to be so much mumbo-jumbo about it, but through all of it, I sensed there was something real, something important. I had an overwhelming desire to come here. I thought, unrealistically I know, that I could find my answers here. So I came to Mexico. Now, I am sure that I am supposed to be here. I know this is what I need to do. I need to protect those secrets, or maybe even help to reveal them; which task is mine - I am not sure yet. But I feel it is for me to do. I can't speak for the others." Jack took a final long deep breath and fell silent. He had gotten lost in his own speech. He had divulged so much and felt a little uncomfortable, at the same time he felt relieved, to finally spill it out. In speaking, he solidified his own resolve.

Eligio nodded but said nothing. He simply turned and stared into Alana's eyes, challenging her next. Alana felt uncomfortable, wondering if she needed to match Jack's level of disclosure. She didn't want to diminish Jack's heartache by going into her own long story. Jack had revealed a lot about himself. Alana didn't really know how to respond to his loss. She had not thought about children much; her life devoted to her work. She could not imagine the horrors of outliving your own child. Her heart clenched at the idea. Still she wanted to let Jack know that she understood where he was coming from. She thought about how different Jack's path was from hers, and yet she felt the same allegiance and certainty to being here, and the same resolve to continue on wherever this path took her. She too was sure and needed to at least let Eligio know it.

"I understand your draw to this mystery. I too have been searching for my own answers and feel that I have been led directly here to this place, in this time. I am not sure what the answers are or what we are to do next, but I am not going home until I am!" Alana stated, looking deep into Eligio's eyes trying to convey her conviction.

Apu knew he needed to say something next, as Eligio had shifted his gaze to him. But what would it be? He also wanted to pass Eligio's test, though he was unsure of how to do that. He did not want it to sound like, 'me too.' But that is what he was thinking. Finally, he decided to simply mention his own personal guidance. "My grandfather, Danvir Chohan, died a few years ago in India. I was very close to him. He was my spiritual teacher; he taught me the Vedic path and traditions. He taught me how to meditate." Apu paused for a moment; a smile creased his face as he remembered his youth. But the smile soon faded. "I was lost after his death. One day he came to me in a vision when I was deep in meditation. He did not say anything, but I knew he was with me again and has remained ever since. Now he guides me. He shows himself to me, as a ghost – a spirit, letting me know I am doing the right thing; I am walking the right path. I have seen him during my meditations every day since we have arrived. But even more amazing, one afternoon in the cave, I saw his spirit walking about while I took pictures. I have no doubt that I am supposed to be here."

Upon hearing their confessions, Eligio knew what he needed to do next. He got up from his seat, turned toward the mountain and began walking in the direction of the cave. Jack, Alana and Apu looked around at each other confused. Then, without a word, they got to their feet and followed Eligio. Jack wondered if he had totally misread Eligio's line of questioning. Carlos saw them following Eligio up the hill again and decided he should follow along too. He still wasn't sure about this old shaman.

Chapter 17

December 13, 2012

This was more than Eligio had anticipated from the three foreigners, and now they had to hurry. The interview and testing process was completed; they had all three passed. He knew it was time to perform his final shamanic duty; to tell the story of the Age of Man. The same story was told to him when he was a little boy, and that was repeated to him many times during his training as Daykeeper. 'It must be told in the presence of the ancients,' he thought to himself as he looked back down the mountain to make sure that the others were behind him.

It was high noon and the sun was beating down on the group as they climbed to the mouth of the cave. Once they entered, the cool damp interior was a welcomed reprieve. They filed in through the small doorway, all noticing that Eligio was making himself comfortable on the dirt floor. Each found a spot, creating a semi-circle in front of the wall. Eligio was on one end, with the wall of secrets to his left side. A small ray of light filtered in through the cave's opening; otherwise the space was quite dark. Apu was about to get up and turn on the battery powered lights placed throughout the cave, but at that same moment Eligio pulled out matches and candles from his backpack. He silently placed two large candles at the base of the wall and lit them. The shaman then set another well burned candle in front of himself and lit it. He seemed to glow, just like the simple flames.

Carlos agreed to translate the story for the others as well as he could. Alana would occasionally help out when necessary.

Jack tried to relax. He thought about what they were going to do about tomorrow, when the authorities arrived, but he did his best to let go. He decided to get through today first.

Eligio's candles smelled funny to the others and the cave took on an eerie air of mystery, filled with secrets and shadows. Eligio sat very still with his eyes closed. The others inhaled deeply, instinctively wanting to create a sense of calm. Apu closed his eyes and soon the others followed suit. Each person was lost in his or her own thoughts when Eligio's barely audible hum vibrated around the room. Soon the hum expanded and turned into a chant of sorts. The others opened their eyes slightly and were amazed at how the cave had changed. The space around them seemed to glow. The flicker of the flames caused the wall to appear in gentle motion, the characters, symbols and etchings alive with energy in their messages. Eligio's chanting, which had gotten louder, seemed to come from every corner of the cave in full stereo sound. The acrid smell of the candles made their eyes water and caused a slight dizzying feeling.

Abruptly, Eligio stopped the chanting. Silence reigned for long moments. Then Eligio spoke, at first it was in a language that none understood. He then shifted a little and switched to Spanish as he told the story.

"There have been many tales told of the beginning of the Age of Man. The ancient Mayas told of the story of the Hero Twins, Hunahpu and Xbalanque, sons of Hun Hunahpu. The Aztecs told the story of Quetzalcoatl and Tezcatlipoca and the creation of the five suns. Many stories originated with the Olmecs and the World Tree sprouting out of Creation Mountain. What I am about to tell you, is much different from all of those stories. This story is descendent from the Ah Tza, the people from over the sea. Countless Baktun have passed since they came to the land of the Maya. The story I am about to relay, was written in several of our books made of bark. Most of the books were destroyed; some were stolen by the Jesus priests. That is when our family was assigned to the position of Gatekeeper. We protect the stories. We were to guarantee their survival. My ancestors also created this wall: the living Wall of Hunab Ku. By your presence here, having found and exposed this Wall, by the timing and by your own admissions, I know these stories are for you to understand and to take into the world.

When the Ah Tza, the People of the Rattlesnake, came here, they were seen as gods. They were beautiful and colorful, richly adorned and made up. We were more primitive than they, thus we saw them as gods. We wanted to worship them. They tried to teach us, to help us. They taught us about the stars and how to track time. They taught us that time was imaginary and that we could hide our own secrets in it. They taught us the wisdom of geometry and astronomy and mathematics and many other concepts that changed our lives. Most importantly, they tried to teach us about ourselves, where man came from and what our destiny was to be.

Our priests became their primary students, since they were our leaders. Later, after these god-people passed on, our priests became enamored with their new knowledge and began to use it as power. In the end, the power overwhelmed them, always demanding more. Then many began to die. Too many of us died. Human sacrifices at the powerful hands of the priests. It was abominable, a gross misrepresentation of the truths that we were taught. At first my own ancestors were among many priests that fought against such distortions. However, slowly each one succumbed to the enticement of wealth and power, or on fear of death. They were persuaded to join the carnage. Eventually, they all believed the lies that they had created; this gave them great credibility with the people. After many generations, no one remembered anything else. All, but one line of my own family, the Gatekeeper priests; we alone would cling to the truth in its original form. We alone would go into hiding, allowing the truths to become fairy tales told to children to help them go to sleep. We wrote these truths down in secret codices but when the western priests came here, they found them and took them. Many of them they burned, but some were stolen."

Eligio paused. It was obvious the sadness and feeling of betrayal was real and had trickled down through the ages to each person who knew the truth. He inhaled deeply and then exhaled, long and slowly - releasing it once and for all.

"These same truths are here before you now. These are the original truths as pure in their content as when they were first taught to us by the Ah Tza, or as they are known to you, the Atlantiens."

Eligio paused again. Each one of the scientists were busy processing all the information he had just shared with them. Of course there was no way to verify it; it was too incredible to be true.

Eligio closed his eyes again. He took several long deep breaths and then fell back into his chanting. The others watched. The air in the cave was heavy. The wall danced about, as the light flickered. The suspense was building, toward what they were not sure. The common feeling was that they had entered another space and time. Jack felt no imminent danger. He was comfortable and yet anxious to hear what was to come next.

Alana experienced acute anticipation, waiting for something really important to be revealed. Her body felt heavy and yet her mind alert.

Apu went deeper into a state of meditation, understanding the process of transcendentalism. He had experienced alternate conscious states several times before, during deep meditations. There was no better moment than this.

The chanting stopped. There was another long stretch of silence. So long in fact, that the others started to think that Eligio had fallen asleep. Finally, he began to speak again. His voice was deep and rich; it reverberated throughout the cave, filling every space. They could feel the words in their very bones.

"All of humanity is a grand, unique and miraculous experiment, but not bound by our concepts of time. Time is important, as we will see. Man's evolution is slow, very slow. Many millions of years ago, we started out as energy, evolved into simple forms, then into complex forms, and finally into even more complex forms. Over much time, each life-form adapted, it learned. However, no amount of time or adaptation can explain the sudden jumps we find in life or intelligence that is evident in *our* history. There is more to the process of evolution than we see, than we've been taught.

The gods knew that this experiment would need help along the way and at certain points in our development we would require major shifts; large jumps in complexity, awareness and intelligence. Many thousands of years ago, the Ah Tza, knew these truths. They instructed us in the creation, manipulation and tracking of time. As humans, we are amazing creatures, we learned and adapted to our teachings well. Our brains became more complex, our thoughts and our creativity blossomed. The gods knew that some were prepared to know the goal, where we are heading, and when the next jump would take place. They were ready to understand - The end of the Age of Man is the beginning of the Age of Gods."

Eligio paused again. The others were listening intently to this alternate history lesson. It was getting very interesting and they wanted to hear more. Eligio felt their eagerness.

"Mankind will not cease to exist; rather the next Age of Man *is* the Age of Gods. We transition into conscious creators. As gods, we understand our connections to each other and to the whole of our world, even to the whole of the universe. We understand the energy of creation, the power of love and the truth in unity. We leave behind the world of duality, where we learned so much through opposition. As gods, we learn and grow through our sameness rather than our differences. As gods we transcend the fear of death and understand its gifts. We understand how to communicate with all other creatures, whether animal or plant, whether alive or dead. For in truth, nothing dies, but only transforms. All is God. As gods, we learn to utilize all of the forces of the universe and our limitations fall away. As gods, we come to live a whole new way; in harmony, in peace and in love. This is our goal, this is our destiny. This is the next age of humanity and this age is now upon us."

"It was foretold to my ancestors, that the end of the Age of Man calculates to be thirteen Baktun, zero Katun, zero Tun, zero Uinal, zero K'in - which on your calendar is December 21, 2012. At this precise time, the forces and energies are in place to facilitate a mass jump in humanity's evolution. This is when we become like the gods." Eligio looked around the room to see if each of them had registered the proximity of the date, hoping they understood the significance of what he was telling them.

"Though everything has been prepared, in order to facilitate such a jump in mankind, there is a process that must be carried out precisely. Humanity, as a whole, is at its most dangerous juncture in its development. Our brains have evolved to the point where our will is very strong and yet our understanding is still limited. We have maximized our polarity training (the teachings of opposites) to the extreme. We have been climbing steadily to reach critical mass. Should we not reach the point of unity in time, we could trigger annihilation in one final destructive act. The moment of critical jump is the moment when all possibilities exist at once, including failure. The gods would love to intervene, but they dare not. Such an intervention now would recess our development. We must choose it ourselves, and we must all choose, or at least a critical number must to sway the masses.

The good news is, we live in a world of opposites, so along with this tide of destruction that we experience daily, there has also been a tide of creation and awareness. It may not be as visible, but it is equally as strong. As soon as the critical numbers of individuals select unity rather than separation the jump *will* happen.

Since the gods cannot intervene, a series of events have been set up to help facilitate this jump in mankind's evolution. Certain individuals volunteered to embody and communicate the necessary vision in the right span of time. These individuals would each have different tasks to perform. If anything went wrong with this plan or these individuals did not carry out their missions successfully, the Age of Man and opposites could rule and the end would eventually be self destruction. I cannot stress enough the importance of this process."

Eligio gave them a few moments to digest the information that he had just shared. Jack sat motionless, soaking it all in, feeling stronger than ever in knowing that he was one of those individuals. The very idea astounded him, but he felt it to be true. Alana knew in an instant that she had found the explanation to the words of her vision. She was confident that Eligio's story included her. All the while, Apu silently thanked his grandfather for guiding him here and wondered if Danvir Chohan had become one of those gods guiding the whole adventure.

Eligio continued, "I will tell you what little I know of these people. The first individual is referred to as Zero. He or she is the beginning and the end of the mission. He is to lead. The second is referred to as the Sky. This person knows the vision of the future and keeps the others on track. The third is known as the Rock. This person gives stability and guidance. There are 8 others, they are all known as Gatekeepers. They each carry a specific key to open the gateway to illumination. Each key has a symbol." Eligio gestured to the wall on his left directly to the set of symbols with the Hunab Ku as their canvas. "These eight symbols are given to you from the ancients; they will guide you to the Gatekeepers. As each key becomes part of your understanding, it also becomes part of the whole of humanity. Each key will have a definite effect on us all, whether it is immediate or not." They each stared at the symbols Eligio was referring to and magically the pictures seemed to stand out. It was now clear that these unique symbols were watching and waiting for them.

"The Zero, the Sky and the Rock must find the other Gatekeepers and receive the messages of the keys. Each gateway you pass through takes us all one step closer to the Age of Gods. When the final key is unlocked and its message is revealed, the jump will take place. In that moment, a final individual will feel the message of the last key and make a choice. This final being to choose is referred to as the Flame. This individual is the last person who needs to understand and he or she, will spark the fire that will set ablaze the rest of the humanity. This fire will ignite the power of *God* in each individual."

"I know that these descriptions of the four are cryptic; their meanings and possible identities have been debated by my family for many generations. The ancients relayed only that the Zero himself would understand.

I, and my family, have been commissioned to protect these secrets until the Zero arrived. My final act as the first Gatekeeper is to destroy the Wall of Hunab Ku."

"WHAT? Destroy the wall!?" Jack exclaimed, suddenly angry. His outburst broke the trance that had overtaken them. "You cannot destroy it. How will anyone believe us, if we do not have the evidence to prove that what you are saying is true?" He was nearly screaming at Eligio, his eyes daring the man to answer. Eligio did not respond or even move. After a couple of moments, the Gatekeeper shifted his body on the cave floor and closed his eyes. Almost immediately, Jack felt calmer and less threatened. This change in sensation amazed them all. Jack allowed the calm to wash over him. After a couple of deep breaths, he questioned him again, this time in a low meek voice. "Why?"

Chapter 18

December 13, 2012

"My ancestors knew when the foreign priests took our secret books, that they would decipher them eventually and thus know the prophecies. They also knew that the enemy would not wish the prophecies to come to pass. The idea of being a god is enticing to those who want power, but the prophecies are clear - if all had such power, no one person could rule over another. Their power now comes from stealing it from others. Should true power be equally distributed to all individuals, each one a creator empowered by God, then they would lose their control. The reality is, that they are correct, their old way of controlling would no longer be effective and this causes fear. When you live by the forces of opposition, it is all you can see. Those who strive for such control have sought out and destroyed many of the clues left here by the ancients. None of them have told the whole story as this wall, but this cave does. The enemy has sought to find this place for many generations and they will not stop until they do. They are very resourceful and have enjoyed their ability to control others for a very long time. They will not relinquish it without a fight. They must not be allowed to stall the mission, the awakening. They are blinded and believe that they are right, and this makes them very dangerous. They are like our priests many ages ago; they now believe the lies that they created. This gives them great credibility and influence."

Eligio paused again giving Carlos a minute to catch up. He had been doing a great job translating Eligio's intricate story. He had only asked Alana for help on a couple of words.

Jack's brain was spinning with all the new information and the danger awaiting them the next day. "I still don't understand why you have to destroy the wall."

Eligio sighed. "Until today I did not understand this directive either. But you have felt the power of this place. I sense that there is a reason, though I may not totally understand. I trust in the ancient wisdom. You must trust also."

"So this Zero person is supposed to decipher these symbols and find the eight Gatekeepers to unlock the gates? All in eight days? How do I do that?" Jack wasn't aware for a moment that he had put himself into the Zero's shoes. When he realized it, he looked around to see if the others had also. He could tell by the looks on their faces that they had heard him and agreed with the conclusion. With the support that he felt, he was able to continue, "And how do I find these Gatekeepers?"

It was Alana who answered him, "I believe that I can help find the Gatekeepers. We must decipher those symbols. I had a vision years ago that gave me a picture of where we are going. It is a wonderful, beautiful, peaceful place," she said dreamily. "Anyway, I believe that I am the Sky and I know I can help."

Apu chimed in, "I know we can figure it out. I have pictures and drawings of the entire wall and cave, so we will always have it with us. We can go to a place that is safe, where they won't find us. I may know a place in the Rockies." Apu smiled when he said this. The Rock was found. Though it was uncanny, the coincidences, they all still saw humor in such perfection. They laughed together for a moment, releasing some of the seriousness of the moment.

"How will we be able to do all of this in only eight days?" Jack directed his question toward Eligio, though if anyone at all could answer his questions, he would be grateful. But this time, no one else chimed in. It seemed impossible in a short period of time.

"You will have to figure the rest out for yourselves. I do not know any more about the mission than what I have told you. You are correct though. You will have to complete it by December 21st."

"I *can* warn you though, the followers of the ones who stole the codices are still here. Their members are everywhere. They will not give up looking for you, to thwart your mission. You must be very careful and ever so vigilant." Eligio said.

"I am not sure how this mission is possible, but we must try." Jack replied. He knew that this was what he must do; he just wasn't sure how to go about it. Jack had done a lot of difficult things throughout his professional career, but in none of them had he felt less prepared or less confident than he did facing this 'mission.' And this was perhaps the most important thing he would ever do.

Apu decided it was time to make the plans for the next couple of days, at least. "Well, we have to get out of Mexico and that may not be easy if we are caught destroying historical relics."

Eligio volunteered, "I will take care of the cave. I'll make sure that they know it is by my actions not yours. You must pack to leave now, before they arrive. Before they start searching for you."

"We can go to my grandfather's home in Colorado." Apu offered. "He had been my guide since he passed several years ago. I know that he would want us to use it. No one will find us there, not if we are careful."

"We can fly into California. I will quickly stop at my place, grab some things and then we can drive my car to Colorado, that way no one can trace our airline tickets or a rental car. They will think we are in California and will be looking for us there." Alana's idea drew nods.

Carlos quit translating for a few minutes and said, "It will take some time to pack up the camp, should we leave any trace?"

"We only need the essentials, anything related to the wall, our personal items, and anything that could lead them to us. Other than that, we will leave the rest behind." Jack informed him.

They began to fidget about the cave, ready to proceed with their plans, anxious to get out of Mexico before the Ministry caught up with them and detained them. Eligio stopped them for a moment to pass on one final warning.

"There is something more I must tell you. The prophecies warn of the moment of transition. It is a very critical moment. The opposition will have the most power at the same time. It is the moment of equal sides, the moment of decision, where the fate of humanity is based, in one decision, in one instant." Jack wasn't sure what that meant, but guessed it would be apparent when the time came. He figured this was one adventure he was going to have to follow from his gut and of course, with the help of the others. He turned and looked at Apu and then at Alana. A bond had formed between them. They could all feel it. The burden was incomprehensible, but wasn't that what heroes were made from; winning against insurmountable odds?

"This *is* your destiny. All things are set up for you to succeed and the gods are with you. You are not alone, you are *never* alone. You must remember this!" Eligio stressed.

They sat there for a couple more minutes in silence, knowing that as soon as they left the cave, they would never see it again. There was some fear, it was mostly a fear of the unknown. Having each other seemed to help . Each one knew that this was what they had waited for, why they were here.

Jack had been searching since his son had died and his family had fallen apart. He felt in his heart that this quest would lead him back to his son.

Alana knew her whole life had been led in preparation for this moment. This was where her alternate self had been guiding her. Those few symbols on the wall, the same that had come to her in her vision, told her so.

Apu could almost see his grandfather standing beside him, sending his approval, leading him, from the other side of life.

Each one knew they would have to rely on each other to fill in the missing pieces. Jack put his hand into the middle of the circle without saying a word. The others just looked at him for a moment, then they understood and one by one, each put one hand on top of his, like a sports team about to go onto the field. But instead of a battle cry or a cheer, they just hung on for a moment. It was a silent gesture of connectedness and commitment. A connection to the mission and to each other. A commitment to the whole of humanity.

Chapter 19

December 13, 2012

Professor Ramirez from the National Museum and University Laboratories in Mexico City arrived early. He brought along a portable gamma spectrometer and other supplies to collect several samples for the lab. Huetzin De Los Reyes was determined to make this official. He would not allow another artifact to leave his county. He could not let it happen and expect to retain his job. He knew this was his last chance.

They were making plans to depart, first thing in the morning, when Huetzin received a call.

"Hello?" he answered. "Yes, sir. No sir, we are leaving at first light. Yes, sir. I was waiting for Professor Ramirez to arrive with his equipment. Tonight? Sorry, sir. No, I did not think they were going to steal anything. Dr. Reese's credentials checked out. Yes, sir. Yes sir, I will take the police with us. Sir, do you suspect that they are dangerous? Yes, sir, I will ask the lieutenant myself. Oh. And he agreed to come along? Thank you, sir." Huetzin's face was turning more red with each word. "Yes sir. We will leave immediately. It should take us only two hours. Yes, sir, I will contact you as soon as possible. Yes, sir, thank you, sir."

When he hung up the phone, he was sweating profusely. He wondered about the urgency. He really hadn't thought there was any real threat, though he did detect that he had not been told the whole truth. 'I wonder who he was referring to as *diplomatic pressures* and *higher authorities*. Well, whoever is pulling my boss's strings is not my concern.' He only knew that he must not fail this time. He straightened his posture as his face became stern.

Lieutenant Munoa knocked on the door. "I have two jeeps ready to go. Are you ready, Señor De Los Reyes?"

"Yes, of course. What about Professor Ramirez?" Huetzin asked.

"He is already outside in one of the jeeps."

"I see. Well, let's go then," Huetzin replied as he walked toward the door. He had a bad feeling about all of this, but was determined to push ahead. He climbed into the jeep with Professor Ramirez. In the other jeep were four more policemen, fully armed with rifles on their shoulders and handguns on their hips. He felt that the situation was spiraling out of his control. He turned to the lieutenant and asked if all the fire-power was necessary.

"Orders," was all he heard in reply. As the jeep took off, Heutzin's mood was sullen, fully expecting it to rain again.

Chapter 20

December 13, 2012

Jack got up from the circle and started to exit the cave. He stopped abruptly and turned. He wanted one last look at the wall. The candles had burned down low and it had grown dark outside. In the dim light he could barely make out the etchings in the wall. He marveled, not for the first time, at the workmanship and wondered about the Maya and their secrets. Then he turned and crept out through the opening. Apu and Alana took a similar last look before they too exited the cave. As Carlos was about to leave, he asked Eligio if he was coming.

"No. I will stay here for a while. I will be down later." Eligio replied.

"Okay, see you in a bit." Carlos said as he left. Eligio got up from his spot on the cave floor, turned on the battery powered lights and got to work. He sensed he didn't have much time.

As they made their way down the hill, the three friends began planning immediately. "We should leave at dawn." Jack said. "I am not sure what time the inspector will arrive, but I would like to be long gone by then. Also, we will want to go a different route than usual. We wouldn't want to pass them on the road. Carlos, we will need to get to an airport, but not the one near Ocosingo. Any ideas?"

"I think I know just the place." Carlos said as he raced to catch up with the others. "Clearly one I don't know." Jack was curious.

"We can go to Altamirano, to the south. They have a small airport where you can get a flight to San Cristóbal de Las Casas, from there we can catch a plane to Mexico City." Carlos informed them.

"Excellent. Where's Eligio?" Jack replied.

"He said he wanted to stay for a little while."

For only a moment, Jack wondered what the old shaman was up to, but immediately switched his attention to the countless tasks at hand. "Everyone pack up just what you will need. We won't have room for much."

It was now completely dark as they reached the camp. Carlos found and turned on two battery powered lanterns. Apu started a fire.

"I will fix some food. We need to eat." Carlos headed for the mess tent. Jack entered his hut and lit a small lantern. He looked around wishing he wasn't leaving so many things behind, but there was no helping that now. 'Who knows where this mission will lead us. I must be nuts, destroying and leaving an archaeological find, and going in search of some unknown keys. I have no idea what these keys are or how to find them.' He shook his head hard. 'Stay focused,' he admonished himself. He grabbed his notebook computer and its rechargeable battery packs. He stashed some clothes, an extra pair of boots and a couple of personal items in his duffle. Then he sat on his cot and began to sort through his papers and notes. After a few moments of remorse, he realized he wouldn't need any of them. He was really starting to believe in Eligio's story. If he failed, who knew what would happen? Eligio had hinted at the end of the humanity. If they were successful, he couldn't even guess what he would need. 'Oh, well. Things will change.' Jack resolved to himself. He gathered his notes and took them outside to the fire and tossed them into the flames. There was a quick blaze and then smoldering ash. 'The end of an excavation. The beginning of an adventure.' Jack quipped smiling. Though he was unsure of many things, inside he felt he was doing the right thing.

Alana made her way over to Carlos' hut. Since she had only just arrived, she had not unpacked much. She knew she had already paired down her belongings quite a bit when coming out here, but repacked anyway, leaving as much as she possibly could behind.

Apu was having a tougher time. He knew he needed all of his notes, papers, pictures and memory sticks. This was what they would use to decipher the symbols - the secrets the wall contained. All of his material would be their guide. He opened his pilot's bag, a gift from his grandfather, and began putting in everything that he had gathered regarding the Wall. His other reference materials he put into another bag. Next, he concentrated on his personal belongings - they were minimal in many ways now. Finally, after scanning the area one last time, he felt satisfied.

It wasn't long before Carlos was calling them to dinner. They each made their way over to the mess tent and sat down. Eligio was already sitting at the small table eating. He and Carlos had been mapping out the fastest routes out of the area. They ate quietly. Tomorrow was the beginning of the unknown. Jack suggested they try to get some rest. He wanted to leave even before dawn, if they could.

Just as they were finishing up, they heard a low rumbling noise echoing up the canyon. It was the unmistakable sound of a vehicle coming closer. As they sat in breathless silence, the noise grew louder.

Jack jumped up. "I'm guessing two jeeps. It has to be the inspector with backup. Get your things. We have to go NOW!" He hollered in a strained whisper, as he ran to pick up his bags from his hut. The others were already scrambling. Carlos ran to his hut, gathered a couple of things, threw them into a bag and was back to the jeep in a flash. He turned out all the battery-powered lights and grabbed two flashlights and the bag of food that he had already prepared from the mess tent. He looked all around for Eligio but couldn't spot him. Finally, he caught him making his way up the hill with a small flash light beam leading his way. 'Good luck, Eligio.' Carlos sent his blessing.

Jack had started the jeep. The others threw their bags into the back and climbed in.

"Where's Eligio?" Jack directed his concern to Carlos as he climbed into the passenger's seat.

"He is on his way up to the cave." He mumbled sadly, "I didn't get a chance to say goodbye."

Jack turned the jeep around and headed in the direction Carlos and Eligio had scouted - toward the back pass, down the south side of the mountain. It was barely a road and would be hard to navigate at night. But they had no choice. As they went past the slope leading up to the cave, they were drawn to look up at its opening. They could see a glow coming from the entrance. Eligio had turned on all the lights.

'Smart,' Jack thought. This would draw the inspector's attention up the hill. It could give them more time to get away. Each passenger in their own way, silently sent Eligio gratitude for all he had shared with them and for what he was about to do. Quickly, however their attentions shifted to the treacherous dirt path ahead of them and the danger they were desperately trying to escape. They could only hope that they would be far enough away, out of earshot and sight, when the inspector actually pulled up to the deserted camp.

Chapter 21

December 13, 2012

When Lieutenant Munoa's jeep pulled up to what was obviously the campsite, he and his officers looked for signs of life. The second jeep pulled up behind carrying Inspector De Los Reyes, from the Ministry of Antiquities and the Professor. He motioned for the others to wait, and with his hand on his hip, gripping his pistol, he climbed out of the jeep. He noticed that the fire pit smoldered with the remains of a fire. Seeing a quick gesture, the other officers cautiously followed Munoa's lead, got out, flashlights in hand and guns at the ready. The group inspected the huts, but found no one. "There is a lot of stuff here," one of the men called to the lieutenant. "They must be around here somewhere."

One of the other officers came out from the mess tent, "They must have eaten not too long ago; there is still fresh food and dishes in this one."

Inspector De Los Reyes stood next to the jeep, taking in the whole deserted campsite. He was more interested in the archeological site than in finding Dr. Reese and his team. Allowing his eyes to adjust by moving into the dark, away from the flashing lights, he spotted a glow up on the side of the large mountain to the right. "Lieutenant. There, over there, a light. Up the hill there, see? They must be up at the dig site." He alerted the lieutenant as he started off in that direction, a flashlight in his hand illuminating the way. Lieutenant Munoa thought he heard something off in the distance but immediately forgot about it when the inspector pointed out the light. Professor Ramirez followed along, but stayed more to the rear of the group. The police made him nervous.

When Huetzin arrived at the mouth of the cave, he heard a deep muffled voice, "Salgan de aquí! Es peligroso aquí! *(You must stay away! There is danger here!)*" The voice echoed as if it surrounded them. This frightened him and stopped him in his tracks, just outside the entrance to the cave. The lieutenant stormed past the others, without pause. He drew his gun and entered. His officers entered right behind their leader. Huetzin and the professor reluctantly followed. What Huetzin saw after his eyes adjusted to the light, was the back of an older man, standing with his arms high, facing a magnificent wall. He was holding something in his right hand. Huetzin didn't notice much else about the man. His attention was fully captivated by the wall. The officers found the shaman much more interesting. Lieutenant Munoa's trained eye noticed something far more attention-grabbing. Around the cave, were small piles of dynamite neatly and meticulously placed. Barely detectable wires led from the piles to the motionless shaman. The device in his hand was clear to Munoa and he immediately understood the shaman's intent.

The lieutenant put his hands up, showing a sign of surrender to sooth the old man. "Take it easy, Señor. We are only looking for Dr. Jack Reese and his team. Have you seen them?" The man did not turn or answer.

"Get out of the cave at once or I will blow all of you up with it." Eligio demanded.

"Wait!" Huetzin said. "You can't destroy such a treasure," he said as he pointed to the wall in front of Eligio.

"This wall belongs to my people, the Maya. It belongs to the Cuscun family, my family. It was created by my ancestors," he bellowed at them. "Now, it belongs to me and I will destroy it. I will not let it fall into the hands of non-believers."

Again the lieutenant tried to calm him. He didn't care what happened to the damn wall; he just wanted to find Reese. "We will leave if you tell us where Dr. Reese is."

"I don't know where he is. You must leave now!" Eligio shouted. They all began to back out of the cave, one by one, each climbing out of the small opening. Eligio turned and followed them to the mouth of the cave, but remained just inside the archway. The lieutenant tried one more time, "Have you seen Dr. Reese at all?"

"No, no one has been here. I was using this abandoned campsite for a day or two while it suited me." Eligio said defiantly. This surprised the lieutenant. Where could Reese have gone?

"When did you arrive here, Señor …?"

"My name is Eligio Cuscun and I told you, I got here a couple of days ago and no one was here." Eligio lied.

This did not make any sense to the lieutenant. Why would this man be ready to destroy this cave with dynamite and where could Dr. Reese and his team, have gone? He knew this crazy man must be lying but he wasn't about to press him for the truth. Instead he tried a different tactic.

"Why do you want to blow up the cave?" he asked.

"The cave belongs to me and my ancestors. I am not going to let you or any other non-believers defile it."

This time Huetzin responded, "Non-believers of what?"

"Non-believers of the prophecy." Eligio responded. He figured the longer he kept them talking the better it would be for the Zero and the others.

"What prophecy?" Huetzin asked, puzzled.

But the lieutenant was getting impatient. "Señor Cuscun, did you know Dr. Reese?" he interrupted.

Eligio knew this was a dangerous question. The lieutenant was trying to catch him in a lie. "I know no one." He answered belligerently. "I am here to protect this cave from those who steal our treasures."

"We do not wish to steal any treasure." Huetzin tried to reassure the man. Again the lieutenant interrupted.

"This is getting us nowhere. We must find Reese and his team. My orders are to stop him and anyone on his team from escaping the country with information about that… the …" the lieutenant struggled for the words to describe what was in the cave. "…that wall or treasure or whatever it is, in there." He pointed to the cave. Fed up with the situation, he turned around, started away from the cave and motioned to his officers to follow him.

Eligio knew, in that moment, that he had to make a decision. He did not believe in taking life. He believed in the connectedness of all things. But he knew he had to give the Zero more time to escape. The inspector and the professor had not yet turned to go. Eligio drew in a deep breath and faced them, he spoke in a deep, raspy growl, "You must go also. Go! Go!" His face turned red and he waved his arms wildly, trying with all his might to scare them away.

Huetzin tried one more time to save the wall. "You do not have to destroy this cave, we will help you protect it," he pleaded.

Eligio looked him dead in the eye and said with an eerie, calm voice, "If you do not wish to die, you must go now, quickly."

Huetzin got the message, turned and began to run down the hill with the professor right on his heels. Eligio, waiting one more brief moment, hoping they would be far enough away. He looked up at the sky, exhaled a slow and grateful breath, smiled a peaceful, satisfied smile and pressed the button.

The lieutenant and his officers were not yet off the mountain side and the inspector and the professor were just far enough away to escape serious injury. The explosion was enormous. The ground shook. The air filled with dust and debris. When it all settled, the top of the mountain was replaced by a crater. The blast stalled the whole group for hours. By the time they got everyone down the mountain and everyone's wounds taken care of, it was early the next morning. They rested before proceeding any further. The lieutenant was frustrated having no communication to his office or the outside world. He lay on a cot, supposing it was Dr. Reese's, his arm in a makeshift sling and cursed the old man with the dynamite. The others suffered from cuts, bumps and bruises, but they had all survived.

Eligio's body was never found. He, his spirit, at least, had moved on. He fulfilled his destiny and passed in peace.

Chapter 22

December 13, 2012

Though they were miles away, Jack, Alana, Apu and Carlos all heard the blast. They knew instinctively that Eligio had been successful in destroying the wall. They also strongly suspected that he had not survived. Jack felt a familiar pang of sorrow. A wave of sadness flowed over the others as well. It lingered in Carlos, for he, perhaps more than anyone else, had connected with the old shaman. No one spoke for a long while, as they drove on into the night. Each individual member of the group understood, like never before, the seriousness of the mission. Its success was the most significant undertaking they would ever attempt. Eligio had guided them on this quest and then infused it with profound importance through his willingness to protect it and them with his own life.

It was dawn and Jack's eyelids were getting heavy as he drove. When he came to a fork in the road, he brought the jeep to a complete stop. Carlos opened his eyes and looked around. Jack planned to ask the first to wake to take over driving, hoping it would be Carlos, "Do you want to drive for a while? I am getting tired and you know better where we are going." Carlos simply nodded, got out of the passenger's seat and came around the front. After settling in, Jack closed his eyes and fell asleep almost immediately. Carlos drove on for another hour. Alana and Apu were both fast asleep in the back seat despite the rocky road.

The loaded down jeep pulled up to the airplane hanger that sat beside a small grass runway. Carlos got out and went inside. The others woke up sleepily. When Jack realized where they were, he became alert instantly, keeping an eye out for the police or any government officials. He felt like a drug smuggler in the midst of Columbia or some other such miscreant. He marveled at how things had changed since the earthquake. An ancient wall of symbols had caused one man to die and an innocent group to be on the run. It seemed surreal and yet here he was – right in the middle of it.

Carlos came out of the hanger and informed them that everything was set. "A small single engine airplane and its owner will fly you to San Cristóbal. It is easy to get a flight to Mexico City from there."

Concerned, Jack inquired about the cost. He had limited resources here in the jungle.

"You will need to pay two hundred dollars now, in cash and one hundred more when you arrive. Can you do this?" Carlos asked.

"Yes. Thank you, Carlos, good work." Jack replied, so grateful to have Carlos along.

"There is one more thing, Señor Jack." Carlos paused a moment before continuing.

"Yes, Carlos?" Jack thought something was wrong.

"I will not be coming with you. This is my home and I cannot be of further help to you on this mission. Since I have no family, I will go to Eligio's village and see if he had any family remaining. I will let them know what happened to him and help them if I can."

Jack was saddened to lose Carlos; he had been invaluable during their stay in Mexico and he had become a good friend. Jack did not know what the future held for any of them, but he was sure that he did not wish to drag Carlos into it any further. He understood and admired what Carlos was feeling regarding Eligio.

"We will miss you, my friend. Please give Eligio's family our deepest sympathy and gratitude."

The others got out of the jeep and gathered their bags. Carlos helped them carry their bags to the plane, which had taxied out onto the field. With the bags stowed in the cargo hold, they prepared to board. Each one turned and embraced Carlos before they got on. Apu's eyes welled with tears as he said his goodbye. "Thank you for everything, Carlos. I will miss you." He quickly turned and got in. Jack was the last one to board. He thanked Carlos again, clasped his hand and then climbed the steps. When Carlos drew back his hand there was cash in it. He was surprised, but grateful. He had a long road back Bachajon - Eligio's village.

As the airplane took off, Apu, Alana and Jack each reflected on the events that had transpired over the last twenty-four hours. To Alana, so much had happened since she had been walking gloomily back to her hotel, depressed about another near-miss.

Apu had expected to be studying the wall for some time in Mexico and then head back to the university. He was puzzled by his grandfather's continuing 'visits,' but had not expected such a sudden turn of events or such a monumental task to be set before him. He was grateful to not be in it alone.

Jack leaned forward in his seat and peered down, through the window, at the fading landscape below. He felt a huge weight on his shoulders. He would feel better if he *knew* what he needed to do. If only he had a clearer picture. He took a deep breath and prayed; not to any god in particular, but to the force of good that seemed to be guiding him. He prayed for continued guidance and strength. He looked around at his companions and knew that he had the best support possible. This soothed his troubled mind some. He further consoled himself with the fact that they, at least, knew what the next step was and where they were heading.

'Rest now Jack, you're going to need all of your wits about you for the coming days.' He heard this in his head. Was that the answer to his prayer? He leaned back and closed his eyes and did as instructed.

Part 2

"A coincidence is when God performs a miracle, and decides to remain anonymous."

~ *Unknown*

Chapter 23

December 14, 2012

Their plane touched down at LAX. It was packed with travelers from all corners of the globe. Alana, Apu and Jack slowly made their way off the plane and out of the airport, into the southern California sunlight. They only had the few bags they managed to escape with.

Their travels through San Cristóbal and Mexico City had been relatively quick and uneventful. They had gone from the small chartered plane in Altamirano to a slightly larger plane in San Cristóbal, to a huge jet in Mexico City, all without incident. The trip however, was not without stress; they expected to be stopped and arrested at every turn. Surely, Huetzin De Los Reyes had gotten back to Ocosingo and alerted the authorities. Jack knew they hadn't done anything wrong, not really. He had only misled him as to the contents of the cave. But he also knew that didn't really matter; he was not above suspicion.

They were relieved to touchdown in the States. Whoever was after them couldn't know where they were now.

Alana gave the cab driver directions to her house. She began to have doubts regarding the validity of their mission and started to wonder what she was doing with these two men and if she shouldn't just tell them to continue on without her. She was now safe at home. There was a dramatic contrast between how she felt at home compared to being in Mexico. Their recent adventures felt like a hazy dream, distant and unclear. Doubts began to flood her mind - doubts of the mission and doubts of the things that Eligio had told them. Alana thought she probably should have paid attention to those doubts before this, before bringing all of this to her home. She even questioned her own gullibility for believing any of it in the first place. She vaguely remembered some sense of importance. 'How could anything I do have any effect on the whole world? What a ridiculous idea. How could I be so naive?' Gazing at the crowds in the city, she thought, 'Look at all of these people. No one here thinks such things. Not one of them even considers that the world could be ending in the next few days. How could I know something that no one else even has an inkling of? Isn't it more plausible that I am the crazy one?' Alana didn't know that similar thoughts were running through Jack's mind as well.

Apu was not entertaining such thoughts. He did not fall prey to the same numbing effects of coming home that the others were experiencing. Perhaps it was due to the fact that this wasn't actually his home - having been born and raised in India. For whatever reason, Apu was more accustomed to extraordinary things happening. He did *see* his dead grandfather more regularly now. Apu, instead, was thinking about the symbols that were to lead them to the keys. There was something familiar about one of the markings. It reminded him of something and he was wracking his brain trying to remember what that *'something'* was. He was unaware of the doubts and concerns of the other two until they arrived at Alana's house. She invited them in politely enough, but Apu sensed there was something wrong.

As Alana unlocked the front door she thought about the things she had sent home from Mexico City, after her stint with the museum. She hoped that her neighbor, Jenn, had put her luggage inside. Alana opened the door and walked in first, side-stepping the mail that was littering the foyer's floor. Another huge pile of mail sat in a basket on the small table just inside the doorway. Alana saw her bags off to the side and all her plants seemed to still be alive. She made a mental note to see Jennifer soon and thank her. Alana put her keys on the table, scooped up the main from the floor, and went to the kitchen, carrying the basket. "Make yourselves at home. I'm just gonna check my mail."

'She is too casual, too calm. That's it.' Apu now was very aware of how the energy of his traveling companions had shifted. He wanted a shower, a good meal and some sleep. But mostly he wanted to decipher the first of the symbols, so they could find the first gateway and discover the first key. Time was ticking away and Alana seemed way too cool for his liking. Just when he was about to say something to Jack, Jack asked their hostess, "Do you mind if I clean up some?"

"Help yourself. The bathroom is up the stairs and to the right. There should be clean towels in the lower cabinet." Alana answered. Jack seemed to have the same nonchalant attitude that he sensed from Alana. 'What the hell is going on?' Apu wondered. He decided to be patient and wait and see what transpired next, before he confronted them. After all, he could use a shower too, he rationalized. While Jack was in the bathroom, he decided to do some research.

"Do you have an active Net port here?" he asked.

"Sure, I didn't want to have to get it reconnected, so I left it active. The office is around the corner, there." She pointed without looking. She was obviously distracted by the letter she was reading. Apu picked up his backpack and headed in the direction of the office. He worried about what could have happened to cause his companions to become distant and blasé.

His worries abated some however, when he entered Alana Borisenko's office. It was lined with books of ancient writings, from around the world. He was immediately enthralled and scanned title after title looking for any that would give him clues to the meanings of the Wall of Secrets' symbols. He pulled a couple and stacked them on the table by the large leather chair. The magnificent chair took up the whole corner of the room. He was about to turn to sit down when one more binding caught his eye. It was an oversized book on the bottom shelf. "Big Sur's lost tribe: The Essalen." It wasn't the title that caught his eye, but more the symbols on the spine. Covering the outside jacket on the book were tiny, bony hand-prints with thin marks scrawled lengthwise on each palm. He excitedly snatched it off the shelf and practically fell into the chair as he started to turn its pages. 'It couldn't be this simple,' he thought to himself. He scanned each page slowly, looking for more information on the hand prints. Within minutes he read about how the Essalen's lived in the upper Carmel Valley in the rugged and densely-forested Santa Lucia Mountains, south of what is now the exclusive Monterey, California. They were a shy and quiet people who revered the earth and each other. He finally came to several small photographs of the handprints and their corresponding descriptions. They created the hand prints nearly four thousand years ago, carefully painting them on the cave's walls.

As Apu stared at the photos, he slowly pieced together the connection between the ancient bony handprints and the Mayan symbols he had been contemplating. Apu knew handprints were a common design - used by many indigenous peoples around the world. The ones in Borneo were some of the most famous. He was unaware of the Essalen tribes though. If you inverted one hand and lay it side-by-side with another, which was not inverted, you would see a group of lines resembling flames, which is what Apu had thought the Mayan symbol reminded him of, flames. Now, he saw something completely different. He laid the book open on the desk and pulled out his disc of pictures of the Mayan wall from his back pack. It took a moment to find the exact picture of the symbols from the wall. But soon he was staring at the digital photos from the Wall of Secrets and comparing them to the photo in the book. They were a very close match. The symbol had found them. Of all the symbols on the wall, the flames, seemingly now to be a pair of handprints, had been the first that he concentrated on. Then to walk in here and have the symbols nearly jump off Alana's shelf at him. Apu knew not to discount coincidences like this. His grandfather taught him that "coincidences are God trying to get your attention." This was too close of a match to ignore.

Apu decided to see if there was more recent information on the Net. He turned on Alana's computer and Googled his way to the Esalen Institute – a spiritual center in Essalen territory. Something more than their well-known hot-springs, drew Apu to the institute. The handprints were only twelve miles east of their campus. Apu wasn't sure if the actual handprints, or the Esalen Institute, would reveal the key Eligio had told them about. But he was sure this was where they should explore first. He hoped when he explained it to the others, that the evidence would be equally compelling to them.

They were not *that* far from the Big Sur area, at least it was in the same state. They could drive there on the way to his grandfather's cabin in Colorado. It wouldn't be that much out of the way, he rationalized to himself. Excited, he rushed into the kitchen to tell Jack and Alana and to share with them the connection he had found.

* *

Alana was sitting at her kitchen table going through the large stack of mail. Most òf it was junk, but a letter from her parents in Romania grabbed her full attention. She missed them. After savoring it, she laid the letter off to the side in a small 'important pile.' The rather large pile beside it was all of the junk mail. Alana stared out the kitchen window for a few minutes. 'I could go and see them now. I am not scheduled to go for Christmas, but I could go now instead of going off on this ridiculous quest, searching for some mysterious secret gates or keys.' She was getting irritated with herself and her continual drive to find an ancient language. 'All because of that vision I had years ago.'

Alana sighed and focused more on the kitchen and her immediate surroundings, making up her mind to stay home. She would let Jack and Apu continue on if they chose to. She glanced over at the back door and saw something that startled her. The door handle was broken and the wood was chipped and splintered. She felt a tremor of fear. Slowly she got up and walked over to the door and peered around the corner into the dining room. No one was there. Here in the small hallway between the dining room and kitchen, the back door had definitely been broken into. The glass was not broken, but the wood frame had been forced and the door handle was hanging loose. She froze. Then without thinking she opened the small pantry closet door in a rush. No one was there. It was actually too small to hold a person. She knew she was freaking out. Alana tip-toed in search of the others. As she came around the corner of the kitchen to the front steps she ran into Apu who was walking with determination in the opposite direction. They nearly knocked each other down as Alana squealed out in fright.

"It's just me, Alana. I found something very interesting. I wanted to show you..." He began excitedly. But before he could continue with his news, Alana interrupted him with hers.

"Someone broke in while I was gone. The back door is broken, come see." Apu relented as they made their way back to the kitchen and the back door.

"I wonder when this happened." Apu had just gotten the words past his lips when they heard a loud THUMP and a BANG upstairs. They both said at once, "JACK!" and ran for the stairs to find him.

Chapter 24

December 14, 2012

Charles tapped lightly on the door himself. He had not visited the Director's home for a couple of months, being too busy fulfilling his duties as Deputy Director. More and more the old man had put things in his hands. He was proud of the trust and confidence his grandfather had in him. Charles was now nearly 40, but men in his family lived a long time. He was only just getting started.

There was a faint call to enter. Charles opened the door and silently walked across the thick carpet toward the leather chair that the Director, his own aged grandfather, sat in. Upon seeing that it was Charles, the old man frowned in concern. "What brings you all the way out here?"

"I wanted to update you myself. I know how critical our timing is and I wanted to get your opinion before we proceed." The old man only grunted, knowing only bad news would bring Charles this far.

"We have not heard from Lieutenant Munoa for over twelve hours and we can only assume that something went wrong. We *have* tracked down Jack Reese's information. It seems that Max McMillan was overly confident. He did not dissuade Professor Reese from seeking further assistance in deciphering his find. Dr. Reese was able to contact Dr. Alana Borisenko, one of the world's foremost Mayan epigraphers, who was already in Mexico. She seems to have agreed to assist him. Dr. Borisenko is who he was waiting for in Ocosingo. Professor Reese is further ahead of us then we suspected."

"I have sent a man to the Borisenko residence in Los Angeles and to Dr. Reese's in Michigan. We believe that Reese also has a graduate student down there with him, from the University of Michigan, where he teaches, by the name of Apu Chohan. We have sent someone to check out his apartment. Should they show up at any of these targets, we will intercept them."

The old man sat silently listening to the report. He added, "Make sure you do background checks on all three. They may take refuge with family or friends, we need to know who and where. I want everything you can dig up on all three of them."

Charles nodded in agreement. "I have already ordered the checks. I also have a team working on this around the clock, until they are intercepted. We will tap our resources within law enforcement here in the U.S. if needed. But I would like to leave that as a last resort."

"Yes, we do not need this being leaked to the press, if we can avoid it," the old man confirmed. "Pull their credit reports and track any credit card use. They have to pay their way somehow."

Charles again assured the old man that all of it was already being done. He knew his grandfather had every confidence in him. But he also knew that it was difficult for him to let go of the reins. That was fine with Charles, he was not offended. It was always better to have two brains rather than one. And this man's brain, no matter the impact of his advanced age, was the best.

Charles sat quietly on the divan, contemplating his position and responsibility. He was proud to be part of this family and this organization – the Veni Victus, and completely believed in its cause. He knew he was protecting their way of life and that of the entire planet. 'Information, such as what Jack Reese and his friends now possess, is dangerous. It could destroy our society, our way of life. It could cause anarchy - throwing off the delicate balance of power in the world. After all, there were those who were born to lead and those who were born to follow. That's the way of things, the way they have always been. Giving everyone equal power was a falsehood - an impossibility. Those who were meant to follow, those who were meant to be told what to do and how, would only flounder in the midst of such power. They would destroy each other and our whole social order. No. I will not let it happen. I will fight to the death, if need be, to keep my family in power, for the good of all.'

'Besides, I know the truth and it is not what the ancients proclaim. It is what we work for now. I worship the one true God and that God had given me and my family the responsibility of leading the others. I know God demands that we protect the *truth*, at any cost. Many have died through the centuries, protecting this truth. We will not give up now, not in the final hour of crushing the heresy that this organization had been fighting for over a thousand years. We have control and we are not about to lose it now.'

His grandfather sat quietly and contemplated the same balance of power, only the Director of the Veni Victus, a.k.a. the modern day Illuminati, *was* questioning *his* beliefs. His resolve to see the annihilation of the ancient wisdom was complete, but his mind plagued him with doubts. He knew it must be his advancing age - death lurking around every corner. He knew that the Reaper was nearby, waiting for the right time to take him. He shuddered slightly, then turned to Charles and looked at him. He knew Charles was not torn with doubt. Charles was like he was when he was young, determined and purposeful. He trusted Charles more than himself now. "You have everything under control. Let me know when you have them in custody."

"Yes, Grandfather. You will be the first to know." Charles replied as he got up to go. "I will do whatever it takes, Director Tyler," he asserted, using a more official tone, "We will not fail in this, our final hour."

The old man only nodded as his grandson closed the door behind him. He knew things were in good hands or the right hands anyway. He welcomed sleep again as he began to doze off. It was his escape. He turned off his mind to the memories that plagued him and relaxed his grip on life, giving in to death to take him whenever it pleased. For now though, it was only a nap that took him away.

Chapter 25

December 14, 2012

Alana and Apu rushed up the stairs as Jack came out of the bathroom, visibly shaken. He only had a towel on, wrapped around his waist and it was slipping. He reached down to tighten it. His eyes were wide and his face was red from obvious exertion.

"What happened?" both asked at the same time. Jack leaned back against the hallway wall and paused to catch his breath.

Then, as he walked down the hall to the window at the end, "He went out this way." He said, still shaken.

Alana was now getting very upset. "Who? Who went out this way?!" her shouting had a distinct tone of fear.

Apu put his hand on her arm, "It's okay, Alana, he's gone now." Apu was afraid they were about to have a hysterical woman on their hands, Jack, in the towel, was already unsteady enough. "Alana, let's go downstairs and get something to drink. Jack, why don't you get dressed and join us? Then you can tell us what happened. Okay?" he said, hoping to illicit calm.

Jack, in spite of being shook up, understood what Apu was trying to do. "Sure, you go ahead. I will get dressed; then make sure everything else is okay up here, and around the rest of the house. I'll be down in a minute." With a deep breath, he turned, went back into the bathroom and shut the door. Apu led Alana back down the stairs.

She was shaking her head and muttering. "Who could be in my house and what would they want?" She wondered if they were common thieves or if they were after something specific. "This couldn't have anything to do with the Mayan wall, could it?" Alana was confused and upset and more than a little frightened. Apu and Jack's presence added *some* security, though minimal. She felt alone – as Apu didn't respond to any of her mutterings. She shuddered at the thought of finding the thief, had she *been* alone.

When Jack closed the door behind him, he just leaned back against it. He had not been in a physical confrontation since he was a freshman in high school. A senior bully had tried to push him around. He slowly walked over to the mirror and looked at his reflection. He could see deep red marks around is neck and shoulders. There would definitely be some bruises showing up soon. He shook his head, trying to clear the thoughts that were racing through it and quickly got dressed, not wanting the others to worry. As he went down the stairs, he thought he already knew why that man had just tried to kill him. Jack's stomach turned upside down with that realization. All thoughts of feeling gullible for choosing this quest had escaped with the man out the window. 'If others believe in it enough that they were willing to kill me for it, then I can take it just as seriously.' He was fearful but he also started to regain his sense of purpose.

Jack was amazed at how the *normal* aspects of life had taken over his mind. The complacency that so many fall into; nearly stalled the mission before it started. People go about their lives never expecting anything extraordinary to happen, and when it does, it is soon dismissed as their imagination. 'Why do we allow the magic to fade into the background, while accepting the mundane without questions?' Jack needed to talk to the others about this. 'Were they feeling the same way?' He ran his hands through his wet hair. He took another deep breath and rounded the corner at the bottom of the stairs. As he entered the kitchen where Apu and Alana were drinking tea, he could not detect their feelings. His cup sat on the table. He sat down and gulped it down. "We need to get out of here. Don't you think?"

After a tense moment, Apu spoke, "Yes, it is obviously not safe. But Jack, we need to know what happened, and I'm starving. I think we are safe for a little while. I don't think the intruder would risk coming back. Did you check that the rest of the house is secure?

"Yes, it's locked up. I think your right. We have a little time and I am starving. The food on the plane was terrible." Jack groaned.

"Perhaps while you tell us what happened up-stairs, I could make us something. Alana, do you have any food? I know you were gone for some time." Apu inquired.

"I am not sure what I have. I will look." But she did not get up from her chair. Both Jack and Apu realized she was very frightened.

"I checked all the rooms upstairs, there is no one else." Jack said. Apu volunteered to check the rest of the downstairs. When he returned, he reported that they were safe. 'For the moment,' he thought in his head; he knew not to say this part out loud. Alana got up and went to the pantry, in search of food. She scanned the shelves for anything they could possibly eat.

"I have some pasta here and a jar of marinara sauce, will that do?" Alana offered.

Apu and Jack both chimed in that it sounded great. Apu was about to start fixing it, when Alana told him to sit and that she would make it. "It will give me something to do with all this nervous energy I now seem to have" she added.

Apu then turned to Jack encouraging him to tell them what happened.

"I had only just finished my shower and was drying off when I heard a noise. But before I could turn around to see what it was, he was on me. He grabbed me around the neck from behind and tried to choke me. I struggled. Fortunately for me he wasn't a large man, and keeping fit for the last few years paid off. He *was* strong enough to hold on for bit. I think he realized that he wasn't going to get me down. When he squeezed really hard, I doubled over and he let go and ran. As soon as I caught my breath and grabbed a towel, I ran after him. He was out the window and onto the top of the garage before I could reach the window. I saw him run across the street and get into a silver Audi." Jack finished the account while unconsciously touching his sore neck.

"What did he look like?" Apu asked.
But before Jack could answer, Alana chimed in, "What did he want, why would someone try to kill you? Why here?"

"I think it has to do with the Wall." Jack replied.

"How could it? How would anyone know?" Alana was perplexed.

"I am not sure, but he tried to kill me. If it were a simple burglar, why wouldn't he just leave when he heard all of us arrive? There was a moment when I could see his face in the mirror. He wasn't a kid or a rough-looking character. He seemed well kept and nicely dressed; a man in his mid-thirties. Also he was driving an Audi - not the car of a thief. He was here looking for something and when we came home, I think he panicked."

They were all silent as Alana served up the spaghetti, each lost in fearful thoughts about what they had gotten themselves into. Alana was the most concerned, but she was also angry. 'How dare they come into my house. They, whoever *they* are, are not going to stop me. I will finish this mission if it is the last thing I do.' She thought as her competitive nature got the better of her. 'I can't believe I was ready to give up my own search. What was going on anyway? Of course I want to find out what this mystery reveals. And if I know nothing else, I

know those symbol are part of my own life's purpose.' All thoughts of
quitting and staying behind were gone, for good.

Apu was very quiet, as if he were listening for something. Jack
looked over to him and asked, "What? Do you hear something?" Jack
looked around. Apu responded quickly, "No, no. I was listening to my
own thoughts. It is a practice I learned as a child. I find that my inner
thoughts, not the ones that skim the surface, have a kind of wisdom. I
often get guidance from listening to them." he said rather shyly.

"What do your inner thoughts tell you?" Alana asked,
genuinely wanting to know.

"That we should not discuss too much here, that others may
be listening." Apu replied. They each one looked at the other,
registering what Apu was saying and then looked around the room.
Bugs, of course. It would make sense if someone were trying to find
out more about the Mayan Wall, or where they were going next, they
would have put listening devices in the house.

"I found something while I was in the library, but I don't want
to discuss it here. After we eat, we should be off." Apu said softly.

"I agree. Alana, do you have a car?" Jack asked in a whisper.

"Yes, it's in the garage. But won't they be looking for it?"
Alana whispered softly back.

"Perhaps, if they checked it out before we got here, but for
now it will have to do. They won't know where we are heading and it
should take a good deal of time to find us."

They finished eating in silence. Apu cleaned up the dishes
afterward, while Alana went off to pack some things. Jack went into the
garage to start the car and check the gas. He was quickly planning in his
head. 'We should use cash as much as possible. I don't know how
much power these people really have, but I don't want to take any
chances. I wonder if the car could be bugged too, or worse, they are
tracking us with some type of homing device. I am probably getting
paranoid now.' Jack reached up to his aching neck as the dark bruises
began to appear. "No, I'm not paranoid." He said out loud. 'Better to
be safe than sorry. We can get a rental car, but that requires a credit
card and then they could know what type of car they have. Oh, well, at
least it wouldn't be bugged or tracked.'

Soon, Apu arrived in the garage with a pile of books in his
arms.

"Alana has some great books that may help with our search."
He said as he put them in the back seat, careful not to divulge more.

He went back in to get his bag. Jack went in and got a local phone book and looked up rental car places. He figured he'd ask Alana which was the closest.

After the car was packed, Alana went into her office to write a quick email to her neighbor Jenn. She asked her to keep looking after the house, explaining that she was off on another assignment and thanked her for all of her help. She pushed the send button, and turned off the computer, wondering if she would be back. She sighed, realizing just how much she was unsure of. Finally, she went out to the garage, locking up the house behind her.

Alana drove them down the street while both Jack and Apu watched for signs of being followed. No one spoke about the Wall, their thoughts or where they were going. The only discussion was about rental car agencies and supplies. Each one had a thousand things to say and twice as many questions, but dared not speak just yet. Their lives may depend upon their silence.

When they arrived at the agency, Jack went in to get the car, while the others waited. He rented a small navy HUV- the auto industries' hybrid replacement of the SUV, figuring that it would be large enough for them to travel in and rugged enough to go just about anywhere. He was grateful for the mandatory switchover to hybrids after the oil wars; otherwise they wouldn't be able to afford a road trip to Colorado. Also, he wanted something that looked like any other common car on the road, so they would be more difficult to spot. He rented it for two full weeks, if they didn't solve the puzzle by then, it would be too late anyway.

They loaded all of their things into the HUV and drove Alana's car to the back parking lot. There was a collective sigh of relief when they drove off the lot in the new vehicle. The stress of danger was lurking about, for the last couple of hours had really worn on their nerves. The first thing Jack asked as they pulled onto the highway was how much cash they each could get their hands on. This took the others back for a second. He explained that it was best to minimize credit card use. "It is too easily tracked."

After some quick accounting, they went to the nearest ATM and withdrew as much cash as they could from their individual accounts. They stopped at the store and got drinks, supplies and a road atlas. They were back in the HUV again, driving, when Jack realized he didn't know where they were going. He asked Apu, "Where to?"

"Head north, according to this map, there is a rest stop about ten miles from here. I would like to stop there and talk." He knew it was safe to talk in the car now, but he needed to see their eyes when they discussed the Esalen connection. He needed to know if it felt right to them – as it did to him, before they went all that way on what could be a wild goose chase. They didn't have time for that. Better to make sure, well, as sure as they could be under these circumstances. Apu was confident that it was the right place, but he needed the others to be sure also. They drove in continued silence, to the rest stop, each one wondering what was next.

Chapter 26

December 14, 2012

It wasn't good news. This was just the sort of thing that happened repeatedly over the centuries. Every time they thought they had information contained, it leaked out again. It seems as though something or someone conspired against them. Joseph Charles Tyler III was tired from the long fight. He had just received word from his grandson that the archaeologist and his friends had escaped. And worse, they had been alerted. It was clear to Joseph that luck was not on their side. All of his years of work would be foiled in just a couple of days; not to mention the work of more than a hundred others before him; if they didn't do something and do it fast.

Joseph struggled with his own internal doubts, but he could not help it. As darkness crept in around the edges of his mind, he grew more and more fearful. 'What if he had been wrong?' The world has changed from when his predecessors were in his position. People are different now. 'We have fought so hard to preserve the illusions that the Christian family was founded upon.' He had always believed that it was the right thing to do. 'Keep the families together, keep man in his rightful place of dominance, keep the control structures in place, and maintain the status quo. It wasn't hard to perpetuate the illusion that things had always been this way. It wasn't too difficult to hide, discard and rewrite history. It was up to the victors to write the stories, and rightfully so. The strongest, the most self-reliant and the most hard-working *should* be victorious. We undoubtedly were directed by God and have long had every right to seize the reigns and direct society's destiny.'

Joseph had been taught and always *believed* that the people needed to trust in this foundation to survive. The sciences of archaeology, anthropology and sociology had suffered the most at the hands of such a tight ideological grip. In truth, all of science had suffered; the constant whipping boy of the church and of his own organization. 'It was necessary to make anyone, who logically sought to pursue their own truth, into godless, valueless people who wanted to destroy our very beliefs, crush our secure foundation and take our children with them.' Sometimes he had been amazed at how well they had pulled it off.

'It had not always been easy though. In the 60's, the solid grip had been threatened. We nearly lost the fight. Love, peace and personal independence had proved to be formidable adversaries. The work to regain the conservative edge has been difficult, long and painful (Joseph half smiled to himself over the use of the word *conservative*. It was beguiling how the most radical, violent and muddled teachings had become "conservative" in the eyes of the world; he credited himself for that triumph.) But in the end, we re-established our stronghold on the people. Of course, the Oil Wars of a few years ago really helped. There is also nothing like an attack on American soil to cause fear in the hearts of its people. There is no better way to control and contain people than with fear. With a few well-placed men in the White House, we have cemented our grip on the course of progress.'

'But have we kept it?' Joseph was no longer convinced. 'No matter how strong our hold seemed, things were changing. No matter how hard we tried to contain the truth, it leaked out in the most obscure places. And the young people were becoming impossible to control; they just didn't care what we thought of them anymore. They know our ways are not for them right from birth. Most of the time, in spite of being unsure of their own motives, they toss aside our values, like the peel of a banana-obvious useless trash.'

He shook his head to clear it some. "No. I must stop these doubts. I am just so tired;" speaking in a low whisper, "we have won, again and again."

Allowing himself to slip back to his private thoughts, 'I have personally been instrumental in preserving the American way of life, prosperity and its place of dominance in the world. I will not allow an ancient prophecy and a couple of rouge scientists to destroy all of our hard work. People don't need truth. They need strength, leadership and guidance. We allow them to stay in that hypnotized state of the mundane, in which they so enjoy.' Joseph Charles Taylor III was determined to make sure they could continue on this way.

He picked up the phone and pushed a single button, he was immediately connected to Charles.

"Yes, sir?" Charles answered on the other end.

"Get the archaeologist that reported the find, the friend of Dr. Reese's. He works for us, right?"

"He has been a field informant for a number of years, yes."

"Well, he is about to get a promotion. Bring him in. Send him through the course. He's a safe choice. I doubt Dr. Reese suspects his friends yet, especially another scientist."

"Yes, sir. I'll get him in today." Charles promised.

"Good. And make sure anyone following them, doesn't get too close. We can't afford another mistake. We have to time it right this time. Do you underst…?" Joseph finished short and lapsed into a fit of coughing.

"Yes, sir." He ran his hands through his jet black hair and smiled, he was not offended by Joseph's brusque manner at all. He always admired his grandfather's strength and willingness to give second chances.

Joseph realized it wasn't Charles' fault that Reese had gotten away, but inside he was angry and frustrated.

"Let me know when you hear anything new." He said in a softer tone. His quick rant was ending and the overwhelming fatigue was settling over him again. They both knew that he could monitor everything from his home office, but Joseph liked to be updated by his people, the way it used to be. He too, liked it the way it used to be. It was comfortable. He hung up the phone and sat back in his chair. Joseph began to make a mental list of the resources at his disposal. He wouldn't fail.

Chapter 27

December 14, 2012

Jack pulled the HUV into the first parking spot at a rest stop on northbound Highway 5. They had only been driving for about 20 minutes. But, a rest was welcomed by all. After a quick trip to the bathroom, they sat at a picnic table and discussed what happened after arriving back in the U.S. and how they each had nearly deserted the whole idea. They decided to stay aware of each other's moods and manners, should such indifference take hold again. Finally, they moved on to discuss their next course of action.

"Okay, Apu where are we going?" Jack asked.

"We need to go back to the beginning, so you can follow my logic in this matter." Apu went into a description of the series of discoveries that led him to the Esalen Institute and its surrounding area. It didn't take long. When he got to the actual description of the handprints and their similarities to the one from the Wall of Secrets, he pulled out the rubbing he was carrying from the Mayan wall and opened Alana's book to show the comparison. He could tell by the looks of their faces that they didn't see the match.

"Here, let me show you," he said as he took out two additional drawings he had printed on Alana's computer, of the Essalen handprints. He flipped one of them, inverted it and more or less, locked the thumb with that of the other. Immediately, recognition registered on their faces.

"Wow, that's it." Jack acknowledged.

"How'd you do that?"

"Good work." Jack smiled as he slapped Apu's shoulder lightly.

Apu was gratified that they saw the same resemblance he did. He then described the online search results that led him to the Institute.

"It is a spiritual center located near the caves where these handprints were painted. I know that there are native handprints all over the world; many of them would be similar to these, should you do the same thing to them." Apu said, referring to the sketches. "But the way this all worked out tells me that this..." he said as he pointed to a map, "is the right place. I believe this is where we need to go. What do you think?"

"I agree with you. We should at least check it out. Don't you think so?" Alana turned and asked Jack.

Jack looked at Alana first and then to Apu and decided to think out loud, "It is interesting that you chose that symbol first. I wrote a paper on Aboriginal art in which handprints were the primary focus. There are archaeological sites all around the world that have handprints. They are especially prevalent in shamanic cultures and are often located in very remote locations, linking them to more of a ritual art form. The ones you mentioned in Borneo, Indonesia are amazing." Jack paused momentarily, and then continued. "But the serendipitous circumstances surrounding Apu's discovery of this place, at this time, seems important. I think we should go, it is our best lead. And besides, the resemblance is uncanny. There is no way to ignore it." Alana and Apu both nodded their heads in agreement.

They got back into the HUV and continued heading north. Once on the highway again, Alana brought up the next question on everyone's mind, "What are we looking for when we get there? Any ideas? Aren't we supposed to meet someone, a Gatekeeper? Eligio was a Gatekeeper, right? Do you think the next one will just show up like he did?" Alana rapidly followed each question with another.

"Yes, Eligio was a Gatekeeper, but I have no idea how we will know where or who the next one is. And will they be looking for us?" Apu replied.

"It's all pretty strange. We are going to a place that we think *might* be connected to an ancient wall in Mexico, to meet someone we don't know and who may not even know we are coming. All I am sure of, is that there are still questions left unanswered and I feel as if they all lie ahead of us. So… we will continue on." Jack said.

Neither Apu nor Alana had anything to say in reply, each falling into their own thoughts. Jack drove on in silence for a while. The traffic was not too bad; they had escaped the rush hour. He struggled with his own doubts, wondering how they could pull off such a monumental task. After some inner wrestling, he let go of the mission and focused on his own personal quest for understanding. If there really was a destiny for humanity, he was willing to help it along, but he left the details of that to the higher intelligence. He couldn't be sure if they were on the right track or not. But something, some part of this mission, made him feel like they were. When Jack let go, he had a sense of peace wash over him. He exhaled long and slow and felt his whole body relax. What happened now, he could not predict, but for the moment, he was content going in the direction he was going.

Jack glanced over to Alana who was sitting in the passenger seat. She looked deep in thought. 'She *is* beautiful,' he thought to himself. 'She is *smart* too. I know she was really freaked out by what happened at her house, I should try and reassure her.' But for some reason, Jack waited. He just wanted to enjoy this momentary sense of peace. He looked in the rearview mirror at Apu in the back seat. Apu had his head back, leaning on the headrest. At first Jack thought he was asleep, but then he saw Apu reach up to scratch his nose. Apu too, had a look of peace on his face, his eyes were closed and he was breathing deeply. Jack thought that he might be meditating. 'Maybe we should all try meditating. Maybe we would understand more of what we are looking for.' Jack knew he couldn't meditate in the car while driving; he would have to wait until someone else took over the wheel, to give it a try.

While Jack was quiet in his thoughts, Alana was lost in her own personal struggle. She was grappling with her fears and with the events at her house. She felt deep inside that something or someone was trying to stop them. This gave their quest more credibility, but it also brought a whole host of fears to the surface. She marveled at how she was ready to quit just before the intruder was discovered. Coming home to a familiar environment had such a strong effect. She could easily have made a serious mistake. After searching for so many years, she had nearly walked away just before discovering the truth. For a split second, Alana was grateful for the intruder. Then she felt badly; Jack's neck was still causing him some discomfort, but Alana knew that the man had changed how she felt about this mission and jolted her back to reality. *And* they now knew someone didn't want them to succeed. She wondered how far that person, or persons, would go to stop them. Danger lurked, she felt it.

'Will they be able to track us?' She looked over in the side mirror at the cars behind them. 'Could one of those cars be them?' She shook her head; she couldn't allow herself to become this fearful and paranoid. She inhaled deeply and tried to release the fear and stress. After focusing on her breathing for a couple of minutes, Alana noticed another emotion bubbling up. Excitement. She had needed the kick in the pants that the intruder had provided. She felt alive and knew she didn't want to miss this adventure, no matter what the danger. The mystery, the only thing in her life that had given her cause, the driving force behind everything she had done for years now, was getting closer, she could feel it. That attacker had really *helped* her. She knew it was no longer only her own inner quest, but she was now part of a bigger journey, one with much larger ramifications. No one would believe her, if she tried to explain, except for the two people in this car. She looked over at Jack. He had a smile on his face and seemed relaxed - even happy. He looked handsome to Alana in that moment. Apu was asleep. These two men knew what was happening, at least as much as she did. She drew comfort from that idea. She was no longer alone. That felt really good. She eased into her seat, put one foot up on the dashboard and just basked in the moment.

After meditating for some time with the purpose of trying to calm the energy in the car, (Jack and Alana seemed to each be struggling with so many divergent thoughts), he sat back and stared out the window. 'There is something about driving a long distance in a car that makes me introspective,' Apu thought. 'Perhaps it is the limitations of space in a small vehicle or maybe it's the concept of traveling through other people's lives and realities that does it. You stare out the window and see people in their cars or walking down the street, or sitting in their houses, and realize that there are millions of other realities happening in the same moment. It is both sobering and mind-expanding.' After Apu felt Jack and Alana calm down, he laid his head back again on the headrest and really closed his eyes. The last thing he thought of before he dozed off was how contented he felt to be with these people on this mission, at this time.

Chapter 28

December 14, 2012

Jack drove for two hours in near silence, save for occasional small talk and single pit stop. He was thinking about the Wall of Secrets and all that it had revealed to them so far, as well as what it had still to teach them. It amazed him. He knew that some believed the Mayans to be much more intelligent and advanced than most archeologists thought. 'It was an astounding idea, that the infamous people who performed human sacrifices were the same people who had developed such understanding of the cycles of creation and had interwoven that understanding into the foundation of their whole society - their calendars. Not many academics would believe that the Maya understood or could foretell the path to godhood. Heck, many academics don't even believe in god. Well, someone else clearly put stock in what the Maya knew or they wouldn't be chasing after us and trying to kill me.' He rubbed his neck again gently when he thought of the attack at Alana's house.

Even though it had scared them all, the attack solidified his resolve and pushed him forward. He could see a definite cause and effect relationship between many things that had happened in the last few days, putting him on the road he was traveling on right now. Some of the things that happened were subtle nudges, others were major events. But looking back he could see how each had led him down this path. As a matter of fact, he could trace his life and outcomes all the way back to birth. In the end, like it or not, he knew he believed in some kind of destiny. Its distinctive mark was clear on his life.

'Ironically, I am now driving someone else's car, with two other scientists, to who- knows-where, to meet who-knows-who, trying to decipher an ancient Maya wall and in the end save the world.' Jack smiled at that thought. Absolutely ridiculous. Good thing he didn't have to convince anyone else of what he was up to. He wondered where this adventure would really lead him, personally. Somehow he knew it wasn't anywhere he had ever imagined. What else was he to do? Go home and forget about the whole thing? That notion was even more impossible than the adventure itself.

Sometime during the second hour of their journey, Jack decided he needed to get some coffee, it had gotten dark and he was getting tired. He wondered if they shouldn't stop for the night and try to find this symbol's Gatekeeper tomorrow when it was light. Then he thought better of it. They had a lot to do in a short amount of time. Better to not wait. He pulled the HUV into a convenience store to get coffee. In the light of the store parking lot, Apu and Alana awoke. They slept well to the monotony of the road.

"What's up?" Apu asked sleepily.

"Coffee break," Jack replied as he opened the door to get out.

"Where are we?" Alana asked, alert immediately. She was still a little jumpy.

"We are about an hour away from our first destination, I think." Jack answered. "Would either of you like coffee?"

"I would love some and maybe a snack. I am getting hungry." Alana got out of the car.

"Sure," was all that Apu could muster.

The lights and sounds of the store were in deep contrast to the dark road. In the corner was a large TV blasting out the evening news. They took in what snippets of the headlines that they could: *The cost of energy was still climbing, fossil fuels in constant decline. There had been another earthquake in Mexico, this one closer to Mexico City and many people were still missing. China's population was continuing to choke supply lines to other needy countries. Many were dying daily in the wars in the Middle East, where the U.S. was still struggling for some control over oil.*

All of this information was disseminated within the fifteen minutes that they were in the store picking out their snacks and beverages and paying for them. 'Things had gotten worse, in just a couple months.' Jack thought. He didn't miss the evening news at all. He always wondered why news seemed to mean *bad news* to the television networks. He actually *felt* the general urgency of their mission. He hoped they were heading in the right direction and towards the correct place.

Jack had poured himself a tall cup of coffee and then went looking for something sweet to eat. He hadn't had a donut for months and all of a sudden he craved a jelly-filled or glazed confection.

Alana had gotten a sandwich from the ready-made section, some chips and a diet soda. Not health food by any stretch, but considering the choices she didn't think she faired too badly. Apu had gotten coffee and a sandwich as well. He also bought a few bottles of water for later.

When they got back to the car, Apu offered to drive for awhile. Jack was grateful for the rest. He climbed into the back seat while Apu settled behind the wheel. He set his coffee in the cup holder, took the keys that Jack offered him and started the car. Alana had just closed her door on the passenger side when there was a loud rap on her window. They all jumped. Alana gave out a yelp. For a moment no one moved. Then Alana looked closely to see who was threatening their lives now. It was an un-kept man asking if they had any change to spare. Alana was trying to calm her pounding heart and shallow breath as she shook her head no, in response to the beggar. But he didn't go away. He rapped on the window again. He obviously didn't understand or couldn't hear her. She began to lower her window just a bit to tell him - no. Immediately, the man grabbed hold of the top of the window and tried to force it down further.

"I need a drink, you must help me," he spat at her. Alana reeled at the smell coming from the man. Alana was instantly sorry that she had put down the window. She wanted to put it back up, but knew she would squeeze the man's dirty fingers if she did. Apu had put the car in gear, but he didn't want to hurt the old man, no matter how annoying he was. He started to back up very slowly.

"I don't have a drink for you, sorry. Please get away from our car," she pleaded. Finally, she decided the only way to get away without hurting him was to give him money. She reached into her pocket and pulled out a couple of dollars and some change and threw it out the open window slot. The old man immediately let go and knelt down to retrieve it from the ground.

The whole scene only took a minute or two, though it seemed much longer. They were all a little shaken by the ordeal; Alana the most. As Apu pulled back onto the road, he exhaled; glad that the old man had not been hurt. They all felt sorry for him, another victim of the financial fallout of the economy going into the gutter.

Jack looked back at the old man, still searching the ground for the money Alana had thrown out. Everyone was so focused on the ordeal they didn't notice that a silver Volvo pulled out just moments after they did. It followed them.

Chapter 29

December 14, 2012

In the dim light of the parking lot, Melvin Cooper was totally unconscious of the rough pavement biting his tired bony knees as he knelt down searching for every cent the lady had given him. He pitied himself and what he had been reduced to. Two years ago he had dressed in suits and driven an expensive car. Two years ago he had a family and a life. It had all changed when the earthquake of 2009 shook San Juan Capistrano in southern California. He lost everything that day. His home slid two blocks away from its original location as the whole mountain side crumbled. His business went up in smoke as the wildfires devoured block after block. But the physical destruction had been secondary to the demise of his family. His wife died in a gas explosion at her work. His teenage son had been hit by a car that lost control in the middle of the second shock wave. He lost it all, including his mind for a while. When he started to remember who he was and what had happened he couldn't bare it. He turned to drinking, and each time he began to remember he would have another drink until he could remember nothing. He could feel nothing. He took to the streets; nothing mattered anymore.

At some point he had been jumped by a group of gang kids hoping to have a little fun with him. He had crawled away missing a tooth and dragging his broken ankle. It had never healed correctly and now he walked with a painful limp. He didn't care. He couldn't. Melvin's only concern now was to find his next drink. There were moments when he wished those kids had just killed him. He wanted to die, like the rest of his family. But he drove those thoughts from his mind and drank more. It would soon be over, he was sure his misery could not last forever. Tonight, he could buy enough liquor to be numb for days. He got up and limped in the direction of his favorite liquor store, saying a silent thank you to the lady in the navy HUV.

Chapter 30

December 14, 2012

  Apu pulled into the Esalen Institute parking lot and turned off the car. No one moved for a couple of moments as they realized they did not have a clue as to what to do next. 'We probably should have called ahead and made reservations,' Jack thought. 'But we don't really know how long we were going to be here.'

  They looked at each other for a moment more and then Alana shrugged. "We might as well go in. What else are we going to do, stay out here in the car?" They got out and walked toward the front door of what looked like the main building.

  The Esalen Institute was built in the 60's but had been updated over the years and looked like a beautiful campus. There were several buildings and though they couldn't see much in the dark, there seemed to be flower gardens all around the property. The night air was cooler and the salty smell of the ocean caused them to relax, but only a little.

  Jack reached out to grab the handle of the front door. But just as his hand touched the metal, it swung in, away from him. Two people came out. They were deep in conversation with each other, nearly causing a collision.

  "I am going to bed now, I want to go down to the caves at first light," the man said. He was tall and thin with a deeper than usual voice.

  "Me too. I will meet you for breakfast at 6:30. I can't wait to see the handprints," the woman replied. "Oh, sorry. I wasn't paying attention to where I was going," the woman said to Jack after just barely avoiding running into him.

  "No, its okay… I'm sorry… but were you just speaking of handprints? The Esalen Indian caves? *The* hand-prints?" Jack asked while trying to control his excitement.

  "Why, yes. We are going there in the morning." She replied, surprised by the man's directness.

  "Wow, that's why we're here. Could we follow you to where they are?" Jack asked. Neither the woman nor the man answered immediately.

"Oh, uh, sorry, my name is Dr. Jack Reese and these are my colleagues, Dr. Alana Borisenko and Apu Chohan. We have come a long way to inquire about the handprints."

The man finally smiled, recovering from his surprise, "You are welcomed to come along. My name is Dr. Sherman Fisher and this is Dr. Alice Cunningham. We are down here from the Simon Fraser University in British Columbia. We have a working theory regarding the paintings of shamanic cultures and are traveling to investigate these relationships."

"It is a pleasure to meet you both. We've just come from Mexico and are investigating similarities between these particular handprints and some interesting markings we found in Mayan territory." Jack offered.

"Really?" Dr. Cunningham's eyes lit up. "We would love to exchange notes. Can you meet us in the dining hall at 6:30, in the morning? We can have some breakfast and then head down to the caves? They are about twelve miles from here."

"Absolutely, we would love to. We will be ready. Thank you for allowing us to tag along." Alana chimed in.

"No trouble at all, we are most interested in your research. We'll see you all in the morning." Dr Fisher said as he headed off toward one of the other buildings. Dr. Cunningham headed in a different direction. Alana, Apu and Jack just stood there for a moment with their mouths hanging open.

"And that is the way it works when you are on a sacred mission from God." Apu proclaimed with a smile. Jack and Alana both turned to slap Apu lightly; but he ducked and they laughed out loud instead.

"Let's go see if we can get a place to sleep for the night. We're going to have an early morning, by the sound of it." Alana said. They went in the door this time with out running into anyone else.

Chapter 31

December 15, 2012

The Essalen Institute had two separate rooms available, one for the men and one for Alana. The next morning they arose early and met in the small but tidy dining hall.

"I slept surprisingly well last night. I feel safe here. It's nice after the last few days of being on the run." Alana commented with a relieved sigh. Jack agreed.

They had already finished breakfast and were enjoying coffee when Drs. Fischer and Cunningham entered the dining hall and joined them at their table.

"Good Morning, Dr. Reese, Dr. Borisenko and Mr. Chohan." Dr. Cunningham greeted them, surprising everyone by remembering their names.

"Please call me Jack; only my students call me Dr. Reese." Jack requested. "And this is Alana and Apu." He gestured toward the others.

"Excellent. I am Alice and this is Sherman. I see you all have already eaten. It won't take us long."

"Take your time; we are still soaking up as much coffee as possible." Alana said smiling, tying to be friendly.

"What type of students do you have Jack?" Sherman asked when he returned from the breakfast buffet bar with a plate full of food.

"I am an archeology professor at the University of Michigan. Apu, here, is one of my graduate students. I have not been teaching for the past several months though, as we were doing field work in Mexico."

"And are you also an archaeologist?" Sherman asked Alana between mouthfuls.

"No, actually I am an epigrapher; I study and *attempt* to decode ancient languages. Jack called me to help out, to hopefully decipher the Mayan glyphs he recently discovered."

"That's very exciting. Have you had any luck?" Alice inquired.

"We're still working on it." Stopping short of what she wished to add, Alana wondered if they should be divulging so much information to these strangers. She decided to remain cautious. "What are your fields of expertise?" She asked trying to turn the conversation away from the Mayan glyphs.

"Sherman is a psychologist and I am a sociologist. We have been collaborating for over a year on a project involving aboriginal art." Alice replied for both of them. "We think there is a direct connection between shamanic cultures, their art forms and the psychological, spiritual and social development of the people of that time." She looked down at her plate, wondering if she was ready to really get into such conversation here at breakfast. Then she looked up, obviously making the decision to proceed. "Don't you find it interesting how we habitually consider these indigenous people to be primitive and sometimes even barbaric; even though they are often more advanced than we give them credit, especially in how they interact within their social circles?"

"And with less psychological disease and afflictions than our modern society experiences." Sherman elaborated on Alice's thought.

"They seemed happier. Of course, that is subjective and very difficult to measure, but we can learn a lot by studying their lives and specifically their spiritual art forms." Alice went on.

This ping-pong recital continued between Alice and Sherman, each completing each other's thoughts. Alana would have normally thought it to be irritating, but between these two obviously close friends, she found it charming.

"Anyway, that is what we are here for. The Essalen Indian site is much closer geographically to us, than many other famous handprint sites and a lot easier to get to. We have read much of the archeological records regarding these people, but thought it would be great to come and see them for ourselves. Not to mention, we were excited to stay here at the Esalen Institute. Have you been here before?" Sherman asked politely.

"No. This is our first time, and I'm sad to say - we don't really know that much about the Institute itself. We came here primarily to see the hand-paintings." Jack answered.

Apu had stayed quiet, just listening to the conversation. He was still working on waking up so early. He had slept deeply, but his dreams were filled with visions of running, while people were in close pursuit. Who the people were, he could not tell. Unlike Alana's current sense of security, he had a sense of danger in their near future. He hoped not too near.

Sherman finished his breakfast while Alice was filling them in. When he cleared his plate, he took up the conversation allowing Alice to finish eating.

"The Institute has been here for nearly 50 years and is a beacon of spiritual growth and development for individuals around the world. I don't believe it is an accident that you have come here. I am looking forward to what the day has to offer us." Sherman sounded optimistic and upbeat. Apu allowed his sense of danger to recede so that he could enjoy the company and the adventure. Once everyone finished they headed toward the parking lot.

"We are in that navy HUV. Can we follow you?" Jack inquired hoping they wouldn't mind.

"Of course. We have directions from the Institute's staff. They have been so helpful. It doesn't seem too difficult. We'll be in that dark green sedan." Alice replied. They eagerly piled into their respective vehicles and headed down the hill to the valley where the Esalen Indians had made their mark. After driving for about 10 minutes, Jack looked into his rear-view mirror and noticed Apu deep in thought. Alana noticed too.

"You haven't spoken much this morning, is there anything wrong?" Alana turned in her seat to look at Apu.

"I had some disturbing dreams about us running away from danger last night." Apu said thoughtfully as if his mind were still trying to figure out his dreams.

"It could be about the running we have been doing for the last few days and the danger we have already faced, don'tcha think?" Alana asked hopefully.

"It could be that, of course. I just sense a threat this morning. Have either of you noticed anything?"

"No, I haven't." Jack answered. "Do you think it has to do with Alice and Sherman? I didn't feel anything negative coming from them."

"I don't think it's them. I am just not sure. It is just a general sense of danger. Let's keep our eyes open and I don't think we should elaborate on the Wall any more than we have; not until we are sure that it is safe."

"But we have to trust some people, how else are we going to find the Gatekeepers?" Alana felt a new level of alarm.

"I think we are doing fine so far. I am just telling you what I sense. I don't know that we *can't* trust Alice or Sherman. They may well

be the Gatekeepers, themselves. Who knows? Let's just be careful, that
is all I'm saying." Apu said, giving up trying to explain himself.

"Agreed." Jack said. But Alana was silent; her earlier feelings
of being safe fell by the way-side. She knew she was letting her fears get
the better of her - *again*. Alana knew she needed to get a grip. She was
quiet the rest of the short trip to the caves.

They turned onto a dirt road and after about a mile, they
pulled off to the side of the road behind Alice and Sherman's car.
There were rolling hills all around. Near where they stopped, there
were gentle slopes leading up to sharp cliffs in the distance.

"This must be it. We probably have to walk the rest of the
way." Jack announced. They all got out of the cars. Apu went to the
back to get his camera.

"The caves are just over that ridge there." Sherman said
holding a small map and pointing to the southeast. "It shouldn't take
too long to walk."

Alana pulled out a water bottle and offered extras to the
others and also grabbed a flashlight 'just in case' she thought. Alice and
Sherman had gathered similar items and they were all off hiking in just
a few minutes. Jack walked in front with Alice and Sherman, Alana and
Apu were just behind them. As they walked, Alana felt a little safer with
him by her side.

Apu was keeping his eyes and ears open. The danger he felt
earlier was not as keenly present at the moment, which led him to think
that *it* may not have anything to do with Alice and Sherman. He hoped
that was true.

Jack was feeling that there was definitely something they
needed to do with Alice and Sherman. It was too much of a
coincidence – the way they met and are now heading to the Esalen
caves with them. He was unsure of how to pursue it further. Perhaps
he just needed to relax and let it happen. He finally asked, "Explain to
me your theory regarding these native handprints and human social,
psychological and spiritual growth."

Sherman was the first to answer. "All of our research into the
health and well-being of these shamanistic cultures led us to believe
that there is a direct correlation between this type of ritualistic spiritual
behavior and a people's general psychological health. It is believed that
the handprints themselves are one of the keys that unlock the puzzle of
their cultures. The handprint is a kind of connection to the 'other
world,' their spirit world. Of course, most cultures have beliefs in

'spiritual worlds;' this is not anomalous at all. But the personal connection *is* relevant. A connection so tangible, that they actually reach out their hands and touch it. This is significant for many reasons." Sherman paused and took a sip from his water bottle, then continued. "Many cultures have obstacles or caveats to reaching their spirit worlds. These shamans believed in a direct connection. Though they act as leaders, they encourage individual enlightenment. This is evidenced by multiple handprints – as each person reaches that state of understanding. But it is even more than that."

Alice took up the explanation. "These handprints are really about personal power. You can't get any more personal than one's own handprint and the work we do with our hands is often *and* has been traditionally considered the manifestation of our personal power- our mark on the world. A *shaman's* power, for instance, comes from that connection to the spirit world, not from muscular strength or force, but from spiritual understanding and connection. It was this connection that guided them in performing their purpose."

Jack was contemplating what Alice and Sherman were saying. It seemed very pertinent, but he wasn't sure why. Sherman continued, "We believe this is important to the evolution of humanity. If each of us had that same type of connection to our own personal power, we would not have the problems that seem so prevalent today. Many of the conflicts and wars that we experience are based on our feelings of insecurity and fear. It is our belief, and one of the theories we seek to prove, that if we all were connected to that type of personal power through spirit, fear would not be such a central motivator.

Alana was listening intently. She had studied so many ancient civilizations and most of them had a sect of leaders who were shamans or sages. What Sherman and Alice were saying seemed too simple.

Since they seemed to be interested, Sherman continued, "We are told continually what to feel, what is in vogue or popular. We are told what to fear, what to reject, how and who to hate. We deny this influence. We like to believe that we are free thinkers, making our own decisions, but we are thoroughly influenced by our society, the news, our governmental leaders, our social expectations and our commercialism. These influences color our choices. They dictate what we think about, what we want and what we strive for. If instead, we had a more internal barometer to direct our thoughts, actions and feelings we would indeed live much different lives, individually and collectively."

Alana agreed with the last statement, still she felt there was more to what they were saying. Their hike took them over a ridge and they now faced a set of cliffs that undoubtedly housed the caves they were seeking. They made their way across a narrow ravine and found themselves in the shadows of the cliffs. They could see the openings, in the most pronounced rock face, scattered here and there.

"The information from the Institute says that the two northern caves have the better preserved prints. I suggest we head there first." He pointed to the northern-most opening and walked that direction. The others nodded and followed. When they entered the cave, the air was dry and stale. Alice wrinkled her nose a little. They were drawn to the back of the cave where they could make out the fading handprints of the Essalen Indians.

"These were made thousands of years ago, and yet I can still sense their souls here. These handprints are definitely personal." Alice said as she reached out and put her hand over one of them, "It is almost as if I can touch *them* - their souls lie just on the other side of this stone wall. It feels so intimate." Her voice softened to a whisper.

The others agreed and quietly echoed Alice's sentiments, as they followed her lead. Each reached out to shake the hands of the ancient people. The initial atmosphere was quietly reverent. After the awe faded some, Apu took a couple of pictures, but the flash was spoiling the mood, so he satisfied his urge with only a couple. Apu felt none of the earlier danger; instead he could almost *see* his grandfather's image standing in the background. He decided to go to the center of the cave, sit down and quietly go within. It was not long before Alice joined him. Eventually, they were all seated in a circle, quietly soaking in the feeling of being in such an ancient and obviously extraordinary part of native history. They felt as if they were communing with the spirits of a people long ago. After about ten minutes, Jack started to feel restless and in need of more information. Hoping the timing was right, he asked quietly, "How do you think they, the Essalen, were able to connect to this personal power you spoke of?"

"The "how-to" is quite varied. They preformed rituals, they used substances. They went into trances. There are a number of means to that end. The how-to part is still being examined and explored. I am personally exploring *my* own methods of connecting to *my* personal power. The actual outcomes are clearer." Sherman explained. "One of the values in connecting to spirit, is the initiate's (the one doing the connecting) purpose. A *shaman's* personal power is the intent to help and heal his people. When each shaman found and connected to the power that lies within, they used that power to determine and then fulfill that personal destiny. A destiny always involves service to your tribe, village or fellow man (or woman). This is not an insignificant fact. Taking on the life of a shaman as your destiny, was not decided upon lightly; going through the shamanic initiations were often difficult and quite involved."

Alice again took up the story, excited to have such an eager audience. "The handprints, we believe, have three primary messages to teach us. The first and foremost is the importance of connecting to the spirit world in a personal way. This is the *key*." Alice stressed. Her choice of words did not escape Jack, Apu or Alana's notice.

"But also, it is very important to understand, that in the process of connecting to the *spirit world*, certain outcomes are revealed. We have identified two very important outcomes through our research. The first is one's personal purpose in this life. In other words, the answer to the age old question, 'why am I here?' is revealed to each person. The next outcome is an aspect of the last one. In answering the question, 'why am I here,' individuals will always find an element of service to humanity." She said the last with a smile.

"You mean the whole thing is about finding and living your purpose? That is what these handprints mean?" Alana hated breaking the flow of information but needed to know if she was getting everything they were saying.

Sherman turned slightly and addressed Alana warmly. "Not just *a* purpose, but *your* purpose. Every individual has certain talents, gifts, abilities and viewpoints that are his alone. Each of these provides us all a unique destiny. You'd be surprised by how many people do not have any idea what they are here to do, and those who *do* know, are often too afraid to follow through... *or* they just don't think they can. There are many, many more people like this than there are people who know their purpose, what their contribution should be and are busy doing it. And yet this is the most important question we can ask and answer for ourselves. *Why am I personally here?*"

He went on, "Of course any purpose can be beneficial. It is called direction and a wonderful combatant for depression and melancholy. In fact when we find our *true* purpose we find life invigorating. We work harder but enjoy it more. We get up early and go to bed late because we love and are so fulfilled by what we are doing.

How can you hate your neighbor, if you are enjoying your own life so much?"

Again, it was Alice's turn to elaborate. "Children should be encouraged to ask this question of themselves at an early age, and finding the answer should be *at least* as important as reading, writing and arithmetic. If only a small percentage of people around the world pursued and lived their true purpose, the world would be measurably happier. Crime of all types would decrease. Prosperity would increase. Major social issues and injustices like poverty, broken homes and racism would lessen. Kahlil Gibran, the Lebanese poet said, *'When you are born, your work is placed in your heart.'* Our whole society has discouraged listening to your heart. We are encouraged to stay in the jobs and lives we hate, dying slowly; all under the guise of being responsible and proper. Is it not more responsible and proper to fulfill the purpose you were born to accomplish?"

"Each person's purpose will *always* have a component of service involved, because at the center of our selves, (or in *spirit,* if you will, which is where your purpose comes from) we understand that everyone is related to the other. We are essentially one big tribe. By helping you, I help myself." Alice's voice trailed off.

Apu, Alana and Jack were engrossed. It seemed too simple and Jack did not understand how living "on-purpose" would cure poverty or stop crime. His internal questions made him uncomfortable. He began to shift around on the floor of the cave again. Sherman noticed Jack's discomfort and intuitively understood its source.

"It is hard to believe that such a simple idea as finding and living on-purpose would have such dramatic effects on our world. But if you think for a moment at where the average human being currently is psychologically, and draw the contrast, it becomes quite clear."

"The average Westerner, some would label civilized, (I would not choose that word), is caught in a life of mediocrity and unhappiness. The magic has been lost, on most. We are sucked into the spell of consumerism, to be left with many things in our garage but nothing in our hearts. We live frustrated, desperate lives of hopelessness, which are only occasionally sprinkled with moments of hope and clarity. The most we look forward to is the next *thing* we can add to our already bulging pile of stuff. We somehow go to jobs we don't actually choose, day in and day out, wondering if there isn't something more to life. We skimp and scrape to get by, never thinking about the next person. It does not often cross our minds, that giving away our time, energy and love to another, gives us more happiness and hope in our *own* lives. We live in fear – fear of dying, fear of living, fear of losing our stuff, fear of our neighbors, fear of the environment, fear of change, and fear of ourselves, really."

Sherman continued as the others focused their attention on him. "If we compare this type of existence to the type of existence the owner's of these handprints lived, we see a dramatic difference. They sought out, discovered and lived in harmony with their purpose, with each other and in their environment. These symbols physically remain to demonstrate to this day, their connection to personal power and purpose – and to the spirit world that brought them that purpose. When we know our purpose we are happier, more centered people. We have direction, hope and something to look forward to, each and everyday. Something to work toward. When we meet people who are living on-purpose we revere them, call them heroes and envy their lives. But we each have our own gifts to bring. Like the "Little Drummer Boy" our personal gifts are all that God wants from us. When our personal purpose is expressed into how we make a living, we are fulfilled and happy. When that purpose also reveals our individual method of service to our fellow man, fear falls away and peace and satisfaction take its place." Sherman felt the others absorbing his words. He paused for Alice to elaborate.

"Imagine a world where each person worked at a job they loved. Imagine the majority of people in the *civilized* world, anxious and excited to go to work each day, because it gave them such joy and happiness. Imagine doing something inspiring every day of your life. Look at the word itself. The word 'inspire' comes from 'in–spirit' – it is the root of each person's personal power and purpose. When you live a life that is *on-purpose*, you live in harmony with spirit – or God. The ancient philosopher Patanjali put it this way:

"When you are inspired by some great purpose, some extraordinary project, all your thoughts break their bonds: Your mind transcends limitations, your consciousness expands in every direction, and you find yourself in a new, great and wonderful world. Dormant forces, facilities and talents become alive, and you discover yourself to be a greater person by far than you ever dreamed yourself to be."

"That is what living on-purpose is all about. Can you imagine a world where everyone thought and lived like that?" Sherman summarized.

Alana was perplexed, "Why don't we do this? It seems so simple and it makes so much sense?"

"Truth is very often simple," Sherman answered. "But we have strayed far from simplicity in our 'advanced culture.' We have to back track some to find these truths today. Fortunately, the Essalen, like many other ancient people, have left us reminders to help us remember. I think the Maya have done the same, have they not?"

Jack had known for a while now that Alice and Sherman were definitely the Gatekeepers they were to meet. He was so busy trying to assimilate all the information that he had not thought of the Mayan wall and their mysterious adventure since he entered the cave. He glanced for a moment at Apu and then at Alana, and immediately received affirming nods from both. It was time to share more about their mission with Alice and Sherman.

"It is hard to sum up all that we have been through in the last few days. But the short story is this: The Maya had a series of extraordinarily advanced calendars that predicted the phases of mankind's changes through time and our eventual evolution to another level of understanding. The time for this evolution is actually now upon us. They left us an amazing story carved into stone to help us understand this jump. Apu and I discovered that stone just a couple days ago. A Mayan shaman, who died helping us, revealed that we are on the verge of a monumental shift in human consciousness. He informed us that this is humanity's transitional time. We must reach a critical mass, in the number of humans who understand and embrace the truths that were given to us by the ancients, on the Wall of Secrets. These truths were *not* explained to us. They were given in the form of symbols that we are commissioned to decipher. The process, of deciphering each symbol and understanding its meaning, is intended to accumulate and add to the critical mass needed, to topple us over the edge, into this new reality. Though we know the process, each new symbol, or *key*, as it was referred to by the shaman, is unknown to us. We do not know the details of the keys, nor do we know how it all actually works. We are essentially clueless. But we are following the signs as they appear to those he called the Gatekeepers, who in-turn expose the actual keys and their meanings. I believe that you..." Jack paused nervously, then continued, "Sherman, and Alice are Gatekeepers and that these truths that you have told us, are the first in the series of the eight that we must uncover and understand."

Sherman and Alice looked at each other and then at Jack. He half-expected them to tell him he was crazy. He, Apu and Alana each held their breath waiting for a response. It was Alice who spoke.

"Sherman and I have thought for years something very similar. We have both felt that we are (or were in a past life) shamans. We have taken our own personal measures to connect to the spirit world. Through that connection, we found each other and our own purposes in life, together. We were led to this place, at this time and we knew we needed to share our work and ideas with you, from nearly the moment we met. We were compelled by our own inner connections to speak with you all."

Apu decided it was his turn to add to the conversation, "You must continue to tell these truths to others. You must tell as many people as will listen. The more who understand and apply such information, the greater *our* chances for success. We may not understand how it all works, but it doesn't take a scientist to know that the more who understand and change, the closer to 'critical mass' we will be."

"People must ask the questions of themselves." Apu deeply felt the words, "*Why am I here? What am I passionate about? What did I dream about when I was a child? If I could do anything, without concern for money or circumstance, what would I do? How can I serve my neighbor? What can I do? What gives me a sense of peace, joy and satisfaction?* These are the questions others must be asking themselves to find their purpose. Right? These questions will lead people to God or Spirit. I believe you; this helps all of us."

Alice felt the excitement that had been growing steadily within the cave. The kind of excitement that is felt only when truth is being stated and shared, and when authentic power becomes an electric current flowing though each person's veins, creating bubbles of joy inside.

"Yes, exactly," she exclaimed. "The answers to these questions can be found in the personal connection to the spirit world, whatever that may mean to the individual person."

Sherman felt as if he were almost floating within the cave, the energy was so intense, he was buoyant. "It is similar to moving out of your logical left brain into your intuitive right. I think this is why there are more women who understand these truths than men. They're intuitive sides are often more developed. It is here, in this side of our being, where our purpose presents itself continually, if we were only able to hear it. This of course, goes beyond our scope of study. This conversation has crossed over into our own personal beliefs on these matters. But we would love to be more involved in teaching this to children and adults of all ages. We know how important it is!"

Alana knew very well the importance of following one's purpose. "Once you find it, it doesn't mean that the path, or your life, will be easy. I have known my purpose for some time now, or at least part of it. It has often been difficult. But when I know I am *on-purpose*, I feel the most joy and peace in my life. After speaking and hearing from you both, I will be more proud of being in that state. We each are here for a reason; I should not be ashamed of mine, no matter how *weird* it may seem. I am very grateful for this meeting and the opportunity to come to peace with that."

The energy moved into a profound level of appreciation and gratitude. It was not spoken of more than what Alana had just voiced, but it was sincerely felt by each one in the circle. It reminded Apu, Jack and Alana of Eligio. For a moment it seemed as if he was there, in the cave with them, as he had been in another cave a long way from there.

No one spoke for a few long minutes. They instinctively allowed the energy to bathe them in warmth and love. It was rejuvenating. It was life-giving and affirming. Beyond wonderful. For those moments the energy was building and then it pushed its way out of the cave and to distant places beyond. Soon afterwards, the energy lessened and quieted. Time stood still and so did they.

Chapter 32

December 15, 2012

"Where are they now?" Charles asked.

"They went out to some caves this morning. It's such a remote area that we couldn't follow them without risk of being seen. We're waiting on the main road. They have to come back this way; it's the only way out of the area." Matt, one of the organization's field agents, said into his cell phone.

"Do not lose them! It'll be your hides if you do." Charles hung up. He had two more things to take care of to insure that his plan would work. In the meantime, it was essential that Matt not lose them. He left his office and went down the hallway. He stopped at the first door on the left, opened it and went in. Inside was a small room hosting a table, a couple chairs and a very large window against the far wall. It wasn't actually a window at all, but a two-way mirror. He was on the two-way side; the other side faced a larger room. In that room, sat two agents briefing Max McMillan, archaeologist, friend to Dr. Jack Reese and newly recruited agent.

Max was frowning now. Charles could tell that he didn't like what he was hearing. He moved to the wall and turned on the speaker so he could listen in on Max's conversation.

"I don't want Jack to be hurt. I don't want *anyone* to be hurt" Max's concern was increasing by the moment.

"No one will be hurt. We just need to contain the information that Dr. Reese now has. We must *convince* him and his colleagues what is the right thing to do." Agent Moyer stressed the word convince a little too much for Max's taste. He knew he didn't have a choice, but he still wanted to be on record. It was one thing to turn people in and report finds that may threaten our way of life. Jack didn't understand the dangers of what he was investigating. But Max couldn't be involved in having him killed. That was entirely unacceptable in his book. He hoped for Jack's sake that he was soon *convinced*.

"What do you want me to do?" Max sighed and ran his hand through his dark hair. He hoped he might have some effect on Jack's decision to go along.

'Good boy,' Charles thought. It would be easier if Max understood his position, without having to *convince* him as well. Charles turned off the speaker and left the room and headed back to his office. He had two more items to attend to. If they both went well, he would not need to utilize Max at all. He was anxious to have this assignment complete, and to be able to report to the director that they were successful and he could die in peace. Charles was ready to take over the agency and he knew this was the last thing he must do in order to guarantee confidence in his position.

Charles picked up the phone and buzzed his secretary. "Charlotte, get me the number for The Esalen Institute in Big Sur, California, please."

"Yes sir, right away."

Charles hung up the phone and waited, going over his plan, looking for holes. He wanted to be prepared for every scenario. Soon, very soon it would be over.

Chapter 33

December 15, 2012

Brad hung up the phone. He smelled a rat. He called out to the outer office. "Tess, when Dr. Cunningham and Fisher get back with their friends, will you let me know. I must see them immediately."

Brad had spent many years developing his intuitive nature. He had felt too many coincidences since yesterday's arrival of so many astute guests; too many Ph.D.s with advanced auras. And now... a call from this Charles Tyler, President of Veni Victus, offering the Esalen Institute a healthy donation, for detaining his newest guests. Something was wrong, very wrong.

Brad sat back in his chair and closed his eyes. He fell into a state of *emptiness* almost immediately. It had taken him many years to become so proficient at it. All was quiet for a while and then he felt a heightened intensity. It washed over him like a wave crashing onto shore. He smiled at first, joy-filled, with this new wave of energy. Then it increased. He laughed out loud as it welled inside of him. It was so beautiful, so perfect, and so simple. He had been hoping and waiting for this. It was the beginning, he knew, in fact it had already begun.

After many minutes of absorbing the energy wave, he felt calm and peaceful. He got up and went outside, marveling at how bright and clean the day was. On his way out, he told Tess not to worry about looking out for the doctors; he would take care of it. He milled around the gardens the rest of the morning, watching and waiting.

Chapter 34

December 15, 2012

Apu's stomach began to rumble; it was loud enough for the others to hear. He smiled sheepishly as the others giggled. "I may need to get some food soon." He stated the obvious. The humor had released them from the silence. They each, in turn, stood and gathered their things. Jack decided that Alice and Sherman deserved to be warned, just in case they were deemed guilty by association.

"Both of you should know that we are being pursued by someone, or more than one someone (we aren't really sure), who does not wish for us to succeed. They tracked us down in Mexico and followed us to Alana's house in LA, and though we've tried to be careful, they may have followed us here. In LA, a man tried to strangle me. Apu here, our resident psychic," he said smiling, hoping Apu would take it as a compliment, "has felt danger close at hand since this morning. I just want you to be prepared." His apologetic tone was genuine and not lost on either Alice or Sherman.

"We understand. I can only imagine who would want to stop you and cause your mission to fail. It must be someone who knows what is going on. The idea that someone would know about your journey, and not want mankind to evolve, sounds scary indeed. Is there anything we can do to help?" Sherman offered.

"I am not sure. We have to stay on the move and hopefully one step ahead of them. I have to presume that they are here, in the area. Perhaps back at the Institute even. I trust in Apu's intuition, he has been correct so far." Jack squeezed Apu's shoulder gratefully.

"I have an idea," Alana offered, although she was still thinking it through. "Would you consider trading cars with us? If they have followed us here, they know what kind of car we are driving. It is a rental. You can return it whenever and wherever you are finished with it."

"It could be dangerous." Jack warned. "And we could not say when we would be able to return your car. If you don't want to, we certainly understand."

"Nonsense." Alice spoke up, almost interrupting Jack. "We would be delighted to help. They will, of course, figure out that we are not you when we arrive back at the Institute, but it may give you enough time to get a head start."

"I think it's a good idea. You must continue your mission - for all of us." Sherman said. "We will stall them as long as possible."

"Excellent. I can't tell you where we are off to, as we really don't know ourselves. But we will make sure you get your car back as soon as possible." Jack said.

"I know, I'm not worried about it. Now let's get going. Apu needs to eat." Sherman said and they all laughed again. The short hike seemed longer on the way back.

When they arrived at the cars, they switched their personal bags and keys.

"You will be in our thoughts and prayers." Alice said, a little tearful. They all embraced. No more words could convey what they felt. Their connection was now beyond space and time. In just an hour or more, they had become friends and comrades joining in the adventure together.

They turned the cars around and headed back up the dirt road, as it was the only way out. As they reached the main road, the HUV headed back to the Institute and the sedan went off in the other direction.

The Volvo that was waiting in the distance, paused a moment more, then followed the HUV. The occupants did not notice that there was one less person in the HUV, as the dust from the road obscured the windows. Besides, they were staying far enough behind as to not alert the people in the HUV.

Sherman was watching for them however, being made keenly aware by Jack and the others of the potential danger. He smiled when he saw that the Volvo followed them and not the others. It had worked, for now.

"Jack was right; their pursuers did follow them out here. And they are following us now." He contently told Alice. She smiled too.

Neither Sherman nor Alice knew what to expect when they got back to the Institute, but they knew they had a job to do. They had no fear, only the residual peace that grew form the connection they had made with their ancient and recent friends.

Chapter 35

December 15, 2012

Melvin Cooper lay in a gutter, passed out from over intoxication and on the verge of a welcomed death. A brown station wagon went slowly by, stopped and then backed up toward him. A large dark-skinned man climbed out from behind the wheel, walked over and knelt down over Melvin. He reached out his hand and touched Melvin's neck, checking for a pulse. Still alive. He bent over and scooped the man up with a grunt. Melvin wasn't that heavy, but his odor was foul. He put him in the back of his car. Got behind the wheel and drove home.

The man took Melvin into his house and laid him on a twin bed in a small room with no windows, at the rear of the house. He covered him with a blanket. He put a glass of water beside the bed on the night stand and went to make soup. When it was done, he then put a bowl on the nightstand beside the water. Finally, as he walked out he turned to make sure everything was just right. As he left, he closed and locked the door behind him.

His last guest had left this morning. It had been a middle-aged woman restored to health and on her way to be reunited with her only surviving family, her daughter.

This was the man's purpose. This was what he was here to do and he knew it. He had once been like them, lost to the world, lost to himself. Someone helped him years ago, on the edge of the worst. Now it was his turn to help others. He was grateful for every day of life that he had now, and he was determined to help others find life again as well.

Today, it was Melvin's turn. The large black man didn't know why Melvin was next, he just trusted in his own guidance and destiny. Melvin was yet to meet his.

Chapter 36

December 15, 2012

Sherman and Alice pulled into Esalen Institute parking lot to be immediately greeted by Brad. "It's about time you guys got back; I've been waiting for you. Where are the others?"

Sherman looked at Alice then turned back to Brad and asked, "Why?"

"Because. There are lots of people looking for them. Listen, I don't know what is going on, but I sense trouble. I got a call this morning from a Charles Tyler, from The Fraternity of Veni Victus, *whoever they are*. Anyway, he offered the Institute a boat-load of money, in donation. The only thing he asked was to know the whereabouts of Dr. Reese and friends."

Sherman and Alice were not sure of what to make of Brad and this information. "And what did you tell him, Brad?" Alice asked.

"I told him that I was grateful for the donation, and before I could stop myself told him that Dr. Reese and his friends had left for the caves and I didn't know when or *if* they would return. That was the truth. Are they coming back?" He looked up the road, half-expecting them to drive up. "And you switched cars?" Brad noticed.

"They had other places to go." Sherman answered, hoping that would be enough.

"Good. I'm glad they're gone." Brad said with relief. "I didn't trust this Charles Tyler guy anyway. Listen, what went on down there? I felt some intense new energy about an hour ago, though I couldn't put my finger on its source."

"We'll have to fill you in later, Brad. We are being followed or at least closely watched. I'm sure it's related to the phone call. They think we are Dr. Reese and his colleagues, because of the car switch. There may be others on the property as well." Sherman looked around for anyone paying more attention to them than usual. "We need to get out of here quickly, and without *them* suspecting that it is not Dr. Reese in this car. Do you know what I mean?" He stressed the last question.

"Absolutely. You, two, get going. I will have your other things shipped to you, will that help?"

"Excellent. If anyone asks, we had to go home for a family emergency. And you don't know where Dr. Reese and the others have gone."

"That is easy enough, I actually don't. Now get out of here, take the back way out, along the beach and the hot springs. Good luck."

"Thanks Brad, and to you too. Be well. We'll call." The car was already moving as they said good-bye. "Here they come!" Alice's voice shook with excitement as she looked in her side mirror at the road behind them.

Sherman looked in the rear-view mirror and yelled to Brad in the distance, "I don't want them to see us, but we need them to follow us!"

"Don't worry; I'll distract them for a bit." Brad waved and hoped they heard him.

Sherman drove the HUV out the back gate, past the beach and hot springs and on up to the northern exit. They were glad to see a car following them, though a healthy distance back. They were both energized by the adventure and talked at length on the trip home about their meeting with Jack, Alana and Apu. All the while knowing that they were buying them precious time. The proof was in the rear-view mirror.

Sherman and Alice decided to drive the HUV all the way to Washington and return it there, then catch a taxi home. And with any luck, it would take some time before their tail figured out who was really in the navy HUV.

Chapter 37

December 15, 2012

The dust from the dirt road cleared just enough for Jack to see the Volvo pull out and follow their HUV in the other direction. He smiled and told the others what he had seen. After turning to watch, they all exhaled, relieved to be free of their tail for awhile.

They headed east back toward Highway 5. Jack wasn't sure what was next, but he wanted to put some distance between them and whoever was pursuing them.

"Apu, where are we going next?" Jack asked.

"I think it is time to head to my grandfathers cabin in Colorado. We can regroup, do some research on the next symbol and it will be safe. From there, I don't know where we will go." Apu replied.

"Very well, to Colorado then. We need to stop for gas and food soon. But I'd like to wait until we are father away." Jack said.

Alana was looking at the map. "Head north on 5, then we can continue east on Highway 80. Also, I can drive for a while. I haven't taken a turn yet."

"Good. After we stop, it's all yours."

They began discussing their latest escape and more remarkably, another enlightening experience - the first symbol was revealed. They felt the effects of its simplicity and truth. *They* each knew their own individual purpose. That had been revealed over time and substantiated when Eligio had exposed the mission and mystery to them. But they wanted to go deeper; they imagined and discussed the types of changes that this new symbol's meaning could bring about on the world and chatted about it at length. It was a long trip, full of speculation and aspirations, paused only when they made pit stops along the way.

'Purpose and service for each individual, revealed through a personal connection to the spirit world,' they summarized and reviewed repeatedly. It was this connection that still seemed somewhat elusive to them, though Apu had more of a sense of it than Jack or Alana. The connection – the how-to of it, was where their conversation and then thoughts dwelled for hours.

Finally, all thoughts surrendered to the monotony of the road. Silence fell upon the group as Jack and Apu both dozed off while Alana took them east.

Chapter 38

December 15, 2012

The afternoon sun shined in the rear-view mirror as they headed east on Highway 80 through Nevada. It was at least eight hours to Salt Lake City, Utah and they had only covered two and a half of it.

After his nap, Apu pulled out his papers from Mexico. Included with his notes was the rubbing. He laid it out on top of a book on his lap. He used a small flash light to see, as the December sun had already set behind them. He knew it was time to decipher another symbol.

He stared at the ancient designs and again marveled. At first glance, they looked somehow familiar, and yet, at the same time, they were like nothing he'd seen before. Also, now for the first time, he realized that the handprint symbol that they had just deciphered and experienced was in the middle of the set. For some reason he had fixated on the flames (now hands) the most intensely. He wondered how his internal thoughts and decisions had triggered a cascade of events that seemed to work out perfectly even though it seemed out of the natural sequence.

This raised a new question in his mind. Which symbol would be next? He held the rubbing at arms length and maneuvered the light. He flipped it and rotated it to gain as much perspective on the whole group of symbols as possible. As he looked at the whole paper, he squinted his eyes a little to blur the image. Then he turned it around to see if his eye could detect anything through the back of the paper. Apu felt he had covered every angle, every viewpoint and every lighting nuance. Sighing, he laid it back down on his lap and let his head fall back against the seat. There didn't seem to be anything new standing out more than the others. He closed his eyes and soon dozed off to sleep.

About an hour later, Apu woke up to bright lights and he felt disoriented. Alana had pulled into a gas station and must have gone inside. It was the car door closing that awakened him. He ran his hands through his thick dark hair and rubbed his face. Then he looked down at his lap and realized the rubbing was gone. He looked all round the back seat, but it wasn't anywhere to be seen. He started to feel alarmed.

He looked up front. Jack was in the passenger seat still asleep. He was puzzled. Panic began to set in. 'Where could it have gone?' he searched though all of his things. He looked under the seat. It wasn't there. He sat back with his mouth open, reviewing his movements in his mind, step by step...

Alana came back to the car and got in. She looked into her rear-view mirror and noticed the look on Apu face. "What's the matter?" She was immediately worried. "What's wrong? Did something happen while I was gone?"

Apu took a deep, calming breath and spoke. "I had a rubbing of the wall here, on my lap, before I fell asleep. Now it's gone. I can't find it."

"Oh, that. I have it. I noticed you studying it before you fell asleep and decided to have a look at it myself to curb the boredom of the road. I have it right here." She pulled it out of her pocket and handed it over. She could see his relief. "Sorry, didn't mean to worry you."

"No, it's okay, now that I know it's safe." Apu responded. "Did you come up with anything?"

"Well, it is hard to study something when you're driving, but I see something familiar in one of the symbols. It resembles a symbol that I know of. The top part looks like an ancient Hindu symbol for the number zero; also known as *sunya* - meaning void or emptiness. It isn't used anymore in that form. The Hindu progressed to using a simple dot for the number zero and then an empty circle – similar to what we use today. But that symbol is one way they used to delineate the place holder we refer to as zero, thousands of years ago."

"Didn't Eligio refer to Jack as Zero?" Apu asked, feeling relieved now that he knew where the rubbing had gone.

"Yes, but for some reason, I don't think it is the same. Or maybe it is. I'm not sure. But I *would* like to find out."

"Where can we find out more information on this old Hindu zero symbol?" Apu asked.

"Well, there are books of course, but most aren't very well known or easy to locate. Perhaps in a large library... It seems to me that I remember something about... Oh, of course. Salt Lake City has a huge and relatively new library. I have read about it and always wanted to see it. And we're headed right through there!"

"Yeah, but we won't get into the city until well after 10:00 tonight. They will be closed by then. We will have to stay over until morning."

"Should we wake Jack and let him know?" Alana realized that they were making plans while Jack slept.

"Nah. Let him sleep, he can cast his vote when we get there. Are you okay to drive for a while longer?"

"Yup, I'm all set. I got coffee when I was in the store. They actually had Starbucks," she said with a wide grin.

Apu shook his head at her, laughing. "Good for you. I am going to jot down some notes on what happened today." Apu pulled out his notebook and began writing as Alana drove on through the evening heading for Utah.

Chapter 39

December 15, 2012

"What the hell is going on? I offered that guy a lot of money." Charles was furious. "Where are they now?" He yelled into the phone. He could never understand when people did not act within their own best interests. 'How could anyone who ran a non-profit business turn down such a large donation? He hadn't asked him for anything really. Just detain Dr. Reese until someone arrived to discuss potential funding for his archaeological endeavors.' "Oh, for ..." He didn't finish the sentence. No need. "What about the others we had on the Esalen Institute's property? Did they see anything? Find them!" He yelled into the phone.

Charles was on the phone in his office, speaking with his top assistant, Nathan, who was in the control room monitoring progress. The control room was in the basement of the eleven story executive building. It was the safest room in the building and had several tunnels that led to transportation centers throughout the city. It was also wired and connected to every available computer hub around the world, many that no one even knew existed.

"I will be right down." An exasperated Charles said, hung up and went out into the hall to the elevators. He used his swipe card and pushed in a sequence of numbers to go to floor 0.

When he arrived at the door to the control room he pressed his hand into the scanner on the wall. After a moment, the computer confirmed his identity. He then used his card key to open the door. This room no longer amazed Charles, but anyone who would gaze on it for the first time, would stand slack-jawed upon entering. It contained row after row of Cray 10 supercomputers. The public thought the Cray computer went defunct – a dinosaur of the '80's and '90's computer revolution. Not many knew that one of its designers, Timothy Reardon, a young graduate from Minnesota State University, had also been an agent of this organization. When The Cray 3 had failed and the Cray 4 had not quite launched successfully, Tim contacted the group directly. He knew the potential of the machines for their work. When Seymour Cray found out that Tim's loyalties were divided, he immediately fired him. Seymour had a well-timed auto accident not long afterward and the Cray supercomputer's development moved in-house and under-ground, with Timothy Reardon leading the way. Seymour Cray's other company, SRC Computer Corporation, went off in a different direction. Now, a decade later, the Fraternity of Veni Victus was secretly operating at over a hundred gigahertz, on the Cray 10, the fastest supercomputer in existence.

Other remarkable features in the room included a solid wall of flat, plasma computer monitors, spitting out information from across the globe. This was command central. It was one of the most top secret places on the planet. Only those of high rank, within the organization even knew it existed. And no one on the *outside* knew about it. Not even those they protected. 'It wouldn't do to have the traditionalists around the world know that they are being manipulated. No. Better to leave them their righteous indignation, their perceived individuality. They are more dangerous that way, but easier to control. There are some that may suspect something's up, but they are too disorganized to come after us. Still even in their disorganized state, they give us trouble, now and then.' He shook his head to clear it; he had enough trouble to deal with right now.

Charles went down three rows to find Nathan sitting at a terminal with three others working around him. "Where are they?"

"They are on the road headed toward Oregon." Nathan answered.

"Okay and where are *our* people?"

"Marty and Sam are pursuing in the Volvo. Mac and Terry are still at the Institute waiting for instructions."

"I want to speak to them. Get them on the phone now."

Nathan turned around and dialed. Then, he handed the phone to Charles. "Terry? This is Charles. What the hell happened out there?"

"The HUV pulled in, the owner here – Brad, I think his name is, went up to the car window. They talked and then the HUV took off. They went the back way out, we found out later. Marty and Sam have picked up their trail again."

"O, for Christ's sake." Charles exclaimed in frustration. "Okay. You guys head to the regional office in California. We have other plans."

"Yes, sir," Terry said as he hung up. He yelled over to Mac, who just shrugged as they got in the car and headed for San Francisco and the California regional office.

When Charles hung up the phone he turned to Nathan. "What is the status of Max McMillan?"

"He is ready. We just need to set it up."

"Good. Now we need Reese to call in. We need to create some type of event, something to cause alarm and make him want to call Max. Get the team together and come up with some options. I am tired of chasing after Reese. I want him to come to us this time. I want options in one hour." Charles turned to leave the control room. He trusted Nathan, but he was handling this one personally. He had to.

'Now what to tell the old man…' he thought to himself. 'This isn't going to be easy.' He pushed the elevator button for the 11th floor.

Chapter 40

December 16, 2012

The sun arose in the sky the next morning to reveal a fresh dusting of snow littering the ground, the trees and all it could find. Everything sparkled so brightly it was nearly blinding.

Jack was the first to rise, having slept the most of yesterday's trip. He went down to the hotel common area to retrieve some of the continental breakfast they offered. When he returned to the room it was just 7:50am and Apu was in the shower. Alana was in the adjacent room. He knocked on the door between the rooms. There was no answer. He knew she would be tired this morning. She had driven all afternoon and into the night. When they had arrived in Salt Lake City, Apu and Alana shared with Jack their information and idea of going to the SLC library. He agreed and they checked in for the night.

Jack rapped again. He heard a faint 'come in' from the other side. He turned the knob and the door opened. He expected it to be locked. Alana was still in bed, she barely squinted her eyes open to look up at him as he approached her bedside. Her hair was fanned all over the pillow. Aside from head and hair, Alana was otherwise snuggled in tight under the covers. Jack marveled at how beautiful she was. He smiled at her. "Time to wake up. I brought you coffee and a danish."

"Thank you. What time is it?"

"It's almost 8:00. The library opens at nine. I'd like to be there as soon as it opens."

"Agreed. Okay, I am getting up." Alana said as she sat up in bed and graciously took the coffee. As she sat up, Jack couldn't help but notice the sheer tank top she was wearing. He decided it was time to go see if Apu was ready yet. He stammered over something about getting more coffee and exited to the other room, the safer space. Jack knew he was attracted to Alana. The more he was around her; the more he wanted to be around her. He also knew that anything that might develop would have to wait until the mission was successful. 'I have to keep my head clear,' he said to himself as he gulped down a swallow of hot coffee, essentially burning his throat. He choked. Apu poked his head out of the bathroom to see if he was alright. He just smiled weakly and said "Coffee's hot." Apu just shook his head and ducked back into the bathroom, continuing to get ready.

* *

Alana had noticed the way Jack had looked at her. She also knew that she was becoming quite fond of him too. But she was glad when he left in a hurry. 'No time for that now.' She got up and went to the shower. 'Still I wonder…'

Chapter 41

December 16, 2012

They each had their assignments when they got to the library. Alana went looking for ancient Hindu writings. She was sure she would find the symbol there. Apu was in search of mathematical symbols and notations. Jack decided he wanted to check out what they had on Mayan hieroglyphs, if anything. After a quick stop at the computer look-up, all three scattered in different directions.

Apu was on the floor, sitting cross-legged in the middle of an aisle with a stack of books on his right and two opened on his lap. He was leaning over reading a particularly interesting section when he realized someone was trying to get past him. "Oh, sorry," he said without looking up. He tried to scoot closer to the bookshelf, making a wider path for the man to get by. He kept his eyes trained on the section he was reading. After a moment more, again he noticed someone. He looked up, paying more attention this time. It was an older gentleman with dark skin. He wasn't actually trying to get by, but was caught looking through Apu's selections.

"Sorry, are you finished with this one?" the man asked, in a stronger accent than Apu had heard in years. He guessed the man to be from his homeland, India. Apu however lacked further curiosity about him and stayed focused on his search through the books.

"Actually, no. These are the ones I am still considering. There are others there on the shelf, but I'll be finished pretty soon." Apu offered, still feeling a little greedy and more than a little irritated. The man lingered.

"This one has what I am looking for, those others do not." He leaned down and pointed to a book in the middle of the stack. Apu looked at the book the man had chosen and wondered what the man was researching.

"Why that book?" Apu asked, becoming less irritated and now much more interested.

"It is for my friend. I have been trying to explain the essential nature of the unified field and I thought that since he is a mathematician, he would understand it more from a point of view presented in this book."

"The essential nature of the unified field?" Apu repeated, as if in a far off voice, gazing off into the distance. Of course, his grandfather had spoken of the unified field. He tried to remember what his grandfather had said. Something about a connection to all things. He decided to inquire more of the man. Both men stood simultaneously. "How can a book on the number zero explain the essential nature of the unified field?"

"Zero is fundamentally a symbol for the unified field."

"Wow. This stuff really works." Apu looked with wide eyes at the stranger, who in turn looked back at him questioningly. "My name is Apu Chohan. I am here with some friends. I need you to… I mean… Do you have a little time to explain to *us* the relationship of zero with the unified field?"

The older gentleman raised his eyebrows and smiled. "Sure son, I guess so. Where are your friends?" he asked while looking around.

"They are here - somewhere. You stay here and I will go find them. You aren't going to leave are you?" For a moment Apu was afraid the man would *disappear* as soon as he turned to go.

"I will not leave. I don't have another appointment until noon."

"Great. I'll be right back." Apu turned and ran to find Jack and Alana. He was amazed at how the Gatekeepers just showed up out of nowhere. At least he *thought* this was another Gatekeeper. Together, they would find out soon enough.

He found Alana first. "Alana, I found something, someone actually." He said as he rushed up to her, trying to keep his voice low. She looked up; she had been deep in the material she was reading. She didn't move. "Alana. You must come with me now, he is waiting."

"*Who* is waiting? What are you talking about?"

"Please, just come with me."

"Okay," She said a little exasperated. "Hey, I was right; that symbol is nearly identical to this ancient Hindu symbol for zero, look." She showed him the symbol in the book. Apu looked at what Alana was referring to. He was impatient but curious. It was a drawing, not a three-dimensional Mayan carving, but the shapes were the same.

"Wow, that's it and the fact that it is coupled with the Mayan symbol for zero clinches it. How in the hell did they know the Hindu symbol?" he questioned without expecting an answer. "Bring it with you." Apu tried to rush her.

Alana slowly got up and put the other books back on their shelves, keeping only the one with the drawing. Apu was getting impatient. "Do you know where Jack is?"

"Nope. I haven't seen him since we arrived."

"Okay, I will take you over and then go and find him."

"Over where?" Apu decided it would be too difficult to explain; he just grabbed her hand and hurried her along. In a minute, she was standing in front of an Indian gentleman of about fifty-five or sixty. He had kind eyes and seemed to be amused with Apu and his urgency.

"Alana, this is… I don't actually know your name." Apu said turning to the stranger.

"My name is Ram Srinivasan."

"Alana, this is Mr. Srinivasan. He is going to explain to us how the number zero is the symbol for the unified field."

"Okaaay." Alana was at a loss for words.

"Wait, don't start yet. I still have to find Jack. I will be right back." Apu ran off again.

"Alana, is it?" Ram asked. "Why don't we have a seat over here? It will be more comfortable."

"Yes, good idea. Thank you. My name is Alana Borisenko. I am an epigrapher from the University of Southern California."

"Ah, yes, most interesting work - the amazing writing systems our ancestors came up with. You must find it very stimulating."

"Yes, I do, even though it can be quite challenging at times. I try to discover what they were thinking, their motivations, when they created their pictures and words. I am not always accurate though."

He smiled at Alana and then turned to see Apu returning with another man.

"This is Dr. Jack Reese. Jack this is Ram Srinivasan." Apu was out of breath.

"Nice to meet you, Ram. Apu tells me you can explain something about the number zero. We appreciate you taking the time."

"It is no problem. As I said to Apu, I was interested in helping my friend who is a mathematician understand the unified field. This book on zero seemed to be an appropriate fit because the number zero is a long-recognized symbol for the unified field."

"What exactly *is* the unified field?" Alana asked.

"I believe officially it has been described as *a universal phenomenon that demonstrates the connectivity of all things*. But zero is much more than its definition. The unified field is that which is outside of time or space but all things are connected to. All things which are manifest, or in our physical reality, come from the unified field, but *in* the unified field they are not manifest. Within the unified field they exist only as possibilities. All possibilities exist in the field. Also we are *all* connected to it at *all* times, whether we are aware of it or not. Unfortunately, most are not. The concept of zero happens to *coincide* (another mathematical term), with the concept of the unified field." He paused.

Jack saw his opportunity, "Wait, before you go on, Apu are we sure that this symbol is the same as Zero?"

Alana interjected. "Yes, we are pretty sure. Here's the drawing that I remembered. It is no longer used by the Hindu, but it is one of their ancient symbols for zero. I found this at the same time that Apu found Mr. Srinivasan here." She said pointedly, raising her eyebrows to deliver the significance of that timing to Jack. Jack understood that these were coincidences too perfect to be accidental.

"Okay. Now how does zero *coincide* with this unified field?" he turned back to Ram.

Ram was increasingly fascinated with this little group of strangers and a little amused as well. "As I said, the number, or meaning of zero can be used fundamentally as a symbol for the unified field. Let me describe some of the attributes of the unified field and perhaps it will become clearer to you."

"The unified field is invisible, silent, without beginning or end, it is empty yet all possibilities exist within it. You can not divide it in any way, but all things are created from within it. It is all places and no place at the same time. It is pure and in perfect balance. It is absent of all matter. It is invincible, infinite and yet extremely simple. Do these things remind you of what zero represents?"

"I thought zero stood for nothing, not everything." Apu said.

"The void and infinity, everything and nothing, are basically two sides of the same coin." Ram said. "The void is seen as nothing, and yet in that void exists all possibilities at one time, as soon as *something* comes into *being*, all other possibilities fall away. The void is zero. Can you see how 'all possibilities' is very close to infinite? Zero and infinite are equal and opposite. They are yin and yang, twin concepts challenging us to expand our understanding of the Universe, ourselves and God."

"I kinda see what you mean." Alana said. She was trying to process it. "But what does this have to do with us?"

"Wonderful question. We are an essential part of, and always connected to, the unified field, to the infinite void. There are many more aspects to this field, but zero comes closer than any other symbol we have, to describe it. Many believe that God is, in essence, what the unified field is made of. I believe that our associations to whatever gods we worship, cloud our full understanding of this field. But if you prefer to think of it *as* God, that is fine too. I believe zero to be a simpler, less cumbersome representative. Though as do all representatives, it too, limits us from the experience of the real thing. In order to really know the unified field you must connect to it."

Jack grew excited. "Yes, we have just learned and understand that we must connect to the spirit world; but how do we do that? How can one connect to this unified field or spirit world or God or zero or whatever it may be called?"

"That's an even better question. Our nature or very being is *one* with this field already. In order to make a *conscious* connection, you must first be aware that it exists. Awareness is always the first step. Then you must get out of the way. What I mean is, you must side-step your mind and its constant chatter and find the silence, or the void within you. This is the way to the unified field. The human mind has an estimated 60,000-70,000 thoughts per day. Most of the time, we have the same thoughts day after day. If we were to calm our minds, have fewer thoughts and more gaps between those thoughts, we would be able to hear God; you would be able to connect to your spirit world. You would find and enter the unified field, the field of creation, the place where God dwells. You must enter those silent gaps between your thoughts with your awareness. You must step into the null, the void, the gap." Ram paused for a moment to let what he was trying to convey, sink in. He knew what he was trying to communicate was a complicated premise for the inexperienced. "Many, many people throughout history have struggled with these very same ideas." Ram continued with empathy, attempting to lessen the breadth of their challenge and help them to understand.

"If you look at our present symbol for the number zero, you would see nothing with a circle drawn around it. This is because there is no way for us to delineate nothing from what is around it with out that line. This makes it a symbol. But it's what is inside that counts. It's what is inside of the curved line that you must enter." Ram paused again. He felt the cloud of unknowing lift.

Apu was beginning to understand the correlation between the unified field and zero. But Apu knew about the void, his grandfather had told him about it many times. He said, "You mean by meditating, right?"

"Yes, exactly. Meditation allows the mind to slow down. It helps relinquish the grasp your ego has on your life. Meditation can be your own personal doorway to the unified field, to God, really. It has been said that if prayer is us talking to God, then meditation is when we listen to God talking to us."

"What is meditation exactly? I mean I have heard of meditation, most everyone has. I am just not really sure I have done it correctly. How do I meditate and connect to God?" Jack asked.

"There are many different techniques of meditation. We must each one find the one that works for us, individually. Meditation is the practice of taking time to settle your mind, and slow down your thoughts, so you are able to slip into the gaps between your thoughts. It is here where the true power of life exists. It is here, where you will find peace, happiness, love, knowingness, your true self. It is here where God resides at all times. The unified field is never out of our reach." Ram put his hand up and pinched the air between his finger and thumb. "God is here." Then he spread his arms wide. "And God is here. God is everywhere. But our minds are too busy with fears and worries; we are too pre-occupied with ourselves or our relationships, to *hear* God."

"Meditation does take practice," he said as he put his arms down. "Your mind, will not relinquish its hold on your life easily. But with perseverance and dedication you can find your own personal connection to the spirit world and step into the void. It does *not* take years before you benefit from meditation. It only takes one time to begin to feel its benefit. To connect to the field of all possibilities, if only for a moment, will change your life. You will know the *feeling*. You will have opened your awareness to the experience of God. You will create a new experience in your brain and in your body that you can return to again and again."

Ram stopped talking for a few minutes. It was quiet at their table. They had chosen a table off in the corner of the library. They all just sat and listened to others milling around the large building. There was a feeling of being isolated and protected in spite of being in such a public place. Ram continued.

"The benefits of meditation have long been scientifically documented. It has been proven to reduce crime, create peace and prosperity, save lives, reduce pain and many more wonderful things. All of this is due to people connecting to zero - to the silence, to the void, to God.

"Many are afraid of silence. And infinity scares us also. Personally, I prefer the idea of unlimited possibilities, to the limits of what I know. The noise that we fill our lives with is old, ancient in fact. But the silence exists purely, and the *things* we have around us are diluted and redundant. I like the idea of always having fresh new possibilities available to me and it is in the *silence* that I find them."

Apu knew that when he meditated he felt connected to his intuitive nature. He felt in tune with his surroundings and not only the possibilities that could happen, but the probabilities that might well come to be. He felt fore-warned or aware of currents in people's attitudes and actions. He really believed that all things were connected. He felt his grandfather close by, right now especially, and was filled with gratitude.

Alana and Jack were quiet, trying to assimilate the information. Ram could sense this and stayed quiet for a while. Finally he suggested, "Meditation is not something you can learn *about*, it is something you must *do*. You must try it for yourself to understand and benefit from it. You may be able to sense that what I am saying is true, but don't let that be the end of it. You must do it yourselves to *know* it."

Jack nodded his head. "Yes, I can sense it, but it still doesn't feel real. I *want* to try it myself."

Ram was pleased. "I suggest using a mantra or a sound. If you repeat it over and over, it helps keep the mind from wandering. Also, do not berate yourself when your mind does stray, because it will many times in the beginning. Just gently bring your awareness back around to the silence, to the empty space between your thoughts. Some find it works for them to recite a favorite poem. As you concentrate on each word of the poem, visualize the words in your mind. Then guide your awareness between the words, to the space *in between* them. This is where the silence is, this is where the field is. You simply slip into the gap between words and thoughts."

"The most important thing to remember is personal practice. Find time each day to embrace the silence. The number zero should

take on a whole new meaning to you from now on. It should remind
you of the space, the gap, the silence, the unified field."

"There are many things that *nothingness* is not. In fact, all that
has substance is no longer *nothingness*; it is no longer at zero state. So
zero just *is*. Zero *is*… as God *is*… and you *are*. This is at the core of our
very nature. It is *worth* connecting to regularly."

Ram was quiet for a longer while now. The moments ticked by
and no one spoke. Apu was the first to close his eyes and slip into
meditation. Jack was next to try and Alana last. She seemed to always
have fears to contend with. Still eventually she trusted that it would be
okay to close her eyes and at least try. After the others had closed their
eyes, Ram closed his as well. He sent silent encouragement to his new
friends and visualized a circle around them all, embracing them all in a
large zero where only silence could be heard.

Chapter 42

December 16, 2012

Marie pushed the grocery cart with one hand and held on tight to the hand of her screaming five year old son, Adam with the other. In the cart sat her two year old, Mark who was also crying. There were moments when Marie wondered why she ever wanted to have children. Just a simple trip to the grocery store could be an all-out ordeal causing stress and unhappiness. She had never imagined her life would be like this. Of course many things had not turned out like she had planned. Her husband was recently laid off, making her the only one bringing money into the household. Why *he* couldn't pick up the kids while she got the groceries was beyond her. He always cited his need to job hunt. What an excuse. Still she knew he was suffering. He was a good man and really wanted to take care of his family. She knew he felt like he had failed them. No amount of reassurance from her had made any difference. She just prayed that he would find something soon or she didn't know what they would do. Her income was just not enough to pay all the bills, and those were piling up fast.

With a surge of effort, its source unknown, she put the five year old in his booster seat against his determined will. The two year old was easier, for now. She loaded the groceries into the back and got in for the short drive home. She started the car and then simply paused. She was tired. She gave Mark a bottle and a sippy cup seemed to quiet Adam for now.

She exhaled. She was sitting in a city grocery store parking lot with the huge Salt Lake City Library looming from across the street. The radio was spouting out the headlines: *Wal-Mart files Chapter 11 – Cites cost of logistics and increasing strength of Chinese currency vs. US Dollar. Queen Elizabeth II in a coma following a stroke. Venetian Seawall finally completed – cost overruns in the billions- the population is still in decline as Italy tires to rescue tourist gem.*

All of a sudden, she felt a peace she hadn't felt for a long while; it washed over her. At first it just made her feel calmer. Then she began to cry. She was on the verge of sobbing. The feelings were intense. She had missed any resemblance to this feeling so much. Safety. She felt okay, taken care of. In that moment she felt as though an angel was visiting her, wrapping her in arms, strong and loving. She smiled through her tears. She looked back at her children who seemed quite content and she saw their beautiful faces for the first time that day, that week maybe. She cried harder. She loved her babies. She reached back and caressed each of their cheeks.

Adam asked, "What's wrong, mommy?"

"Nothing honey, Mommy is just happy."

"But, why are you crying?"

"These are happy tears, baby. Mommy loves you very much."

"Love you too, Mommy" said Adam as he went back to his sippy cup, not really understanding Mommy's happy cry.

Marie turned around in her seat, brushed away her tears, looked up into the sky and said a silent, 'Thank you,' before putting the car in gear and heading home. She felt like things were going to be better from now on. New possibilities lay just around the corner for them. She drove home in silence - a sensation of connecting to God had washed over her and remained. She welcomed the quiet. She knew she had much to be thankful for. That is where she decided to stay for the rest of the day, no matter what happened, she wanted to stay deep in gratitude.

Chapter 43

December 16, 2012

Melvin was going through withdrawal. When he wasn't retching into the bowl on the floor next to his bed, he was shaking in pain. He had yelled and screamed to his captor. He had begged and pleaded but all to no avail. He was still locked in this room. He was brought food and water; most of the time he only drank the water. He was so thirsty. But he couldn't keep the food down anyway. There was a small porta-potty in the corner. It was cleaned out twice that day.

He knew he was not being ill-treated but that consolation remained in the back of his mind. The only thing he could really think about was a drink. He needed a drink, a real drink.

Once while experiencing a few moments of lucidity, he read part of a magazine that was left in the room. The few magazines in the nightstand were old but they helped to provide a distraction now and then. The room had no windows and most of the time he couldn't care less. He didn't know what day it was.

Melvin read a little of the National Geographic. For a moment, he was reminded of the life he used to live. Then he became angry and threw the magazine across the room. He didn't want to remember. He didn't want to feel how much he missed them.

All of a sudden, he felt a wave of peace sweep over him. He imagined his wife was there looking at him, she was standing next to his son. He could see them both, there with him, supporting him.

He broke down and he gave in to the tears. He sobbed from his core while his fragile, tortured body was wracked with wave after wave of grief. He missed them so much. Why hadn't he died too? He wanted to be with them. He cried out in so much pain and anguish that the walls seem to rattle. Why, God, why?

When he could cry no more, he was reduced to a limp pile of humanity quietly lying in the corner. In that moment of silence, he heard her. She spoke to him. At least he imagined it was her, his beautiful wife. "You still have a destiny to fulfill, my love. There is still time for you. You must live, my dear. You must get better. There is something left for you to do. Then we will be together again. Remember that I love you. I will always love you."

He allowed himself to see her; he looked into her eyes and cried out to her. His pain was so strong that the room pulsated with it. But he felt her love too; he felt love again. He nodded his head. He would try, for her, he would try to live.

In a few moments, the room felt dark again, but he still felt her love in his heart. He had a purpose. He would get better and find out what it was, so that someday soon he would be with her again. He crawled over and got into his bed. Melvin dreamily dozed off and slept peacefully for the first time in years.

Chapter 44

December 16, 2012

There was no way to tell how much time they had been meditating; it seemed like hours and only a few moments at the same time. Apu looked up to see Ram smiling at him. Ram knew he had another appointment to get to and gently nudged the others back to present consciousness. He wasn't surprised to see that Apu was the first to respond, as he had the most experience with meditation. Soon though, Jack opened his eyes and looked up. He felt so much peace flowing that he knew he was close to tears. They all waited quietly for Alana.

Alana had drifted into a state of awareness she was unfamiliar with. She saw snippets of scenes with people she had never met. An old drunk crying out in pain, a mother of two children overwhelmed with life's struggles. She watched as the same peace that was growing in her heart, and in the library room around her, seemed to reach across the distance and touch their lives, as well as her own. She couldn't imagine that they were real. Yet they seemed so real - in their struggles and pain, and in the joy and peace that had just transformed them. She thought it was her own mind making it up. But then she thought that it really didn't matter. She was amazed at the scenes, and much more amazed at the level of peace and joy she felt in her own heart. In that moment, as she came back to the library in space and time, she knew their mission would be successful. Later on, she would forget this confidence and assurance, but right now it permeated her being. When she finally opened her eyes and looked up, silent tears streamed down her face. She smiled at the others and wiped her eyes.

"It is okay to cry. It is your body's way of processing intense emotion. Sometimes crying also helps us to ground the energy of the void into our bodies, it is a physical expression for something that isn't really physical, but is more emotional." Ram told her.

Alana nodded her head but couldn't really speak yet. The others knew that Ram had to leave soon, but didn't know how to say goodbye - after such a deepening experience. To have such an intense connection with someone so quickly was disconcerting. And yet breaking the connection immediately was even more bewildering. Jack knew he had to tell this man something about their mission. But Alana asked a question first.

"Is it common to have visions when you are meditating?"

Ram raised his eyebrows, something they had seen him do several times and often seemed to denote his amusement.

"When you connect to the gap, to the silence, your destiny is revealed; sometimes your destiny is directly interwoven with your ability to 'see' things. Maybe this is one of your gifts." he asked her. "Do you know what I mean?"

"Yes, I think I do, thank you. We just learned the importance of personal purpose and living the life you were born to live."

"Ram, you should know that we are... 'on a mission from God.'" Jack informed him and they all laughed at the reference to an old movie line. "Actually, even though it seems absurd, I believe it is true." Jack went into a short explanation of their adventure. He spent a little more time on recounting the last key, feeling that to reach a critical mass each one of the Gatekeepers should be told the whole story.

Ram listened intently then responded with obvious sincerity. "I would like to thank you all for your commitment. Through meeting each of you and hearing of your adventures, I am recommitted to share my part with as many people as *I* can." He reached down and picked up the book that he had gotten from Apu's pile, smiled at Apu and tapped the cover. "In fact, I will begin now with my friend, the mathematician. Did you know that absolute zero – the temperature in Kelvin, is not possible in the physical world? All things are so intricately connected and interwoven that you can not separate the item you wish to freeze from its surroundings, enough to reach absolute zero. Everything is constantly interacting with everything else.

I also believe that this further demonstrates that what is in the void (at zero state) is not manifest or physical. Anyway, I know my linear-thinking friend will find all of this most interesting." It was obvious that Ram enjoyed learning and then teaching such advanced concepts to all types of people.

Ram got up to go and they all instinctively rose to their feet. Jack asked, "Ram, are you a teacher?"

Ram reached out his hand to shake Jack's. "Of a sort. I was a very successful engineer who climbed the corporate ladder to the very top, which is where I discovered just what the top will get you, a heart attack. I actually died. The paramedics brought me back. I experienced the unified field in those moments, when my heart was no longer beating. After I recovered, I quit my job and bought a small coffee shop on the east side of town. I spend my days reading, meditating, doing yoga and teaching my two dozen or so faithful customers what I have just shared with you. I believe zero is a wonderful introduction into the world of spirit, and is the most apropos symbol for the unified field."

"Well, keep it up; you are very good at it! I think it is truly *your* gift." Jack said.

Alana gave Ram a hug. Apu bowed first and then warmly shook the older man's hand with both of his. "Namaste," they both said in unison. Ram finally turned around to go, visibly emotional.

"It is so weird how they just kind of pop into our lives, change us, give us the keys and then pop right back out again. Do you think it is just because we are on this mission or does this happen to other people?" Alana asked.

"I think it could happen to anyone who was open and looking for it." Apu said.

"I agree. We just happen to be really looking for it and for them. You know I've been thinking about this critical mass thing. I wonder how that will happen, who will be the final person to get *it*, and therefore take us over the edge. Do you think it will it be at the end of our mission, when we have solved all the symbols' mysteries, and the Maya have revealed all that they knew?" Jack asked.

"I think so. But it is impossible to know how many lives we will touch or how many others the people that we connect with, will touch. Who knows who the last person will actually be?" Apu replied in a questioning tone.

"I think we will know who the last person is." Alana stated without really knowing why she surmised such a thing.

"Well," Apu teased, "since you are the one with the 'sight,' I'm sure you will know and you can tell the rest of us." They all laughed as they made their way out of the library.

Jack thought that he would never see libraries in the same way again. "Let's make time every morning while we are traveling together to meditate."

"At night too." Alana added. Apu and Jack agreed with gentle nods.

"My turn to drive," Apu said.

"Yeah, but no meditating when you're behind the wheel." She teased back.

Chapter 45

December 16, 2012

Apu informed his passengers that they were approaching Interstate 70, after taking a shortcut south on US Highway 6 through Utah's back country. When they turned onto Interstate 70 heading east, the sun was setting behind them once again. They decided to stop in a little town called Green River to fill up the gas tank and their bellies.

While sitting at the table, waiting for their food to arrive, Apu was reviewing the map and the distance to his grandfather's cabin. "It is about 300 miles from here."

"Wow, that far? I thought when we would be closer by now." Alana replied.

"We are *closer*. It's a big country." Apu teased. "The cabin is on the other side of the Colorado mountain range, closer to Denver, though we aren't going quite that far east." Apu informed them as he continued to study the map.

"Do you know how to get there? You look like you are trying to figure it out as we go." Alana teased back.

"Hmm?" Apu had become distracted by something on the map. He looked up. "Wha...? Oh. No. I know where I am going. I was just looking at something else." He paused deciding whether to broach the subject. "Arches National Park is not far from here, you know. I have always wanted to see it. I don't suppose we have time to go check it out, do we?"

"Not really. Not unless it holds one of our keys." Jack laughed at the thought. "What *is* the next key we are trying to uncover by the way?" he asked dismissing the sight-seeing idea almost immediately.

"Good question," Apu said wondering why he would even think of touring a national park at a time like this. He took one last look at the map, put it to the side and pulled out the rubbing from the Wall of Secrets. He spread it out on the table in front of them. They all just stared at it.

"The two we *have* uncovered are not near each other and are not in any type of order that I can tell." Alana said. "That doesn't help us much, does it?"

Jack rotated the paper around to face him and gazed carefully into its images for a few more minutes. "This looks sort of Celtic, this looks more Asian, and this looks Egyptian. Any ideas?" He looked up at Alana and gently turned the rubbing around to face her.

She stared down at it for a while. "I agree with you, but nothing is standing out for me right now." Alana said giving it back to Apu.

"Hmm? Who me?" Apu replied absent mindedly.

"Yes, you. What is your 'sixth sense' telling you?" Jack asked him.

"Well, I don't know *which* symbol is next, but my gut is telling me to go to Arches National Park." Apu stated quickly feeling like a giddy tourist with a wish-list.

"Just to sight-see or because of *divine guidance*?" Alana asked, only half joking.

"I am not sure really, but that is all I can think of right now, so I think we should go and find out." Apu said.

Jack was quiet for a moment, thinking over the possibilities. At first the notion of checking out the scenery seemed ludicrous in light of the pressing nature of their mission. But then he considered all the things that have happened so far. He decided that in the absence of other options, the one in front of them seemed to be the way to go. Things had worked out perfectly so far. Of course, if they wanted to see the park, they would have to wait until morning. This meant another night in a hotel. 'Oh, well...'

"Okay, after dinner we will find a hotel. Tomorrow morning early, we'll go see the Arches. I have not been there either. This should prove interesting." As soon as the words left his lips the waitress arrived with their food. They all looked around at each other, once again silently acknowledging one more small coincidence.

"How far away is it from here?" Alana wanted to know, while picking at a small salad; she was more interested in the entrée.

"Not too far. We should actually drive down to Moab; it's a small town just a few miles south of the park's only entrance. Then we will be close by for an early start. Moab is about an hour from here, I'd guess." Apu filled them in, having taken out the map again.

"Good, after we eat, we will go to Moab and find a hotel. They do have hotels there, right?" Alana asked, wanted some basic assurance of a roof over her head before agreeing.

"I am sure they do." Apu answered, finally feeling a morsel of confidence.

After she finished her meal Alana asked to see the rubbing again. Apu pulled it out of his bag and handed it to her. She cleared the area of the table in front of her and laid the rubbing from the Wall of Secrets out flat. She stared at it for a few seconds, and then said, "This symbol looks like it could be two-fold, like the last one was. The lower part looks like an *ouroboro*." She looked up to see if the others knew what she meant. Jack and Apu both had blank looks on their faces. She smiled and said, "An *ouroboro* is the snake eating its own tail. It is a symbol for infinity. And this one, on the top, see here?" she said pointing, "I didn't see it before, because I was seeing them as conjoined. But this top one is a twisted ribbon, in Latin it's called *lemniscate*, also known as a Mobius strip. It is the symbol we still use today for *infinity* in mathematics. Both symbols represent eternity, continuous renewal, or infinity. The *ouroboro* – or snake, also can mean resurrection or continual rebirth." Alana was both excited and pleased to have come up with probable meaning for one of the symbols.

"It is interesting that it didn't even occur to me until after we decided to go to the Arches. I think we still need to go there; with our track record - we'll find the Gatekeeper and find out what it really means." She concluded.

"It is also interesting how related each of the keys seem to be to the one before it. This definitely resembles the Zero key." Jack said.

"It reminds me of something I learned a long time ago." Apu was trying to remember exactly how it went. "The Veda says, 'if you remove a part from infinity or add a part to infinity, still what remains is infinity.'" Everyone was left thinking about that through the rest of dinner.

There were several decent hotels. They checked into one that advertised a free breakfast on their marquis. They got two rooms with the joining door again. After settling in, Alana suggested they get together to meditate. Jack and Apu thought it was a great idea so they all gathered in the guy's room and situated themselves on the floor in a circle. Apu naturally took his yogic position of 'seated mountain' which meant his legs crossed over each other, his back was straight and his hands rested on each corresponding knee. The others had seen this done before and decided to try the same position. They each closed their eyes and it was very quiet for a long while as each tried their own version of going into the void. Time marched on, but no one noticed, each lost in their own connections to the spirit world.

Alana was having trouble at first. Her thoughts kept getting in the way. She tried not to get upset about it. Each time she gently guided her mind back to her meditation. Finally she decided to use the method Ram had spoken of. Instead of using a poem though, she used the words she had heard in her vision years ago. She visualized each word in her mind's eye and then she moved to the next and visualized it. After she could see each word clearly, she would peer into the space between the words. The first time she did it, she was amazed at the feeling. But as soon as she felt surprised, she lost it. So she tried it again with the next two words. Finally, by the time she had completed the phrase, she was getting better at staying in the gap. She felt freedom, expanse and release gracefully compressed into those moments. She felt free of fear. She didn't feel driven in those moments, just peaceful and happy.

Jack was having a similar experience, only he decided to use a poem he read and loved as a boy. He hadn't thought of it in a long time, but as soon as he closed his eyes, it came back to him. Meditating on that particular poem gave him a sense of innocence; a pure innocence that he had not felt in a very, long time. He felt content.

It was nearly an hour later when Apu arose from the floor stretching his back. Alana and Jack got up too. Alana rubbed her legs some to get the blood flowing again. Her simple movement was not lost on Jack, who tried not to watch. He decided to quickly excuse himself, to go down to the office and see what kind of maps and literature they had on the park. Apu turned to Alana after Jack exited the room and said, "He likes you, you know."

"Who? Jack?" she acted nonchalant. "I like him too." Making light of the idea.

"No, I mean he *likes* you." Apu smiled.

"Whatever. I think you are imagining things." She said as she went through the doorway into her room, but she was smiling to herself. Apu quietly hoped the two would have a chance to be alone at some point. He thought they would make a nice couple.

About an hour later Jack finally came back to their room. Apu had dozed off. "Apu, wake up. I want to tell you something… Apu, wake up." Jack shook him. Apu opened his eyes and then jumped up.

"What's wrong? Is something wrong? Is Alana okay?"

"Calm down; everybody's fine. I just wanted to tell you who I ran into down in the hotel lobby. Man, you were really asleep, sorry."

"Yeah, I do that after meditation. It really helps me to relax and sleep better." Apu said. "Who did you run into?"

"There is a group of graduate students, from all over Europe, who just checked in. They are going to the park tomorrow too and invited us to join them." Jack said.

"That's nice, Jack. What are they studying?" Apu asked yawning.

"They are actually physicists, but they are sight-seeing and decided to stop here to see the arches."

"Okay." Apu squinted his eyes. He was having trouble seeing the significance of this encounter and was wondering why it was important enough to wake him up.

"The part I wanted to tell you about was, when I walked in, two of them were having a heated debate about the nature of the universe and how it related to the unified field. I found this far too coincidental, so I went up to them, introduced myself and listened in on their conversation. I think we need to explore this further. I think these people are why we are here tonight and not heading over the mountains. And I think this is why we are going to Arches National Park tomorrow, because that is where they are going."

Apu remained silent. He was taking in everything that Jack had said. The good news was that his intuition was still working. He was not worried, but the idea that he could be wrong had crossed his mind. "Excellent. That is great news."

"Okay, now go back to sleep," Jack said with a sheepish grin. "We'll discover the next revelation tomorrow." Jack winked at Apu.

Jack looked amused and confident. And Apu thought he looked more relaxed than he had seen him in a long time. 'Probably has something to do with the amazing adventure we are on, not to mention the fact that he is following his own purpose, meditating and, last but not least, a newly blossoming fondness for a certain Dr. Alana Borisenko.' Apu smiled too and rolled over. He was glad that Jack was happy. Jack had become more than his teacher, he was his friend and co-conspirator in helping humanity to evolve.

Jack crawled into the other bed and fell asleep immediately. Peace settled upon the room.

Chapter 46

December 16, 2012

Charles couldn't catch a break. It seemed as if someone or something was conspiring against him. Not only had they lost Dr. Reese in California, but as it turned out, he had completely given them the slip. The HUV was driven by someone else entirely, a couple they had met at the Institute. Charles' crew had been led on a wild goose chase all of the way up to Washington state.

With this news, he couldn't bare to face the Director again tonight. He decided to wait until tomorrow morning to inform him of this latest screw-up. He wanted this day to end. He closed up his desk, locked it and left his office. He still had an ace up his sleeve and that part of his plan would work, he hoped. He wasn't giving up. He couldn't.

He got into his fire red Corvette, a personal indulgence, threw his briefcase into the passenger's seat, and started the engine. It was nearly 11pm; there shouldn't be too many people out on the roads tonight. He punched the gas, revved the engine and put the car into gear. Charles sighed with an 'Ahh,' as he squealed the tires leaving the parking lot. He decided to take the expressway, and gather some speed. He turned onto the highway and shifted gears as the car jumped into action. In only moments, he was cruising along in the far left lane with all of the windows down. He shifted gears again and jammed the pedal closer to the floor, the Corvette responded eagerly.

Charles was feeling the stress of the day fade away with the miles. He was soon going nearly 100 miles per hour. He was two miles from his exit when a merging car came into his field of view. He saw the car in just enough time. He swerved to go around it. He missed the car completely, but was going so fast that he lost his usual precise control and caught the uneven edge of the highway with one tire , causing the opposite tire to propel the car into the air like a rocket, flipping end over end. It landed on the right shoulder, over a hundred yards from where the other car had merged into traffic.

Charles did not feel any pain. He saw himself and the car flying through the air and he knew he was about to die. He silently apologized to his grandfather. He had many regrets in those last milliseconds, but not for his work. He believed in their cause. He was sure that God would reward him well. In the last flash of his life, before the car hit the ground, he had a brief twang of fear, but it only lingered a moment before his car exploded into a million pieces. He died instantly from the impact.

Chapter 47

December 16, 2012

Joseph was sound asleep when the phone rang. He didn't pick it up until the 5th ring. "Ye…," he said groggily. He cleared his throat and tried again. "Yes, what is it?"

"Sir, there has been a terrible accident. Charles…" Nathan, Charles' first assistant, didn't know how to say it. He knew how close the Director was to his grandson, even though they were always completely professional on the job. Charles always said 'yes, sir and no, sir' to Joseph and he always referred to his grandfather as The Director. Still everyone knew there was a real pride in their relationship, a respect and even love. Nathan hated to be the one to have to break the news.

"What accident? Where is Charles, why isn't *he* calling me?" The old man coughed, still trying to get a little more awake.

"Director Tyler, it is my grim duty to inform you that Charles Tyler, your Deputy Director died about an hour ago, as the result of an automobile accident on Highway 10. At this time we do not know the exact cause, but the rescue workers believe that he was driving very fast at the time." Nathan decided to be as official as possible; it was the only way he was going to get through it.

There was no sound on the other end for some time. Finally, Nathan gently inquired, "Sir, are you there?" Still there was silence. Nathan started to worry that the news had killed the old man. "Director Tyler, are you there sir?" Finally, a tired, beaten voice spoke on the other end, but not in the raspy sleepy voice he had first heard. Nor was it the firm authoritative voice, he associated with the Director, from time to time. No, this was a weak, frail voice, filled with pain.

"Yes, I am here. I'm coming in. Where are they taking the body?"

"I believe that he was en route to General Hospital via ambulance about 30 minutes ago."

"I will be stopping at the hospital first, then I will be at the office."

"Yes, sir."

"Nathan…"

"Yes, sir?"

"I want a senior staff meeting at 6:00 a.m. Call them all and get them in. Also, I want to speak with everyone who was working on all of Charles' latest projects, most importantly - the Reese matter. Do you understand?"

"Yes, sir. I will take care of it."

"Good." The old man barely got the phone back in its cradle before he collapsed in pain. He landed heavily on his pillow, coughs wracking his whole body. Rufus, his butler arrived at his door in time to see the collapse and rushed to get the old man's medicine and a glass of water. After a few moments, Joseph was breathing easier. But uninvited tears began to stream down his face. He didn't bother to conceal them. He let them fall. Rufus didn't know what had happened, but hung on to Joseph's hand for a few moments.

"Can I get you anything, sir?"

"Yes, I must get dressed and go to the hospital and then to the office. Charles has been killed in an automobile accident." Joseph choked out through sobs. "Probably that damn Corvette he loved so much. I told him it went too fast!" Joseph cried out.

Rufus held Joseph's hand firmly, trying to comfort the distraught old man. After a few more minutes, when Joseph seemed to have a little more emotional control, he got up to prepare for the night's journey. When he came back he said, "Your clothes are ready, sir. I have gotten Baron up to prepare the car. Also, sir, I am going with you." Joseph looked up at Rufus, but did not protest. He simple nodded, took a tissue and wiped his eyes and face and got up to get ready. He reminded himself that he had to think of the job. No matter what, he had to pick up where Charles left off and complete the *job*. There was no other choice. He slowly made his way to the bathroom. It would be a long night. Joseph thought that the rest of his life, however long or short it was, would be - from now on - one perpetually long night.

Chapter 48

December 17, 2012

Joseph made his way down to the morgue at the General Hospital with the help of Rufus. He wasn't sure he wanted to see Charles' body, but he knew he needed to. He had to be sure. He had to see that Charles was really gone. The attendant behind the glass lifted the sheet to reveal a very broken up and charred body. Charles looked hideous. Joseph, astounded, thought of how horrible the human body could look when it is so abused. He lowered his head into his hands and the attendant covered the body again. They silently made their way out to the office. Rufus handled everything. He told Joseph that he would call to make the funeral arrangements later that day. They made their way slowly to the car. It was more than his advanced age that was slowing Joseph down.

However, by the time they arrived at the downtown office, Joseph had collected himself. He stood up as tall as he could and walked in the front door with all the dignity available to the Director of Fraternity of the Veni Victus.

When he entered the conference room where Nathan had gathered the department heads, they all stood. He took his place at the head of a very long, deep mahogany table. All of his doubts were gone. They died with Charles; leaving only a stern and unwavering resolve - to finish the job in these last couple of days. He would live that long, he was sure of it.

"Thank you all for coming. As you all know I'm sure, Charles Joseph Tyler, our Deputy Director died late last night on his way home from work. He was in a car accident. There is no reason to suspect wrong doing. It is up to us to move on. Charles had more or less taken over many of my duties and was in line to become the next director. However, now with his death, I will be resuming command. I will be here everyday until our latest threat is handled and I will not tolerate anything other than complete success." Somber eyes regarded him from around the room.

"There will be no Deputy until after we have turned the New Year. Nathan, you will be my First Assistant for now. Everyone else will remain where they are and perform their duties as required. Any questions?" Heads shook. "Good." Joseph stood up and everyone else stood with him. They slowly filed out of the room, save for Nathan James. Nathan's family had worked for the organization for many generations. He was smart and capable. Joseph had approved Charles' promoting him to First.

· "Director Tyler, before the group that is working on the Reese case comes in; there is something you should know. Last night we learned that the tail on Reese's HUV was bogus. I mean, he wasn't the driver, as we had thought. Reese switched cars in California with another couple. Our guys followed the HUV to Washington State only to realize it was the wrong car. Right now we have no idea where they are."

Joseph was quiet for a moment. "Very well." He wondered why Charles kept this from him last night and if this news had any part in the accident that killed his grandson. He suspected it had at least been weighing on Charles' mind. Joseph pushed away the disappointment that threatened to weaken him further. "I want to hear everything we have on these people. We will find them. They will turn up or we will make them turn up. Understood?"

"Yes, sir." He waved to the person waiting in the hall and another line of people filed into the conference room and silently sat down.

"I know everyone knows who I am, so let's just get on with it. Tell me everything you have discovered so far."

Nathan started, "Most of *you,* the Director doesn't know, so why don't you introduce yourselves and tell him what your individual research has uncovered. Samantha, you start."

Joseph listened as the tall brunette gave him the run-down on Jack Reese, his history, education, family, credit standing, investment portfolio, professional publications he had published in, field of expertise and many more personal details. Next he heard about Alana Borisenko and then Apu Chohan.

Nathan also explained the connection to and communications with Max McMillan and what Charles had been planning. Most of what he heard he already knew from Charles or from reading the daily briefings, but he wanted to see if anything new had turned up.

After reviewing every detail of the case, he sent them all back to their posts to search for more. Reese was heading somewhere. They needed to find out where. In the meantime, he spoke with Nathan about the ideas Charles had been brewing for getting Dr. Reese to reconnect with Max. They were busy for most of the day with plans and alternate plans. He wanted this sewn up as quickly as possible. He had a grandson to bury and needed to mourn.

Chapter 49

December 17, 2012

The next morning Jack was up early as usual. He went down to the lobby in search of coffee and whatever breakfast the hotel provided. He soon returned with several cups coffee and plates of food on a tray. Apu was in the shower. He yelled in, "Hey, coffee's here. I'm gonna go see if Alana is up."

"Okay, thanks." Apu yelled back from the shower.

Jack went over to the adjoining door and tapped. There was an answer but it was hard to make out. He tapped again, this time he heard clearly a request to come in. He opened the door. Alana was just coming out of the bathroom. She was showered and dressed. Her long hair was wet and hanging down her back. She smiled. "Sorry, I was brushing my teeth."

"No problem. I have coffee and breakfast if you would like some. Also I have news." He told her what he shared with Apu the night before.

"Well, it is nice to know we are still on the right track." Let me dry my hair some and then I will be over for coffee."

"Okay. Do you want to do a short meditation this morning?" Jack asked.

"Actually, I already did mine earlier. I was up very early." She smiled at Jack again as she turned to go back into the bathroom. He thought she looked very happy this morning. It must have been a good meditation, he mused as he returned to the coffee and food.

Apu was already drinking his first cup. "Is Alana up?"

"Yeah, she said she already meditated early this morning."

"Oooh, *she* is with it today." Apu joked.

"Yeah, seems so..." was all that Jack could say. Apu suspected Jack felt a little left out.

They finished breakfast and went down to meet the grad students. When they got to the parking lot Jack introduced Rene and Fritz, the two who were debating quantum mechanics the previous evening. They decided to drive in two cars to the park, since Jack wanted to continue on east after their tour.

They weren't even in the Arches Park before they could see huge formations that nature had carved along giant rock walls. Apu thought that it didn't seem much like a *park*. There were large structures of red rock as far as the eye could see. Some were connected to others creating flat-topped mesas, while others were single monoliths like the famous Balancing Rock. As they drove further in, there were places to pull over and walk around. They drove toward the far end of the park to the area called Devil's Garden. The sights were truly breathtaking.

No one was talking beyond a whisper or sigh; everyone was taking in the magnificence of the rocks and the views. They pulled their cars into one of the empty lots and got out. Hiking was required to truly experience the arches. Again, it was quiet as Jack, Apu and Alana were joined by the students. Everyone was taking in the grandeur of the tall pinnacles surrounding them, astounded by the way the rock splendidly reflected the early morning sun. Rene and Fritz were walking some distance behind Jack and Alana. Apu had ventured off with his camera.

"They are so big," Alana shared her first impression.

"I know." It was hard to find the words to describe the sights around them. They were humbly walking between sheer walls reaching sixty to one hundred feet high. Off the paths, some walls converged to mere cracks, which seemed to close in from the top. "It is so quiet and…so beautiful out here." Jack said. It wasn't long before Apu found them again.

"You guys have to see this," he whispered excitedly. There was a peacefulness that even excitement shouldn't break.

"What is it?" Jack asked.

"Just come look." Apu answered.

They followed Apu around the end of one particularly large outcropping of red pinnacles and fins, to see the sprawling valley ahead of them, with mesas as far as they could see. It was magnificent. "Beautiful," Alana said, closing her eyes and taking a deep breath.

"Wow," Jack exclaimed.

"Do you see that over there? Does it remind you of anything?" Apu asked. They turned their heads. Rene and Fritz had caught up with them and looked where Apu was pointing.

Alana felt a shiver run up the back of her neck; she was the first to recognize what Apu was seeing. "Oh my god." She stared with her mouth open. The implications were quickly sinking in. At first, Jack was confused by Alana's reaction, but then he saw it too. He started giggling. "Too amazing." Rene looked at Fritz questioningly. They were beginning to think their new friends were a little crazy.

"Uh, guys… what are you talking about, and what's so funny?" Fritz thought the area was beautiful and didn't understand Jack's laughter.

Jack looked at the others and then back to Rene and Fritz. He realized that these two must be the next Gatekeepers for they were undoubtedly staring at their newest key's symbol.

Off in the distance there was a particular rock formation that formed an unusual silhouette against the blue sky beyond. The arch before them formed the most perfect circle. Rene and Fritz were still waiting to be included in the significance of the discovery. As they walked closer, Apu read the description of the rock formation in the guide book he had grabbed from the hotel. "The arch we were staring at is called the Double O Arch. We are actually looking at it from the far side. The natives believed that to walk through the arch was to enter a different realm – a different spiritual dimension, one with every possibility imaginable. Doesn't that remind you of the *ouroboros* symbol we were just discussing last night?" Apu finished.

"Yes! Exactly, and the ouroboros (the snake eating its own tail), like the circle, stands for infinity." Alana said

Apu was still reading parts of the guide book. "There is another arch further back, (we must have passed it), called the Ribbon. We were just talking about the *lemniscus* – the Latin word for ribbon, which also means infinity?"

"Infinity - *or* the field of all possibilities." Jack added clarification.

Fritz and Rene weren't sure what they were really talking about, but 'a field of possibilities' was something they were passionate about. They had come on this trip in order to discuss the implications of what they had been studying and working on together at Cambridge University. They needed time to really explore the ideas they had been discovering in their own personal lives. "Quantum Physics *is* the physics of possibilities, even rather strange possibilities." Rene said looking up at the arch and then focusing again on their new friends.

Jack was overwhelmed with so many coincidences at once, he decided it was time to sit down and hear what these two young scientists had to say. "Let's go over and sit in the archway. We can sit in *infinity* and listen to what you two know about Quantum physics, specifically as it relates to the field of all possibilities." Jack invited.

They all found a spot to settle under the expanse of rock. One arch was clearly more circular than the other. The atmosphere changed as soon as they sat down. Alana looked down, and there at her feet was something else truly remarkable. "Look!" she squealed, pointed down to her feet. There on the desert floor was a snake skin left behind, all coiled up, yet vacant. Apu and Jack recognized the coincidence and laughed heartily. Alana just sat there awe-struck, then shook her head and looked at the others who were laughing out loud. Finally, she laughed too. "Well, I'd say we are in the right place." She chuckled.

When Rene and Fritz again realized that they were not included in the conversation Fritz asked, "What is going on with you guys?"

"We'll tell you all about it later, for now we would like to hear what you can tell *us* about quantum fields." Jack insisted.

"Yes, please do." Alana encouraged.

"Well…" Fritz said adjusting his thoughts, postponing his own questions for now. "Well, it is not widely known, how reality, or rather what we think reality is, really works." Fritz started out slowly in a distinctly French accent.

"Quantum Physics has proven to us that matter is not solid at all. Matter is made up of tiny building blocks called molecules, right? Most people know that. People think of these molecules as solid little balls, but they aren't solid at all. They are something much more mysterious. First of all, molecules and *their* building blocks – atoms, are made up primarily of *space* – just empty space! The amount of what we thought was solid in an atom, we found out is actually quite insignificant compared to the huge amount of empty space that occupies each atom. Atoms have a nucleus, which electrons revolve around. But elections aren't solid either. As a matter of fact, *they* are also made up of mostly space. What is not space, however, is also not solid; it is more like a fuzzy cloud of information that pops in and out of existence according to certain factors - or probabilities. No one knows where they go when they are not actually visible to *us*. I think they go right back into the field of all possibilities."

"It gets worse (rather, more confusing)… The *nucleus* of an atom is not solid *either*; it will also pop in and out of existence. So if electrons and atoms and molecules are all mostly space, how does *matter* – or how do objects really exist?"

"This makes all of the things that we consider solid an absolute enigma. All of these solid objects..." Fritz said as he patted the rock he was sitting on, "...are not really solid and what's more, molecules, atoms and electrons don't behave according to the "normal" laws of physics either. When you examine what atoms are really made of, strange things begin to happen."

Rene took up the conversation. "At the sub-atomic level, reality is quite bizarre. What is *real* to us, a solid particle of matter, isn't solid at all *and* it is continually emerging or rather "collapsing" from an infinite field of possibilities, where it presumably resides. And what's even more bizarre is that all of these possibilities seem to exist simultaneously, on the other side of our veil of 'reality.' To take the mystery one step further, it seems that we, the scientists, are who observing this strange behavior, actually have an effect on that behavior, or upon which possibility emerges. That really starts to blow the mind."

Fritz tried to clarify. "Electrons exist in waves of probabilities (out of all *possibilities*), or what mathematics refer to as wave functions. As waves, an electron's "position" can actually be in multiple places at the same time. This is called superposition. Think of a sound wave. If you are attending a concert, the people on the other side of the auditorium can hear the same music that you are hearing. Or you are in a room with a light bulb. If someone else enters the room, they can also see around the room. The light fills the whole room. But the moment we look at the light wave (with the correct equipment, an electron microscope), the electrons snap into one of the probable positions. The electrons "hold still" or "collapse" into one position. So, they are waves, everywhere at once, until we look at them, then they are particles, holding in one place for that instance. When we are not looking, they are back to being waves of possibilities, or 'probability amplitudes.' When we look at them, we cause the wave to collapse into a particle. This means not only that matter is not *solid*, but that it is not completely separate from you, or me. I have an effect on how and when matter appears."

Rene picked up the train of thought again. Alana was reminded of Alice and Sherman and for a moment wondered how they had made out with the rental car. But Rene soon pulled her back with his explanation.

"The implications of this are astounding, if you really think about it. This is where we have been studying on our own; we began to

see the connection between physics and metaphysics. The world is not
a fixed place in time and space. It is affected by me, for example, and
therefore I am no longer powerless to change my world."

Jack thought that this alone was a fantastic statement. It made
sense. To have science supply evidence of the unified field was very
exciting and felt reassuring to Jack.

Rene went on: "To Fritz and I, these insights into the sub-
atomic world have proven that the universe is made up of endless
possibilities. My personal experience -equaling to which one of those
possibilities enters *my* reality, is *directly related* to me and my expectations
as the observer. When and how these sub-atomic particles of matter
perform their dance of emergence is directly related to how and when I
observe them."

Fritz could detect a gap and spoke again. "Matter, is not solid
at all, but is more like thoughts, tendencies, bits of information,
consciousness actually, and it is directly connected to *our* consciousness.
We think we have no choice, regarding the direction or circumstances
of our lives. We are conditioned this way. We believe that the world out
there is separate from us in here." He said pointing to his head. "Solid
matter has always been separate from us. This rock is separate; the trees
are separate, etc. But in truth, matter is made up of information, of
energy and it is *not* separate from us at all. We have an effect. What we
see in our world is what we believe we will see or what we expect to
see. That is why the saying 'when I see it, I'll believe it' is backwards.
You actually will 'see it *when* you believe it.' That seems impossible, but
quantum physics has proven it to be true. We have a choice and that
choice has an effect on everything around us. Sometimes this is hard to
handle, but it is true, all the same."

Rene tried to describe further, "The science of quantum
mechanics calculates from all possibilities, the *probabilities*. Mathematics
can help us determine the probability from a multitude of possibilities,
but it can *not* tell us exactly where or when the wave *will* collapse into a
particle. Only the observer has the ability to choose."

"The universe is a sea of possibilities. Once those possibilities
become matter, or solid, in that instant, they are now known and
therefore limited. The nature of the Universe is unlimited, just as God
is unlimited. Once this subatomic *stuff* collapses from a wave into a
particle - it no longer is in many places at once. It is no longer infinite.
It is now in *one* single place. It no longer is a *multitude* of probabilities, it
is *one* solid particle. This is limited. When we speak of sub-atomic

particles; when we know their positions we can not know their energy. That stays infinite. The flip side is, when we know their energy, we can not know their position. Position is then infinite. This is the uncertainty principle. Cool, huh?" Rene smiled, obviously enjoying sharing such ideas.

"The unified field, that you were speaking of earlier, is the same as the 'field of all possibilities,' is it not? This is why it is better to be in the *unknown*, then in the known. But we are very often afraid of the unknown. When we relinquish our limitations - when we embrace the unknown - all new, wonderful and exciting possibilities open up to us. The *known* is your past. This is *why* Rene and I have been studying independently of others. We believe that limitations, problems, frustrations and even pain revolve around our belief in the past, the *known*, in other words – around solid matter. But if we can let go of the idea that matter is what is *more* real; relinquish the past and open our minds to the potential of the quantum universe, we realize that our past does not need to dictate our future. Since *I* am the observer, *I can choose something different*."

Rene tried to sum it up, "Einstein once said, 'The problem will not be solved by the same minds that created it.' I always thought that meant that different people needed to come in to solve our problems. But what about our personal problems? Someone else can't necessarily come in and solve them for us. I, we…" Rene looked over at Fritz and smiled warmly, "…realized that it isn't someone *else's mind* that is needed, it is a *change of my mind* that is needed. We can change our own minds! We have the choice to relinquish our past and choose a new set of possibilities. All we have to do is *change our minds*. Einstein also knew it wouldn't be easy." His eyes twinkled, in obvious appreciation for Einstein. "He said, 'Reality is merely an illusion, albeit a very persistent one.'"

Fritz got in the last word, "We become accustomed to what we believe reality to be and we are overwhelmingly convinced that we are limited in our ability to make that reality any different. We must give up those convictions and limitations. I think it was Richard Bach who said, 'Argue for your limitations, and sure enough, they *are* yours.' I love that."

"We must return to innocence, to the time before all our notions of what is real and not real, and what is possible and not possible, are formed. We must give up our attachment to the past, our personal history, and become like children, each day realizing that all possibilities await our choices."

When they finished their discourse, their audience was reaction-less; motionless. Rene and Fritz wondered if they had overwhelmed them. Still no one spoke. Not able to stand the silence too long, Rene said, "I hope we have not overwhelmed you. We get very excited as I am sure you could tell. We are trying to integrate these ideas into our own lives and speaking of them helps that process."

Jack spoke up first.

"I think it is fantastic, almost too fantastic to believe. Except that our lives seem to be running on *fantastic* right now." He smiled, and looked at the wondrous place around them. Fritz and Rene both felt relieved. Apu chimed in next.

"I have heard many of these ideas before, though never woven together so well," he nodded to the two Belgians. "It is still hard to *understand,* however I think it is *much* harder to *integrate* these ideas into my daily thoughts. You have made things much clearer for me. Thank you."

Alana finally spoke, "I really like the idea that matter isn't more real than our thoughts or beliefs. Though it feels pretty real when I stub my toe." She smiled as she tapped her foot against the rock that she was sitting on. "I'm anxious to try *changing my mind*. It's a lot to think about."

"I fully agree," Fritz said. "That's why we are on this trip, to take the time away from our studies to discuss and integrate these ideas. We are very excited, having observed and experimented with these sub-atomic truths in the laboratory."

Jack was thinking, trying to remember everything they had just said. Finally, he said slowly, "I think just opening one's self up to the idea that reality is malleable and that we have choice in the matter, pun acknowledged, and that the possibilities are endless; these are the main *keys* to your quantum mysteries. These are not *too* difficult to understand." Jack was trying to distill so much information into the main *key*. He knew that he, Alana and Apu would be discussing this for a while. But he felt confident in his understanding of the basics.

"Exactly. You've got it!" Fritz was proud and thrilled that they were able to convey their conclusions.

They all were quiet again for a few moments. Jack decided to tell Fritz and Rene about the mission and the amazing symbols that had shown up for them in this place. They had certainly earned the right to know. He went through the essential story. Apu and Alana had not tired of hearing it themselves. It always seemed so outrageous and yet they were living it. Jack also tried to sum up the first two keys for them. Rene and Fritz sat in wonder.

After further discussion among the whole group, Fritz said, "I am happy that we were able to meet and share our stories. There has been much written on the concepts that we have shared with you, but maybe we should also begin *telling* others, considering what you've just told us regarding the end of our age and the Mayan's predictions."

"Absolutely! You both have done an amazing job of condensing a lot of information into a couple of truths that we can learn and use. The more people who know about these truths and begin to integrate them into their lives, the closer we are to reaching the critical mass needed to make a different choice as a people." Jack said.

Fritz looked at Rene and they nodded to each other. It was clear, the power and the clarity of the connection that they were all experiencing. "This will be the beginning of our speaking tour." Rene declared with a smile.

Alana got up from the rock and stretched. The sun was high in the sky now and she was getting warm in her jacket. She was glad that it had been such a temperate December so far. Apu also got up. The mood had shifted and they all knew they needed to be on their separate ways.

"We wish you all the best on your mission. We will do everything that we can to support the shift in consciousness." Fritz said, sad to leave their new friends.

"Thank *you*, and thank you for explaining another *key* to us." Jack said sincerely as they began the walk back to the path. He turned around and gazed one last time at the natural ouroboro made from rock. He shook his head in amazement at how the symbols and the keys had joined together perfectly directed by each of the Gatekeepers. He smiled to himself, wondering what and *who* would be next.

Upon arriving back at the cars, Jack, Alana and Apu shared affectionate good-byes with Rene and Fritz. It was always an emotional moment, the connections were quick but they ran deep. They waved good-bye as both cars headed towards the main road. When they reached Highway 70 the Gatekeepers turned west; going to Salt Lake City. Apu, who offered to drive, turned east, toward Colorado. He wondered if the next stop would be his grandfather's cabin or if they might find more detours along the way. It didn't matter. He knew they were on the right track no matter what.

Jack turned slightly from the front passenger seat, to look at Alana in the back seat. Her eyes were closed. He could not tell if she was asleep or if she was just thinking. Either way he didn't want to disturb her. He turned toward the front, closed his own eyes and thought about clouds of electrons.

Chapter 50

December 17, 2012

Chuck pulled his rig into the truck-stop to fuel up. He had been driving for six hours straight and knew that he needed to rest. After filling up, he pulled the eighteen-wheeler over into truck parking and got out. He headed toward the trucker's lounge and restaurant for a shower and a bite.

He stood under the hot water and wondered if life would ever be any different. He was so lonely since Martha, his wife, had died last year from cancer. He didn't think he would survive at first. But he had somehow. 'If you call this survival,' he thought. He went from one town to the next delivering his load, never really making a connection with anyone. It paid the bills. But the long hours on the road left him too much time to think. He tried listening to the radio and to MP3s but still his mind would wander to the 30 years they had together. They never had any kids - she was unable. He would have liked kids, but they made a life with just the two of them and their little dog, Brandy. Brandy had been so depressed after Martha died that he decided to give her to the kids down the block. Some time later she seemed to be back to her chipper old self. At least Brandy was happy again.

Chuck went into the restaurant and ordered dinner. He pulled out his log book and recorded his hours. When his food came, he ate it in silence, as he always did. He wondered if he would ever be happy again. He finished his meal, paid his bill, went out to the truck and climbed into the back of the cab for a quick nap. This simple routine was his life.

He was laying there looking at Martha's picture when he heard a loud crash come from outside. He looked out and could see, from his vantage point, there had been an accident. No one else seemed to have noticed yet. Surely others had heard that crash. Still he watched for a moment but no one else went running. Quickly, he climbed down from the cab into the driver's seat and got on the CB radio to call it in. Then he grabbed his crow bar from behind the seat and went running up the road.

Two cars had plowed head-on into each other. The closest car was upright. Chuck rushed over. The driver was sitting straight up and looked stunned, airbag powder further whitening his face. "Are you alright?" Chuck asked the man. The driver looked over at him and just nodded. Chuck looked over at the other car; it was upside down on the pavement, about thirty yards away. Its wheels were still spinning. He rushed over to it, knelt down to look inside the passenger side. There was a young boy, about twelve, in the back seat. He looked shook up, but seemed alert.

"Are you alright, son? How do you feel, anything broken?"

"No, I don't think so. I hit my head and my arm hurts. How is my mom?"

Chuck looked in the front seat. There was a woman unconscious. She seemed to be pinned by the steering wheel. "I'll get her in a just a minute. Let's get you out of there first," he said to the boy. Chuck was worried about the mom, but wanted to get the kid out right away. He opened the passenger door and pushed the seat out of the way. The boy tried to get out, but realized his seat belt held him tight. "I can't reach the seat belt," he said. Chuck was a large man and had trouble, but he reached in as far as he could and managed to push the lever to release the boy. Then he pulled the boy out and carried him over to the grassy area nearby. "You sit here while I go and get your mom, okay?" The boy just nodded.

Chuck went around to the other side of the car. He looked in at the mother. She was bleeding from where her head had hit the door's window and she looked like she was pinned tight. He worried that he would cause her further damage if he tired to pull her out. Chuck looked around. Only a couple minutes had passed. He made a decision, since the ambulance had not yet arrived. He tried to open her door. It was bent and jammed. He grabbed his crowbar and tried to pry it open. He pulled with all of his might and still the door would not budge. Chuck didn't give up. He reached in and felt the woman's neck. He was relieved that she still had a pulse. But he knew she might not make it. He tried to talk to her to rouse her, but there was no answer, no movement. Chuck decided to try another angle with his crow bar. The door creaked slightly. He was able to push the end of the bar in a little deeper and then he really tugged; the muscles in his arms and neck bulged with strain and effort. Finally the door sprang open as Chuck fell hard to the ground.

He dropped the crowbar and crawled up next to the woman. She still was held into place, but by more than the seatbelt. He decided to deal with one thing at a time. "Son?" He yelled over to the kid sitting watching. "What is your name, son?"

"Jason."

"Okay, Jason. My name is Chuck and I am gonna try and help your mom." He tried to sound infinitely calmer than he felt. "But I can't reach her seatbelt latch from this side. Do you think you can reach in and release it?"

"I don't know," he said tearfully, "I will try."

"Good boy, Jason. You give it a try." The boy crawled over and reached in, but he could not reach it from the outside of the car. He climbed in further and was able to punch the lever. Then he crawled back out. He was visibly shaken - seeing his mother up close. He started to cry again. "Is she going to be okay?"

"I don't know Jason. We're gonna do what we can, okay?"

"Okay."

Chuck tried to push the seat back to release the woman. He had read how spinal injuries could happen by moving the body after an accident. He worried about this, but worried more about her bleeding to death. He could see that the steering wheel was really pushed into her torso. She could be bleeding internally too. The smell of gas fueled his decision to get her out. He pushed hard on the seat again while lifting the release to make it go back. It shifted a little and he was able to pull the woman from the car and onto the ground. He was careful not to move her too much and continued to support her head.

It was in that moment that the ambulance arrived and a fire rescue truck as well. They were upon them asking questions and attending to the woman immediately. Another attendant went over to the other car and was attending the man who was still sitting, dazed inside his vehicle. A police car soon arrived and Chuck stepped back after answering everyone's questions. When he did, he saw Jason sitting alone on the curb wrapped in a blanket, crying. He went over and sat beside him. "It's going to be okay, son. I am sure they will take you to the hospital with your mom."

"I am scared that she will not be okay, that she will die like my dad did. He died in the war."

"I am sorry to hear that Jason." He didn't know what else to say to the boy.

"Will you come with me to the hospital?" Chuck was a little taken back by the request. But he thought about it for a second and then agreed. He put his arm around the child and said, "Sure. I can come. How is your arm, what did the attendant say?"

"They said is only looked bruised, but I would get an x-ray at the hospital."

'This boy has been through so much; at least I can go to the hospital with him. Besides I was just wishing for someone to come into my life and give it meaning again. Looks like I got my wish, at least for a today.'

They took the woman to the hospital immediately and the police offered to take the boy separately. Chuck told the officer his situation and included the boy's request. The officer said that he didn't mind if Chuck rode along. He climbed into the back seat with the boy. Jason immediately scooted over closer to him. Chuck smiled and put his arm around him. The police cruiser pulled onto the highway and headed toward the hospital. He turned on his lights and siren. Normally the kid would have been thrilled, but today, he was just glad this big guy next to him had stopped to help them.

Chuck marveled at how things had changed in a moment. You never know the possibilities that lie just around the next corner or on a lonely stretch of highway.

Chapter 51

December 17, 2012

Melvin was now able to have his meals with the stranger-turned-friend, who had saved his life. He found out that his name is Tom Shift. He is a union pipe-fitter by day and savior by night. Melvin knew he wasn't the first or even the second that Tom had taken in, and he was sure he wouldn't be the last.

Ever since Melvin had seen his wife and son visiting him in his vision, he had worked hard to get better, to recover his life in the last couple of days. He was able to take walks outside and he had moved from the room with no windows to a nicer room with a view of the street outside.

Melvin wasn't sure what was next for him. He didn't have a home or a job. He didn't have any money. He didn't even know what he would want to do. But today, despite all of these unknowns, he felt good.

He went out to the front porch, sat on the chair and watched the cars, trucks and people go by. Everyone was deeply involved in their own busy lives.

Tom was at work and wouldn't be home until dinner time. That was okay by Melvin, he decided to just sit and enjoy the afternoon sun. He had an overwhelming sense of joy, although aside from being alive and sober, he didn't really know why. It was more than his miraculous recovery; more than his capture from the brink of death. It was more than seeing the wonderful vision that had given him new purpose and meaning in his life. No, today there was something more.

He heard a noise and looked down the street. It was the mailman coming up the block.

"Good day to you" the mailman said smiling.

"And to you, sir. It is a fine day." Melvin replied.

"Are you a guest of Tom's?" The mailman asked.

"Yes, sir. Mr. Shift is a very kind man"

"That he is. Would you please give him his mail?" The mailman handed over the stack and turned to go.

"Sure will. You have a good one..."

"I will and you too. Oh, and tell Tom that the Christmas season has started and we are looking for help down at the main office."

Melvin thought for a moment and then quickly yelled after the retreating mail man. "I sure will tell him."

The mailman was already off to the next house. Melvin just sat there slightly stunned. This was something he could do. He used to help his dad out at his office the whole time he was growing up. Life seemed brand-new to Melvin, and it was offering a whole host of new possibilities that he had never thought of before. He laid his head back against the back of the chair and basked in the gratitude he felt for being alive and having a new purpose.

Chapter 52

December 17, 2012

Marie was going home from work early today. Her boss had just landed a big deal and had let the whole staff go home early in celebration. She was even more amazed that her husband had offered to pick the boys up from their schools today. She smiled to herself as she drove home. Ever since that angel appeared to her yesterday, things seemed better.

When she pulled into the driveway, Adam was on his tricycle and Mark was on his scooter. Their dad was working in the garage. Marie had not seen him outside working since he had been laid off. She went up and kissed him on the cheek and then hugged the boys who came running over to her.

"I got a job today," Joe said with a side smirk on his face. Marie just sunk to the ground with Mark in her arms and sat there with her mouth open. There were no limits to what this day had to offer. The possibilities seemed endless.

Chapter 53

December 17, 2012

Apu decided not to stop for lunch right away; he wanted to get over the mountains before nightfall. Besides the others had dozed off, so he figured hunger hadn't set in yet.

Snow began to fall as they reached the higher elevations, getting closer to Vail, Colorado. If the weather didn't get any worse, it should take about two hours to arrive at the cabin. The trip had been amazingly successful so far, but he was ready to stay put for a day or two. Of course, there was no way to tell if *that* would actually happen. They only had four days left before December 21ˢᵗ. They may be on the road again very soon. Still, he was anxious to be in familiar territory.

Danvir Chohan, Apu's grandfather, had come from India to Colorado on business, many years ago. His company bought out a smaller company in Denver. Since he had to travel here at least once a year, often many more times, he bought a cabin. He had brought Apu there often. Apu especially remembered the times when he graduated from high school and from college. When Danvir died, he left the cabin to Apu. He was the only one in the family who seemed to love it as much as his grandfather had.

Jack woke up to see a darkened sky and snow coming down rapidly. He imagined mountains were looming all around but low dark clouds blurred the normally majestic views. "How are you doing?" he sleepily asked Apu.

"Okay for now. I hope it doesn't get any worse."

"Do you want me to drive for awhile?"

"Nah, I'm fine. Besides, I know where we're headed."

"True enough. Okay, but let me know if you need a break." Jack looked back to see that Alana was still out. "Where are we anyway?"

"We're near Vail. Under normal conditions we would have about 2 hours to go."

"And *where* is this cabin?"

"It is in Evergreen, just west of Englewood."

"Do you think we will be safe there?"

"No one except my family would know about it. I am sure that it was in my grandfather's records, but it would be hard to trace him to me, I think, since our family origins and records are all in India. I think it will be safe."

"Good. We need a little time to rest from the road and regroup, even though things have worked out brilliantly so far. It's amazing really, if you think about it."

"I know what you mean. It would be hard to plan it and have it work out as perfectly as it has." Apu agreed.

The snow was falling a little harder, so Apu slowed down some more. 'At this rate, it will take a lot longer to get there,' he thought to himself. He was just about to say it out loud when they both heard a loud, "Pop!" They jumped, startled from the noise and the bump. They had definitely run over something. Apu didn't slam on his breaks, but he slowed down considerably. "I didn't see anything, but with the road covered like this, we wouldn't be able to anyway." Apu said a little alarmed. It was only another moment before he knew that they had blown out the tire. He pulled over to the side of the road and pushed the button for the flashers.

By this time Alana was awake and knew that something was wrong. "What happened?" She asked worried, but trying to remain calm.

"We have a flat tire." Jack informed her. "Let's hope that there is a spare in the trunk." He added as he got out. Alana rolled her eyes. She hadn't had much luck with tires this week. Apu popped the trunk and got out to look. He and Jack met at the rear of the car and each searched around in the trunk. The compartment was bare; Jack then looked under the car. No use. There wasn't a spare anywhere. Neither of them had a winter coat, so they rushed back to the car and got in, shivering.

"No spare." Jack broke the bad news.

"How can there be no spare? Doesn't every car have a spare tire? I thought every car had a spare and a jack." Alana was frustrated and alarmed by how quickly the snow was coming down. "Where are we anyway?"

"We are in the mountains of Colorado. Vail is about 20 miles back, so that means we are right about to the Vail pass, which is over 10,000 feet." Apu said trying to be informative. Jack frowned at him. A little less information about their elevation would have been okay for the time being.

"Well, this car has two 'jacks' but no spare." Jack said trying to make light of the situation.

Alana relaxed a little at the joke, but still wondered out loud, "What are we going to do?"

"We are going to wait 'til someone comes by and hopefully helps us out." Jack said confidently.

No one had a cell phone, since they didn't have reception in Mexico; they each had left theirs at home. Alana had not thought to grab hers at the house, especially under the circumstances of their departure.

"I have a warmer jacket in my bag in the trunk. I think I will get that. Apu pop the trunk again, will you." Jack requested. He was calm, though he wasn't sure why. This was really not a good situation. He knew that if they ran out of gas, they could freeze to death before morning. That was not a comforting thought. He decided to trust in miracles that had led them flawlessly this far. Panicking seemed like a ridiculous option in light of the last few days. He grabbed his jacket, put it on, closed the trunk and got back in the car.

"We should remember the keys - especially the last one Rene and Fritz just told us about. The unknown is simply the field of all possibilities. It is in the unknown where the magic lies. Haven't we proven this to be true over and over again on this trip?" Apu said.

Alana knew that Apu was right, yet she was also a little annoyed that he was so calm. She closed her eyes and tired to take a few deep meditative breaths. It proved to help.

Apu went on, "I am sure that there will be someone coming by soon. This *is* a major highway and it is still early."

Sure enough a few moments later a car sped by. However, it didn't stop and no one had enough lead time to get out and wave them down. Jack realized he was going to have to get a lot colder to get some help. He got out without sharing his plan and stood at the front of the car to hide from the wind; he watched the road for another vehicle to approach. He wrapped his arms around himself and put his hands in each opposite armpit to keep them warm. He stomped up and down to keep his blood flowing. He kept chanting "in the unknown is the magic, in the unknown there are unlimited possibilities."

After five minutes or so, another car sped by, he waved his hands, but they didn't stop. He wasn't sure they had even seen him; the snow was falling pretty heavily by now.

"He will freeze out there. We are going to have to take turns." Apu admitted to Alana. "I will go next." He got out. "You go in and warm up Jack, I will try for a while."

"Thanks." Jack said gratefully and got in the car, vigorously rubbing his hands together.

"I'm next, if no one stops." Alana announced.

"You don't have to, I can go out again." Jack offered chivalry.

"Why, because I am a woman?" She smiled. "It just so happens, Jack Reese, that a woman's body temperature is slightly higher than a man's. So it doesn't make sense for me to be the only one that doesn't take a turn in the cold."

Jack just raised his eyebrows and smiled back sheepishly. He was caught caring about her comfort. She touched his shoulder and said softly, "But thanks for the thought."

"Well, here, take my jacket then." He took it off, shook off the snow and gave it to her. She took it gratefully and got out of the car a few minutes later to relieve Apu. "My turn," she told him." Maybe I can get more of a response," she said as she winked. Apu smiled and said, "Let's hope so!" as he got back into the car. He checked the gas tank, they were half full. That would last for a good amount of time, though he wondered how long the snow storm would last.

Alana had been outside for about five minutes, jumping up and down trying to keep warm and constantly watching for any cars headed their direction. Suddenly, she heard and felt a loud rumble; she strained to see what was approaching. She only had a moment to recognize the tow truck before it sped past. She had waved her arms and yelled, but it was no use.

She was losing faith as her hands and feet began to feel numb. She stood there looking to her right, where the tow truck had disappeared into the wall of snow. The white fluffy stuff was enveloping them. Finally, she heard another noise. She strained to see. She could only make out red tail lights coming back toward her, from the east. The tow truck was backing up on the shoulder of the road. She waved and yelled again. She realized she probably didn't need to yell anymore, but she kept yelling, waving, she was so excited.

Jack and Apu quickly recognized what was happening. Jack figured that the driver of the truck might think it was only a woman stranded. They both got out of the car, and waited with Alana for the truck driver to climb out into the blizzard.

A very large, bearded man got out from the truck and came over to where they were all standing. "Trouble?" he asked.

"Boy, are we glad to see you. We have a flat tire and no spare." Alana answered.

"Tough luck on a night like this." He said. His voice was gruff. He was wearing jean overalls and fleece-lined coat, open at the front. He looked like he never really got cold. He had a plain grey cap on his head. Although his face was covered in hair, his smile was kind, if ever so slight. He walked around them, looked at the front passenger's side tire, which was entirely flat. He came back to the stranded three. "I can tow the car and take you all to my shop to fix it. It is about 35 minutes east of here. That work for you all?"

"That would be fantastic. Thank you so much." Again it was Alana who spoke. Apu and Jack chimed in their 'thank you's too, but decided to let Alana's feminine influence work to their advantage. They stayed close by though.

The large tow truck driver went back to his truck and pulled out chains. Jack decided he should ask if he could help. "Nope. Won't take me long. Why don't you all go and get into the cab of my truck, it's warmer in there. I will have the car jacked up and ready in a few minutes."

"Thank you…what is your name sir?" Jack asked.

"It ain't sir, that's for sure. I'm Jake. Jake Jenkins."

"Well thank you, Jake."

"No problem."

Jack and the others went around to the cab of the large tow truck and got in, grateful for the warmth. True to his word, it wasn't long before Jake had the car hoisted up and was back in the truck's cab pulling out onto the highway.

Alana tried to make small-talk in the very cramped cab. "So how long have you been a tow truck driver, Jake?" She thought she sounded silly after she spoke the words.

"'bout 10 years now, I guess." Jake was a man of few words and it turned quiet again in the truck for a long while. Finally Jake asked, "Where you all headed?"

Apu answered, "To Evergreen to visit family." Jack raised his eyebrow at the comment, since it wasn't exactly accurate, unless you considered going to a dead man's cabin, a "visit." He didn't say anything though; he didn't want to contradict Apu and trusted his judgment.

"Evergreen's nice." Jake replied. It fell silent again, for the remainder of the trip to Jake Jenkin's shop. They pulled up to a large barn-like structure next to a small log house. Jack instantly imagined that Jake had built it all himself, single-handedly, of course.

"You are welcome to have dinner with us. My wife will be making food 'bout this time, I'm sure." They were all taken back by such a generous offer from their giant, yet quiet rescuer.

"Oh, we wouldn't want to impose on you and your family, Jake." Alana said.

"No trouble." He led them through the front door of the house. "Sal, we have company. Flat tire near Vail." He yelled down the front hall. A small woman came around the corner of the kitchen. Jake dwarfed her. Their size difference was quite remarkable. Jake turned and went back out the front door. 'Sal' was all smiles and welcomed them into the house.

"My name's Sally. Can I get you some coffee or hot cocoa?" She kept going; there was no pause for an answer. "You'd be surprised how many people Jake brings home, especially in winter snow storms. It's fine, don't worry. I am used to it. I made pot pie for dinner. There's plenty. It will take some time for Jake to get your car fixed anyway, might as well eat. You all aren't from around here are you? Well, we get people from all over the world, you'd be surprised." It was no wonder Jake was so quiet, this woman talked non-stop. There was no need to try and answer her questions, most of the time she answered them for herself. But the food was very good and they were warm. In a little more than an hour, Jake returned and announced the car was fixed. It was a nasty blowout, he informed them and they needed a whole new tire, which he happened to carry. Jack wondered what the bill would be, knowing he would gladly pay whatever it was. They were all very happy to no longer be stranded out in the snow storm.

Chapter 54

December 17, 2012

They were sitting around the table having coffee, after eating the best pot pie Jack had ever had, when Jake sat down at the table to eat. He had taken off his coat and was wearing a faded green t-shirt under his bibbed overalls. His large arms and chest made the t-shirt bulge. Apu was sitting on Jake's right and was staring unabashedly at the tattoo carved into his huge bicep. His jaw dropped open in stunned recognition. He knew he should no longer be surprised by the miracles that seemed to occur hourly on this journey, but this truly seemed unbelievable. Jake Jenkins had to be the most unlikely Gatekeeper Apu could ever imagine, and yet there it was, there *he* was, right in front of him.

Jack noticed Apu's fixation on Jake's arm, but he was on the opposite side and could not see what he was looking at. Alana, however, had a full view of the tattoo, though at first she didn't notice it from the angle of her seat at the table. She saw and followed Apu's line of sight and finally took time to really examine it. She looked at it, looked up at Jake, who was busily eating his dinner and then she looked back at the tattoo. She again looked at Apu who had gazed around at the others to see if they were getting it. He and Alana locked wide eyes. Jack didn't know what they were up to, though he could tell something was going on.

Alana decided to ask their host, "Jake, what does the tattoo on your arm mean?"

"It means unity." Jake replied through a mouthful of food. Apu immediately wondered if he really was a Gatekeeper. How would this non-talkative one share the vast information as did the others? How would they learn the next revelation, if he didn't speak? Jack was still in the dark, since Jake hadn't turned his arm.

Sally had been quiet for a while, which was nice since she hadn't really stopped talking since they entered the house. But now she spoke up.

"Now, Jake tell them what they need to know." She said cryptically. "You'll have to let him eat first. Once you get him going, he really can get quite chatty." This seemed a ridiculous assertion in that moment.

They all sat quietly and sipped coffee, and waited for Jake to finish eating a very large portion of chicken pot pie. Sally got up and poured Jake a cup of coffee. Then she instinctively sat in down directly next to him, once he had finished his dinner. He took several sips, adjusted in his chair by pushing it back from the table a little and evoked a loud screech on the floor, when he did so.

"I knew who you all were first time I saw yous." He began. "I have been giving my speech to strangers like you for years, but I always knew there would come a day when someone would come through and they would be *looking* for what I had to say." He took another sip of coffee and cleared his voice. The lead-in was nearly comical, as if Jake, the giant, was auditioning for a part in a local school play.

"I had a vision a long time ago. Changed my life that day. I saw this shape in that vision and I decided to have it permanently put on my arm." This time he shifted in his chair and pulled his large arm around in front of his chest to show it to everyone at the table. Jack finally understood what the others had been so amazed about. He too was astounded.

"I was close to death that day; a logging accident. As I lay all alone in the dirt, my leg crushed under a log, I saw a bright light. That light came down out of the sky and circled around me. All the way around the outside of that light was this same design." He traced the figure around the marks in his own flesh.

"Then there was a woman standing there, in the light, with this same design in a braid, hovering over her head. She was beautiful. She absolutely sparkled with light all around her. She told me I wasn't going to die that day. She said that I had a job to do and that someday, someone would come and I would pass on the information that she was about to tell me. Until that day, I was to tell everyone I could, anyone who would listen, the message that she gave me, the message of Unity. I expect I have told hundreds of people over the years."

"Today when I woke up, I had this feeling I was to meet those special people she told me about. When I saw yous broke down on the road, I *knew* it was *you*. I just felt it in here." He pointed to his own chest.

Jack, Apu and Alana had experienced many amazing things in the last few days, but to watch this big burly mountain man sit and speak of such things was truly miraculous. They listened intently to every word he said.

"The message she told me, the *light lady* I mean, was simple. That everyone is connected to each other. That we are all part of the same thing - like separate patterned squares on a large quilt. And that we should treat everyone, no matter what, no matter who, with respect and love. 'Cause it was the same as treating our loved ones or ourselves that way."

Jake's simple way of explaining this was endearing to the three travelers. It was abundantly clear that no matter how different his vocabulary, his message was heart-felt and clear.

"The *light lady* also said that though this world is made up of opposites, that one day soon we would understand that those opposites are made up of the same material, the same stuff. 'Like two sides of the same coin,' she said. You can't have a quarter with out the head *and* the tail. And no matter how *different* things seem to be from each other, they really aren't so different, and some day, and she kept saying 'soon,' we would know this. She called it a para-dox."

"Now, I am not a very smart man, I know that. Though I ain't no idiot neither. What she said made sense to me and I have tried to live by it ever since."

Jake drew in his breath and allowed them a break. He took several sips of coffee. He could feel Sally's eyes on him; beaming so proudly. It was obvious - their love for each other and how proud she was of him. Apu, Jack and Alana just sat and listened and watched, afraid to break the spell that must have fallen on them.

"Now some of the information she told me was more complicated. As soon as I was able (I was quickly rescued and taken to the hospital), I wrote down everything I could remember. I spent the next six months recovering and readin' up on what she told me. I can say that I understand most of it now. But for a long time I didn't get it. It took a long while. I have been studying it ever since, really. Some of the townsfolk wonder about the books I get at the library and in the mail. Heck, even my friends get the courage to ask me, tease me. But that's okay; I know I am a better person for having my leg crushed that day and for having my light-angel visit." Jake smiled so genuinely they all had to smile in return.

"Anyway, here is the information I was told and have since learned - this is in addition to the message I already told yous.

All of life is on a continuum, meaning that it is all connected, and in more ways than one, I've found out. We are related. Do you know that we each share each other's molecules? Through a complete lifetime, all of the molecules in the world have been in my body and in every other person's body on the planet. People in China have had my molecules and I have had the molecules of people in the Middle East and Africa. We are all made up of the same stuff. Not only that," he said with still a note of surprise in his voice, "we have the same molecules as people who are gone, dead, like Michelangelo or Leonardo Da Vinci, or Abraham Lincoln or Hitler even. Isn't that amazing?"

"And there's more. Not only are our bodies made up of the same molecules as everyone else, but genetically speaking we are all 99.99% exactly the same. Everyone on the planet is *that* closely related." Jake shook his head, obviously still stunned by this truth.

"She told me that not only are all things related, but that all things are possible and we are connected to all things and to all possibilities. She stressed to me that when one of us changes it affects all of us. How'd she put it? Oh, yeah, the *whole* of us. When *many* of us change, it affects the *whole of us* further. She said that there will come a day, not far in the future, when we will be on the verge of a big change, for the good. She called this change a couple of different names. I didn't know what they were at the time, but I do now. She called it the "*evolution of the human species.*" She also called it "*our next punct-uated equil-ibrium.*"

"Now, I will admit that the second one, well, I really struggled with it. I couldn't figure out what that meant for some time. Finally, I found a book that described it to me like this: Punctu-ated equili-brium means that in the evolution of a species, us of instance, individuals gradually build themselves into more and more complex organisms. Life continues toward more organized and complex life, it's in our nature. This happens very, very slowly over millions of years. But there are times in that development, where there is an inex-plicable," he said the word slowly, like so many others, as if he had practiced them, "jumps in that growth or adap-tations. This is called punctu-ated equili-brium and *this* is what human kind is going to experience very soon. We are building up to it now." Jake paused, taking time to regroup; then he continued.

"She also called this change *critical mass*. Our people began to change and become aware, a long time ago, but there were too few to make the jump, too few to create the punctu-ated equili-brium. But the numbers have been growing. More and more people have been waking up, understanding that we are all the same and changing. It makes it hard to go to war with someone who is so similar to you, dontcha think? Oh, sure we are different, but not enough to kill over. As soon as we realize *that*, things will really start to change."

"The angle, she described this critical mass shift as a slow build up and then a quick topple over the edge. She said that the time when we are close, the last few days before we reach critical mass, will be the most crucial, because we will actually be in a super-state. We are capable of anything in those couple of days or weeks, and due to our vola-tility, we could also destroy ourselves instead of shift. All things that are possible will be hyper-possible during those days."

"Now, I don't have to tell you that all of this sounded amazing to me. I had to actually look up the words she was using. I had never heard anything like this in my whole life. Nor had anyone I knew. I always wondered why she chose me and not some smart professor or someone like that. I never knew why it was me, but *I* am glad. What she said changed my life, that's for sure."

There was silence in the room. Jake got up from his seat, went across the room, poured himself more coffee, then back to his seat to sit down. He looked as if he was intently thinking, making sure he didn't leave anything out of his speech. He looked up as he remembered something else.

"Another term she used was very strange; she said something about *the hundredth monkey*. This confused me for a long while until I finally found the story about it. The hundredth monkey is the term given to an experiment that took place in Japan decades ago. Scientists were studying monkeys on the islands, and to lure them out so they could look at them, the scientists fed them sweet potatoes. Well, they would just drop bags and bags of sweet potatoes in the sand. The monkeys liked the sweet potatoes a lot, but they didn't care for the gritty sand in their mouths. One day one of the female monkeys went over and dunked the sweet potato in the ocean water and then ate it. Seems she liked it much better without the sand, and it even added a salty flavor." Jake kind of smiled at that comment. You could tell he was imagining the scene on the beach in Japan.

"Well this female monkey taught her family of monkeys to do the same thing. Pretty soon all the younger monkeys on her side of the island were washing off their sweet potatoes before they ate them. In

no time, most every monkey on the entire island was doing the same
thing. Even those that weren't related to the first group. The idea just
spread. That's not the most amazing part. At some point in the
experiment, *most all* of the monkeys on *all* of the islands were doing the
same thing! Now, how did the others hear, about it? How does a
money tell another monkey on a different island far away, how to wash
sweet potatoes? And all at the same *time*? Well, they didn't. The monkey
species just reached a critical mass in understanding and behavior and
all of a sudden the whole monkey species knew how and did it. The
scientists don't really know what the critical mass number actually was.
They just symbolized it by saying the hundredth monkey phenomenon.
That is how critical mass works, or so I've read. Only now it's *our* turn.
So I guess you could say we are *now* looking for the *hundredth human
phenom-enon*."

He smiled as he made up his own terminology. Jack, Apu and
Alana just sat there in awe. It was surreal. The air in the room was
tingly. Alana had butterflies in her stomach, like an excitement that
came from somewhere deep inside the truths that Jake was relaying.
Apu was trying not to show how amazed he was, but he was not doing
a very good job of it. Jack had to get up and walk around the room. He
couldn't help the huge smile on his face.

"You all look pretty smart, I 'spect you all understand what all
this means already. But that is what I am supposed to share. Believe it
or not. It is just all about being connected to each other and being
unified, like monkeys on an island. She called it *unity consciousness*. That
is what I try and have now. Unity Consciousness. That's why I put her
braided Celtic circle on my arm, to help me to remember that we, our
lives, are all interwoven, we are all one."

Alana wanted to get up and hug the big man, but didn't want
Sally to be alarmed. She just sent him warmth and gratitude through
her smiles instead. She loved him in that moment, and she was amazed
at how much. She had absolutely fallen for this over-stuffed, hairy man
and his tiny, chatty wife. Her heart was full.

Apu was feeling much the same; he reached up and touched
the tattoo. Jake didn't seem to mind. Jack finally came back over and
sat down. He looked up at Jake.

"I don't think there are words enough to thank you for all you
have shared with us. It is a very important message, perhaps the most
important of our whole mission. Your message gives me an amazing

amount of hope for our future!" Jake didn't say anything in response, he just smiled wide.

Alana began to tell Jake and Sally about their adventure and why it was so important that they know what Jake had just told them. Jake was impressed with their story and was visibly excited about their mission and being able to help out.

They sat in the warm kitchen for another hour, discussing what Jake had told them and what it all meant. They were careful to include the other keys as part of the story, feeling that each new Gatekeeper should know as much of the entire story as possible. Upon realizing how late it had become, Apu looked out the window at the weather. He could see that the snow had more or less tapered off to occasional flurries, and knew they should get going.

"Jack, we still have to get all of the way to Evergreen tonight, I think the snow has let up." Jack agreed and they all reluctantly got up to go. The familiar connection and following sadness, to leave their new friends was present, yet again. Still, they knew they must go on. They all embraced and wished each other well.

"Don't stop giving your message to everyone who will listen, Jake. It is more important now than ever." Jack said.

"Oh, don't you worry, I won't. I know my job and I take it seriously." He said with a contented smile. "Y'all be careful now."

"How much do we owe you, Jake, for the tire and the tow?" Alana asked.

"You don't own me nothin' mame; it's my pleasure to help you on your way. Please except it as a gift." Jake said.

"Thank you so very much, Jake, Sally." Alana said. This time she did give him a big hug and a kiss on the cheek. She could see that he actually blushed. Sally had been pretty quiet, understanding the importance of Jake's message. Alana thanked her for a wonderful dinner and hugged her too. Sally stood in the doorway with Jake, waving good-bye.

When they got into the car, they found three large parkas in the back seat. They just smiled and waved with a yell of, 'thank you' as they drove off.

Chapter 55

December 17, 2012

When Tom got home, and learned of the Post Office position, he called his friend who was one of the managers. Before, he knew it, Melvin was employed.

He began his new job the next day. He was both excited and nervous. He thought about how he had so often used alcohol to deal with his nervousness. But that was before. He would never do that again. Tonight he sat on the porch and listened to the crickets and looked up at the stars.

Tom came out of the house and sat beside him, but didn't speak for a few minutes. After a comfortable silence he finally said, "Don't be nervous about tomorrow, Melvin; you will do great."

"Thanks, Tom. I hope so."

"You know, last week I was working at a new apartment complex. I went in early only to see my boss's boss come in right after me, completely drunk. I found out later that the night before his teenage son had gotten arrested for stealing a car. It was only a prank, but the boy is in serious trouble. Terry, the boss, couldn't handle it and he went out and stayed out drinking all night *tying one on*. So you see we are all are human, we all have troubles, we all have weaknesses and we all make poor choices. We can't judge or hold grudges, 'cause when we do, we are judging ourselves. And a grudge will only hurt the one who holds it."

"Point is, we are all equal and connected. So don't go feelin' bad about yourself or thinking you can't do the job. Everyone has their troubles. Treatin' people kind is the way to go, no matter if they understand it or not. And treatin' yourself with kindness is the most important." With a gentle sigh, Tom grew quiet again.

"I can't thank you enough, Tom. You have given me so much. You have given me my life back."

"Well, seems the least I can do, someone gave mine back to me a while ago. Since we are all so connected to one another, I'm just returning the favor." He laughed lightly at his own turn of phrase.

"I'm off to bed, Melvin, see you in the morning."

"Yep, me too. Good night."

Chapter 56

December 17, 2012

Marie was tucking the kids into bed when the phone rang. She kissed the boys goodnight and went to answer it.

"Hello?"

"Marie? It's Claire."

"Hey, Claire, what's up?" Marie could always tell when her little sister was in a mood.

"I am so upset." She said in tears.

"What's wrong, is Mandy okay?"

"She's fine, she is asleep. Doug just left. We had this huge fight and he stormed out. He says he is tired of me nagging him all the time." She sobbed. "He said we should separate."

"Oh, Claire, I am so sorry. What can I do to help?" She was amazed that Claire was even calling her. Her sister had been so condescending to her after Joe had lost his job. 'I don't know why you stay with him.' Claire had told her. She kept telling her she was crazy for putting up with his bad moods and not making him help out with the kids.

Now it seemed that the shoe was on the other foot, as they say. But Marie understood what it was like. For some reason, she didn't want to rub it in as she usually would. She felt a new connection to her sister. The thought occurred to her out of the blue, 'Aren't we all really the same?' This surprised Marie, but in that moment it somehow made sense.

"Maybe Doug just needs to blow off some steam. Do you want me to come over and be with you for a little?" Marie offered.

"Oh, could you, Marie?" That would be great. I just don't know what I would do without Doug."

"Sure. Let me talk to Joe. The boys just went to bed so I'm sure he wouldn't miss me for a little while."

"Thank you, Marie." She sniffled.

When Marie got in her car to drive the 10 blocks over to Claire's house, she decided to release all her resentment toward her sister. 'It won't do either of us any good. I can help her more if I just love her for where she is right now.' Marie thought. 'Maybe if everyone realized that, the world would be a better place.'

Chapter 57

December 17, 2012

The doctor came out to talk to Chuck and the boy, who had been waiting patiently, for quite a few hours, in the hospital waiting room.

"Are you June Turner's husband?"

"No." Chuck answered quickly. "I am just a friend. I think the woman is widowed; this is her son, Jason. How is she?"

"She is stable but serious condition." The doctor asked if it was alright to speak frankly in front of the boy; Chuck nodded. "She had a ruptured spleen and a lot of internal bleeding. We operated, repaired her spleen and stopped the bleeding. She also has a concussion and we suspect that the blow to her head has caused the coma. It could be a temporary condition, we will have to wait and see. Is there another relative that might live near by?"

The police officer had already asked the same question. Jason informed them that his aunt Janet lived pretty close. They called her immediately

"We are waiting for Jason's aunt to get here."

"Good, have her check in at the desk, we need the patient's medical information and records." The doctor said and walked away.

"I don't want to go to Aunt Janet's. She hates me. Can't I stay with you?" the boy whined to Chuck.

"I don't live around here son and I don't think they would let you stay with a complete stranger, and they shouldn't; why would they trust me?"

"But *I* trust you." Jason said.

"Well, thank you, Jason. I trust you too."

Aunt Janet arrived. She instantly seemed angry and yelled at Jason. "What happened?" Chuck stepped in front of the boy and answered for him.

"There was an accident and your sister is in serious condition. Her spleen was ruptured, plus she has a concussion and right now, she is in a coma. They don't know when she will come out of it. The doctor asked for you to check in with the nurse at the desk over there."

"And who are you, her latest boyfriend I suppose?"

"No…, I am just a friend. My name is Chuck Adams. I pulled them from the wreckage."

"Oh, well, ah, I guess I should thank you. You can go now, I'm here. Come on Jason; let's go see just what is going on." She grabbed for his hand.

He flinched and moved away. "I don't want to go with you. I want to stay here with Chuck."

"It's okay, Mame. I will stay here with the boy if you want, while you go and talk to the nurses." She looked down at the boy and then back at the large man who he was hiding behind. She decided she would fight with him later. "Oh, all right. You both stay here."

After she turned away from them, Chuck bent down to talk to the boy. "Listen son. I understand your feelings about your aunt. But you have to understand, they are not going to let you stay with me, 'sides I haven't got a place for us to stay at." Chuck paused for a minute - thinking. "I tell you what I am going to do. I am going to go and deliver the load on my truck. Then I will get in my car and come back here. I will stay in this area, and visit you and your mom until we know that she is going to be okay. You still won't be able to stay with me, but at least we can spend time here visiting at the hospital while your mom recovers." The boy smiled, excited to have Chuck there with him.

"I know you're scared. Your mom is real sick and you aren't real fond of your aunt. But don't judge your aunt too harshly; everyone has their own problems and she doesn't seem too happy, if you ask me. Just keep that in mind." He could tell that Jason understood.

Chuck was suddenly overwhelmed with a thought - which he immediately shared with Jason, "Listen, Jason, every chance you get I want you to send your mom your love, even if you aren't in the same room with her. Send it from your heart to hers. She will feel it. You and your mom are definitely connected. So send her all the love you have. Okay?"

"Yes, I will." Jason said as if he really took to heart what Chuck was telling him. Chuck then reached out and gave the boy a hug.

"It's gonna be okay, you'll see." Chuck didn't know where his optimism was coming from, but he believed it was true. He then turned and went over to Aunt Janet to say good-bye and tell her he would be back. She was just as rude as before. He felt sorry for her and saw that underneath all of her harsh walls, she was an unhappy and quite frightened person. He reached out and put his large hand on her shoulder, looked into her eyes and smiled warmly.

"Don't worry, mame, it's gonna be okay. I will be back in a couple days."

Janet didn't know what to say or how to react. It seemed that Chuck had gotten past her defenses in a single moment. She just nodded her head and fought back the tears, tears that let loose and spilled down her cheeks for no apparent reason. She was relieved that he had already turned to go

Chuck walked out of the hospital, glancing back once to wave to Jason and smile.

Aunt Janet wondered about this stranger who could make her melt in an instant. She hadn't cried in three years. She remembered the exact day the last time it happened. She shook her head and then turned to Jason. "Come on, hon, they said we could go and see her now. But she may not look so good, so don't be upset, okay?" He nodded his head. Jason reached up and held her hand as they walked down the hall toward his mother's room.

Chapter 58

December 17, 2012

It was past eleven by the time they pulled down the long driveway toward Apu's cabin. During the ride they had discussed at length the conversation with Jake and Sally. It had been another remarkable day but a long and tiring one; they gladly allowed the discussion to die down.

Apu retrieved the key to the front door from under a nearby rock and unlocked the very dark but welcoming cabin. It was cold inside but the atmosphere was pleasant.

"All the amenities of home." Apu said as he went out to get wood to start a fire in the wood stove.

Alana and Jack brought in their bags and looked around the cabin. They very much liked what they saw. It looked rugged on the outside, rough hewn logs and chinking. But inside it was quite modern and comfortable. There were two bedrooms; one with two twin beds and one with a large queen sized bed. They decided that the queen would be Alana's and the guys would stay in the smaller bedroom. After the fire was blazing and the cabin was cozy and warm, Alana started to yawn. "I am off to bed, you guys, see you in the morning."

Jack and Apu agreed with Alana and soon they were all sinking into dreams of magic and monkeys. They had no idea what the next stage of their adventure would entail, but for now they were safe, warm and peaceful and that was more than enough.

Part 3

"The power and capacity of learning exists in the soul already; and that just as the eye was unable to turn from darkness to light without the whole body, so too the instrument of knowledge can only by the movement of the whole soul be turned from the world of becoming into that of being, and learn by degrees to endure the sight of being, and of the brightest and best of being, or in other words, of the good."

-- Plato, The Allegory of the Cave

Chapter 59

December 18, 2012

The next morning the warm sun shined on the little cabin in the woods. Jack was up early as usual, searching the kitchen for a coffee maker and coffee. He found the coffee maker in one of the lower cupboards but was not as fortunate in finding coffee. He knew there had not been any visitors to the cabin in over a year but made one last attempt, the freezer. 'Voilá!' he thought with a smirk. He found a small bag of frozen coffee beans. Jubilant, he started searching for a grinder. Then he discovered that the coffee maker itself did the grinding et al. He dropped in what he thought was the appropriate amount of beans and let it go to work.

Next, Jack did an inventory of what food was available. The freezer contained other less recognizable packages, and he wondered how long they had been there. There were some canned goods in the pantry. Overall, Jack decided a trip to the grocery would be next on their list of things to do. He didn't know how long they would be there, but he hoped it was at least a day or two. They needed to rest, if only for a little while.

Jack was sitting at the kitchen table drinking coffee and staring out the window when Alana came into the kitchen. She poured herself a cup of coffee and sat down without saying a word. After the third sip she finally mumbled, "Good coffee."

"Yeah, I found it in the freezer. But there isn't much to eat. We will have to find a grocery store if we are going to stay long."

"Do you think we will be able to stay?"

"Don't know. I mean I think it's safe, but we don't have a lot of time before the 21st and there are four symbols left to decipher. So far we have 'coincidently' run into the Gatekeepers along our travels. That won't continue to be the pattern if we stay here, unless, of course, people start knocking on the door."

"After the miracles that we have seen in the last few days, I wouldn't be surprised." Alana said.

"I know. But still I don't think that is the way it will work -just a gut feeling. Actually, the more I think about it, the more nervous I get. I don't really know how it will all work out. I don't know how it could." He looked into his coffee cup, as if the brown liquid would reveal some clue. 'Maybe tea would have been a better choice.' he thought to himself.

"Well, for today we should just relax, re-group and review what we have learned so far. Also, Apu said that there is a Net connection here, so we can do a little research. I, for one, would like to check my email."

"Yeah, me too. Everyone knew I would be off-line for some time, while I was in Mexico, but I would like to see if there is anything happening at the University. It is *time* to check in, I think. We may only have three days left, but it feels as if we have been given a short reprieve and I think we should take advantage of it while it lasts."

A few more moments of coffee and contemplation followed; they were content to patiently sip and enjoy the sunlight coming in the kitchen window. The design of the cabin was very open except for the bedrooms and bath off to one end. The kitchen was adjacent to the living area, but completely open to it. Connected to the kitchen was a small study area, complete with a desk, chair and bookshelves lining one wall. A computer monitor and keyboard sat silent and dusty on the desktop.

Not too long after Jack and Alana had finished their first cup of coffee, Apu woke up and joined them. He smelled coffee and went over to get some. "Any food in the house?" he asked as he poured the steaming dark liquid into a clean cup.

"Not really, where is the closest grocery store?" Jack inquired.

"I think I remember a small store about ten minutes from here. It isn't a supermarket, but it should do."

"Good, in a few minutes, I will head over there, if you tell me where it is. I think the fire needs stoking. Oh, and is there hot water?" Jack was trying to think of everything.

"Yeah, should be. My grandfather had a solar water heater put in a while back. I'll make sure it is on." He got up and went to a large closet between the kitchen and study. He came back a minute later. "It looks like everything is working fine. We should have hot water soon."

"Excellent. I would love a long hot shower." Alana announced.

"Okay, shower's yours first. I'll take one when I get back with food."

"I will feed the fire." Apu volunteered. "Jack, just go down the lane, take a left onto the main road. Go to the first stop sign and make a left again. It is about four miles up on the right. It shouldn't be too hard to find."

Everyone went off in different directions. It all seemed quite mundane compared to the adventures of the past few days. They welcomed the solid connection to a single place. Tomorrow may bring all new surprises, but right then typical mundane tasks felt wonderful and were deeply appreciated.

Chapter 60

December 18, 2012

Joseph sat at his kitchen table eating eggs and toast, while reading the morning paper. He had been up late the night before thinking of Charles, going through his office and looking for any clues about a further plan that he may have left behind.

Joseph learned from Nathan that they had convinced Max McMillan to work with the organization by bringing in Dr. Reese and his associates. They had carried out the beginning of the plan. Max was to email Jack Reese, cryptically hinting at news of a similar find in Egypt. He would request that Jack contact him immediately to discuss possible correlations. Charles had been convinced that if Jack Reese checked his email, he would not be able to resist contacting Max, if only out of professional curiosity. They were monitoring Jack's email accounts, watching for him to connect and retrieve his messages. Even if Jack didn't bite, they would be able to track him to a general location as soon as he logged-in. Joseph figured that any bit of information would be more than what he was looking at now.

He was proud of Charles and thought that the plan was a good one, but it was not enough. Joseph decided to also use Jack's ex-wife as possible bait and sent one of the field agents to her home to speak with her. The agent was to act like FBI, with questions for Dr. Reese regarding a recent archeological find in Mexico and an explosion and subsequent death of a local.

The agent assured Mary Reese that Jack wasn't in any immediate danger or trouble; they just needed to speak to him as soon as possible. She offered to leave him a message to call her, but that was all she knew to do, to help the agent. It might turn out to be enough though. She left Jack a phone message at his house and wrote him an email, requesting that he call her as soon as he could, it was important.

Joseph also ordered the agents to monitor Apu's and Alana's email. They contacted Alana's parents in Romania under the guise of a new research grant that Alana had pursued in recent months. Joseph figured that the lure of money would get a reaction from her, should she check in.

Finally, they sent an imposter email from the registrar at the University of Michigan to Apu, informing him that his enrollment status was in question and if he didn't contact them by the end of the semester, they would assume he was withdrawing. Joseph knew all of the tactics they were using relied on Jack and his colleagues getting online or calling in to check their messages. Now, there was no choice but to wait.

Joseph finished his breakfast and asked Rufus to bring the car around. He planned to go into the office early to see if the team had turned up anything new. All could be managed from here, but since Charles' death Joseph needed to be busy. Plus, he wanted to be on-hand the moment any one of their prey were to connect online.

Chapter 61

December 18, 2012

Jack returned to the cabin with groceries and a newspaper. He busied himself with putting everything away in the kitchen.

Alana was showered and sitting by the fire writing in a notebook. Apu was taking his turn in the shower.

It was cold outside but the sun was shinning and everything seemed bright and beautiful, calm and peaceful. The peace was welcomed by the cabins' new occupants.

Jack soon took his turn in the shower while Apu and Alana made breakfast. They all sat and ate quietly, grateful for the serenity. Finally, after clearing his plate Apu spoke. "I've been really thinking about the events of the past few days, the Gatekeepers we've met and the keys they have given us. I would like to take some time and discuss it more, in depth if you both don't mind. I feel like it is important that we really understand these keys – that we really know them, especially in light of what Jake was saying about the 100ᵗʰ human and critical mass."

"I agree." Alana said. "I was trying to write down things this morning. So much has happened; I don't want to forget anything, not a single detail. It is so important."

"Good idea. Let's get comfortable, by the fire and go over it." Jack suggested. They moved away from the center island in the kitchen that also served as a table with stools, into the living area where several small couches and chairs circled the wood stove. In the center of the room was a square coffee table settled on a striking Turkish rug.

Jack grabbed some paper and a pencil. Alana retrieved her notebook and Apu went to find his case containing his notes, the rubbing, his laptop and all the materials from Mexico that he had been able to grab, as well as a couple of books from Alana's library. His arms were full.

Jack sat his cup down and took one of the pieces of paper out and wrote down the word Mexico, much like a teacher at a blackboard. Under it, on the left, he wrote the words 'Cave of Secrets.' On the right, he wrote 'Eligio.' "Let's start with what Eligio told us about the Cave of Secrets and the Wall of Hunab Ku."

"He told us that the next Age of Man is the Age of Gods. He described this next age as a time when we would be connected to all things, including each other. He said there would be no limitations or fear. We would live in peace and harmony. It sounded too good to be true. It still sounds that way, but for some reason - I believe more now that it *is* possible." Jack was writing the main points down on the piece of paper as he spoke. Apu and Alana listened and nodded as he went along. When Jack took a moment to breathe, Alana spoke, while referring to her notebook.

"Eligio told us about a jump in evolution. A jump that is necessary to bring us to this Age of Gods. Isn't it amazing that *that* is just what Jake was telling us? How did Jake put it? Oh, here it is… *'Punctuated Equilibrium.'* Fascinating."

"There are actually many correlations between what Eligio told us and the keys we have discovered so far." Apu added. "To live in a time without limitations, isn't that the field of all possibilities – the third key?"

They sat for a moment thinking of Eligio and the incredible journey he had begun for them. "According to what Eligio said, and the Mayan calendar we only have three days left to find the final four keys." Jack said. "He also said that mankind was at a critical juncture, Jake explained this to us further, that 'anything could happen in this time' in our development." Jack paused for a couple seconds and then said what he was thinking.

"It's funny. I have felt responsible to the *wall*, since the first moment I saw it after the earth quake, and then to the *mission*. I want to carry this through to the end, even though I know that danger is creeping in around us at every turn." Jack thought he was dramatizing a little; but he couldn't help it.

Apu concurred. "I have felt that too. But I have also felt a cloud or bubble of protection around us. Eligio said that the 'gods' couldn't intervene but I do feel their presence, their protection and maybe even their guidance along our path. Don't you?" he asked openly. It was Alana who answered.

"I have felt the danger, many times. Sometimes I wonder if that isn't my own fears or if they a real dangers, but looking back - I think it might be a little of both. I *have* seen the *evidence* of the protection you speak of," she said looking at Apu, "but I don't always feel it. I would like to open up to that more."

There was a lull in the conversation as they each considered their role in the adventure. Finally, Jack remembered something else Eligio had said. "Eligio also told us that I am called Zero, you are Sky," he said gesturing to Alana, "and you the Rock," he said to Apu. Anyone have any more of an idea what he meant by these names? I have been thinking about it, but haven't come up with anything more concrete than what we already know."

"Well, in my vision," Alana took a stab at it first, "the one I had a long time ago, I saw a place and a people. I could not tell if they lived in the past, the future or in an alternate reality. But the look, feel, atmosphere and energy coming from that place is what I imagine the Age of Gods to be like. So perhaps when he spoke about the Sky as having a *vision for the future* that is what he meant." She wondered out-loud.

"Yes, that makes sense." Jack said.

"Actually, I, in contrast, feel like I have had a grounding effect of this mission. I do not want to sound egotistical, but there are times when I feel you two are distracted and my role is to help bring you back around. For instance, when we first arrived back in the US, when you felt lost, that was similar to other wandering moments along the way. I tried to bring us back to the task at hand, I worked to ground us." Apu tried to humbly make his point. "Could this have been what Eligio was referring to as the stable Rock?" He didn't need to worry about the others though. They were very aware of Apu's constant steady mind and centering affect. They nodded and smiled.

"I am very glad you have been on this adventure with us Apu. Your sixth sense alone has helped us many times." Alana reassured.

Jack responded next. "No doubt about it, we may have gotten dangerously side-tracked many times had you not been along. Besides we are now sitting in *your* cabin in the Rockies." They all laughed at coincidence. Jack paused for a moment but quickly proceeded with another question. "I see how each of you have lived up to your titles, but how am *I* the *Zero*? How did Eligio put it? – the beginning and the end. I mean we have had many references to zero in some of the keys, but how do those relate to *me*?"

"Well…" Alana spoke slowly trying to figure it out as she went. "The mission began with you and ends with you; can't that be it?"

"Yes, but Apu actually discovered the Wall first. And isn't there some other being called the *Flame* that is supposed to come in at the end?" Jack asked obviously confused.

"I don't know exactly what it means, but I'm sure you will know before it is all said and done." Apu concluded.

"You are probably right." Jack accepted. "Let's move on…"

"It just amazes me," Alana continued, "how all the keys fit together. Not to mention how we have come to all this information. The seemingly random circumstances alone are astounding but if you look at the keys, their actual revelations are perfectly interlinked. The first Gatekeepers were Sherman and Alice at Esalen. The symbol was the handprint which represented our *purpose* and our *personal connection* to the spirit world. Alice and Sherman didn't give us any information about how-to, but told us how important living and finding your purpose is to each person's life and to the world as a whole."

"See how that fits perfectly with the second key?" Alana questioned. The others were listening intently with an occasional nod of agreement or subtle 'ah-ha' along the way. They allowed Alana to continue. "The second Gatekeeper was Ram and his key was zero, or the void or silence. He had many words to describe it, but it was all about the 'spirit world' that Alice and Sherman had spoken of. So Ram just picked up where they left off. He gave us the 'how-to.'"

Jack continued to jot down the highlights of Alana's recall. "Next we *accidentally*," she said with a smirk, "run into Fritz and Rene who were the third Gatekeepers. They explained to us the third key and infinity, the *field of all possibilities* with the help of quantum physics. Part of their explanation included us being connected to and a part of this field. And this tied directly into Jake Jenkins, our road-side savior.

"Jake was the forth Gatekeeper, and a wonderful one, I have to add." Alana smiled warmly, thinking of how fond she was of Jake and his wife, Sally. "His key was unity or connection. He also summed up a lot of Eligio's points from the Cave. Didn't you think so?"

Apu agreed whole-heartedly. "Absolutely. I understood more of the bigger picture after Jake gave us the fourth key."

"I wonder what else there is to learn?" Jack asked. "This seems like a lot already. I can't imagine what the other four keys would be."

"Neither can I." Apu added.

"But they must be important…" Jack allowed his comment to gently trail off as each got lost in his or her own thoughts.

Finally, Apu suggested, "Perhaps we should meditate like Ram showed us. We haven't had a chance since Utah."

"Good idea." Alana agreed, "Can we put another log in the stove? The wind seems to be picking up outside." She was right, the wind was now howling through the trees. The sun was still shining, but scattered clouds were sailing quickly across the sky. "I wonder if it is going to snow again."

"I actually bought a newspaper! Let's look and see what the weather is supposed to be." He picked it up, looking for the forecast section. The headline read: *'Earthquake topples the Hagia Sophia Mosque in Istanbul. Stood for over 1500 years.'* Jack shook his head, sad to have lost such a architectural treasure. He turned to the back section, "Yup, we are supposed to get a storm, tonight through tomorrow morning. We could get up to eight inches. Temperatures will be in the mid 20's. Apu, do we have enough wood to stay warm?" Jack asked.

"We have plenty. A couple of trees fell last winter and we had a neighbor chop and split it for our pile. We will be warm. But I wonder if this storm will hinder our progress?" Even as Apu said it, he knew it was a silly question

"After what has happened, I doubt anything will get in our way. Everything will happen exactly as it is supposed to." Alana said, not knowing what lies around the corner and how that belief would be tested.

They all got comfortable in their seats around the stove. Apu had stoked the fire and put on another log. Soon each closed their eyes and fell into meditation.

The room filled with peace and warmth. Their minds stilled and the Keys and their meanings settled within their beings. A *knowing* and a trust settled over them like a blanket and for the next hour they *knew* unity, not just thought about it. They experienced their connection to the field that unites everything and everyone. Each one personally connected to God and to their truest potential. The wind howled ever louder outside, while inside the small cabin - silence permeated everything, dismissing all questions and doubts.

Chapter 62

December 18, 2012

Apu went to the door, grabbed his parka off the nearby hook and declared that he would bring in more wood, before the storm got worse. Jack joined him.

"I'll help. By the sound of it out there, we may need a lot of wood." They went out the door as a rush of cold blew in.

The meditation time had been wonderful, followed by an equally nourishing lunch. They joked around with each other and enjoyed the time to just relax.

Alana went over to the study, sat down at the desk and turned on the computer. She decided to do a little research on the remaining symbols. It couldn't hurt. After the computer booted and the Net connection was established, she figured that a quick check of her email was in order. She went out to her web-mail and logged in. Soon she was sorting through her emails folders in search of anything important, or even interesting. She had several professional eZine subscriptions which she filed for future perusal.

Alana noticed a message from her sister. She read through it: pictures of her niece and nephew, information on Bella's new job and general news. It was nice to hear from her and Alana was glad things were going well. The kids had really grown. Alana wondered if she would ever have children of her own. It hadn't been a priority, but as she got older, she thought about it occasionally. She then thought of Jack. 'He would make a good father, I think.' She caught herself. 'No time to be thinking of a family now. We have to save humanity first.' She giggled to herself with that thought. She *did* believe that what they were doing was extremely important but cautioned herself not to take things too seriously; she knew she could get obsessed. If her sister knew what she was thinking, she'd think Alana crazy. 'Oh, well, maybe I am. But right now it is the only way I can be.'

Alana continued to sort through her email. She saw a message from her parents and opened it. The Foundation for the Advancement of Mesoamerican Studies had finally gotten back to her regarding her grant application; or rather they had tried and couldn't find her, so they had contacted her parents. 'Wow. I should call them. But what would I say?' The idea of going back into research seemed far away right now. 'Still, when this mission is over, won't I need to work? It couldn't hurt to call them and secure the grant.'

Just then the door blew open as Jack and Apu came in with arm loads of wood to stack beside the stove. They went back out again. The cold air swirled around Alana. All at once she felt a rush of dread. She shivered. She just sat there frozen with feelings of foreboding and danger. She wondered what it meant. 'The grant? The next key? The people chasing them and trying to stop them?' She didn't know.

The guys returned with more wood and went out a third time. As the cold air filled the small cabin once more, Alana still didn't move. She mentally scanned everything she could think of, trying to discover what the dreaded feelings were associated with. When Jack and Apu came in with the third load, Jack noticed Alana sitting very still and looking pale.

"Alana, you okay?" She nodded her head, inhaled deeply and looked up at Jack.

"Yeah, I think so. I just had the weirdest feeling… You guys done with the wood? You're freezing me out." She said forcing a smile.

"I think that will hold us through the evening and night." Jack said.

"If not we know where there is more. Did you find anything out online?" Apu asked, noticing the computer was on. Alana told them about the email from her parents, the impulse to call and her related experience.

"Hmm." Jack said. "Perhaps we should wait to contact anyone from the outside. Maybe you could just send the foundation an email." Jack suggested.

"I think you are right, I will send one, later on." Alana agreed, feeling better with that decision.

"I would like to check my email also." Jack said. "No one has heard from me for weeks." Alana moved out of the chair and went over to the stove to warm up. Jack tapped in another web address to check his web-mail. Soon he was sorting though his own email folders. He noticed one from his ex-wife. He opened it and read. His posture changed, he felt himself becoming tense. She mentioned the FBI and he immediately knew they were onto them. But how? Jack decided that it must be the people that were after them and had already tried to kill him. He knew he could not contact her, but at the same time he hoped she was safe and wanted her to know that he was okay. 'Why would our pursuers let us know they are looking for us, why would they reveal themselves at all?' He thought to himself. 'Unless, Mary is in danger and they want me to know that. It could be a threat.' He began to really worry about Mary.

He noticed another email with a priority flag on it. It was from Max McMillan. A shiver ran up his spine. He read the message. 'A new find in Egypt? No, I doubt it. It is another ploy. It has to be.' He no longer trusted Max, not since the phone call in Mexico. 'Am I getting paranoid?' Jack felt confused and scared for a moment. He looked up at the other two and decided to let them in on the suspicious messages that *he* had received.

"I don't think they know where we are. They are using everyone we know to get us to reveal ourselves and our location." Apu stated. I'll bet there is some similar threat or enticement in my email. We must be very careful."

"I think Apu is right. We must not let them know where we are. I have had a very bad feeling since I first read my email." Alana said.

"It may be too late. We have logged in and retrieved our personal emails using this area's local Net provider. That connection can be traced to this area, even if not to this specific cabin. They will know what state we are in at the very least." Jack informed them

"Well, thankfully it's a big state." Apu smiled trying to calm the worries that had cropped up with this new link to the outside world.

"You're right. We are fine. Let's stick to what we know and our research. Did you find anything out about the remaining symbols?" Jack asked Alana.

"No, not yet. I got side-tracked by email and now I wish I hadn't even looked."

"It's okay. We will just be very cautious from now on." Jack smiled at Alana trying to reassure her.

"Right." Alana tried to sound confident, while she thought to herself, 'I want to just crawl under the covers to meditate more, it is the only thing that seems to help with my overwhelming fears.' She continued to stand by the fire to keep warm.

Chapter 63

December 18, 2012

There was a tap at the door. "Yes." Joseph replied. Nathan opened the door.

"We have a bite. Dr. Reese and Alana Borisenko have both logged onto their emails. We have a general location. They are in the Denver, Colorado area."

"Excellent. Cross reference Colorado with their files. See if there is any other connection to Colorado for any of them. They are there for a reason. Find it." Joseph demanded in a raspy voice.

"Yes, sir." Nathan closed the door and went down to the control room.

Nathan had seen a real difference in the Director since Charles death. He worried about the old man's health. But he never worried about his ability. It was clear that his mind was in tact.

Nathan was anxious to get to the control room. He wanted to find the Colorado connection quickly and give the old man some good news. He hadn't slept much since hearing of the accident two days ago, but he didn't need to. He was determined to succeed, for Charles, his mentor. He smiled to himself.

When the door opened to the control room, he began barking orders and sat down at a terminal himself to quicken the search. It wouldn't be long now, he could feel it. 'I will catch and kill these people *myself* if I have to. The old man will be so happy and relieved; he will make me the next Director.' His conniving smirk went un-noticed.

Chapter 64

December 18, 2012

The sun set behind the mountains, leaving only a muted glow behind as heavy clouds rolling in. The three friends spent hours online searching for anything regarding the last four symbols, but to no avail. Nothing seemed to match up. Nothing felt right.

"Maybe this isn't how we are supposed to find them. It certainly isn't how it has worked so far. Maybe we just have to get out there again," Apu said pointing outside, "and wait for them to just show up like before."

"You're probably right." Jack agreed. "I guess I was just hoping to have a clue first. It is a little un-nerving to just wait. It happened so fast last time. The hours are now ticking by and we have no idea what we should do or where we should go next," He said gloomily.

"Yeah, last time we had a destination, this cabin. And everything seemed to just happen along the way. Now that we are *here*, what do we do?" Alana chimed in. "Don't get me wrong, I am happy to have a break, but shouldn't we know what we are doing next? Time is running out."

"We have to trust in the power that has led us this far." Apu answered, again the voice of stability and strength.

"I know, Apu. You're right. It's just hard to sit here." Jack said. "And now I'm worried about Mary. She may be in danger. Why else would they let me know that they have gotten to her? I think it is a threat." Jack said.

"Why don't you email her? That can't harm us, or give them any more information than they already have. As long as you don't tell her anything specific. Just find out if she is okay." Alana suggested.

"Yes, of course. I think I will." Jack went over to the computer to write a quick email:

Dear Mary,

I am fine, busy with work. I am traveling a little, doing some research on the finds in Mexico. I heard of some trouble in Mexico after I left, but it didn't involve me. I will

check in with the FBI when I return in a couple of weeks. In
the meantime, I hope you are doing fine.
Love, Jack

After he read it through again, he shared it with the others.
"What do you think?"

"Sounds good, you aren't giving away anything. Very
nonchalant. Seems fine to me." Alana said.

"Me too." Apu said. Jack pushed the *Send* button and felt
some relief. If she answers him, he would know that she is okay.
'Unless, they answer for her and she is already hurt.' Jack kept his
thoughts to himself. 'No, I won't go there. I must trust and stay
focused. Remember the knowing during the meditation. Remember…'
He kept telling himself. He got up and went to the kitchen. "How 'bout
some dinner?" He needed to do something to occupy his mind.

Apu and Alana pitched in. They had fun cooking together;
they teased each other and laughed. It was a great dinner and a peaceful
evening. They talked about the Keys and the Gatekeepers. They
marveled at the miracles and they felt their connection to each other.

After dinner was over and cleaned up, Apu went over to the
study and pulled out his notes and the rubbing. He looked at the titles
of the books on the shelves. He pulled a couple down and began to
read.

Alana and Jack went into the living area and sat down. Jack sat
down first on the end of one of the small couches. Alana was behind
him and brushed past his leg as she made her way over to the same
small couch and sat down. This maneuver surprised Jack, but he was
pleased. Alana kicked off her shoes and then folded her legs under her
as she sat down. She leaned back to look at Jack.

"Do you still love her? Your ex-wife I mean." She asked in a
quiet voice. Jack was surprised again, this time by the question.

"Yes. I mean I will always love her, I guess." He stumbled. But
I am not *in* love with her anymore. I do not wish to be with her or
anything like that. She isn't the same person I married. I just want her
to be happy." He figured that he had offered enough, more than
enough in fact.

"I understand."

"Have you ever been married?" Jack asked.

"No. I seem to always find people who are emotionally unavailable. It's okay though. I have been emotionally unavailable also. I am too driven." Alana admitted.

"I know what you mean. I have buried myself in my work since my son passed away. It seemed easier than the idea of finding another relationship. Scared I guess. I have been looking for answers. I think that I have put off everything else, until I find them."

"Me too." Alana smiled at Jack. It was warm and friendly and their connection seemed so real that one might be able to actually see it between them. For a moment Alana nearly got up to go. She wanted to go anywhere, anywhere but here…too close to someone she cared about. She felt vulnerable. But she didn't move. She decided to stick with it, to see where it went. 'Sitting here on this couch right now seems the most natural thing I have ever done, and yet it scares me almost as much as finding out we had a trespasser in my house.' Alana thought to herself, but for some reason she didn't run. She suspected it had to do with the keys and all that she was learning, all that she was gaining.

Jack didn't move either. He too was feeling a little panicked, but at the same time it felt nice to be here with Alana. He reached out and touched her hand. She didn't draw back. He held it for a few moments. She just left her hand in his. Finally, Jack pulled her hand toward him and gestured. Alana understood the request. She adjusted in her seat and moved closer, sitting right next to him. He put is arm around her shoulders and she leaned her head onto his. They sat snuggled up together for a long while. The attraction was real; something neither could deny. But they were not ready to move beyond sitting snuggled together on the couch. It was enough, for now. It was perfect in fact. Peaceful and right.

Apu looked over at them briefly and noticed the intimacy between them. 'It's about time.' He smiled.

Apu hadn't really found anything in any of the reading he was doing, but the task had passed the time. He decided it was time for bed. He went over, filled the wood stove and said good night.

Jack looked down at Alana and confirmed what he already suspected; she had fallen asleep on his shoulder. It felt wonderful. He kicked off his shoes and propped his feet up on the coffee table. He pulled a nearby blanket over them and held Alana tightly as he dozed off.

Chapter 65

December 19, 2012

Sometime during the night, Alana had gotten up and gone off to bed. Jack woke up alone on the couch. He had a thought as he groggily got up, stretched and headed to his own bed. He went over to the computer, logged in and checked to see if Mary had emailed back. He noticed he was holding his breath as he waited for the page to load. Sure enough there was an email from her. He opened it and read:

"Jack, I am fine. Where are you? When will you be home? I need to see you soon. Mary."

This message made Jack's churn. He could tell it wasn't Mary, or at least not only her. Something was wrong. Why would she need to see him, they haven't seen each other in years. Something is definitely wrong. 'Perhaps I need to go there. Maybe that is where the next Gatekeeper is.' He didn't think that Mary was a Gatekeeper, but he felt he should make sure she was okay. He sat there, staring at the message; stuck there for more than a few minutes. Finally, he decided he could do nothing tonight. Tomorrow morning he would see what the others thought.

Jack went to bed, but it was some time before he slept. He knew he should meditate, that it would help him find peace and even perhaps the right course of action. But he couldn't seem to clear his mind. He tossed and turned until nearly dawn, then fell into an exhausted sleep.

Morning came with Alana and Apu up before Jack. This was very unusual. Apu recalled the last time he was up before Jack and that was following a night of too much wine – the night of the earthquake that had started them on this whole adventure.

"What's up with Jack? He is usually up first." Alana asked.

"I don't know. It's not like him." Apu replied.

"Should we wake him?"

"Nah, we don't have anywhere to go yet. Let's let him sleep."

"Right." Alana wondered if her going off to bed had upset him.

"I am going to do some research. When I was looking at the rubbing last night, one of the symbols reminded me of some type of Arabic writing, though it didn't occur to me until I woke up. I figured I would do a little more digging." Apu declared.

"Ooo, let me see. Can I help out?" She offered eagerly.

"Sure, I'd love your help." Apu said. "Maybe together we can figure it out."

"Let me get my coffee and I will be right there." Alana was excited to be on the hunt; she so loved ancient writings and symbols.

Apu pulled out the rubbing and pointed out the symbol he had referenced.

"I see what you mean. Funny, I didn't notice that before." Alana said puzzling over the image. "It looks more Hebrew, than Arabic, and it also sort of looks like a stick figure."

"Yeah, I see what you mean."

They spent about an hour searching online for clues. Finally, they found an ambiguous reference on a website about the Kabbalah, Jewish mysticism, which sounded similar to their symbol. They didn't understand the meaning and there were no actual pictures. They remained unsure if they were on the right track.

"I wonder if the local synagogue would be of help, maybe the rabbi would be able to explain this to us." Alana said.

"There is a large synagogue in Denver. They have a very remarkable rabbi. He often writes a column in the newspaper here." Apu's excitement grew.

Alana had a thought and went over to the coffee table to open yesterday's newspaper. She scanned through the pages. *War continues between the former Iraqi states of Mesopotamia and Kurdistan. London Olympic Bomber trial continues. Wright Whale Believed Extinct – none sighted off Greenland – melting ice caps and loss of krill populations cited as factors. "Indigo Children" top MP3 download chart.* "Here. Is this the guy?" She handed the correct section over to Apu. Surprise spread over his face.

"Wow. That's got to mean something. He only writes occasionally, and on the day Jack picks up the copy of the paper, Rabbi Zimmerman's column is in it."

"I think this is the sign we have been waiting for. We need to go speak to him."

"I totally agree." Apu mumbled while still reading through the column.

Jack entered the room and went straight for coffee, after taking a few sips he inquired, "You agree with what?"

"I agree that we need to go see Rabbi Zimmerman in Denver." Apu said looking up from the newspaper. Alana was worried by how out-of-sorts Jack looked. "Are you okay, Jack?"

"Yeah, I'm fine. I got a reply from Mary last night." He told them what was in the message. He had memorized it. It was short and he had stared at it long enough to take it in, all the while trying to glean from the words - the truth about Mary's safety.

"I think I need to talk to her. I need to know that she is really alright." Jack said as he rubbed his tired eyes.

The idea of a phone call to someone they suspected was under surveillance by the very people who were trying to stop them, concerned everyone. But Alana and Apu could see that Jack was genuinely worried. They discussed it and decided that if he felt he really must, he should call, but he should keep it short. They would have to go into town to call. There were no phones at the cabin. "My grandfather just always used his personal phone when he was here." Apu gave as an explanation.

"You can call when we go in to see Rabbi Yosef Zimmerman." Alana explained to Jack about the symbol and the sequence of events that led them to the decision to go to Denver. Jack agreed that a trip to see the rabbi might be helpful; they had learned to follow synchronicities.

After breakfast they bundled themselves in the parkas that Jake had given them, started the car and headed down the hill toward Denver. The going was slow at first, as the mountain roads were not yet cleared from the previous night's snow fall. But once they got close to the city, the roads were fine. As they pulled up to the Mile High Synagogue, they hoped the rabbi was in.

They ascended the steps of the old stone structure and went inside. It took a moment for their eyes to adjust to the difference in lighting. They were in a large foyer, thickly carpeted, muting the sounds from down the hall. Faint voices coming from the left hallway captured their attention; Alana decided to ask for assistance. An older bearded man was standing in the hallway, talking to a much younger man. As they approached, he looked up and smiled at them. "Can I help you?" He had a kind face and bright twinkling eyes. Alana liked him immediately.

"Yes, we are looking for Rabbi Yosef Zimmerman." She inquired.

"You have found him, what can I do for you?"

"My name is Dr. Alana Borisenko, I am an epigrapher specializing in Pre-Columbian cultures. This is Dr. Jack Reese, archaeologist and Apu Chohan, research assistant. We have been trying to decipher some Mayan symbols that we discovered in Mexico."

"Wow, very interesting, very interesting indeed. Come. Sit down. We can go into my office, here." He bade good-bye to the younger man and led the way into a spacious, yet comfortable office, containing a heavy, dark, ornate desk and many comfortable chairs seated around it. They all picked a spot and sat down.

"How can I help with your Mayan symbols? I don't know much about the Mayans."

"Well… we thought you might be able to help us with one symbol in particular." Apu said. "Alana and I found a reference online, on a Kabbalah site that may be related to our symbol. There were no pictures though, so we are not sure. It is a long shot, we know, but does this look familiar at all?" Apu pulled out the rubbing, folded to the symbol in question and pointed to it.

Rabbi Yosef Zimmerman raised his eyebrows and sat back in his chair. He thought this was all very intriguing. He had just explained this very symbol to a young student the night before. He knew there was something important going on, even though he wasn't sure what it was.

"I do not have a photograph, if that is what you seek, but I have a drawing. He opened the top drawer of his desk and pulled out the same drawing he had just recently used in illustration. He set in on top of his desk and then watched the reactions of the three strangers in his office.

Jack was the closest to the behemoth desk. He got up and stared down at the drawing. Apu and Alana were quickly on their feet also looking at the drawing.

They glanced at each other and then at the rabbi. "Is that it?" the rabbi asked.

"Almost exactly, without the hat." Apu replied quietly, humbled by such perfection. It would seem they could not fail.

"Where did you say you found this symbol? I am very interested." The rabbi asked. Jack looked at the others and they shrugged. They had to trust the signs.

Apu unfolded the rest of the rubbing. "This was taken off a wall in Mayan territory, in Chiapas, Mexico. It was put there over a thousand years ago." Apu said.

The rabbi just stared with his mouth open. Finally he whispered, "Impossible."

"I assure you, rabbi, it is possible. It is the truth. I made this rubbing myself." Apu said.

"Yes, yes. I'm sorry, I didn't mean…" Regaining his composure, he looked at them and smiled. "Amazing."

"What exactly does this symbol mean to you, to the Kabbalah?" Alana asked.

"The symbol is the *Tetragrammaton*, which is the four letters that represent God in the Jewish faith. Although there is no direct translation, it is often transliterated as YHWH. If you were to write the Hebrew letters vertically, the letters look like a stick figure of a man - that is exactly what you see here." He said pointing to the rubbing and his own drawing. "It means *man is created in the image of God.* The actual letters are *Yud, heh, vav, heh.*" He pulled out a blank piece of paper and wrote out the Hebrew letters he was referring to.

"These are often correlated to the *Sephirot* or the *Tree of Life* – also part of Kabbalah training. The Sephirot demonstrates the ten attributes that God created to transmit himself into the universe and man's life. The top letter is yud, which corresponds to *Keter* on the *Tree of Life*. *Keter* is the crown attribute. Your symbol there is stressing *Keter*, because it actually has a crown or hat on the Tetragrammaton. Very interesting."

Keter is the first and last gate you enter; depending on if you are ascending or descending the *Tree of Life*. *Keter* is the beginning and the end. Its Divine name is *Ehyeh Asher Ehyeh,* which means: *I am that I am* - it is the past, the present and the future all at once. It is *present moment awareness.*" The rabbi looked around the room to see if his guests were following his explanation. Their rapt attention encouraged him to continue.

"In *present moment awareness* or *Keter Consciousness*, we are all One and in harmony. We also are filled with the desire to live our true purpose when we are in *Keter Consciousness*. At this level, we are in wholeness and identity with God's wholeness. *Keter* is the link between our mind and life and our direct communication with God."

"Through this connection we are able to *know* God, which is beyond faith. *I* call it *perfect faith*. Faith is often explained as believing in something that is unknown or unseen. But perfect faith is much more. Perfect faith is not actually faith at all. Because when you really *know* God and are in *Keter Consciousness,* you *see* God, therefore it is not faith or a belief, but a *knowing.*" Rabbi Zimmerman paused. It was obvious by the looks on his guests' faces that he was giving them a lot to comprehend at once. "Do you want me to continue or have I gone on too much?"

Alana responded immediately, "No. Please go on, it is fascinating. I have only heard of the Kabbalah. I never realized it was so involved."

"Oh, there is much more to it than what I am telling you. People spend their entire lives studying Kabbalah. I am but a student myself, though I often end up teaching others as I learn."

"Please continue, we want to know all you can tell us about this symbol and *Keter Consciousness.*" Jack urged.

"Very well. Where was I? Oh, yes. Knowing God. To know the God force is also to have infinite patience. To *know* you are taken care of, to *know* you are loved, to *know* you are *One* with this force, dispels all worry or anxiety and you have no trouble being patient. With God, the best outcome is always inevitable. The foundation for such patience is in the *knowing,* it is in the relationship with God through Keter."

"As humans, we continually identify with our physical world instead of our true identity as children of God. When we do this we identify with *things.* These things take on too much importance, they become our idols - we identify with what we have, what we do, or what others think of us. Our true identity is *not* any of those things. Man was made in God's image. Unfortunately, most religions try to *make God into man's image.* God is effable and we can only know God through direct relationship, communion and *re-identification.*"

"When we identify with man's ideas, man's things, we separate our consciousness from God consciousness, from Keter consciousness. We must sever or detach ourselves from this habit and re-attach our thoughts to God. This symbol is telling us to embrace the Keter and detach from the *things* of this world." Rabbi Zimmerman paused his lesson and looked into the faces of his three students. He was pleased with the level of understanding he recognized in each of their eyes. "These are difficult concepts, I am happy that you are able to grasp what I have said so far."

"We have had some recent training in these types of ideas. Please, rabbi, continue." Alana again urged. "Does this mean that we should not have wants or desires for things in this world?"

"Our wants and desires are part of our destiny - the reason that we are here, our purpose." The rabbi maintained. "But the outcomes, or results, are of the ego, of the part that does *not* know God. The ego is just an idea of who we are; a human idea of ourselves. It is the cloak we wear, but it is not who we are. We are more. You will recognize the signs of ego by six different identifiers. These are: I am what I do, I am what I have, I am separate from God, I am what others think of me, I am separate from everyone else and finally, I am separate from what is missing in my life. When we identify and think that this is who we are, we are running our life on an idea, a façade, not the real thing."

"The truth of who we are is much different and is based on one fact: We are connected to God, in ways we have yet to imagine, and in everyway we *can* imagine. To *know* this, is to know God. To know God, *is to know yourself,* because you were made in God's image. When you know this completely, intimately and unequivocally, you release expectations, outcomes and will."

"This does not mean we should cease to do things or not work toward goals. It only means that we ought not allow ourselves to become attached to the results of our labors. The result is the creation, the reflection. If we identify with the reflection we lose sight of our true nature."

"*We are the creators, not the creation.* The creation is powerless and static. If we act from the level of a creation, we must impose great will and force. To force creates counter-force. This is why we have war. We live from force instead of power. Power comes from God. Our power comes from our connection to God. Force is what we do when we are not connected to true power. But if we detach and let go of outcomes, we release our addiction to force; then ultimately, we can embrace true power, the power of God."

"The only place you will find God is in present moment awareness. This is Keter consciousness. It is *Ehyeh Asher Ehyeh*: *I am that I am* - the past, the present and the future are all contained in now. It is now that you have the power to change anything. The past is gone and the future is unwritten. Now is where all power resides. It is in the *present moment* that you can create your future and understand your past. *Now* is just another term for *God*." The rabbi paused. Seeing his newest students hungry for such information, he had been lecturing non-stop. He found great personal joy when he discovered these truths. As he looked into the faces of the others in the room, he saw, mirrored, this same joy.

"I have spoken of this only to a few. I have been studying Keter for some time. I am excited to share with others what I have discovered."

"Wow. That is a lot to process. But I think I understand, though I may have to think about it for a while before it can sink in." Apu said, kind of dazed as his brain was working overtime to understand and remember everything the rabbi told them.

"I think it is wonderful and it makes sense." Alana said. She felt like the rabbi's words gave her a new perspective on why she struggled with her past, her fears and her failed relationships.

Jack was still trying to get the entire lesson. "Does this mean we don't pursue our dreams, or our destiny?"

"Absolutely not. It means that you pursue your dreams with passion. But it means that in knowing that you were created in the image of God and connected to God at all times, you need not worry or fret, or attach your happiness to the results of those dreams. Your success is assured. You *know* that it is. Therefore you release it. This whole idea is very, very important. It actually could accelerate our evolution, because as we detach from the past - we are free to create our future. You have only to intend your dreams and goals, with complete clarity and passion, and then release them to the power of God; without any attachment to how it will look or feel or be. Because you *know* it will be perfect. Because God is perfect and because you *know* that you are made in God's image."

Apu said thinking it through, "So the real *key* here is *knowing* and correctly *identifying* ourselves with God. If you have not experienced God, there is no way for you to know and correctly identify with God, and you will become entangled in wishing and worrying about the things of this world. This causes force. You must *know* yourself to be connected to God first and foremost."

"Precisely, all else we attach to in this world is idolatry." The rabbi concluded.

Again the perfect way *this* key fit with the others amazed them. It seemed to Jack that a priceless gem was being revealed to them, one beautiful, sparkling facet at a time. There was a knock at the door. "Yes?" The rabbi answered.

"Your next appointment is here, rabbi." The younger man they had seen earlier peeked in as he delivered the message.

"Very well. I will be ready in a minute. I must go. Have I explained the symbols of Keter and the Tetragrammaton to you well enough?" He sincerely inquired.

"Yes, absolutely." Jack said and looked around at the others. They looked deep in thought, but each subtly nodded. "But before you go, we must share our purpose for being here."

Jack quickly filled the rabbi in on their adventures. He told him of the Cave of Secrets and the Wall of Hunab Ku, as well as of the other keys and Gatekeepers. The rabbi was thrilled with this information and declared that he would not only teach what he could to his people, but he would also immediately write an article for tomorrow's newspaper publication.

"I am so excited to have met you. You have given me new determination and clarity in my work. I feel quite humble and yet rewarded in being able to share this with you and with many others soon. I will do everything that I can to aid you in this mission. You all will be in my prayers." He rose and started toward the door. He turned before he left. "Thank you," came directly from his heart and obviously meant more than the mere words could convey.

They got up. Apu retrieved the rubbing and they made their way out into the cold winter sunlight. As they walked, each replayed the rabbi's words within. Apu and Alana were both looking forward to writing it down in their journals.

As soon they pulled up to the cabin, Jack remembered that he had forgotten to call Mary. "I am going down to the grocery store. They have a phone there and I want to call Mary and see if everything is okay. You guys go ahead in. I will be back soon."

"Just be careful and don't stay on the line for long." Apu reminded him. Alana just waved as he pulled away. She had a sinking feeling but wasn't sure why.

Chapter 66

December 18, 2012

Benjamin Bradley sat at his desk staring off into space. He had spent the morning power brokering for two small manufacturing companies. Ben had always loved his job, even though there were times when he knew the deal could have financially ruined more than a few lives. The important thing in his mind was the growth of the whole, with him in front, of course. *His* overall economic picture was thriving. He didn't allow himself to look too closely into the face of the average small business owner who lost everything in the deals he negotiated.

Today had been the same as most other days. The deals were similar, the profits good. He should be quite satisfied as his profits were nicely adding up to his early retirement fund. He was on top. A financial guru. A rich one. It seems that he had it all.

But today he felt unsatisfied. 'Why today?' Why am I feeling so empty and lost? Why today am I looking around for the high that usually comes naturally with my work? Why today don't I care how much money I have in the bank or how many powerful people are intimidated by me?' he thought listlessly to himself.

Maybe it was because he hadn't had a real date in over a year. He always had a woman on his arm at social gatherings and PR opportunities, but those were *arrangements*, not relationships. For the first time, maybe ever, Benjamin Bradley felt that perhaps there was more to life than making money. But what that was, he wasn't sure. And he had no idea of where to look for it.

Ben got up from his desk and put on his overcoat. He walked out into the foyer where his secretary Terri sat. "I am taking an early lunch and I may not be back until later. You can reach me on my cell for any emergencies, otherwise just take a message and I will get back to them." He directed.

"Yes Mr. Bradley." She said as he left the office.

Ben was reaching his mid-thirties and even his mother quit calling to see if he had anyone in his life. He always figured he had plenty of time. He still felt there was time. What was really bothering him was how his work and success were no longer bringing him any joy. He walked down the street in contemplation. The recent deals he had closed made him more money and respect than ever. And yet he was feeling increasingly empty. He had worked harder, trying to ignore these feelings, but they just got stronger, refusing to be dismissed or ignored.

Why was today the breaking point, Ben was not sure. He just knew he needed to find something to fill the large gap that seemed to have replaced his guts. His reflection stared back at him from a shop window as he walked down the street to his favorite restaurant. As he stared for a minute at his angular face, dark brown hair, brown eyes, nice jaw line, he shook his head and asked 'Who are you really?' With no answer coming forthright he continued to question himself. 'This is ridiculous, men aren't supposed to feel like this, I am not supposed to feel like this. I have got to get a grip.'

He entered the restaurant, found a seat and ordered a drink. Even as he took the first gulp, he knew it wasn't the answer, alcohol would just numb the pain; it wouldn't make it go away. He knew this because he had tried it many times before. He took another gulp nonetheless. As he sat there staring into the glass, feeling miserable, a woman walked past his table with an infant in her arms. She was making her way across the room to her table. He watched her glance behind her at another child, a tiny little girl who was following along behind her mother. "Come along, Mandy, stay with Mommy."

Just as Ben glanced down at Mandy, he noticed a waiter with full arms, rushing out of the kitchen. He obviously did not see her at all, and was undoubtedly going to run right over her. Ben reached down and scooped up the little girl, narrowly saving her from wearing a tray of hot food. He delivered the child to the woman's table without injury.

"Thank you so much." The woman said with tears in her eyes as she held the little girl close to her side.

"No problem." Ben said to the mother. To the little girl he knelt down and said, "You must look up from time to time." He suggested with a wink and a smile as he reached out and gently touched her rosy cheek.

In that moment, Ben realized something was dramatically different. In that very instant, he didn't feel empty or lonely or in pain. Instead, he felt warm and loving and *loved*. This sensation really surprised him. It was not as if he had never done anything *kind* before. But the extreme contrast from how he was feeling just ten seconds before, and now, was hitting him squarely in the chest. He felt tears well up in his own eyes. He stood up, looked at the woman and said, "You are a very lucky woman. You have beautiful children to give your love and attention to." He smiled and went back to his table, but didn't sit down. He put some money down for the drink and walked toward the door.

"Wait, wait. sir," he heard behind. He turned to see the woman walking quickly after him. He looked back at her table and saw the two children in the care of an older woman, who must have just joined them. "I would love to repay you, would you like to have lunch with us." She asked him.

"Huh? Oh, no thank you. I couldn't. But thank you for the offer." He declined, knowing that he needed time to figure out what had just happened. "Perhaps another time?" He warmly suggested, surprising himself. She was also surprised but happy he didn't refuse completely.

"Tomorrow then, we will meet you here tomorrow for lunch. We'll expect you at noon." She insisted. "My name is Catherine Woods and I won't take no for an answer." She held out her hand.

"Ben Bradley, nice to meet you." He shook her hand.

"Then you will come?" She asked.

He thought for a moment and then smiled. "Sure. I would love to. You will bring the children won't you?" He couldn't believe what he just requested.

"Yes, of course. Tim and Mandy will be with me."

"Good. I will see you tomorrow for lunch." He smiled again and left.

Ben was feeling euphoric. Not only had the moment of saving the child from harm, changed him somehow, but he now had a date. He walked down the street in the opposite direction of his office going nowhere in particular. As he walked he thought of Mandy and her innocent face. But it really wasn't only the child that made him feel so full; he realized it was his own act of kindness. It was the selfless act in which he had no expectation of payment. In a moment of clarity, he knew it was an act of complete giving, but he was the one who ended up with the greater gift. He was amazed at the paradox. Any other time the event may have been routine, without remark. But today, these feelings were so overwhelming and in contrast to what he had been feeling that he couldn't dismiss them.

After awhile, he began to think about the child's mother. 'She is pretty, but she must be married.' All of a sudden he felt the old familiar fog begin to spread around the edges of his mind. He stopped that line of thought and halted his steps so abruptly that the man behind him nearly ran into him. 'No. I won't go back. I can't. It is too painful there. Forget about what may be in it for you, Ben, just let it happen as it needs to. Maybe it will just be a pleasant lunch and that's it. And that's okay.' He could think of nothing better than having lunch with that woman and her children.

As he continued down the city sidewalk, he resolved to himself that he would look for more opportunities to give, unconditionally. No longer did he want the hole in his chest. He would now look for ways to fill it, no matter what.

Ben nearly skipped to the subway station. He saw a man with a ragged paper cup, a man he'd seen so many times before and so many times passed by, along the side of the road. Ben stopped to drop money, more than just change, in the cup. He passed a book store with several motivational titles propped in the window. He went in and bought two; he began reading the first while riding home. He didn't care what happened next. He was not going to worry about what it would all look like tomorrow. Right now, he was feeling great about himself and his life.

Chapter 67

December 18, 2012

Melvin came home from his first day at the new job. It had been a good day. At first he was too nervous to enjoy it. But after getting in and meeting some of the other seasonal mail handlers, he felt great. It was so right to be working again. He felt his self-worth improving with each hour he was there.

By lunch time, he was cheerfully joking around with his colleagues when one of the area supervisors came in and called him over. "Melvin Cooper, right?"

"Yep, that's me." He smiled back in reply.

"My name is Ronald Burley. It is my job to supervise the seasonal help and make sure that everything runs smoothly and without incident." He said seriously. Melvin realized this man was not very good humored.

"I have read your file Melvin, and I want you to know that I am keeping an eye on you. Any alcohol abuse whatsoever and you are out of here. Do you understand what I am telling you?"

Melvin was taken aback by the harsh treatment. His earlier light-hearted mood and boosted self-worth drained away quickly. He hung his head. "I understand."

"Good." Mr. Burley said as he walked away, leaving him feeling worthless.

Melvin went back to his work station and didn't say anything for over an hour. His mood continued to spiral along with his feelings about himself. 'It's no use. I am a bum and a drunk and always will be.' He thought to himself. He was nearly ready to just walk out when a lady walked by and winked at him. For that split second, she looked just like his beautiful wife. He closed his eyes and shook his head and then looked back at her. She turned and settled into a work station down the aisle from him. When he looked at her the second time, he saw that she looked nothing like his wife. Not even similar. But he could have sworn just a moment ago that this woman was her twin. He sat down on a nearby stool and closed his eyes for a second. As he did, he heard his wife's voice in his head.

"Melvin, don't judge yourself by what you can or can't do. Don't judge yourself by your past or what someone else thinks of you. You must know yourself from the inside. You are equally as wonderful as anyone else, even if they are not *all* kind people who tell you so. We all have similar fears, weaknesses and challenges. Be kind to yourself, and to others - always."

Melvin felt his chest swell. He smiled openly remembering the miracles that had happened in the last few days. He knew they were real. Whatever else he had been thinking was secondary.

He decided not to let anyone else's issues be his own. He was given a second chance at life and he was going to enjoy it, without living in his past or projecting into the future. Melvin was determined to live each day knowing how blessed he was.

The rest of the day went without incident with Mr. Burley. When he was punching out at 5:00, Melvin passed him on his way out and wished him a good evening.

It was a good day for Melvin Cooper and he was determined to make each day the same.

Chapter 68

December 18, 2012

Marie was working at her desk, lost in all the numbers, names and figures scrolling across her computer screen. She frowned when she glanced at the clock; another hour before lunch and she was already tired. She had been putting in so many long hours since her husband's lay-off that even with the early day yesterday, she was thoroughly exhausted. Joe would begin his new job on Monday, but with Christmas around the corner, they had decided she needed to stay on her current schedule at least until after the holidays.

Marie thought about Christmas for her boys and cringed. They wouldn't be able to afford much this year. The boys were of the age where they wanted everything they saw and although she didn't succumb to their extreme wants, she *did* wish that she could buy them a couple of the things they desired. Besides there were things that they actually *needed* as well. Her heart sunk when she thought about how little they would be able to afford.

As money problems and fatigue weighed her down, Marie dozed glassy eyed at the computer monitor, not really able to focus on anything. Just before she nodded off, Charlene, her co-worker, came by and tapped on her cubical wall. "Hey, you going out for lunch?" she asked.

"Nah, I brought a lunch."

"Oh." Charlene looked disappointed, but didn't leave. She stood there thinking for a moment, then decided, "Nope, you are going out to lunch." She declared. "I am taking you out to lunch to celebrate Joe's new job. Besides I need someone to talk to. So get your coat, lunch is on me. We'll just clock out early and be back early."

Marie looked up at Charlene, surprised at first but allowed a smile. While lost in feeling sorry for herself; she had forgotten about Joe's new job. Besides she knew that Charlene wanted to talk about her health issues. "I'd love to have lunch with you, thanks, Charlene."

As Marie got up to get her coat, she remembered her sister Claire and the problems *they* were having. She decided that her problems weren't so bad. 'I am not going to be so attached to having *things* for Christmas and be happy that we are all together and healthy this holiday season,' she thought to herself as they walked out the office door. 'It's not about *things* anyway. It is about our love for each other.' In that regard, Marie knew she was blessed. The last few days had been miraculous; she would not allow herself to get attached to what everyone thought Christmas was supposed to be. She knew what it really was all about that she was blessed.

Chapter 69

December 18, 2012

Chuck had driven his truck home to St. Louis to drop off his load. He was a little late but when he told his bosses about the accident, they were just glad Chuck hadn't been *in* the accident. The company had lost a driver just two months prior, to a fatal highway pile-up.

Chuck drove home in his car, from the trucking company's office, showered and ate a quick dinner. He looked around his house. There were so many things that reminded him of his dear, sweet wife. The house truly felt dead now. Jason had brought him back to life and he now wanted to leave his house; take the good memories and go. He decided, on the trip home that no matter what happened, if Jason's mom recovered or not, he wanted to be a part of his life. He went to bed that night making plans in his head and in his heart.

The next morning, Chuck woke up early. He wanted to get back to the hospital and Jason as soon as possible, but he had some things to take care of at home first. After breakfast, he packed a couple of bags. He waited until eight o'clock to call his cousin, Matt, who was a real estate agent. Matt was surprised by Chuck's call but even more surprised by his request to put his house on the market. "I am moving to Wichita" Chuck announced.

"Wichita? What's in Wichita?" Matt asked.

"I met someone." Chuck said vaguely, he didn't want to get into the whole story.

"Wow. That's great Chuck. I am happy for you."

"Listen, Matt, I am on my way out of town, now; just call my cell phone if you need anything. But get the ball rolling for me, please."

"Okay, Chuck. How long will you be gone? We will need to get some things ready around the house to show it."

"I will come back when you need me, just call." Chuck said before hanging up.

Chuck went to his computer to transfer money from his savings account to his ATM account. He looked around again, then grabbed his bags and shut the door, happy to be on his way. He was on his way.

Chuck was accustomed to long hours on the road, but this time it was different, he was anxious to see how Jason and his mom were doing and didn't trust the aunt to take good care of Jason. He wondered about the recent events and thought maybe he was being too rash in his decision. But in his heart he knew he had to make this move. A part of him had died with his wife and for the first time in years, he felt life again. He had to at least try.

Chuck started thinking about what could happen. If Jason's mother passed away, he didn't want him to be without someone to care for him. Chuck didn't think the aunt would be excited for that opportunity. He wondered if he could adopt the boy. Or at least take him in as a foster child.

But if the mother lived, would she let Chuck be a part of the boy's life? Hopefully she would, he had saved her life, after all. His mind was busy with rationalizations.

Chuck spent the next couple hours of driving analyzing every scenario. He was beginning to feel anxiety over the many possible hindrances to being a part of Jason's life. As the miles sped by, Chuck got more and more depressed. He began to entertain thoughts of turning around and going home when something surprising happened. As Chuck drove, the radio played softly in the background, and he felt bombarded with memories of the day before. *Running to the car with a crow bar. Pulling the boy from danger. Freeing the woman after a struggle. Going to the hospital. His heart opening up to care for Jason and his mother.*

It was as if he were reliving the whole series of events, all while driving along normally in his car. Chuck's throat clenched as he was overwhelmed with emotions, mixed and explosive. He slowed and pulled to the shoulder of the road.

Chuck realized he had been offered an amazing miracle and was cheapening that gift by worrying about the future. Clearing his throat, he decided to just let go and trust in the same power that had brought this wonder into his life. If this broken heart was able to feel hope again, even for a minute, then he was capable of living whole again. If things didn't work out with Jason, he would be sad, but he would live. Live. He wanted to live now. Not in the past, with his wife. This came to him clearly. The only way he was going to be alive again was to be aware and grateful of each moment and the miracles that accompany those moments.

Chuck picked up his soda and swallowed a large gulp. Looking at himself in the rear view mirror he smiled at his own reflection. 'You are going to be alright, Chuck Adams.'

He pulled out on to the highway again and continued his journey, wanting to trust in whatever was meant to happen. His heart was full of gratitude. He let go of everything else as he turned up the radio a bit. A Christmas carol was playing and Chuck hummed along, smiling.

Chapter 70

December 18, 2012

The only lights on in the command center were the emergency exit signs and Nathan's desk lamp. He yawned, stretched and ran his hand through his hair after glancing down to the lower right corner of his computer to see the time. He knew he should go home and get some sleep, but he was determined to find the archeologist and his friends. He was going through public records of all three. Somewhere there was a connection to Colorado. He just knew it.

Nathan got up and went over to the kitchen area to pour himself another cup of coffee; then sat back down at his desk and typed another search string into his terminal. In today's world everything about everybody was available online. And if it weren't so available, *he* could still get to the information desired. Post-Modern America, if not the entire world, lived and died on the Net. It had become a detailed reflection of civilization's true lives and sometimes it was hard to tell the difference between it and reality.

Nathan pulled up Apu Chohan's family history one more time: his parents were still living in New Delhi; his brothers were also living in that area with their wives and extended families. His grandparents were dead.

'Wait.' Nathan thought. 'Maybe it isn't a living connection after all.'

He punched in Apu's grandfather: A business man who traveled to the U.S. quite often on business. Nathan pulled up his company's records. "Bingo! They had an office in Denver, Colorado." Nathan felt victorious.

Nathan then went looking for property owned by the company but did not find any records. 'Maybe it was owned by Danvir Chohan himself. But Nathan still could not find any records. Nathan felt sure Danvir Chohan had been in Denver. He decided to check Chohan's last will and testament. Nathan was scanning through the long document looking for any references to Colorado. Finally he found it. Mr. Chohan had bequeathed a small piece of property and a cabin in Evergreen, Colorado to Apu upon his death. Nathan was elated to have found them. He was not sure why the property hadn't shown up in any of the other records. It didn't matter; he had them now. He dialed the directors' private number.

"Yes?" Joseph answered.

"I found them, sir. I have the address of a cabin in Evergreen, Colorado that Apu Chohan's grandfather left him when he died."

"Good work. I want you on the first flight to Denver to oversee their capture. I don't want any mistakes this time. I will be in the office in a couple of hours. Report directly to me. Do you understand?"

"Yes, sir. I will make sure we have them this time, sir."

"Good, I'm counting on it."

Nathan hung up the phone, excitedly tapped his computer keyboard and instantly booked the first flight to Denver. He would arrive by 11:00 am. He called and woke up the organization's Denver office manager, James Covert, who had already been put on alert as were all the managers in the western United States. Nathan gave James the address of the cabin in Evergreen and told him to send a car out, but only to monitor. "Don't move in or alert them in any way. Wait till I get there, Director's orders."

"I understand." James said. "They won't know we're watching them."

"Good. Pick me up at the airport" Nathan instructed, gave him the flight information and hung up. He had just enough time to go home, shower and change before heading out. Getting up, he switched off his lamp and breathed in slowly to savor this moment. He was jubilant; the fatigue faded away with the light from his computer.

'This capture is sure to guarantee me the director's position when the old man dies.' He smiled to himself. All that must be done now was make sure those elusive scientists were in custody by the end of tomorrow. As the door locked behind him, he had no doubts that success would be his.

Chapter 71

December 19, 2012

Jack returned to the same small grocery store he had patronized the day before. In the parking area was the old payphone he had noticed yesterday, as they were very rare now-days, with the proliferation of personal cell phones.

Jack pulled up to the side of the phone and got out. He punched in ten digits followed by twelve quarters and soon a phone was ringing in Whitmore Lake, Michigan.

"Hello?"

"Mary. It's Jack. I got your email. Is everything okay?"

"Jack, what the hell is going on? There are people looking for you. They've been relentless. I told them I didn't know where you were and that I hadn't seen you in years, but they wouldn't listen. They kept insisting that I try to contact you. Is everything all right? They acted like you were in some kind of trouble."

"I'm fine. It's just some rare archeological find that a lot of people would like to get their hands on. Some people will stop at nothing. Don't worry about me. I just wanted to make sure you were okay." Jack said looking at his watch. He had been on the line for nearly two minutes and knew he shouldn't stay on much longer.

"Oh. I am fine. They keep coming around and I keep telling them the same thing. But thanks for checking in on me." She said and Jack smiled. He felt a warm familiarity and knew he would always care about her.

"No problem. Don't worry. I will have this all wrapped up soon."

"Okay, take care of yourself."

"You too, Mary." Jack said before hanging up. He felt reassured, glad to hear that she was okay. But he also knew that they had access to her email and that the message had come without any knowing on her part. He knew they were probably monitoring her phone as well and hoped he had not been on the line long enough for them to track the call. It had been a three and a half minute phone call. He looked around the parking lot from his position in the small phone booth. People were milling about the store front, but no one looked suspicious.

Jack got in the car and headed back to the cabin. 'Only two days to go. They had three symbols left; three keys to unlock. He hoped it was enough time. 'Knowing and correctly identifying was the last *key*.' The rabbi said. Jack had experienced from the previous keys, that *knowing* came by way of meditation. He decided that when he got back to the cabin they would have a group meditation. His was nervous, and he knew peace came in those moments of silence.

Chapter 72

December 19, 2012

Todd and George were sitting in the car just down the road, with a clear view of the cabin. They had followed Dr. Reese's car into Denver to a Jewish synagogue and back to the cabin again. They were under strict orders to follow the three, not to lose them and *not* been seen.

They watched through binoculars, as two of the three went into the cabin. They soon realized that Dr. Reese was still in the car and heading back onto the main road and toward them. They didn't have much time to react. "Duck!" They both ducked down under the window-level of the car and waited until they heard the car pass by. "Now what do we do?" Todd didn't like when targets surprised him.

"I will stay here and watch the cabin. You follow Dr. Reese's car. Hopefully he isn't going far and you will be back soon so I don't freeze." George said as he zipped up his coat up, grabbed the binoculars and got out. "Don't lose him."

"I won't." Todd pulled out slowly and followed the only car on the road.

George walked over to one of the tall pine trees and used its protection from the wind. He pulled the binoculars out and trained them on the cabin. He waited and watched.

Chapter 73

December 19, 2012

Nathan departed the terminal at the Denver International Airport at 11:15am. He walked outside into the brisk cold and got into the blue sedan waiting for him. James filled him in immediately.

"I just got a phone call from Todd, one of my men. He and George are on surveillance at the cabin. It seems that, when Dr. Reese and his friends got back from the synagogue, they split up. Todd followed Reese to a nearby grocery store where he used a payphone to call his ex-wife. We just got confirmation and specs off that phone call from the Command Center. It was quick; you can call into Command and listen to the conversation if you wish. It was recorded. George stayed behind and kept an eye on the cabin and the other two scientists. As soon as the call was finished, Dr. Reese drove directly back to the cabin. Todd and George are watching the cabin from a distance."

"Good. How long till we get there?" Nathan was anxious.

"It is about forty-five minutes from here. Will we need additional agents to bring them in?" James asked.

"Yes. I don't want to take any chances. Have four more agents ready to arrive when we do. I want a car at each end of the road while you and I, along with Todd and George, approach the cabin. We will not lose them this time." Nathan's jaw was set; a familiar headache was coming on. He knew he was close to getting the promotion of a lifetime, but he was also cautious. He wasn't about to jump the gun. He would not fail as Charles had, *he* could not afford to.

Chapter 74

December 19, 2012

When Jack entered the cabin, he closed the door behind him, but not before quickly glancing back at the car up the street. After he pulled out of the parking lot at the grocery store, he noticed a car off to the side. It was running. The man sitting behind the wheel looked off in the opposite direction as he passed. Something in his subconscious nagged at him as he drove up the road.

Jack made his way slowly back toward the cabin and kept watching in his rear view mirror to see if anyone was following, especially that black sedan. He didn't see anyone. But now as he closed the cabin door, he saw it come to a stop far in the distance. It looked like the same car. His stomach flipped violently and the color drained from his face. He knew they were in danger.

Jack looked around the cabin for the others. He saw Apu at the computer but didn't see Alana. His mind was racing for options. "Where's Alana?" He asked rather urgently.

"She's in the bathroom. What's wrong? Is Mary okay?"

"Yeah, she's okay. I know now that the email was not from her. I was only on the phone a little over three minutes. It was long enough to know she is fine." Jack was thinking of how to tell them without sending Alana into panic. Alana came out of the bathroom and immediately could tell something was up. "What's wrong?"

"I think they have found us." Jack said simply. No one spoke for a few seconds; Alana couldn't hold her breath any longer, "What do you mean? Are they here?"

"There is a black sedan up the road watching the house, I think. It followed me to the grocery store and now it's parked up there. I don't know what they are waiting for, but I am sure they are here for us." He explained, as he pointed out the window in the direction of where the car sat.

"What are we going to do?" Alana was immediately alarmed.

"I'm not sure. Any ideas?" Jack asked them both. Apu did not say anything. He just stood there stunned. Jack could tell that both Apu and Alana were really frightened. He was also. They seemed to have run out of options.

"We have to get in the car and go. We have to try and lose them." Alana's voice had gotten high with fright.

"What if we can't lose them this time? I think they are probably more desperate to capture us than before. But they are waiting for something, or they would have confronted us already." Jack said.

"Well, we can't just stay here and let them come in and take us." Alana demanded.

"I can't think." Jack said impatiently. Strangely, he remembered that he wanted to have a group meditation time. He couldn't imagine being able to clear his mind in order to meditate, but he also knew that this was exactly when he needed to. He needed to be able to hear God. They needed guidance now, more than ever, and possibilities. The only way he knew to tap into those possibilities was through meditation. He exhaled a long breath and said, "Let's meditate."

"What? You've got to be kidding me." Alana almost screamed.

Calmly Apu added, "No, Jack's right. It's the best option we have right now. *Remember* the keys Alana. Purpose and Personal Power and Possibilities – this is our purpose. I am more convinced of that than ever, and the way to find our Power is through Silence. In the Silence we're connected to all Possibilities. What we need right now are possibilities - options. We must connect, perhaps even to survive." Apu was thinking out-loud, but convinced himself and the others that meditation was the right thing to do.

Jack walked over to Alana and touched her shoulder. "Alana, let's try. We have to trust in the power that has guided us this far. Besides they are just out there watching, we may have plenty of time yet." When she looked up at him, he could see the fear in her eyes. He gently held her hand and led her into the living area. They sat down side by side on one of the couches. Apu took a spot opposite the other two. They each took a deep breath and closed their eyes. At first, Alana could not still her mind at all but as the silence continued she soon found a way to let go.

Each felt a warm light bathe them in peace. They stayed in a state of connection and peace for over twenty minutes. Even Alana was able to relax and feel free from her fear. She felt the presence of her other self, that one from her vision long ago, and immediately she knew their mission would succeed, even though she couldn't see how.

After another few moments, they heard a noise outside. They felt the connection broken as renewed fears invaded their hearts and minds once more. Even if capture didn't mean personal harm, it would surely mean they would fail and that could mean the death of everyone. That is what Eligio had warned against.

Jack went over to the window and looked out. Nothing had changed. The car was still parked up the road. "It must have been the wind." He said relieved.

"Um, I had an idea while we were meditating." Apu was obviously still thinking it through. "My grandfather had a couple of four wheelers in the shed for getting around when it really snowed. I haven't seen them in years, but they should still be out there." Apu started toward the back door.

Alana was thinking about how cold that would be, but it was better than being captured or worse. Jack brightened immediately, anything was better than the other ideas in his head. He could deal with his own capture, but the thought of the others being hurt was more than he could bear and his heart pounded at the thought.

"We could sneak out the back, push them down the hill until we are out of earshot and then take off. I am sure we can find shelter or help somewhere." Jack said.

"Let's get our things and get out of here." Alana was ready to be away from the immediate danger in spite of the cold.

"Be quick about it." Jack said as he stood by the window. "Two more cars have joined the car on the street. I think our time has just run out."

Apu rushed over to the office area and shoved all their papers and references into his bag. Jack and Alana each ran to their rooms and grabbed all the personal items they had with them, bagged them up and rushed back to the center of the house. "I have your other stuff." Jack told Apu. "Did you get everything we'll need?"

"I think so. Let's go! They won't be able to see us if we go out the back door." They threw on their parkas; Apu grabbed gloves and hats and offered the others the same from the drawer by the door. Soon they stepped out into the fresh snow, on the path that led straight to the shed. Apu lead the way.

Chapter 75

December 19, 2012

Nathan and James rendezvoused with Todd and George up the road from Apu's cabin. Nathan asked, "Any movement?"

"Nothing. It has been quiet since Dr. Reese returned from the grocery store." Todd informed the boss.

"He didn't make you at the store did he?"

"I don't think so. If he had, wouldn't they have taken off immediately?"

"Probably." Nathan relented. "Okay, you two, stay here. You two, go down the street the other way and be prepared to block the road should they try and run." Nathan commanded. "James, you and I will go in the front. Stan, you and Dave make your way around to the back in case they try and go out the back. No foul-ups!" He barked. "We want them in custody, alive. Got it?" They all nodded and started off in different directions. Nathan and James waited a few minutes, until the others were nearly in place, before driving down the driveway toward the cabin. Nathan started to feel giddy. This was it. He was looking forward to calling the director with the good news.

Chapter 76

December 19, 2012

Inside the shed Apu checked the four-wheelers for gas. One was full, but one was not. He quickly looked around for the gas can his grandfather had always kept at the ready, praying it had gas in it. It did. He filled the tank on the second four-wheeler as Alana and Jack piled bags on the back of the other one. Jack grabbed some nearby bungee-cords to tie the bags down. "I'll take this one. Jack, you and Alana take the other one."

They didn't hear any movement up the street, as they quietly opened the door. Their hearts were pounding as they rolled the vehicles out of the door and down the hill toward the tree-line behind the cabin. As they reached it, they heard a car approach the cabin. Alana looked back, but could not see around to the front entrance. She turned and followed Jack and Apu as they pushed the four-wheelers as fast as they could, out of sight and hopefully out of earshot. Fortunately, it was all down hill.

When they got to the bottom of the hill, just inside the line of aspens that populated the entire mountainside, they decided to start the engines and put some real distance between them and who ever was chasing them. The engines sputtered and spit at first. Alana felt sure they would be heard and captured any second. Soon the engines roared to life and the noise filled the whole valley. Jack hoped they had enough time and space to escape.

Apu climbed onto his four-wheeler and was off. Alana quickly climbed on behind Jack and wrapped her arms around his waist. She glanced back once more just before they headed off, following Apu. As she did, she saw two men running down the hill after them. She heard the loud gun-shots reverberate thought the countryside, echoing over and over again through the valley, muffled only by the snow. Branches and leaves began to fly all around them. She squeezed Jack harder and buried her head into his back, praying she would not be hit. She heard Jack grunt.

"Are you hit? Are you alright?" she screamed into his ear.

"No, I'm fine, you are just squeezing really tightly," he yelled back over the noise of the engines. He reached down, pulled at one of her hands and she immediately loosened her grip. He smiled and held her hand for one more moment, gave it a reassuring squeeze and then concentrated on the terrain ahead. Soon they were completely out of site of the cabin.

They had been traveling for what seemed like an hour in the cold, Colorado mountains. Evergreen and aspen trees sped by as they negotiated the rough landscape. Large boulders often bared the trail, causing them to slow down and go around; but they didn't dare stop, not yet.

They knew the people chasing them were serious. None of them had *ever* been shot at before. If they ever wondered about the importance of their mission, now was not one of those times. Their pursuers were willing to kill to stop them. This further convinced them how important it was to continue and succeed.

Alana again was feeling overwhelmed by fear. The idea of being shot caused her insides to turn to mush. She tightened her hold on Jack again. Jack reached down and patted her arm. He wanted to tell her not to worry, but he couldn't take his eyes off the trail for fear of losing the minimal control that he had.

The fringes of the forest faded into a blurred dimness as the afternoon sun began to set. As the darkness crouched in around them, Alana's hold on Jack nearly suffocated him. Finally, he reached down and pulled her arms loose again. He heard her whisper in his ear, "Sorry."

Apu had been leading them deeper and deeper into the mountains, further away from civilization, people and roads. He knew this was a dangerous tactic. They were not prepared to survive the night in the outdoors, especially in the middle of winter. But he also knew it would take longer and be harder for those men to track them the further into the woods they went. He knew the general direction they were going, but after a while and as it grew more and more dark, he was sure they were lost. His own fears were about to get the better of him. His mind was desperately scrambling for a way to survive in the bitter cold all night. As they drove on into the night, Apu began to wonder how long their gas would hold out. If they were stranded before they found shelter, they could freeze to death.

Just when he was about to be overtaken with fear and anxiety, Apu spotted lights through the trees ahead. For a split second he was not sure if he should go toward the light or away from it. It could be their hunters. But as soon as the thought crossed his mind, he dismissed it. His intuition told him it was safe. Besides, he could no longer feel his face or hands. Apu led them in the direction of the light.

Soon they came to a small clearing with a little cottage and a small barn at one end. There were lights on and smoke coming from the chimney. They hoped whoever lived there was friendly, for they had no choice but to ask for help.

They stopped along the snow-covered road that led to this mountain retreat and gladly dismounted. Apu cautiously approached the door of the cozy cottage and knocked. He heard a shuffle inside just before the door opened. There, in the doorway, framed by the light glowing inside, was a beautiful, sweet face. It was an older woman, her face wrinkled with age and experience, but her smile was bright and her eyes seemed to twinkle with delight.

"Yes, yes, how are you, how are you all?" She asked sweetly, as she peered around Apu to the others. They were stunned by this greeting, but very glad she seemed friendly.

"We are lost and cold. We were wondering if we may impose upon you, until we can see clearly enough in the morning to make our way out of the mountains." Apu asked as politely and unthreatening as he could manage.

"Oh, Yes. Yes, of course come in. By all means come in." she invited.

They were grateful for the warmth of the fire and huddled around it trying to melt the cold that had crept into their bones.

"My name is Ida. Ida Homberger." She seemed very open and welcoming. Her eyes continued to dance and twinkle as if she had a wonderful secret.

"So sorry, mame. My name is Apu Chohan, this is Alana Borisenko and this is Jack Reese. Thank you so much for opening your home to us. We are very grateful."

"No problem at all. This is wonderful! I am happy for the company. As you can imagine, I don't get many visitors up here. Besides I was expecting you."

This last part really surprised them. Still skeptical, Alana wondered for a moment, if this old woman was working with the men who were after them. She got the words out, "What do you mean, *expecting* us?"

"Not to worry, my dear. There is nothing here that will harm you, and those who are pursuing you will not find this place, no matter how hard they try. You can relax. We have much to discuss. But for now, how about some dinner? I made a big pot of stew and fresh bread."

The little cottage smelled wonderful and in spite of the strangeness of this woman and her more than accurate insight into their situation, they trusted her. They let their fears drain away and gratefully sat down for a bowl of stew. When Alana finished, she took her bowl to the small kitchen, which was off to the side of the small cottage. She offered to wash up but the old woman 'wouldn't hear of it'. She demanded that Alana and the others go sit by the fire and relax. It wasn't long before all of their defenses dissolved. Soon they were wrapped in knitted blankets, and dozing off to sleep. The stress of escape and heaviness of their fears left them exhausted.

Ida Homberger went over to her rocker by the fire, picked up her knitting and continued crafting her latest blanket as the silence and warmth engulfed them.

Chapter 77

December 19, 2012

Nathan was yelling at the others. "What the hell are you doing?"

"They, they were getting away." George, one of the shooters whined in defense.

"Didn't I tell you that we need them alive? Put your gun away, you idiot." Nathan was furious - furious at their failure to capture the scientists and furious that his promotion had just driven off into the woods on a pair of four-wheelers. He had underestimated Dr. Reese and his friends again and had obviously given his agents too much to handle. 'Reese must have seen them at the grocery store and was preparing all the while,' Nathan rationalized to himself.

He replayed the sequence in his head: When he and James got out of their car and headed for the front door, they knocked but there was no answer. Nathan didn't hear any noise and immediately knew something was wrong. He opened the door and went inside. The other agents had rushed in the back door. "This way!" one of them yelled from outside. Nathan followed them out the back door to see three sets of foot tracks going to the shed and then wheel tracks heading towards the woods. "They're on four-wheelers!" someone announced. Just then, an agent fired several shots at them. Nathan rushed over and pushed him down to the ground.

'Our next move?' Nathan questioned himself. 'It will be dark before we can get vehicles to pursue them. We will have to wait until morning to follow the tracks.' Nathan decided to also put agents at the airport, the train stations and rental car agencies, just in case. Nathan's mind was going through every possible avenue of escape. He was not giving up. "Let's go. We have a lot to do before morning."

Nathan stared out the passenger seat window as James drove the car toward the city. He silently vowed, 'Dr. Jack Reese, you will not get away from me again.'

Chapter 78

December 19, 2012

It was two hours before Jack, Alana and Apu started to revive. If the atmosphere was more threatening, Jack would have thought that they had been drugged. It was very strange, the way they had all dozed off to sleep right after eating. Jack tried to think if he had seen Ida eat any of the stew, but couldn't remember. 'Well if we were drugged, it didn't harm us.' He kept these thoughts to himself.

Ida was still sitting in her rocking chair. Behind her, in the flickering light, hung a black and white portrait of Franklin Delano Roosevelt – the former President. She didn't say anything when they awoke; she just smiled and kept on knitting. The blanket she was making was huge, and lay in a pile at her feet. Ida epitomized the idea of the sweet old lady, yet the twinkle in her eye gave hint that she had a deeper story to tell.

"He's a hero of mine", said Ida, gesturing with the knitting needle toward the portrait.

"Oh!" said Jack – realizing that the old woman had just read his mind. He had been wondering about the significance of the Roosevelt portrait.

"We have nothing to fee-ah – but fee-ah itself!" Jack could hear an old radio broadcast in his mind – the one everyone had heard in History class about the darkest days of the Great Depression – 1930 something... He looked back up at Ida – and the portrait. Both the old woman and the long dead President smiled back.

Finally, she tied off the yarn, laid down her kitting needles and declared, "All done." She rose from her seat and gathered the blanket. She walked over to the table and laid it out fully and flat across the table top. Jack rose up to see it and complement her expert work. When he got to the table he stared down at the blanket all laid out. He shook his head in puzzlement, "Ahh. Apu, Alana, you have a look at this." They got up and went over to the blanket and looked down at the amazing workmanship. It only took a second before they realized that the expertly woven design that was knitted into the beautiful blanket possessed incredible significance.

Ida had gone to the kitchen to put on a pot of water. "Would anyone else care for a cup of tea, it refreshes me when I wake up." Each nodded, mindlessly agreeing to the tea, still so transfixed by the blanket's design.

Jack looked over at Ida and asked in wonder, 'Who are you and what does this mean?"

"I told you my name is Ida Homberger and I have known that symbol since before you were born..." She answered, amused.

Apu went over to his case and pulled out the rubbing from the Wall of Secrets. He laid it out on the blanket, beside the design. They were unmistakably related, though not exact. The orientation was different.

"I *know* what it means!" Alana blurted out excitedly. As she stared at the design, she suddenly recognized the symbols and remembered their meanings. The direction of the symbols in the rubbing had thrown her off completely. Satisfaction washed over her face as she smiled brightly up at her companions. "It is pronounced *amagi*. It is a cuneiform inscription." Alana was happy that some of her research over the years was paying off for them. "It's the earliest-known, written appearance of the word for *freedom*, or *liberty*. It was written around 2300 B.C. in the Sumaria."

"Yes, I remember reading something about that, a long time ago during my undergraduate studies." Jack added, trying to remember when he had last heard of the a*magi*.

"Ah, yes, very good. We shall discuss *amagi* – freedom, in depth, first let's have our tea and sit down again by the fire." Ida suggested. It was now evening, but after the nap, they were very awake and anxious to hear what Ida had to tell them. Apu was thinking about how another amazing set of circumstances had led them to exactly the right place, at the right time; when Ida began to speak.

"As Alana has told us, the symbol's name is *amagi* and it means freedom in the old Sumerian language. But it is not just about national freedom, personal freedom or financial freedom, or freedom from slavery or freedom from tyranny. No, it's not just one of those ideas; it is *all* of them combined. It represents the liberty *inherent* in Life. It is what the American fore-fathers were talking about when the Declaration of Independence was created and signed. *"We hold these truths to be self-evident, that all men are created equal, that they are endowed by their Creator with certain unalienable Rights, that among these are Life, Liberty and the pursuit of Happiness."* It means more specifically the freedom from oppression from without *and* from within."

"What I mean is, amagi also means, *freedom from fear.* This is very important for our world right now. Terrorism has become a very real threat to our freedom. But terrorism's *power* comes from *fear.* And we, each one, give it that power with our own fears everyday. Fear is the number one thief of joy, love, peace and happiness. It robs us of the destiny we are here to live out. *Fears* keep us from enjoying the lives we have, and it keeps us from the lives we *could* have." Ida's tea seemed to be calling, for just a quick sip. Her lined and aged face somehow glowed with vitality and her eyes danced with the knowledge that she shared. She swallowed, smacked her lips a little, enjoying the honey she had generously put into her tea.

She continued. "Fear is based in the past *or* actually on a limited *interpretation* of a past experience. The reality of a past situation, or experience, is never *bad*, but your idea of it often is. We also fear the future. But usually this too is based on an *interpretation* of a past experience; one that is often inaccurate or limited in some way. Fear does not exist in the present moment. I will say that again. Fear does not exist in the present moment." She paused again trying to let that settle into their minds, and then gracefully went on.

"As soon as you feel fear, you are living in the past or the future; where you are powerless, thus you feel even more fear. You see, you have no power over the past or the future, because they do not exist *now*. But in the *present*, you are power-full, knowing and connected to a million possibilities, and therefore fear is irrelevant, mute and non-existent." Her tone gave them the feeling that this was possibly the final word on the matter.

The combination of simplicity and complexity were not lost on her audience, they all contemplated her words. Alana was about to ask a question when Ida began speaking again, as if she had never even meant to pause.

"Fear is based on conditionings - which are mental and emotional constructs about something in the past. The past has no bearing whatsoever on what *is*, today. There is no rule, force or law that says what happened yesterday will happen again today. As a matter of fact, it is ridiculous to think that with a huge endless universe, with unlimited potential, that the same thing would happen more than one single time, *ever*. And yet in our human lives we very often experience the same things over and over again. This is because we *are* powerful, whether we know it or not, and if we are continually living in the past, in the old experiences and beliefs, in old paradigms, then we will continually create the same happenings again and again."

"Amagi is based in truth. Truth is what you have already learned on your journey: Purpose, Silence, Possibilities, Unity and correct Identification with God. These are the keys you have already uncovered, are they not? One more truth is Freedom; freedom from your past."

"You must first give up your past. Relinquish it. It has served you, but no more. Let it go. When you give up your past, you give up the *known*. This is hard for many people. They like what they know. It is comfortable, even if it is unhealthy or makes them unhappy. What I am trying to tell you is that it is in the *unknown* where miracles exist. It is where all the answers are, where all the power resides. Let go of what you have *known* and open yourself to the unknown – remember the field of all possibilities." Again Ida declared the last sentence in triumph, as if she spoke from the pinnacle, the climax of her speech. She gulped down the last of her tea and set her cup on the coffee table. She looked down and smoothed out her lightly flowered skirt. This time Jack had a question, but only got as far as inhaling prior to speaking, when Ida resumed her lesson.

"Fear and flight are mental mechanisms of the animals. Animals use these mechanisms well to perpetuate their species. We, as humans, were also able to survive due to this natural perfunctory instinct. However, this very instinct; could very soon be the end of us, if we do not grow past it. Humanity is at a stage of great *understanding* of machine and technology, and yet far away from the *understanding* of truth. It is now, as we tread this tight-rope, when the most danger exists for us. It is now, when we must evolve beyond this animal instinct of fear and flight and grow into knowing, into truth and into love.

Understanding requires us to see our fears for what they truly are – simple ideas from the past that we carry around with us continually, stifling and smothering us. Let them go and learn to live only in the present moment. It is in this space, the *now*, where we are free to choose. It is here, where we can choose happiness, peace, love, joy and *freedom* in every moment.

Many have said to me, 'You don't know what I have been through.' I have heard this over and over. And yet I tell you, as I have told them all, 'What you have been through is the past and is only relevant in as much as you let it be. You have only to change your mind. Free your mind from the thoughts it repeats over and over again." Ida stated pointedly. Her three students waited for her to recommence and explain her last point, which she did after only a few moments.

"Changing your mind is only as difficult as a choice - to think of something else. Are you not able to visualize a summer sunset in your mind? Can you not picture the brilliant yellow, orange and red colors stretching out into the fading blue sky? You can almost smell dusk's musty fragrance, can you not? You can imagine the cooling air caress you skin. Your mind can conjure this image as if you are looking at the sunset in front of you. *Now,* think of running from your pursuers, of the bitter cold whipping past your face while escaping on your motor vehicles. Imagine the bullets screaming past your ears, biting into the trees and branches around you, as you try to escape. Immediately your brain triggers a response. As a matter of fact, your brain doesn't know the difference between the real thing and the memory (or your imagining) of it. Your brain sends out the same exact chemicals into your body when you remember it as it did when you actually were in the thick if it. This is why what we think of is so very important and why living in the past can create the same experiences over and over again.

If you want to know how to change your mind, you just did it. You went from the images of beauty, perfection and peace to fear and suffering in a moment of thought. This is how you change your mind. You simply decide to think something else in *each* moment."

In the last key you learned about knowing and identifying yourself with God. When you are able to do this fully – in that moment you will know freedom from fear. It is the most liberating, wonderful and powerful experience one can have." This time when Ida paused in her speech, she smiled broadly and leaned back with a sigh.

The room was quiet. Jack, Alana and Apu had listened intently, wondering quite often how she knew so many things about what they had been through and all the keys. But when the old woman finished they thought only about the truth she was telling them and knowing full-well how their fears had gotten the better of them in recent days.

Alana was the first to respond. "Are you saying that we have nothing to fear? That nothing can harm us, cause us pain and suffering or even death? I know that isn't true. Many things have harmed me and those bullets were real."

"Ah, yes. Argue for your limitations and you shall have them." Ida said somehow kindly. "Life does happen, even as we are learning how to direct our lives more. However, I will say, if you are living in the *present moment* and you do *not* judge events based on the past, or your fear of the future, then your suffering is a matter of choice in each moment." She said this slowly, hoping to impart the importance of her words. Then she smiled and said quickly, "I, for one, choose not to suffer. I choose happiness and freedom.'

"I think I understand. At least I can feel it. My brain is still trying to reconcile what you are saying; but it feels true." Jack said.

Apu could stay quiet no longer. "How do you know so much about us and the keys? How do you know about the keys?" He tried not to be so abrupt, but could not help himself.

"I know because I have been watching you all along your adventure. I have the gift of sight. It is not the sight of the future but the sight of the present. That is where I reside - in each moment's present awareness. I am able to enter the silence and see what *is* happening. I have been waiting for you, because I have been following and aiding your progress as best I can." Ida's calm demeanor seemed protective.

"How have you aided our progress?" Jack demanded curiously.

"I have sent you love and insight from the unified field. When you connect to God, you are connected to everything that *is*, outside of time and space. Your mission is very important to me, to us all. You all have done very well, I must say."

"Do you know what will happen next?" Even as she asked the question, Alana knew her motive was fear-based.

"No, I do not." The old woman said patiently with a smile. "But I would highly recommend a good night's sleep and then you can open your eyes to what the morning brings." She suggested warmly, and knowingly. "I have two small bedrooms and a bathroom upstairs, you are welcome to stay where-ever it suits you. I sleep down here in the back room. I prefer not to go up and down the stairs any more at my age."

They thanked her for her generous hospitality and all that she had shared with them. Each took a tea cup to the kitchen and then went upstairs. The bedrooms were indeed small, each had a twin bed.

The guys took the bedroom at the top of the stairs and offered the
other to Alana. She went in, changed into pajamas and went to see if
the bathroom was free. Jack was just coming out. They smiled a little
awkwardly to each other and Alana took her turn. She wanted to ask
Jack to stay in her room. She didn't think now was the time for
intimacy, but she would welcome his closeness. This new sense of trust
amazed her, but she wanted to be free of the fears she carried regarding
relationships. When she opened the bathroom door she decided to ask
him, besides she didn't think it would be comfortable bunking with
Apu in such a small bed. She tapped lightly on the door. Jack opened
the door quietly. "Is something wrong?"

        "No, I'm fine, but I was wondering if you wouldn't mind
sleeping in my room tonight." She asked sheepishly, then rushed to
clarify. "Sleep, just sleep." She whispered and wondered how that
sounded. Jack smiled and looked into her eyes. He reached out and
pulled her to him, circling her in his arms and kissing the top of her
head.

        "I would like nothing more." He declared. He poked his head
back in to tell Apu, but he was already asleep. She held his hand as they
walked down the short hallway and into the small room. She climbed
into the bed and lifted the covers to welcome him in. As Jack reached
down to turn off the tiny lamp next to the bed, he noticed a message,
so delicately embroidered within a frame, with simple stitching in light
blue: *There is nothing better than a good night's sleep and open eyes to see what the
morning brings.*

        Jack climbed in beside Alana and reached up his arm. She
snuggled into his side. They laid there for a few moments not speaking
and eventually drifted off into fearless slumber.

Chapter 79

December 20, 2012

The next morning Apu was awake early. He went down to the kitchen in search of coffee, another cup of tea just wouldn't do it. How anyone survived without the kick-start coffee gave him in the morning, was beyond him.

Ida was in the kitchen, dressed in a long night gown and a cozy robe; she shuffled around in fluffy slippers. She smiled warmly at him and asked how he had slept. "Very well, thank you so much for taking us in." Apu replied sincerely.

"It is my pleasure to help. Can I offer you coffee?"

"Yes, please."

Apu was still wondering about the breadth of her knowledge. Ida poured him a cup and began cooking breakfast. In no time at all the whole house smelled wonderful.

"Where are you from?" Apu inquired. Ida knew exactly what he wanted to know.

"I was born and raised in this area, actually. I was named after my paternal grandmother. But my mother, who was Scottish, was my real teacher and mentor. We traveled all over the world, when I was much younger, of course. I also learned from sages and enlightened gurus everywhere. When I was a young woman, my thirst for understanding was unquenchable. As I learned more, I realized that all I sought was *inside* of my being, not outside. I learned to access and then commune with the inner world. I always had the gift of sight, but I didn't understand how it worked or why. When I was able to access Oneness, I began to understand. I live back here in Colorado now, traveling only occasionally. As for my work - I serve others as they find me and I find them."

"Well, I am very grateful to have found you." Apu said truthfully, finishing his first cup and helping himself to another.

Jack had come down while Ida was talking and didn't wish to interrupt. Alana soon followed.

When there was a break in the conversation, Jack said, "Good Morning." Then asked the first question on his mind, as he poured a cup of coffee for himself and Alana. "How do you know the amagi symbol?" he pointed to the blanket now lying on the couch.

"I learned about that symbol and many others during my training, when I was a young woman in the order." Ida answered.

"Which *order*?" Jack didn't mean to be rude, but he really wanted to know.

"I am a member of an ancient order of priestesses called the Nine Maidens. There are not many of us left now. My mother was a priestess and she brought me into the order at the age of six. I did not have a daughter to continue that tradition." She said with a twinge of sadness, which disappeared as she drew the conversation back to the topic. "The amagi was taught to all the initiates."

Alana found this all very interesting and marveled at how the key symbols came from all over the world, creating the Wall of Secrets in Mexico. She mumbled to herself, "But how did the Mayan's get them?"

Ida's answer surprised Alana, "It has not been understood, in modern times, how ancient people were able to travel. Our arrogance keeps our ancestors immobile and unintelligent. We often directly correlate technology with intelligence. This creates the illusion that we are quite advanced and civilized today, and that the ancients were backward and barbaric. But the truth is, mankind long ago was much more learned in the ways of nature, instinct and intuition. Through this knowledge, many very brave souls traveled and advanced their understanding. Besides there are wonderful ways to travel that do not include the body." Ida chuckled, her eyes twinkling as they had the night before. "I think you are aware of this type of travel and knowledge transfer, are you not?" Ida looked into Alana's eyes.

Alana just smiled knowingly and sipped her coffee. She really liked the old woman. She knew they would not be able to stay long and that thought clouded her face with a subtle sadness. Ida noticed it immediately.

"Remember to stay in the moment, and not in the past, Alana, dear. It is in the present moment that your freedom resides. You felt it - purely, for a moment, didn't you? Go there again, whenever you can. Now, let's have breakfast."

They ate a delicious, nurturing meal. Clearly, Ida was an accomplished cook. Actually, she seemed truly accomplished in most everything she tried, to the point of seeming magical. They enjoyed a wonderful morning of comfort and camaraderie, concentrating on each moment, enjoying and appreciating their time with Ida. Their hearts and bellies were full, their bodies warm and comfortable, and their minds stimulated and *free from fear*.

Alana could not remember a time when she felt so safe and happy. She had slept soundly in Jack's arms, feeling loved. It had not been awkward or weird in any way. When she woke up this morning she was facing the wall and Jack was snuggled up behind her, his left arm over her body. 'It felt so right,' she thought to herself.

Alana decided to really try and release her expectations and old fears regarding relationships. Whatever happened next was not something she would worry about. She would attempt to trust in her purpose and in the power that had miraculously led them this far.

Chapter 80

December 20, 2012

The four friends had gone into the living room of Ida's small cottage to relax after an early breakfast, and decided to join in meditation together. It had been silent in the room for nearly an hour; their increasing connections had allowed them to enter the silence easily. This meditation time with Ida was the most profound connection to the silence, to God they had experienced thus far. At first, it was quite emotional - feeling so interconnected and unified with each other. A stream of love washed through them and seemed to heal all of their worries. The silence became profound, and peace reigned.

It was gradual and yet with purpose when they came back to consciousness, awake and aware. They sat serenely, consciously intending the experience of Oneness to be in their wakeful state as well as their meditative state. Soon, each one got up, stretched and began to move around, looking out windows and tending to the fire. Ida was the first to speak. "It is time for you all to be off. There is more adventure waiting for you."

"Yes, we know." Jack was sad to leave, but anxious to see the mission through to its end. "Tomorrow is the 21st of December, when the Mayans predicted the end of this age. We have two more symbols to decipher before that time. You wouldn't be able to give us any more clues of where to look, or what to do after we discover them all, would you?"

Ida's eyes sparkled. "There is not much more I can tell you, except to trust in the power that guides you."

"But how are we supposed to know who will be the final person to tip the scale? Will we know who the 100th human is? Will it be the final gatekeeper? Or will there be someone else, beyond the gatekeepers?" Jack puzzled out-loud.

"I can not say. That is in the future. Today it is not known." Ida responded.

Normally Alana would begin to feel anxious with their moving on, but this latest key and Ida had made her feel more confident in the power that she was connected to. While in meditation she could hear

Ida's voice in her head, telling her to admit to the power that motivated her. As soon as she acknowledged it in her own heart and mind, she felt less fear. "I'm gonna freshen up and pack." She declared on her way up the steps. Jack watched her for a moment and then jumped into action also.

Soon they were all ready to leave, bundled in their oversized parkas, with their bags loaded on the four wheelers. Ida came out in her boots and coat and gave them each a pair of hand-knitted gloves and a hat. She had also prepared food for the trip. They wondered when she had knitted such perfects gifts for each of them. They donned them gratefully. They embraced and thanked her warmly for everything. Alana had tears in her eyes. She knew she would miss the old woman, naturally wondering if she would ever see her again.

"Don't cry, child. Remember our connection." Ida said as she hugged the younger woman and then momentarily holding Alana's face in her hands. Alana just nodded her head and brushed away a tear.

Just before they took off, Ida yelled to them above the noise of the engines, "Go south." She pointed in the correct direction. "The terrain is less rugged and I have a feeling about it." She smiled and winked at them. Jack smiled back and yelled, "Thank you!" as they took off down the hill and into the dense forest.

Chapter 81

December 19, 2012

Melvin was walking home from work in the evening, on his second day. He was very happy with the job he was doing. As he worked, he often thought about all of the packages and cards that were heading to loved ones all around the world, for the holiday season.

He also thought about his own lost family and was a little sad that there was no one else in his life to look after. The only other family he had left in the world was his sister Dorothy who lived in Wisconsin. As the cold December moon rose in the sky, he wondered how she was. He hadn't seen her since his wife's funeral. She may have tried to contact him afterwards, but he was lost to everyone in the years that followed. He thought he might try to contact her, see how she was doing.

Melvin and Dorothy were close as children, especially after their older brother Roger's death in Vietnam. After a couple of years, Dorothy married a farmer. They raised four children, all were grown by now. He wondered if they all went home to the farm at Christmas time. 'Were they there now?' Melvin had only visited twice, a long time ago, in the early years of his own marriage. But when they found out that his wife was pregnant they stopped going to visit Dorothy and her crew. It was just too difficult to make the trip.

When he arrived back to Tom's house he asked for his opinion. "I think it is a great idea, give her a call. Let her know you're alive. See how she is doing."

"I'm a little scared and I don't really know why."

"You've come along way, but if you feel you aren't ready yet, that's okay too. I think it would be good for you to re-connect with your family, especially around the holidays." Tom always tried to be supportive.

"Maybe I am afraid that she will be angry with me or not want to speak to me. I mean, that would be understandable."

"There are too many unknowns to be predicting. You just have to do what your heart tells you. I am going to go fix us some dinner. You decide. Just know that either way it is okay, and that the long distance on my phone is free." Tom said with a smile and a wink then went into the kitchen.

Melvin sat on the chair in the living room for a while thinking about dialing. Every time he reached for the phone, he had an overwhelming fear that she would reject him and then he would be without any family, and completely alone. It seemed easier to just let her stay out there and to let him be the one who keeps them apart, not her. He decided to give up. He ate dinner and read a little, but he kept thinking of Dorothy. 'What if she was glad to hear from me? What if she welcomed me with open arms? I will never know, unless I call.'

He struggled throughout the evening, until his bed time. Finally, he picked up the phone off the nightstand, and began to dial the number. Just as soon as he dialed, the phone was back on its cradle. 'I don't want to wake her up, that wouldn't be kind.' He remembered Wisconsin was in a later time zone. He sat there staring at the phone, wrestling with his fears when something inside him let go. It was an overwhelming feeling of peace, and unfamiliar *freedom*. Immediately, he was able to let go of his fears about calling, of being rejected. He decided to take each moment as it came, determining *in* each moment what to do next. Melvin loved his sister and hoped that she still cared for him, but if she didn't, he would not give up on caring for her. He had been feeling sorry for himself and quite selfish; he let it all go instead of letting *her* go. *He* picked up the phone and confidently dialed.

It was a moment before it connected and began to ring on the other end; once, twice and had started the third ring when a male voice answered.

"Hello?"

"Hello, is Dorothy there?" Melvin asked, feeling some apprehensive.

"Yeah, she's here, who's this?" Melvin felt a little intimidated but continued.

"This is, uh…Melvin, her brother." He said as kindly as he could.

"Oh, okay, hold on." The voice sounded surprised. Melvin wasn't sure if it was Hank, Dorothy's husband or not. It could be one of her sons. The next few moments until Dorothy came on the line were painfully long, but Melvin kept reminding himself to release his fear and not think of the past or the future. Right now, in this moment, he knew he was doing the right thing.

"Hello?" a woman's voice said tentatively on the other end of the line.

"Dorothy, is that you? It's Melvin."

"*Melvin*?! I thought you were dead. Oh, Melvin is it really you?"

"Yes, it's me. I did almost die, but a very kind man helped bring me back to life. How are *you* Dorothy?" Melvin could hear her muffled cry as he spoke, teary eyed himself.

They talked for nearly an hour. She was so glad to hear from him. Melvin felt his whole being fill with joy. She invited him to come for Christmas. He explained that he was working at the local post office as a seasonal worker and wouldn't be able to leave until Christmas Eve day. She was thrilled and wanted him to come as soon as he was able. Melvin told her a little, though not all the details, of what had happened over the last few years. He could hear how heartbroken she was over his pain and the devastation in his life.

"Why don't you come here and live for a while, after your job there is done. It's seasonal right? So you won't have a job after Christmas. You can work here. Hank is always looking for help on the farm, ever since the boys went off to college and their own lives."

"Let's take one step at a time." Melvin was excited by the offer, but he didn't want to get ahead of himself. He had another couple of days before he would finish his job here. Tom was so generous to let him stay this long, but his time here was nearly up. Still, he didn't want to rush. "We can decide all that when I get there for Christmas. I will take the first bus I can on the 24th, heading your way. It may be an over-night trip, but I should be there by Christmas morning."

"Wonderful, I will have a room ready for you. I am so glad you called. And I am so glad you are okay, Melvin, I was so worried about you." She paused and teared up again… "And… I feel badly that I assumed the worst. Please take care of yourself. I don't want to lose another brother." Melvin could hear her sniffle with sadness.

"Don't worry Dorothy, I am okay now. I will see you soon. Take care."

When Melvin hung up the phone he felt amazing. Taking each day at a time, or even one moment at a time was the only way he could think to go on, without being crippled with fear. He wanted to be free and tonight, as he laid his head on his pillow, he felt free and loved.

Chapter 82

December 19, 2012

Marie put the boys down to bed, and then sat down on the couch with a load of clean laundry to fold. After dinner, Joe declared that he needed to go over to his buddy Roger's house, to help him with his car. "He has been having trouble with it starting and they really can't afford a mechanic right now. I shouldn't be too long. Hopefully we can find out what's wrong right away and fix it."

"I'm glad you're helping him out. Tell him and his family I said *Hi*," She called out sleepily, with a yawn. It had been a tough year and many of their friends were financially tight. 'Maybe if we each help each other out, it will make things a little better.'

Marie had already cleaned up the kitchen and was chipping away at some much needed laundry. She was tired, but there was so much that needed to be done. She had to take advantage of every available opportunity to keep ahead of the house and kids.

As Marie watched TV and folded, she switched around the channels for a while; there wasn't much on. Finally she flipped over to a Christmas story. It was one of her favorites – "It's A Wonderful Life." She decided to leave it on until Joe returned. The movie was at the point where Jimmy Stewart's character – George Bailey - was stumbling around Bedford Falls.

'He should be home any time; it has been over two hours.' She reassured herself as she stacked the clean, folded clothes in the basket and leaned back on the couch. Before long she was asleep, the television played on in the background – the family singing Auld Lang Syne – George Bailey tearfully reunited with his family – his brother Harry declaring him the "richest man in Bedford Falls".

It was another hour later when the phone rang. Marie jumped, confused. She thought the movie might be at the point when Clarence, the angel, earned his wings. 'Every time a bell rings, an angel earns his wings', she recited in her mind. But, the ring came again – it was the phone! It could be Joe! She rushed to pick it up before another ring woke the kids. With her other hand, she turned off the TV.

"Hello?"

"Hey, Marie, it's Roger. Sorry to bother you, is Joe there? I have an idea about the car and I needed his opinion."

"No." Marie said with alarm. "I thought he was there with you."

"He was here, but he left about a half hour ago, I thought for sure he would be home by now. It's only a ten minute drive." Roger became a little concerned as he spoke. "Where could he have gone? He said he was tired and going home. Maybe he decided to go to the store or something."

"That's true but very unlikely at this time of night." Marie replied. "I'm gonna try his cell. I'll have him call you as soon as I get a hold of him."

"Good, thanks." He said and hung up.

Marie dialed Joe's cell. As soon as she heard it ringing in the receiver, she also heard it ringing in the kitchen. She went in and there was Joe's phone on the counter. He had forgotten to take it with him. Now she really had no idea how to locate him or how to find out if he was alright. She began to worry. 'What if something happened? Her mind wandered to George Bailey again. He will call,' she tried to reassure herself.

As the seconds ticked by and turned into minutes - still no sign or sound from him, Marie got more and more worried. Her stomach began to turn sick and she started to imagine all the horrible things that could have happened. Just when she held the phone in her hand to call Roger, her hand loosened its grip – so much so that she almost dropped it. Her worry felt different and eased somehow. With a long, gentle sigh, Marie put down the phone. She knew Joe was fine, that her deepening worry could be let go. 'It really is pointless to fear what I do not know. Right now, all I know for sure is that Joe is simply delayed in getting home. There are all kinds of possible reasons for that and many of them are innocent, safe and quite predictable.' She knew she needed to stay out of the 'what-ifs' and set herself firmly in what-I-know.

Her eyes closed as she searched her intuition for Joe. It took only a few moments for her to feel him. Marie lingered in that feeling of peace for a moment. 'Fear is such a sneaky thief; steeling your peace and making you a victim to anything and everything.' She could not identify the source of this new and clear understanding. Still, she accepted it and took a long and deep breath. Just as she let it out she heard a noise and saw the car lights in the driveway. A smile came over her face.

When Joe came in the door he looked cold and dirty.

"What happened to you?" she asked, genuinely interested. "Roger called and said you left over an hour ago."

"I know. I kicked myself for forgetting my cell. I wanted to call you so you wouldn't worry." He was out of breath from worrying that she would be worried. "I was on my way home, coming down highway 29. I watched an accident happen right in front of me. This young kid didn't know how to drive in the snow and lost control of his car, skidded off the road and into a tree. He was not seriously injured, just some scrapes and bruises, but I stayed to help him out of the car and up the snowy, muddy hill. He was really shook up. I waited with him for the police, the ambulance and his parents to show up. I should've asked to use his cell but things were kinda crazy. Sorry, honey."

"Oh, don't be, I'm just so glad you were there to help the poor kid. I was worried when Roger called. Oh, by the way, call him back, he has some idea about the car, and he was concerned too. Anyway, I was worried, but then I realized you were probably fine. I could feel that you were."

Joe looked over at her and raised his eyebrows. Sometimes, Marie could act just a little weird. He smiled. 'She is also right most of the time, weird or not.' He went over to her and kissed her on the cheek. "You, go to bed, hon. You look tired. I will call Roger and then jump in the shower. I won't be long."

Marie didn't argue, she *was* tired. As she crawled in under the covers, she thought about how she had released her fears and claimed her power to reach out and *know* how Joe was. 'Another miracle?' As she fell off to sleep, she wondered if something was happening in the world, or perhaps just to her. So many miracles seemed to be happening every day.

Chapter 83

December 19, 2012

    Chuck arrived at the hospital and went directly to the front desk to inquire about June Turner.

    "She has been moved to a room in the west wing, room 204." The woman behind the desk informed him. When she saw his confusion, she directed him to the elevator and gave him directions.

    Chuck made his way through the winding corridors of the hospital, hoping that Jason would be there too. As he approached the room he looked around for a waiting room. There was a large one toward the middle of the floor. All of the rooms were situated along the outside corridor, surrounding it. There were several people in the waiting room. Chuck scanned the occupants but didn't see Jason anywhere. He turned back and headed across the wide hallway to 204. He tapped lightly, but didn't hear anyone; he slowly pushed the door open and peered inside. The bed closest to the door held an old man, who was sound asleep and snoring rather loudly. Further inside the room Chuck could see June in the window-side bed. In a chair by the window, the young boy was curled up fast asleep.

    Chuck went over and lightly touched Jason's shoulder. Jason woke up and looked up into Chuck's face and smiled. "I knew you would come back." His voice was sleepy. "I didn't want to hang out at Aunt Janet's house today because I knew you would come here."

    "I told you I'd be back." Chuck smiled down at the boy. "How is your mom doing?"

    "They moved her to this room this morning. It's much better. There is more room here and I can stay with her. She hasn't woken up yet, though. The doctor said she is doing okay from the surgery, but he doesn't know when she'll come out of the coma." Jason was somberly reciting his mother's latest prognosis, at least what he could remember. Chuck wanted to cheer him up, his heart broke when he saw how sad Jason was.

    "Have you had lunch?"

    "No. Aunt Janet dropped me off this morning on her way to work and said she wouldn't be able to pick me up till after work, because her job was too far from here. She gave me five dollars though." Jason proudly pulled the bill he hadn't spent out of his pocket.

"You won't need it today, save it for later. Lunch is on me. Let's see what they have in this place to eat." Chuck announced as he led the boy down the hall toward the nurses' station. "We are going to go get some lunch." Chuck informed the nurse. "If anything changes in Jason's mom, June Turner, room 204, will you have us paged please?"

"Sure thing. Great idea," She said smiling at a sleepy eyed Jason. "He needs to get around some. Poor thing's been sitting in there all morning without making a peep." The nurse smiled and looked up at Chuck. "What is your name, sir?"

"I am Chuck Adams, a friend of the family." Chuck winked at the boy as he said it.

"Okay, Mr. Adams, we will page you and Jason if there is any change what so ever."

"Thank you." This time it was Jason who spoke up.

"You're welcome, young man." Chuck was glad that the nurse was so sweet to Jason.

They made their way to the cafeteria and had lunch. The food wasn't horrible, though they both decided they had had better. They then went to the gift shop and bought some fresh flowers for his mom and some comic books to pass the time. Chuck got himself a notebook and a pack of pens. He decided to write down some of what had happened and jot down his plans for the future. Though, even as he thought of the task, he cautioned himself not to get too wrapped up in the results.

They spent the afternoon in the waiting room writing, reading and going into June's room to check on her. Chuck could tell that Jason was getting worried because there had not been a change in his mom yet. He tried to keep the boy's mind occupied but there was no way to get around the fact that they were in a hospital.

While they were in room 204, the doctor made his rounds. Chuck asked how their patient was doing. "Her wounds are healing well. Physically, she is progressing nicely. However, with the type of head trauma she experienced, it is unknown how long she could be in a coma. It may be hours, days or even longer." He said the last part softer, glancing over at the boy. "Let's hope for the best." He smiled. "She may be able to hear you, even if she can't answer you right now, you should talk to her."

After the doctor left, Chuck took the lead, went over to June's bedside and introduced himself. Jason was surprised at first and then thought it was kind of funny and laughed a little. Chuck was happy to have gotten such a response from the boy. They talked to each other for an hour or more, including June in the conversation, even if she couldn't speak to them yet. Later in the day, they played cards and dealt June in. They took turns playing her hand for her. Chuck could tell that including his mom was comforting to Jason.

The day wore on and as evening arrived, so did Aunt Janet. She was surprised to see Chuck, but didn't look altogether unhappy about it. She checked in with the nurse to see how her sister was doing and announced that she had to get home to make dinner for her family. "Get your things, Jason, it's time to go."

"I don't want to go. Can't I stay with Chuck?" Jason pleaded.

"No. You can't stay here all night." She said.

"Actually, if you don't mind, mame, he could have dinner with me and I could drive him to your house. You'd have to give me directions, of course." Chuck ventured.

Aunt Janet thought about it for a few moments and then said, "Oh, I don't care. But he must be home by nine or I will call the police."

"Yes, mame. I will have him home well before nine."

Aunt Janet gave Chuck directions and left. Chuck turned to Jason, "Let's get out of the hospital for a little while. I can give the nurse my cell number if anything changes with your mom." Jason liked that idea and soon they were in the car headed toward the town's shops and restaurants.

They had fun. Jason acted as a tour guide and felt very grown up when he was with Chuck. Chuck was happy to see the boy laugh and play and open up to him. He thought that Jason hadn't had much fun in his young life. They ate burgers, fries and shakes at a local diner. Then they went and got ice cream. All in all, it was a good evening. On the way to Aunt Janet's house Jason got quiet again.

"What if my mom never wakes up?" Chuck cringed at the sadness in Jason's voice. He stopped the car so he could look Jason in the eye.

"We will cross that bridge when we come to it. You can't let your worst fears get the better of you. They will only make you miserable and feel unsafe. You are safe, Jason. I am here and we will face whatever happens together. Okay?"

"Okay." Jason whispered. "Thank you for saving our lives, Chuck." Chuck almost cried at the earnest sentiment Jason conveyed.

"Thank *you*. You have actually helped me, too. And another time, I will tell you how, but for now, we have to get you to Aunt Janet's before she calls the cops on us." They both laughed.

Later that night, as darkness crowded in around the top bunk of his cousins bed, Jason wondered if it was all black where his mom was. He began to fear for her and for himself. 'Didn't she want to wake up and be my mom again?"

Just when the darkest thoughts seemed to take over his mind, Jason saw a light off in the distance. Before long it felt as if it entered his heart. He would do like Chuck had said - he would take it one day at a time. 'I will not let fear steal *my* happiness. Besides Chuck said he would stay with me.' An innocent peace entered his heart and he fell asleep dreaming of the moment when his mother would wake up and smile at him again.

Chuck, incredibly, felt the struggle that Jason had inside himself. He saw and felt the same light of peace as it washed over them both. As Chuck went to sleep, he too recited: "Freedom from fear is living each moment as if *it* is all there is."

Chapter 84

December 19, 2012

Ben spent the afternoon reading his new books. Every time the phone rang he ignored it. He checked the messages after a little while, but decided that nothing was so important to allow it to interrupt his day off. He had not taken a day off in two years, and he was due.

Around three o'clock he called Terri, his secretary and informed her that he would be taking the rest of the week off as well. She worried that he was ill. He assured her that he just needed some time off, and some perspective. He told her to take the rest of the day off also and to call him in the morning with anything pressing. Otherwise, he would see her next week.

Ben went to the large leather chair in his living room, turned on the reading lamp overhead and leaned back with his book. He moved only subtly for the next several hours, finishing one of the books he bought, pulled out a note pad and a pen, and started to write down his thoughts and ideas. He didn't want to forget what had happened and the new concepts he was learning. He was excited to be learning so many new things. He remembered feeling this excited at the onset of becoming successful in his work. Too many deals and too many lives destroyed had taken all the joy out of his work.

Ben got hungry at some point in the evening and went to the kitchen to see what was in the refrigerator. All it contained was a couple of beers, some sour milk and two very old TV dinners. He wasn't surprised, in fact, he expected worse. Ben went to the drawer under the telephone, pulled out a stack of takeout menus, chose one of his favorites and called to order. Opening a beer, he waited for the food to arrive and went back to his chair to begin the second self-improvement book he had purchased.

Once delivered, he opened all of the packages on the coffee table and filled a large plate with an assortment of Chinese food. He switched on his sound system and flipped over to a jazz station. Growing up in the south, he had always loved jazz.

Ben felt full and content as he sat in the same living room he had lived in for five years. 'Why such joy? Why now? Same old room, totally *different* feelings.' He wondered if it was wise to question it, but decided if he should try and understand how he got here in the first place. He couldn't get beyond the simple answers of innocence and selflessness and after thinking about it decided it was enough to just except it and be with it.

It had gotten late and he was about to head to bed when a thought crossed his mind, 'What if I wake up and this was all a dream? Or what if I can't bring back these feelings and I wake up in the same old rut I was in before?' Fear gripped his heart and mind. He didn't want to sleep, or to feel empty inside *ever* again.

Suddenly, he followed a strong urge to just close his eyes. A surge of peace overtook him. He opened his eyes only to navigate to the chair, then let go. Everything was okay. He *would*, in fact, feel this way again tomorrow and for many days to come. He needed to give up the fear of the past and of the future. 'The past did not make today. Each day is new. The past has no power over the future, except for what I give it. Wow. This is intense. Something must really be happening to me.' He grinned and was content.

Ben climbed into bed and let his head sink into his pillow. He let everything go, his past deeds and his feelings of emptiness. He let go of tomorrow and decided to let tomorrow take care of itself. Chuckling to himself, he drifted off into a restful sleep.

Chapter 85

December 19, 2012

     Nathan and the others went back to Denver to wait out the night. He didn't sleep at all as he made plans to follow Dr. Reese's group into the mountains. By early morning, they had enough snowmobiles and supplies to spend several days in open country if needed.

     Nathan had called the Director to tell him the bad news - another escape. It had not been a pleasant phone call and Nathan was determined to never make a call like that again. He concentrated on all the things he thought they needed to do to be successful this time around.

     At dawn, they were at the cabin again, unloading the cross-country vehicles from the large trailers that had carried them this far. The supplies were loaded onto the back racks. Nathan and each of the four other men had donned black down parkas, ski caps and goggles. He knew they were prepared. Nathan was glad that the next snow storm had held off; they were able to easily follow the tracks from the night before.

     He pulled his automatic pistol out of his shoulder holster and examined it. Today would be much different. Nathan had persuaded the Director to authorize lethal force. Since they would be in the mountains and far from witnesses, he ordered Dr. Reese, Alana Borisenko and Apu Chohan to be stopped at all costs. Their time was up. He did insist that Nathan make it look like an accident. Nathan decided to just bury the bodies in the snow; they wouldn't be found until spring, if at all. 'We will be long gone by then and the Mayan threat will be long past and The Fraternity of Veni Victus will retain control, with a new Director - me' Nathan grinned to himself. He gave the very simple and direct order to his men. "Shoot to kill."

     Nathan frowned. Things had not turned out in the manner that he had planned, not since he sabotaged Charles' car. He knew he could complete what Charles had not: capture the three scientists. He reconciled his actions he had chased them into the mountains, 'a perfect burial spot.'

Nathan looked around; all of his men were packed up and ready to go. He put his gun away and pulled out a topographical map, making sure the location of their deaths was perfectly remote. They started their engines and headed down the hill, following the tracks from the night before.

* *

Joseph slumped into his big leather chair, knowing the end was drawing near. He had failed, Charles had failed and now Nathan had failed. He could hear the anger and resolve in Nathan's voice, but he wondered if Nathan did succeed he wouldn't destroy the organization in the process. Joseph could not see how the ancient Fraternity of Veni Victus could survive if the Mayan secrets were revealed to all.

Joseph sunk deeper still into the oversized chair, his pending defeat too much to bear.

Chapter 86

December 20, 2012

They had been driving the four wheeler south for nearly two hours. Apu knew they would need gas soon. He had been steering clear of the roads, trying to avoid being seen and possibly found by their pursuers. But as time wore on, he increasingly feared that they would be stranded. He had been looking for signs of human development and fuel.

They came upon a small road running north/south. Apu decided to follow the road south, but they stayed in the trees. Soon they came to a larger road, a blue highway, running more east/west. Apu knew civilization was more to the east and mountains and forest to the west, so he decided to go east for a while. After another twenty minutes, they came to the out-skirts of a small town with a gas station. A relieved Apu pulled in, picked a pump and turned off his motor. Jack pulled up to another pump behind him.

It didn't take long for them to fill the tanks, but Alana needed to warm up so she went into the small mini-mart. She poured three large cups of coffee and grabbed some snacks, knowing they had Ida's food with them, but figured loading up on more couldn't hurt. Even with the cold, discomfort and uncertainty, it was still easy for Alana to recall all of the wondrous happenings of the past few days, especially after her time with Ida.

It was just past mid-day, but Jack was already thinking about where they would spend the night. He thought about getting a hotel room just to take a shower and warm up, but felt there was too little time.

A big, old pick-up truck, pulling an empty trailer, rumbled into the gas station and up to a pump. A young black man in his early twenties got out and started pumping gas into the tank. He looked around at the four-wheeler crew, "You've gotta be crazy four-wheel'n in this cold," he said with a friendly smile.

"Yeah," Apu said looking around at their outfits and means of transportation. "It looks that way. We have to get south and we don't have other transportation right now." Apu said. "But maybe we are crazy, now that you mention it." He laughed at how they must look to others.

"Where south?"

"Ahh… not sure really." Apu answered awkwardly. 'We are crazy.' He thought to himself. The pick-up truck owner raised his eyebrows and laughed.

"Well, I can take you as far south as Bailey. That's where I live and I'm headin' home, about an hour from here. I just dropped my load of wood, so it'd be easy to haul your rides." He offered.

The thought of being in a nice warm cab for the next fifty or so miles was overwhelming and wonderful to Apu. He turned to Jack, who was just getting back from the bathroom.

"This nice guy has offered to take us as far south as Bailey, the four-wheelers too." Apu excitedly told Jack.

"That'd be great!" Jack eagerly accepted as he walked up to the young man, with his hand extended.

"I'm Jack. This is Apu and Alana." Jack pointed to her as she emerged from the store. "We'd really appreciate a ride. It's really cold out here." Jack said as he shook hands with their newest friend.

"Scott Tanner. A ride's no problem. If you help me load up the four-wheelers onto the trailer, I'll strap 'em down."

Alana watched the guys push the now fully fueled four-wheelers onto the metal trailer and Scott, her new *best* friend, secure them. They all piled into the cab of the pick-up. Soon they were traveling down the road feeling toasty warm.

"Apu said you don't know where you all are headed. But how do you know you are going south?" Scott asked.

"Well, we are on kind of a scavenger hunt. We were told to head south, but know little more than that." Jack said, realizing how vague he must sound.

"That's cool. Are you dudes on some TV reality show or somethin'? Is this like 'The Great Race' or somethin'?" Scott got excited. "Shoot! This might be my 15 minutes of fame."

"Nope… Sorry." Alana answered, knowing he'd be disappointed.

"It's okay, knew that would be too good to be true."

"What's south of here anyway?" Jack asked.

"Well, a lot of mountains and trees, back country mostly. There are cities on the front-range to the east. You know… Denver and Colorado City. If you go west, you run into ski resorts. Most of the towns between the ranges are small. It's just open country and a lot of it."

"Oh," Jack was deep in thought and could muster little else in reply. He really didn't know where they were headed.

They were all quiet for a few more miles. Scott turned on the radio and they listened to music whining from the old speakers. During a short commercial break, the news headlines crackled in over the airwaves.

War continues between the former Iraqi states of Mesopotamia and Kurdistan.

Hybrid Auto sales top 10,000,000 units in USA.

New Pope – Alexander IX, whom everyone is referring to as "The Charismatic Pope" – calls for world peace – as he replaces the late Benedict XVI."

In the back seat, Apu tried to meditate; hoping for some guidance, but the news was not helping. Finally, he gave up and pulled his backpack up from the floor and fished around inside for the rubbing from the Cave of Secrets. There were two symbols left to decipher. The truth was that most of the symbols had *found them*. Apu wondered if they were going to have to search for the next one. He stared at the symbols. It seemed to him as if there was only one left really. But it was hard to tell. Nothing was jumping out at him. He silently handed it over to Alana, who studied it for a while.

Alana felt like she should be able to decipher them. 'It is *why* I was asked on this adventure.' She chided herself softly. As hard as she tried, nothing came stood out clearly. The backdrop of the whole group of symbols was familiar; Eligio had identified the wall in the cave as the "*Wall of Hunab Ku.*" That symbols was clear, though she still was not sure why it was the backdrop for all the other more strange symbols. After a few frustrating minutes, she just relaxed and stared out the window.

As the miles sped by, the sun began to set off to their right, which made the snow sparkle even more. She was about to give the rubbing back to Apu when she had an idea.

"Scott, we may not know where we are going, but we do have a possible clue. Do any of these symbols look familiar to you?"

Jack instinctively put his left hand on the wheel; his confident look confirmed to Scott that it was okay to momentarily look away from the road. Scott took the rubbing and curiously scanned the worn paper as he drove. It took a few seconds to review the whole thing. At last, he said, "Not really. This one sorta looks like a elephant. That reminds me of Elephant Rock in Pine, but that's pretty lame, ain't it? No ma'am - sorry, I don't recognize anythin'." Scott said as he passed it back.

"Wait a minute. Which one?" Alana asked. "It looks like what?"

"A elephant. See the ears and trunk. Not real clear, I know. Like looking at clouds and thinking you see shapes of things. Looks like a elephant to me. Elephant Rock is cool though. I love to go climbing there in the summer months. I go whenever I can. Course there are other Elephant rock formations in Colorado, they have one further south that the Elephant Rock Bicycle tour goes by, but the one in Pine is closer to home for me. 'sides I can always get some fishing in on the Platte while I am down there."

"You mentioned Pine. Where is Pine, Colorado?"

"Actually I could take you there if you want, it isn't far from Bailey, where I live." Scott offered.

"That'd be great. Are there any places to stay in Pine this time of year?" Alana asked.

"Sure. There are a few Bed & Breakfasts open year round. I know one of the owners. I'll take you to that one, if you want."

"Thank you so much, Scott. Looks like we found where we we're supposed to go next." Jack said.

"For real?" Scott asked excitedly. "You mean that's how you guys find your next stop? Just by chance? Sweet."

"I know, sweet, huh?" Jack said and they all laughed.

Chapter 87

December 20, 2012

It was afternoon when they arrived in Pine, Colorado, a quaint little town situated alongside of the Platte River. Scott drove them through the town to the other side where Robert Banks and his wife Patricia owned a Victorian bed and breakfast called the Bells & Whistle Inn. When they arrived, Scott introduced everyone and asked Robert, who Scott called Bob, if they had a room or two available. "Absolutely, I have a few rooms empty right now; it's slow this time of year. We have only Professor Hutchison staying with us through the holidays," Bob said.

"Thank you. We'll take two for the night. We'll probably be off early in the morning, though." Jack said. He surprised himself with the last part, but when he thought about it, it made sense. 'With those shooters on our tail, it won't be long before they find us. Besides tomorrow was the twenty-first.' Time was almost up.

After the three seemed settled on staying, Scott announced that he needed to get home. They all went out to the truck and unloaded their four-wheelers and gear.

"Thank you so much, Scott, for everything." Alana said sincerely. She didn't want to think about traveling that far in the open cold. She was very grateful that they didn't need to again today. 'Who knows what tomorrow would bring.' She thought to herself, then asked, "One more thing though, where's Elephant Rock from here?"

"It's easy, Bob will get you there. And you're welcome, glad to meet y'all. You're an interestin' bunch." He said as he shook everyone's hand. "Good luck on your scavenger hunt." Soon, he was rumbling down the road, noisier now with an empty trailer following behind.

"I would like a hot shower and some food, but not sure which one I want more." Alana said, patiently allowing the anticipation the build.

"I know what you mean." Apu said feeling increasingly tired.

"I agree with both. Let's ask Bob where we can find a restaurant." Jack led them back inside.

"There are a couple places in town, but if you don't want to weather the cold again, Patty could make you something in the kitchen." He offered.

"We don't want to be inconvenience to you or Patty."

"It's no trouble, we just had lunch a bit ago, I'll see if there is any left."

He promptly returned from the kitchen, with a smile.

"Come on in." She still has vegetable soup on the stove. She is heating it up now." They sat down at the large kitchen table. Patty came over and introduced herself, dismissing their concerns over being a bother.

"Don't even think about it, I haven't even cleaned up from our lunch yet, so it's no trouble at all." She dished out three large bowls of soup and passed them to her guests. Then she brought over a fresh baked loaf of bread and a huge block of butter. They were all happily full in no time.

After thanking Patty, they went up to their rooms. There was a moment in the hallway when Jack hesitated. He didn't know which room he should stay in. He certainly didn't want to presume to stay with Alana. The decision was made for him as Alana came up behind him and took his hand and led them into her room. Apu was happy for them both. 'That gives me a whole bed to myself.' He grinned as he entered his room.

Alana said that she was going to take a shower and went into the bathroom and closed the door behind her. Jack stood in the middle of the room, frozen for a moment, not knowing what to do. He decided to get the rubbing from Apu and study it, again. He went next door and tapped on Apu's door. No one answered, so Jack went in. He heard the shower going in the bathroom, and stuck his head in, "I'm taking the rubbing next door to study it for a little."

"Okay," Apu gurgled in reply.

Jack went back to their room and sat in the chair near the window. He was amazed that he had not seen the resemblance to an elephant in the symbol that Scott had. It was a stretch to think the symbol had anything to do with Pine, Colorado, or Elephant Rock, but they had to follow whatever coincidences came their way. They were no better leads at this point. Traveling around the Colorado countryside on a four-wheeler in December was not his idea of fun.

Jack knew that time was getting short. Eligio had said tomorrow was the day of the shift. *The day the hundredth human awakened to reality, changed their minds and therefore shifted the whole species into a new reality.* Tomorrow. He remained in awe of such high ideals; and wondered what exactly would happen. 'Oh well, for now, we have to uncover the final keys. I wonder if we have enough time. Eligio said there were eight; that leaves two more to go. But I don't see how there are two separate symbols left in the set. I guess we just have to trust. If the way things have been happening could be any indication, the next gatekeeper should be nearby.' Jack sat and puzzled over the rubbing and then stared out the window as the sun arched downward in its western descent.

Just then Alana came out of the bathroom wearing clean clothes and a towel on her head. To Jack she smelled wonderful. She walked directly over to Jack's chair, bent over and kissed him. At first the kiss was soft and delicate but Jack pulled Alana into his lap as the kiss deepened. They were wrapped up, tightly entangled in each other, when there was a gentle tap at the door. That broke the kiss. Jack closed his eyes and took a deep breath. He lifted his head and looked toward the door, "Just a minute." Alana smiled and got up from Jack's lap. He reached for her hand and kissed it, before she headed toward the door. Jack jumped up and quickly went into the bathroom to shower.

Alana opened the door and let Apu in. "Jack took the rubbing. I wanted to have a look at it again. I had a thought." Apu went over to the chair that Jack had recently vacated and picked up the paper.

"I remembered that the elephant carries a special meaning in my country. Actually, it can mean multiple things, but there was something quite specific… it is nagging at me. I just can't put my finger on what that is. I thought if I looked at it again…" Alana waited, allowing him time with it, then asked, "Well?"

"Nope, I can't get it." He laughed, though frustrated. "I mean I know it's a symbol for good luck, especially if the elephant's trunk is up. And of course, the Hindu god of sacred wisdom is Ganesha and he has an elephant's head and face. But there is something else… I just can't remember what."

Alana exhaled, "Maybe we'll just have to wait for the next gatekeeper to explain it to us."

After Jack took his shower, they all decided to go find Elephant Rock, since it was the only clue they had. When they reached the bottom of the stairs, Alana paused for a moment, causing the others to nearly walk into her. She had glanced to the right; into the study of the large Victorian style Inn. It only took a second for Alana to truly focus on the tall bearded gentleman browsing through a rather large book, clearly sporting a picture of elephants on the cover. Soon Jack and Apu realized why Alana turned directly into the study. They followed without hesitation.

"Excuse me, sir. What is that book you're reading?" Alana asked directly.

Professor Sam Hutchison looked up at Alana, a little surprised by the intrusion. "What, this?" he looked back at the book, then back to Alana. "This is about Hannibal crossing the Alps on elephants. It's very interesting history. Why?"

"Sorry, my name is Alana Borisenko and these are my friends Jack Reese and Apu Chohan. We happen to be quite interested in elephants."

"Well, there aren't too many around here. Unless, you count Elephant Rock, that is." He smiled mockingly.

Alana smiled back, recognizing how funny she must sound. "We are actually more interested in what elephants represent. What they stand for."

"I thought as much." He laughed. "My name is Sam Hutchison; retired professor of History, and general pain in the ass. Maybe I can be of help, maybe not. Why don't you have a seat and tell me why you are so interested in elephants. It's not everyday I run into someone who is comfortable telling me something like that, at least not here in Colorado."

"Thank you, Sam." Alana was happy to spar with the older professor. Jack and Apu were just as pleased to stay out of it. "Are you staying here at the Inn?" Alana asked, though she already figured this was the same man Bob had mentioned to them.

"Yup, this is my annual retreat. I lost my wife three years ago – this was our favorite place to come before Christmas. You know, to get away before the hubbub of the kids droppin' in and all the dinners and presents. Bob and Patty are such nice folks – putting up with an old coot like me – always complainin' about the ways of the world and all. Some say there is nothin' ornerier than an old professor with no one to lecture…" He trailed off. It certainly seemed to Alana that he needed an audience.

Chapter 88

December 20, 2012

Nathan and his men had just left Ida Homberg's cottage. She had not been any help at all, citing that three people had stopped to ask for directions but they had left right away. Nathan suspected she was lying, but didn't hang around to argue with the old woman. It was obvious that Dr. Reese and his friends were gone now. Fresh tire tracks led away from the cottage heading south. Five snow mobiles were now following those tracks.

A few hours later they pulled into the same gas station where Jack, Alana and Apu had met Scott. As much as Nathan's men searched they could not find tracks leaving the gas station. Nathan could not figure out why they had taken to the actual road, since they had avoided the road so carefully up to that point. He radioed the scouts that he had placed in towns all around the area. No one had seen two four-wheelers anywhere. Nathan was scratching his head when his radio buzzed.

"Yes?"

"Sir. Tad, here. I'm in Pine. I did see a truck and trailer go through town a while ago. It had a couple of four wheelers tied down on a trailer. I couldn't tell how many people were in the cab of the truck, though."

"Good. Did you follow them?"

"No. I didn't think they were our guys. The driver didn't fit the description we have. It just occurred to me now that it could be them." He answered through the static.

"Well, go find them, you idiot! Call me as soon as you spot them. I am on my way." Nathan yelled.

Dr. Reese had given him the slip too many times and Nathan's temper was beginning to get the better of him. He was furious. 'How did they get a ride for themselves *and* their four-wheelers? How do they continue to get so damn lucky?' He paced around the parking lot for a couple of minutes, trying to think.

'We will have to go cross country to Pine since we don't have other transportation from here.' He got on the radio again. "Have four more men meet us in Pine. This ends now. I am tired of freezing my ass off trailing them all over the Colorado back woods. I want them dead by morning. Understand?" He screamed at his own men as well as the scout on the other end of the radio.

They loaded back on the snow mobiles, consulted the topo map and took off at full speed. Every passing hour of feeling cold and defeated fueled Nathan's anger. 'I will shoot them myself.' He thought. 'Just one chance to get close and they are dead. I *will* be the most powerful man in the organization, maybe even the world.'

Chapter 89

December 20, 2012

"Funny you should ask about elephants. I just was thinking about them this morning. Must have had another dream." Sam remarked a little absent mindedly, as if he was trying to recall exactly what it was about. "Anyway, that's not what you are interested in, is it. You want to hear about elephants?"

"No... I mean, Yes...I mean, I think so." Alana wasn't so sure she didn't want to hear about Sam's dream. She was having the strangest feeling and from experience - she knew to pay attention. Still she decided that if she got Sam talking, somewhere in the vast information he delivered, he would probably tell them everything they needed to know.

"Having a hard time deciding?" Sam's eyes squinted half shut as he smiled again. "Okay, elephants. Hannibal rode elephants into the Punic wars against the Romans. I'm not sure what they mean all over the world, but they certainly amazed the Roman's the first time they saw them. And I am sure Hannibal was very grateful for their stamina as he crossed the Alps on them."

"Of course!" Apu interrupted. "That is what the elephant means," Apu slapped his forehead with the palm of his hand. "I just figured out the link to the symbol. In some eastern traditions, the elephant is regarded as a highly intelligent and loyal creature. It never leaves the path by itself and it often stands as a symbol for *gratitude*. Elephants experience deep connections, as highly social creatures – they even mourn those who have died. Gratitude is a very sacred quality." He said smacking himself again, lightly on the forehead for not connecting his memories any sooner with the form of an elephant. "I learned that when I was a child."

"Seems your friend here knows more about elephants than I do," Sam said to Alana. "But I agree with gratitude being a sacred thing. I just don't think that you want to get me going on that topic. Gratitude, I mean."

"Actually, I, we would really like to hear what you have to say about gratitude." Alana encouraged.

Sam looked at Jack and Apu and noticed that they really did seem interested. "Okay, but just know that I gave you every opportunity to escape." He laughed as he hinted at being held captive for one of his lectures.

"Gratitude *is* most sacred," Sam began. "It is not a state of subservience as some might interpret it; though humility is an inseparable part of gratitude. But the type of gratitude I speak of does not worship God *as* some might assume, it rather communes with God, which is considered to be far more reverent."

You see, two years ago I had an epiphany. I had already known about the Mayan Calendar and the long count ending date. I am a professor of history and I teach students all the time about ancient civilizations." Three sets of eyebrows shot up at the mention of Mayan Calendar, but they didn't interrupt. "A couple years ago, I was up here at the Inn during the Christmas season again, reading about all the terrible things happening in the world and wondering what the result of such chaos would be. Being a realist, I figured eventually we would annihilate ourselves. I only hoped I would live another ten years before it happened. That night I was sitting in this same chair when it occurred to me that man could evolve past this stage of destruction and violence, and evolve toward one another." Sam was sitting up straight in his chair, relaxed but intent on his speech. He often rubbed his chin and the hair growing there.

"I believe we are in a time of hyper-growth in our *knowledge and abilities* but stunted-growth in our *understanding* of the nature of life and reality. After that night, I began to feel hopeful again. I thought about it for three months. I felt purpose. I knew that I needed to do something to facilitate this evolution in our behavior. I realized that under the right circumstances, we could leap past all the hatred and destruction. During this time, I picked up a newly published book on Mayans, thinking I would include it in my next syllabus. I read it through and was really drawn to the author's conclusions. It was then that I began to believe that our jump could be related to the Mayan time table."

"After a couple more months of investigation, I had another lucid moment. I understood fully that each and every one of us affects the other and that we can join our energies together to make a difference. I knew that my choices counted."

"I began to understand that I might have one of the keys needed to make this shift or jump. I knew what my message was to be.

After I gave in to the dreams, I started working to tie this message into every lesson I taught, no matter what subject I was actually teaching," His voice strayed from its initial excitement and was quiet for a few moments.

Sam was tall and handsome. He had a full beard and mustache which were turning white, and light blue eyes sparkled with intellect and passion. His smile was warm and playful, though he was definitely serious about his task, his message.

"What *is* your message?" Jack went straight to the point. He had been feeling a crunch for time, even though he knew everything had worked out perfectly so far. He thought he may have came across as rude and was about to apologize when Sam went on.

"Yes, of course. Tomorrow is the twenty first… My message is simple. Gratitude." He paused letting the tie into the previous conversation about elephants, sink in, he then continued.

"Gratitude is not just something you should feel when someone gives you something. It is a state of mind, a state of consciousness, if you will. You can not feel gratitude in the past or future. You can think about it outside of present time reality, but you can't experience it. The true experience of gratitude requires several things. It requires you to be in the present moment, completely devoid of past regrets or future projections. When you experience true gratitude as not only an emotion, but as a state of mind, all traces of being a victim, or of self-pity wash away and are replaced with power and connection to God."

"Now please understand that I am not, nor have I ever been, a religious man. As a man who has studied every religion, I find them all to come up faulty. However, I do believe in an intelligent power that permeates the universe and binds it together in a perfectly choreographed dance. I believe in *that* God. And gratitude is not something I feel toward God for blessing me, as much as it is how I feel when I *commune with* God."

"Many people I have met, and I dare say, many of the people who walk the planet, are addicted to the habit of being victims. We are so expert at this behavior that even when we become the victimizer, we are somehow not guilty because of how we have been victimized prior. This habit, behavior and addiction, is in direct contrast to being in a state of gratitude. When you are in gratitude you understand unequivocally that you are connected to God and are part of it. You can not feel a deficit in any part of your being, if you are communing with that *force*. In other words, you have the power to change - everything, but most importantly your mind, or your perceptions. Remember there is no reality, only perceptions of reality." Sam was on a roll.

"Gratitude is also unique in that you can use it as a tool to *connect* to God and to your deepest states of consciousness. What I mean is, when you are feeling victimized, self-pity, worry or fear – all you have to do is think of something you are grateful for and your mind and energy will change. It doesn't matter how "holy" that thing might be. Hell, it could be feeling grateful for your dog or for a meal or for your most recent life lesson. No matter what it is, your state of mind will change immediately. And if you can stick with it, you can enter the *State of Gratitude.*"

"Our paradigms of understanding our circumstances are based on our own *perceptions* of reality, not on actual reality. So all you have are your perceptions, and these are all based on conditioning (your past) and comparison (duality)."

"If you must compare yourself to others, compare down. Compare to people who are less fortunate than you. No matter your place in the world, there is always someone who you perceive to be worse off than you. I do not tell you this so that you can judge or pity others, or excuse yourself from trying to better yourself, your circumstances or your environment. But by comparing down, you can *feel* grateful. Once you begin to *feel* grateful, you can have access to higher states of gratitude consciousness and realities. It is a powerful tool."

"You may have heard this before – 'like attracts like,' which of course means that people attract to themselves others who are similar to themselves. But it also works with emotions and thoughts. For instance if you are always worrying about not having enough money; you will attract more circumstances that will *allow* you to worry more about not having enough money. It is hard for most people to understand this and even if they do, they have a hard time kicking the worrying habit. The key to moving past worry is to be in a complete state of gratitude; which, by the way, will attract, to you, more circumstances that will *allow* you to feel more gratitude. This is very important in the shifting of our fear-based, dualistic (us versus them) existence."

"Without duality, there is unity. Gratitude is one of unity's faces. Gratitude is part of the *experience* of unity. Another simplified way

to put it is – what you think about expands. Ponder that for a
moment." Sam stopped speaking, figuring that some think-time would
be a relief. He had been going full speed ahead since Jack asked about
his message. Apu wondered if Sam was always swift in his speech, and
similarly in his life; or was this rush of thought only due to their tight
time frame. Alana was working hard to comprehend and integrate
Sam's lecture.

Jack applied it to the feelings of grief he and his wife fell into
after the death of their son. He began to understand how she had
stayed in that state so completely, whereas he went on with his life
searching for an answer, grateful for whatever lesson could be gleaned
from the bliss of their baby's life, albeit brief. In light of everything, he
realized that his son's death had created that search and had been the
catalyst to ignite the whole chain of events that followed. He was
grateful for the baby, his job and his love of learning and he used that
appreciation to move on, to search for meaning in tragedy.

Alana now knew that knowing *of* something and the
experience of it, were entirely different. During a couple of her recent
meditations, she had actually *experienced* gratitude similar to what Sam
was explaining.

After what Sam considered to be a sufficient pause, he spoke
again, anxious to finish. "Gratitude is a tool, a power and a state of
consciousness all at once. It creates miracles in our lives and expands
our hearts to the point where we can invite God in. I urge you, as I
have urged my students: embrace gratitude in every way that you can,"
Sam ended. Having rested his case, he grew silent. He had delivered his
message – the 7th key.

It was so quiet in the room, without forethought or mention;
each of them had gone into meditation. They wanted to experience this
gratitude – now. They each one began with one specific thing there
were really thankful for, then let the feeling of gratitude spread to other
things. As they did so, each of their hearts expanded. Gratitude
embraced them, lifting them, empowering them and then reassuring
them. Smiles sprang up on each face and joy filled the room. It was
wonderful and quite euphoric. They stayed in that state for more than
20 minutes, each aware of the other, but more aware of the *one* power
that brought the universe into existence. Each one personally
experienced gratitude as a state of mind and of being. Every new key
built on the prior and gave them amazing joy and power as their
connection to God became a real and tangible communion.

Chapter 90

December 20, 2012

Abdul Rahman Qadeer's resolve faltered for a moment as he drove down the dirt road to the missile site. They had worked so hard and paid so much for this opportunity. Many had died. Now they would win. The infidel Israelis and Americans were about to pay, and pay with their lives. He and his brothers would spend eternity in Paradise. He wondered what it would be like to have 72 virgins at his beck and call. He was ready to leave the poverty and violence behind.

Abdul looked in the rear view mirror at the large, heavy metal case that contained the weapons-grade Plutonium. It was a perfect plan. They would take out Jerusalem and Washington, D.C. both in one moment. The fallout would cripple, if not kill, both of their governments. The nations would fall. Abdul was carrying the final piece that would guarantee the mission's success. 'The arrogant Americans will fall along with the thieving Israelis.'

He had suffered from the fighting all of his life, and lost two brothers to the battle to keep the godless from stealing their resources and land. 'This will stop them. No more of our people will have to die.' Just as the American's had done in World War II to the Japanese, Abdul would now do the same to them. Only these missiles were better and more advanced. 'American ingenuity and technology was to be admired, but their greed for power would lead to their demise,' Abdul's passion had reached its height.

As he drove along, rejoicing and preemptively celebrating American deaths, and the final blow to Israel, he felt a sharp pain shoot through his chest. He grabbed at his throat, for a brief moment, thinking he was having a heart attack. Then a strange and completely alien thought entered his mind, like the enemy infiltrating through barricaded lines of defense. The thought was that he and the American's and the Israelis were from the same family, having the same father. 'If you kill them, you kill your own brothers,' he heard in his head. He shook his head violently, trying desperately to clear the voice and the message from his mind. In the next moment, he had to actually slow the car down. Deep sadness and loss swept through his being.

Again his chest tightened and his breathing became labored. He looked around and tried to speak louder than the voice inside, "What the hell is happening to me?"

As he pulled the old, beat up Mercedes off to the side of the dirt road, he saw horrible scenes of death and devastation all around him, mangled bodies lying everywhere. It was not only the Israelis and the Americans. He saw his own father and his once beautiful mother, his beloved brothers – all dead and rotting along the road. Abdul's body shook viciously; he had to open his door to vomit onto the ground. The repeated convulsions exhausted him.

Abdul finally slid out of the car and tried to walk, desperate to erase the grotesque and heartbreaking images. He wiped his eyes and stumbled around the car, trying to get a hold of his emotions. "It is not true!" He insisted to himself aloud. "I will not weaken now. We have worked too hard. I will not fail my family. I will not fail Allah." He prayed to Allah for strength and forgiveness for such a lapse in faith. After walking around for a few more minutes, he got back in the car, clenched his jaw and sped on down the road, stirring up a cloud of dust along the way.

Abdul hoped that whatever had just happened did not materialize again. He gritted his teeth, determined to block out anything else that could distract him. He pushed the accelerator harder. 'Less than eight miles to go,' he thought to himself. 'Allah will be with me. It was just the plutonium making me sick, I'm sure of it."

Chapter 91

December 20, 2012

Melvin had fallen asleep. The three-hour bus ride and the monotony of the road had lulled him into closing his eyes and letting go. Life pictures flashed before him as he fell into the abyss of gratitude that had overtaken him in the last couple of days.

As he bought his ticket and waited for the bus, the intense thoughts of how things had changed for him distracted his every task. He had been on the verge of death and longed for release. Now he was alive again. Melvin possessed little money, but here he was - on his way to see his only sister, whom he hadn't connected with in years. It was the 20th of December and he was going to arrive at Dorothy's early. The postal season had been light this year, so after a quick consult with his supervisor, he had thankfully been laid off nearly a week early. Though the job had been short it had been good for Melvin and had made him just enough money to buy the bus ticket.

The more Melvin thought of all the things that he had to be grateful for, the more his heart felt as if it was expanding. He felt empowered, more connected to God and to his beloved wife and son. He smiled even in his groggy state.

In the next moment, Melvin heard a loud crack of thunder invade his slumber. He startled and looked out the window. The rain began to fall in large pellets beating into the side of the Greyhound bus. The wind howled through the trees and the lightening severed the dark sky.

Melvin felt something brewing in the air, and the storm was only part of it. It was as if the thunder was trying to get his attention. His heart jumped to his throat; it was difficult to swallow.

The bus driver turned on the radio, perhaps sensing that something was approaching. At first, Melvin couldn't make out the words, between the static and the noise of the now incessant thunder and rain. As he strained, he could just make out snippets of news.

"North Korean leader Kim Jong II was assassinated early this morning. His train exploded in a fiery crash killing

everyone on board… North Korean citizens react by storming the
borders – some compare it to the fall of the Berlin Wall…

President elect Richardson, while in New York for the
dedication of the new World Trade Center, cautions China about
assisting the North Koreans, insisting that they have been given the
freedom to decide their own future.

The Dow plummets 3,500 points – largest drop in
history as the threat of war with North Korea frightens investors,
internationally."

Melvin felt the turmoil engulfing the globe. He tried to hold
onto the hope and gratitude of only a few moments ago. Just before
the bus driver turned off the radio, Melvin heard:

A freak winter tornado seen in Kansas, as the latest
storm-front whips through the mid-western states heading directly
for the east coast.

Melvin leaned back. 'Such chaos and confusion. Just get me
through this!' he thought as he leaned his head back again. Outside, the
miles passed by as the bus made its way through the blackness on its
way to Wisconsin.

Chapter 92

December 20, 2012

Marie was gathering her things from her desk, getting ready to go home, when her computer monitor went black. 'That's weird. My screen-saver's not set to go black,' she thought to herself.

Just before she had gotten up from her chair, she was reflecting on all of the amazing changes that had been happening and the overpowering feelings of gratitude that followed. Marie was quite consumed in her thoughts. It took several seconds to register that something might actually be wrong with the computer systems.

She sat back down, wondering if she should stay and try to fix the problem. She punched a couple of keys on the keyboard, nothing happened. Marie stood up and looked over the cubical wall to see if anyone else was experiencing the same problem. As she looked, she could see all the other terminals were black too, accompanied by confused faces and murmurs of possible causes.

The boss came out to inquire, but immediately saw that everyone was having the same difficulty. "It's that damn virus!" he mumbled. The power lights were on, but even with all of the button-pushing, the computer screens remained dark. Marie shrugged as did her co-workers. She got ready to go, grabbing her coat and purse. "I'm sure they will have it all fixed by morning," she commented to another woman, who immediately agreed.

As Marie walked out of the glass office door, she heard the unmistakable scream of emergency and police vehicles in all directions. The hair on the back of her neck stood on end as she felt something really wrong was happening somewhere, maybe everywhere. She rushed to her car, started the engine and made her way out onto the highway. Her attention turned from herself to her children as she turned on the radio. The announcer was cautioning everyone to avoid certain routes, as there was a massive pile-up on one of the highways. This news relieved Marie of some of the anxiety that had taken hold.

More curious and disturbing though, was the news regarding an extremely pervasive and destructive new "Grim Reaper" computer virus that seemed to be infecting computer systems world-wide, causing millions of computer monitors to go black. 'This is not good, definitely not good.' Marie thought to herself. She tried hard to remember the gratitude she had been feeling so recently, as she impatiently made her way home.

Chapter 93

December 20, 2012

Chuck had spent the day at the hospital with Jason again. They played cards, read books, went to the cafeteria for lunch and overall had a pleasant visit. June had not stirred at all. The doctor came in to check on her incision and to assess if there were any changes in her condition, but he did not stay long.

Soon after lunch Chuck could see that Jason was getting sleepy, so he took one of the extra blankets and snuggled Jason up in the chair. "Why don't you take a little nap, I will stay awake and keep an eye on your mom, okay," he suggested. Jason thought it was a good idea and soon drifted off.

Chuck sat in the other chair and looked at June's face. She seemed like a peaceful woman. Her bruises and cuts were healing and the lines around her eyes and mouth had smoothed out in the past couple days. Chuck wished he could convey to her that everything would be fine, no matter if she was able to come back to them or not. He sincerely hoped that she would revive, for Jason's sake, but if she could not, Chuck wanted her to know that Jason would be cared for and loved.

Just as Chuck considered those thoughts, two things happened simultaneously. First, he was sure that the corners of June's mouth turned up slightly in a subtle smile. In the same moment, Chuck felt as if he was immersed in warm water that filled him from the inside out. He felt unbelievably grateful for such an opportunity - to care for these people. As his heart stretched to hold all the emotion rushing in, he reached up his right hand and touched June's. She would wake up, he knew it. She just needed time to heal.

Chuck looked over at Jason and smiled. 'Everything is going to be okay,' he thought to himself. Chuck wanted to stay in the feelings he was experiencing as long as possible. But the next set of events caused him to question everything.

Suddenly there was a loud beeping noise. It took a second for Chuck to realized that it was June's set of monitors registering something wrong. In the next minute, he was being pushed aside and told to take the boy and leave the room, as a host of nurses swarmed in around June's body. Jason had been roused by the noise and commotion and when he realized what was happening he started to whimper. In no time Chuck scooped Jason up in his arms. He held him tight as he soothingly told him it would be okay, though in that minute, Chuck was really not sure. Jason refused to leave his mother's side, so without permission, they stood against the far wall and prayed that all the good luck of the last few days had not expired and that there was still one more miracle left for them both.

Chapter 94

December 20, 2012

Ben had been excited to have lunch with Catherine Woods and her children. He got ready early and went to buy a small gift for each of the children. It was Christmas and the perfect time for gifts and, after all, they had given him such a wonderful gift.

He arrived at the restaurant and waited at the same table that the family had occupied the day before. He couldn't help but smile as he felt such overwhelming gratitude for the changes that were happening in his life.

As the meeting time approached, he grew a little nervous. It was just about then when a waiter came over and gave him the message. "Mr. Bradley. We just got a call from a Ms. Catherine Woods. She said to give you her deepest apologies, but one of the children was not feeling well and she would not be able to meet you for lunch."

"Oh…" Ben's heart sank. "Thank you," he said to the man.

"Would you like to order sir?"

"Huh?" Ben was lost in his thoughts, immediately losing the intense feeling he had just been immersed in. Finally he realized what the waiter was asking him.

"Oh, yes. I will have the usual, Frank. Thank you," he said absent mindedly. Frank, the waiter went off to put in the order, thinking that Mr. Bradley, who had always been distracted with business was now distracted by something else.

Ben just sat there blankly for a couple of minutes, disappointed, but even more confused. He thought for sure that meeting with this family was destined. He ate his lunch in silence and then headed down the street toward the subway.

Ben pulled out his cell phone, called information and asked for Catherine Woods, there were several. He was willing to try each one but realized that he should first try the one that was closest. The operator obliged. Of course it may not be her, but he figured it was worth a try. He was already going in the right direction and wanted to deliver his gifts for the children. Ben decided to also stop and get

Catherine something. He picked up a beautiful bunch of fresh cut flowers at the corner vendor.

When he arrived at the correct address, he rang the doorbell and waited. No one came. He rang the bell again and also knocked this time. Still no answer. He tried one last time, feeling desperate and hating that all too familiar feeling of emptiness creeping in. There was no sound coming from the house.

Feeling dejected and foolish, Ben turned and began the journey back toward the subway and home. He questioned how all the wonderful feelings had melted away and left him so empty. As Ben walked up the street, he was mystified at how quickly things seem to change.

Chapter 95

December 20, 2012

Nathan and his men stopped to consult the map. It wasn't too much further. He was cold and angry and ready for this assignment to be over. His radio squawked.

"Yes?"

"We found them," announced the stoic voice on the other end. "They have checked into the Bells & Whistle Bed & Breakfast. What do you want me to do, sir?"

"Just watch them. I will be there within the hour. If they go anywhere, follow them, but wait for me to take them. Do you understand? And Don't Lose Them!" Nathan yelled the last command. He put the radio inside his coat and revved the engine on his snow mobile. They took off again spitting snow and exhaust in every direction.

Chapter 96

December 20, 2012

    The B&B's study was still quiet as the four souls sitting around came out of meditation with a refreshed sense of peace and tranquility. It permeated their beings. Jack smiled and spoke at last, telling Sam of their whole adventure, the danger and what they were attempting to do. He didn't need to convey the urgency, as Sam seemed to already understand.

    "While I was in the pure state of gratitude, I saw a mountain that seemed special or sacred." Apu said. "It feels like a clue; might there be something like that close by? I think we need to go there next." he asked Sam.

    "Maybe... There is ancient Indian land several miles south of here. I have been there twice and each time was a very moving experience. I believe *that* may be where you need to be tomorrow – the twenty-first day of December, 2012." Sam affirmed.

    "Can you tell us how to get there?" Jack asked.

    "I can do better than that. I will take you there."

    "Excellent." Jack didn't want to waist any time getting lost in the woods.

    Alana was not looking forward to going back out into the cold but she was anxious to go to this mountain, for she too had seen it during her meditation. She actually felt as if part of herself was there already, waiting for her. She didn't understand how that could be, but was excited to find out. "Will we be able to get there on the four-wheelers?"

    "Yes, that is actually the best way. But I don't have one. Do you have room for one more?" Sam replied.

    "You can ride with me." Apu answered. "When I saw the mountain, it felt as if there is an energy building there already. But I have also felt another vibration out in the world, one that is not so pleasant, and it has gotten stronger since this morning. We should get going right away." The concern in his usually calm voice was clear.

    "I agree." Sam said. "I can go up to my room and pack up some warm clothing. I will bring some extra blankets; do you all need anything else? It will probably get quite cold tonight, and it looks as if we will be spending it outdoors."

"I could use some extra warmth," Apu took Sam up on his offer as Alana eagerly nodded. Sam smiled and started for the stairs to gather his things.

On instinct, Jack peeked out the front window, barely pushing the curtain to the side. He saw movement off in the distance. There were several cars coming to a stop along the quiet road about 500 meters away. "They are here!" Jack whispered. "How are we going to get out without them seeing us?"

Sam yelled back, having not made it all they way up the stairs yet, "Remember, everyone, no matter what happens, stay in a state of gratitude and in the present moment. It is most important. I think the opposition is getting stronger, angrier and closer."

"Me too." Apu confirmed, grateful to not be the only one bothered by their presence.

It was dusk as the sun began to set early. Jack remembered that tomorrow, the twenty-first of December was also the winter solstice and the shortest day of the year.

Bob came around the corner and nearly ran into Jack peeking out the front window. It didn't take long to explain that there were some unkind people after them and that they needed some help to escape. Sam explained briefly to Bob, that he needed to go too. "They will need my help to find where they are going." Bob didn't really understand, but he knew and trusted Sam.

"Go up stairs and get your things. I will keep watch." Robert informed as he took up the look-out, where Jack had been.

Soon they were all back downstairs, with their things. "Your four-wheelers are parked in back, under our little carport. But they will hear you if you start them up." Robert said.

"Don't worry; we have been in this situation before. We will wheel them down the hill toward the river and take off from there." Jack reported with a smile, though he doubted it would work a second time. Then he reminded himself to stay in that state of gratitude. He used things he was grateful for as a tool to not fall into the trap of worry and fear. He was definitely grateful they had gotten this far, so it wasn't too difficult.

They quickly thanked their hosts and slipped out the back door, into the trees. In the carport they piled their things high on the back rack and tied them down. Jack and Apu took the handle bars and followed Sam down the hill, working hard not to let the vehicles get away from them and tumble ahead. When they reached the bottom, Jack and Apu were panting and sweating. Alana had been the last one to reach the river, staying behind to see if the men milling around the cars on the road, heard or saw them escape. They seemed to get away clean again. That fact helped her remain grateful, and surprisingly calm.

When Alana caught up with the others, they all climbed on board and were ready to start the engines -- they suddenly heard a high pitched buzzing sound. Alana's heart skipped a beat and Apu's throat tightened as they all looked up the river. Far up on the west side, were five snow mobiles headed in their direction. Immediately they each knew they were in grave danger. If they didn't get moving the snow mobiles would be on top of them in only a few minutes. They started their engines and took off.

They went south along the river. Sam had offered to drive, since he knew where they were going. He quite naturally took the lead. Darkness descended heavily upon the group like a suffocating blanket. Imminent danger crowded in faster than ever before. It became a true challenge to stay in that much needed state of gratitude let alone remember any of the other keys.

Chapter 97

December 20, 2012

Nathan and his men were closing in on their destination in Pine, Colorado. They had come down the Platte River as a more direct route. Just when they were around the final bend before town, Nathan called ahead on his radio. He was told that Dr. Reese was still at the B&B. Nathan started mentally planning ways to get them out; he didn't want any witnesses. It needed to be a clean job or he would be the one mopping up the mess afterward.

Just when they rounded the bend and were breathing sighs of relief, Nathan spotted something moving up the river. He pulled out his binoculars, stopped the snow mobile and peered into the distance.

"You Idiots!" he yelled into his radio. "They're getting away!" At the same time, he punched the accelerator on the snow mobile. "No, Jack Reese, you will not escape me this time. Not again." He said out loud, though over the roar of the engines, no one could hear him.

Nathan saw the four-wheelers picking up speed. He fearlessly pursued them, speeding along the river bank, working to stay in the snow and yet not slip into the river. Slowly, he was gaining on his target. The snow mobile was clearly faster in the snow. Unfortunately, they are not worth much without the snow, which became a harsh reality as the four-wheelers crossed the river.

'There must be a shallow spot.' Nathan thought. He pulled out his binoculars and scanned the river up and down for options. He didn't see any.

Infuriated, Nathan was forced to stop at the crossing. He got a final glimpse of them looking back just before they sped up the hill, into the trees and out of sight. He thought of shooting them from where he was stranded, but knew his revolver would not do the job on a moving target. He'd need a hi-powered rifle to make that shot. His men finally caught up to him.

"Is there another way to cross this damn river?" he exploded. One of the men seemed to know the area a little better. "There is a cattle bridge about five miles up the road. We can cross there."

"Lead the way, and Hurry!"

Chapter 98

December 20, 2012

Sam continued to lead them up the hill and finally down the other side. Once again they were astonished at their good fortune, knowing full well it was much more than luck. There was an energy leading them and it was getting stronger as they progressed into the mountains. Maybe it was just their proximity to the final key. Whatever the reason, they could feel it pulling them, drawing them to the next location, to the mountain they had each imagined.

Jack thought about the final symbol and corresponding key. He wondered if there would be someone just standing in the woods waiting to deliver the final message. 'Stranger things have already happened.' He had been questioning for some time if either he, Alana or Apu were the 100th human. Again and again he grappled with the same loaded questions: 'Is it one of us or could it be one of the gatekeepers that will be the last person to feel the influence of the keys, adopt the principles and be the final straw breaking the back of duality, desperation, war, loneliness and limitation? Or will it be someone else entirely, someone we don't yet know about, someone who is getting the messages through some other means?' He didn't know the answers to his own questions. 'We may never know who the last person is to say, *Yes*.' He thought, but could feel things were close at hand, whoever it was. The air itself seemed to tingle with energy of an unknown origin.

While Jack was asking such questions of himself, Apu could feel the other side of the struggle, equally as intense. He could sense the strength and determination of those who did not want to change and were invested in the way things are and have been. They would stop at nothing, believing they are right. 'The energy of darkness is as strong as I have ever felt it. And yet the energy of Light is equally as strong. The conflict is heightened. The end is near. I can feel it so clearly. The age of duality is reaching its most critical point.' Apu prayed that Unity would prevail.

A cold, darkness had fallen upon them completely and Sam was very happy to be out of sight of their pursuers, even if the darkness hindered his own vision as well. He knew that he was following a different light, the light in his heart.

As the stars began to bespeckle the sky, Alana could hear the voices in her mind, in the language of the ancients, the language of her visionary self, the mysterious language she had been trying to find throughout her career. It played over and over in her head, causing her spine to straighten and her breathing to deepen. The words gave her comfort and a strange feeling of power. Her cloudy and dark view of their ride suddenly cleared, in a miraculous way. The formerly darkened landscape took on a glow that she was now sure had always been there. She was just finally able to see it.

'It's alive!' she thought. 'The whole planet, all the plants, the animals and now the ground, all of it. It's alive!' she was amazed that she could feel it and see it with her own wakeful eyes. Her breathing quickened and goose bumps rose on her arms and neck. The night air became electric.

Apu could see it too, and much more. His grandfather seemed to be behind every tree and rock on the road ahead. And not only his grandfather, but he could vaguely make out many, many more beings. Some perhaps he recognized others he did not know at all. But they all knew him, knew them, of this he was sure. Apu understood that they were all waiting for them, waiting for this moment in time.

'They are the Mayans!' The thought hit Apu with force. He began to turn, trying to see their faces. His eyes were wide in amazement.

Sam continued on toward their destination, not stopping for anything. His mission, he knew now was extremely important. He was to get them there. The rest was up to God and all the souls that had worked so hard to bring humanity to this place in time and space. He knew the end was close at hand.

Chapter 99

December 21, 2012

Abdul had arrived at the missile site with the plutonium. He was greeted by his other freedom fighters. This would be their finest hour. He did not mention the relapse he had endured on the road there. It was long gone and now, surrounded by his comrades, he knew they would see the destruction of their enemies.

The first instrument of death was an atomic bomb, now fully operational and being loaded onto a mid-size Lear Jet, which had multiple stops before it reached its American target, the White House. The second instrument was a series, six in all, of automobiles that were loaded with bombs and ready to drive directly into the Knesset in Jerusalem, Israel's parliament building.

There could be no mistakes. They had this single opportunity. The autos had to be ready, but out of site from the Israeli police and the jet had to make the trans-Atlantic flight. Their jamming devices had been tested and proven. Everything was set. Both had to strike the correct coordinates at exactly the same time. The timing was extremely critical.

The jet took off. Only the wait remained now, until everything and everyone would be in position. The atmosphere of the underground bunker was tense. They knew that this was it. The stakes were the highest possible. But they believed in their reward after death. They were not afraid of death and hoped to be martyred for Allah. Abdul could think of no better way to die, then to take out so many of the infidels. He paced around the room, trying to be patient, not wanting to upset the process, but he was anxious. Only hours to go, mere hours to wait.

Abdul also knew he was tense with anticipation. 'We are so close. I want to do it, before something happens that could stop it, stop me, like what happened on the road.' With that thought he left the room and decided to find the men's room. He threw-up what little remained in his stomach. His nerves were completely frayed. He was in the bathroom another hour as he prayed for faith and strength.

* *

Nathan was pushing the snow mobile to its top speed. He too could feel the energy. Everyone in the organization knew the prophecies. He knew he must succeed. Dr. Reese and his friends must be stopped. No one in the organization ever really knew what would happen if the prophecies were actually realized. It was certain that their present way of life would cease to exist. His own power, and the power and influence of the Veni Victus would be obsolete and anarchy was sure to follow.

Something *was* happening, that was for sure. Nathan could almost hear the Director in his own head, and Charles and every other director and leader in the organization for thousands of years. They were all screaming at him, pushing him onward, insisting that he not fail.

"I will not fail you. I will not!" He yelled out, clinching his jaw and grinding his teeth together. A few weeks ago, he was third in line, and only remotely responsible to assist in this mission. Now, it was all up to him. 'I will do it to not disappoint anyone who came before me.'

The cold air cut into the skin on his face and caused tears to roll down his cheeks. That was his excuse for the steady stream that had begun to flow into his scarf. Nathan knew he had to be getting close to the crossing where the four-wheelers disappeared. They couldn't be more than forty or forty-five minutes ahead of them.

The hatred for Reese that he carried in his heart grew, was somehow compounded by the increased energy around him.

"There, there are the tracks!" He yelled to the others, pointing to the left. He made a sharp turn onto the tracks and followed them, pushing onward, his resolve set. His mind trained on one objective. He glanced back at the four snow mobiles behind him. 'We will not fail.'

* *

Abdul entered the main room again; dingy white walls seemed to close in around him. He nearly turned to go back to the bathroom when he heard the voice on the speaker squawk, "We have just passed check point four, ETA is two hours. We are on target. Be ready!"

A cheer rose up from his brothers, but it died quickly as their fate weighed heavy on each of their minds. Abdul felt a new hatred build in his heart. His doubts subsided as he sat with the others to wait for the final word.

Chapter 100

December 21, 2012

Jack, Alana, Apu and Sam traveled over snow and rock, through a frigid river, dense forest and open fields. It seemed, at times, that they would never arrive. Jack figured it was long past midnight and if it weren't for Alana's body heat behind him and the excitement ahead, he would have frozen solid by now. Everyone else was feeling much the same but still they pressed on.

Not long after, what Jack considered, their possible freezing point - something in the atmosphere shifted. As the group crested the tree line, Sam looked back to Jack and yelled, "We have just crossed the boundary onto the sacred land." Apu and Alana had heard him as well, but they already knew. There was a dense fog moving into the valley before them. Pine and Aspen trees thickened the landscape below, giving off a crisp, clean fragrance. The half moon now reached high in the sky, but the fog muted its illumination, causing a hazy glow to blanket the area.

Sam slowed down. The barely detectable path ahead of them now seemed clear. He pulled the four-wheeler off to the side and stopped. He turned off the engine. Jack followed his lead. As both engines were silenced, the air around them seemed to hang with unspoken words. Nothing moved, not one sound echoed through the valley for long moments. Off in the distance the unmistakable howl of coyotes cut the silence and allowed the travelers to breathe; strangely, it was a sigh of relief.

Sam and Apu dismounted only a second before Jack and Alana. Alana was momentarily distracted from the amazing scene unfolding before them, as she tried to get circulation back into the lower part of her body, allowing her legs to work properly. The guys were feeling the same temporary diversion. When Jack was sure his legs would carry him, he instinctively took Alana's hand and slowly started up the mountain path toward the summit.

Apu and Sam mindfully fell into step behind Jack and Alana. The air was sweet, reminding them of a spring morning filled with lilac and honeysuckle. This essence struck Alana as quite astonishing - in the middle of such a cold winter night. Even the cold had lessened. As she inhaled, the air was crisp and fresh, no longer bitter cold. She absorbed the smells deep into her lungs and felt newness flow into her blood and into every cell in her body.

Sam knew he no longer needed to guide the small group, there was an opened path cutting the mist, stretching out before them. He knew Jack, the Zero, belonged in front.

Jack could see the path wind its way up to the top of a tall rounded mountain. He couldn't quite make out the top, but he could sense it. It beckoned to him. "The power of this place is amazing, overwhelming. It is like a dream." He mumbled to himself.

Unexpectedly, they detected a soft beat in the air. Jack stopped silently questioning its source, 'The wind in the trees, thunder in the distance?' they could all feel it in the ground, in the air, in their bodies. At first it seemed like a low primal beat – of drums maybe, but soon it carried with it a full-bodied melody, accompanied by a deep rumble within the earth. It was beautiful, and it drew them onward. They had no idea where it was coming from. It just seemed to fill the air.

Gradually, their *eyes* were opened. They could see them in the moonlight. Everywhere, even beyond the horizon, were the glowing apparitions of thousands of people - ghosts, souls unencumbered by bodies. They intrinsically understood that these souls, these ghosts, were the cause of the heavy mist and cadence surrounding them.

They felt only happiness when they saw them. It was as if all of the souls were sending them their energy, their love, their encouragement, their power. It was an awe-inspiring effect. Apu and Jack immediately recognized many of the faces to be Mayan. Alana poked Jack, "Do you see them too?" She whispered. He turned his head a little in her direction, but without redirecting his gaze, "Yes," was his muted response.

Jack was overwhelmed by the attention being bestowed upon them by the beings that were everywhere now. 'Angels, ghosts, dead Mayans?' Whoever or whatever they were; they were silently applauding them. They were not physically clapping their hands, but Jack felt their adoration none-the-less. They each felt completely humbled.

Jack clenched Alana's hand as they slowly began walking again, following the long path to the top of the mountain, surrounded by a multitude of beings, young and old, Mayan, Egyptian, Native, African, Asian, and every other type of being who had ever walked the earth.

There were even some that Jack was not quite sure *where* or *when* they lived.

All of the way along the path, the adoration and adulation continued from the throngs of spirit people. Jack tried to dismiss such food for his ego from his own mind, 'I just needed to find out why my infant son had died. I'm not anything special.' But as soon as the thoughts came, he heard another voice, "You are made in the image of God, you are special. You are the Zero." This completely surprised him. He paused in his step, and looked around to see who had answered him.

Almost immediately he saw a young man standing beside a tree some distance a head of him. Jack was drawn to him from something deep down inside his gut. He swallowed hard and his body began to react in strange and unexplained ways to the sight of this man. Jack gently released Alana's hand and walked ever so slowly, though with complete deliberation toward the being.

Jack stopped abruptly, directly in front of him. The man did not have a corporeal body, but his spirit was so strong, that Jack could clearly make out his delicate features. Jack looked deep into the young man's eyes and immediately knew him. This was his son, grown. The young man smiled at Jack. Jack cried out as the emotions hit him squarely in the chest, and overcame him. Jack's whole body tingled – and he was aware his soul and flesh were separate – but one. He fell to his knees and cried out again, "Jacky!"

Alana's hands came up to her mouth as she nearly screamed out too. Tears ran down her cheeks. Apu came up behind Alana and touched her lightly on the back. He too was tearful. Sam, only one step behind, wiped his own face as the final Gatekeeper began to speak.

"You are special, Father. You said *yes* at every turn. You answered the call. You braved the dangers. You would not stop until you had the answers you sought. Now you are here, and I am here with you. I have always been with you, encouraging you to fulfill your destiny. And you have Father, you have!" Jack looked into his precious son's face. He wanted to embrace him, but knew he could not. Jack's state of gratitude was complete.

Jacky turned and addressed Alana, Apu and Sam. "You, each one of you are exceptional. You are here because you chose to be here, because, no matter the danger, distraction or difficulty; you would not walk away from your destiny. It is every person's destiny to be here this night." He paused for only a moment, not wishing to give the others a chance to doubt what he said. "The final symbol from the Wall of Hunab Ku has a double meaning; it combines the sign for the Sun and also the *Son*." He smiled allowing his words to sink in as his father somehow managed to make his way to his feet. "The Sun represents God and is the giver of all life on earth, and the provider of *unconditional* love. The sun is a symbol of deity, appearing all around world. The ancient Indian Vedas referred to the sun's radiance as the supreme truth. It gives light, warmth and energy to each and every object below, forsaking none, for all are *one* to the Sun.

The second part of the mark is the actual sign of Hunab Ku. This Mayan symbol means: *One source of energy*. It represents the passage linking two worlds, the joining of opposites. Only through love can opposites transcend. Together they are joined in this moment – this moment of transition, this moment in time - when we transcend our bonds of duality and become One in Life and Love. The final key is Love – unconditional love, and reverence for each other as we come together in complete Unity."

Jacky, raised his arms out wide and high. Everything stopped, the music, the coyotes, even the crickets ceased their song. Soon, all of the other beings raised their arms out wide. There was a collective intake of breath, as the multitudes proceeded to do a Sun Salutation – raising arms wide, then high over-head, they pressed their palms together and while exhaling, brought those hands down in front of their faces to rest directly before their hearts, as if in prayer. The next motion brought each being to bow low, to Jack, to Alana, and to Apu. Finally, in unison they fell to their knees in reverence and gratitude.

Jacky knelt before his father. Jack finally understood how he was the Zero, he had conceived the child and in turn the child had brought him here. The beginning and the end wrapped into one - reflecting the perfection of life.

Love, the strongest power in the Universe, rippled through the crowd. It was the first perfect moment to exist in such a large crowd in the history of mankind. After the wave immersed them completely, they stood silently for what seemed an eternity.

Then Jack lowered his arms and looked up the mountain. All heads turned in the direction Jack was looking. He realized there was more to be done this night. With Jacky silently walking at Jack's side, they all began to make their way up to the very pinnacle of the mountain. Apu recognized another spirit. He saw Eligio, who clearly looked happy and proud. Jack and Alana laughed joyously when they

saw him fall in line behind them. As they walked, the music began again
and the crowd began to sing in an ancient language that everyone
seemed to understand - they sang in unison. The sound was angelically
harmonized, and its energy intensified as they ascended to the top of
the mountain, louder and more powerful than before.

As they reached the top, Sam stepped back and into the
crowd. Jack, Alana and Apu held hands and looked around them. The
mist had cleared at this elevation, revealing a stunning panorama of
nature and light stretched out as far as they could see. They could feel
the energy of the planet herself; her blessings seemed to envelope
them. No one even tried to still the flow of tears that ran down their
faces. The three stood, surrounded by the multitudes; the singing and
rhythms filled every molecule of space from the earth to heavens
above.

Out of the blue, Alana saw her Visionary Self step through the
crowd and come to the edge of the mass of souls. She went up to her
and smiled broadly, though she was shocked and overcome with
emotion. This beautiful woman that looked so much like Alana,
dropped to her knees before her, touching her head to the ground, in
respect and acknowledgement. Then she rose.

"You made it, I knew you would. You struggled with your
fears, but you continued to allow your visions to guide you. You bring
the female elements of water and air together, from the Sky, to our
union." Alana understood her words, the language of the ancients, the
same language that had played in her head for so many years. It was
Alana's turn, and with a glowing heart, she knelt down to this ancient
being. She wept in gratitude and love. Alana understood that this
woman was her future, though truly on this day, in this moment, there
was no past or future – there was only now; the all-powerful Now. The
being faded back into the crowd. Alana rose to her feet, looked over to
Jack and smiled warmly. He had become part of her Now and she
trusted that they would be together for a very long time. He came over
and put his arm around her, and whispered into her ear "I love you."

"I know." They giggled, then she finished, "I love you, too."

Apu, witnessed Alana's destiny come full circle. He was
overtaken with emotion and the connection to each of his companions.
As he turned, sensing a new aura, he met and locked eyes with his
grandfather. He smiled and walked over to him. Apu put his hands
together in front of his chest and then to his forehead as he bowed and
then knelt down and kissed the man's ghostly feet. Through his tears

Apu thanked him for everything he had taught him. When Apu rose to
his feet, Danvir Chohan repeated the same gesture, a reciprocal
honoring and giving of thanks a physical Namaste. "You bring your
connection to the earth with you always. You remain stable as a Rock,
no matter the situation, knowing always your true being is inside. And
you have brought us to *this* Rock. Thank you, my young grandson. You
brought me here as surely as I brought you."

Though time seemed to stand still, they *all* knew dawn was
upon them and, save for Alana, Jack and Apu, they also *all* knew what
was to happen next. Jacky began to speak to everyone at once, his voice
somehow carried across the miles to the vast amount of souls that
continued to gather on every side of the mountain.

The angelic chanting continued – like a million monks in perfect
harmony in the sanctuary of the greatest cathedral.

Jack, the Zero, was moved to speak above the music "It is
time to connect with *Everyone* else. The 100th human approaches. It is
time to reach out to all of those who are actually *in* body. It is the end
of time and the beginning of time."

Alana, Jack and Apu again clasped hands and held on tight.
Soul after soul joined in the link; though their hands were not solid the
connection was impermeable. As the sky ever so slightly began to
brighten, a vacuum of silence fell.

Then in the next moment it happened. Nathan reached the
outside rim of the massive group of souls encompassing the
mountainside, as he did he felt the tremendous power assembled and
saw the beings slowly surround him. Defensively, he fumbled with his
gun. But, he was astonished by the aura of the gathered mass. He heard
the music – the sweet voices in the air . His gun slipped from his
loosened grip and was instantly covered with snow. The song – that
song - reached into his heart and ripped it open exposing him to the
power of Love. He immediately collapsed, and sobbed. His lust for
power melted away, along with his misunderstanding of the very secrets
he had tried so hard to conceal. Abruptly, he was effortlessly scooped
up by the spirits - carried to the top of the mountain and brought to
stand before Jack, Alana and Apu. Confused and beset with so many
new emotions, Nathan stood stunned before the crowd. He surveyed
all of the faces he could see, most of them un-embodied. With a jolt, he
noticed someone he recognized. Staring directly through him was
Charles Tyler. Nathan felt his already thundering heart skip a beat. He
slumped and resolved to be condemned.

Jack silently drew him back with his genuine forgiveness and felt only love for this man. He spoke with a voice that was hardly his own, a voice that seemed to be joined by all the other beings in attendance.

"Nathan James, you, who have sought to conceal the truth, to kill us and stop this moment in history, it is you who we choose to represent us. *You* are our past. *You* are our fears and our ambitions. *You* are our duality. We embrace you in complete acceptance, love and reverence. We are One with you. You shall be the representative, for in this moment there are too many who come to the well, to count. But you are here, *you* shall be the flame that ignites the conscious shift of the whole, you are *the 100th human*." The last part was spoken in unison by every being present, the words thundered loudly and rolled throughout the mountainside and beyond. As the last syllable was uttered, every soul knelt down, including Jack, Alana and Apu. They gave forgiveness, unconditional love and reverence to their enemy. Only Nathan's shocked intake of breath could be heard as he stood in complete bewilderment.

As they rose to their feet again, Jack asked Nathan, "Do you accept this gift? Do you choose Love, Reverence for all life and Unity?"

"Yes." Nathan responded as his heart continued to expand. He knelt down in return, reciprocating the sentiments.

As soon as Nathan voiced his acceptance, a single, piercingly clear female voice rang out. All could hear her haunting melody encircle the mountain and then spread as if on wings. It carried to the far ends of the planet. In that moment, the sun flashed over the horizon, bathing the mountain in brilliant rays of orange, yellow and white light. Apu, Jack and Alana held on tight to each other's hands as the whole mountain began singing in unison. The energy was building, higher and higher, lighter and lighter. Light pierced every bit of darkness. Love encompassed the earth and all its inhabitants as a single halo, enveloping it, wholly. Each soul who was present on that mountain top was so encompassed with light, it beamed from their pours, from their eyes and from their finger tips. The Love filled every space possible. The song and energy reached a harmonic crescendo and spread with such force - to only equal a tidal wave of God's Love and Unity. *Instantly, it reached into every person on the planet.*

Total compassion reached deep down in their lives, their hearts and their minds. As if someone threw back the dim, dark curtains exposing the sun for the first time, light flooded into every nook and cranny of the globe. Each and every mind opened at once.

In that same identical second, on the other side of the world, Abdul was about to give the word that would launch two massive attacks trained on Israel and the U.S. When he felt the wave hit him, he saw the truth and fell to the ground. This time, he was not sick but, but full of love. The pilots on the plane carrying the bomb, felt the wave and for an instant, lost control of their airplane. After recovering, they turned around to head home. The drivers of the explosive laden automobiles, felt the wave hit them too. They turned around in retreat. Mission aborted.

Melvin rang his sister's doorbell worried about the late hour, only to be embraced so fully that he could hardly breathe. The wave hit them both, causing them to fall down on the stoop entangled in each other's arms, crying and laughing.

Marie was awake early, having been up with one of the boys. When the wave hit her, she dropped her cup onto the floor as she collapsed into her chair. Her husband was just coming into the room; he ran to her side and held on tightly.

Chuck had stayed that night in the hospital, after June's trouble the day before. They had almost lost her. Under the circumstances, Aunt Janet had allowed Jason to stay as well. Chuck sat by her bedside praying she would revive. The wave hit them; Chuck, Jason and June. Chuck gasped out as the air was knocked from his chest. He felt the hand in his move. June was smiling up at him and Jason. Chuck and Jason both bent over to hug her, crying like babies into her hospital gown.

Ben had been sleeping at Catherine's in the spare room. Before he had gotten down the block from her house, she had come running after him. Both of the children had the flu and Catherine wasn't feeling well either, so he offered to stay and help out. For some reason, for which Ben was very grateful, she trusted him and excepted his offer to help. He woke up when Mandy called for a hand the bathroom. On his way to her room, the wave hit him. He embraced the beautiful child and held on. His new life was in his arms. Catherine, with tears in her eyes, found them in the hallway. The new family embraced.

Joseph Charles Tyler felt the shift take place and instantly knew that Nathan had not succeeded but also felt completely thrilled with that failure. He finally comprehended the error of his ways and understood that they had it wrong all along. Veni Victus didn't mean to 'control life', it meant to *discover life*!' He realized that in the end the Veni Vici *provided* the 100th human. His heart expanded and then rested, releasing its long life. Joseph died over a sadly wasted life, but found a way to rejoice as he was granted forgiveness and insight in the final moment.

These and many more countless stories were told after that day. "Where were you when the 100th human accepted?" or "What were you doing when the 100th human wave hit you?" This remained the topic of conversations for years to come.

The news headlines were dramatically different that day. *In the Koreas – families reunite in the DMZ- soldiers put down their guns. Pope Alexander IX was delivering a morning prayer at St. Peters Basilica when the crowd was overcome by the wave and chanted, Hominae Centi, Hominae Centi – the 100th human. Rare white Buffalo was born in South Dakota.*

Jack, Alana and Apu knew intimately every other person on the planet when the wave hit. They could hear their thoughts and give theirs back. It was a massive telepathic link. In that moment, the exact time of the shift, their own bodies became fluid light, transcending all the limitations of duality.

The shift caused each person to open their hearts and minds to each other. Each individual knew beyond any doubt that they were truly the same, all connected, all One in God's Love.

It was a moment of opening, of changing, of being. It was a moment that could never be taken back. In that moment, we all knew each other, really knew each other and deeply loved. We all heard the same music, no matter the tongue. We connected at the deepest levels, heart to heart, mind to mind, and soul to soul. We finally and saw and *felt* each other for the first time.

Each of the Gatekeepers felt the leap in consciousness and shouted out, rejoicing. Sherman and Alice, Ram, Rene and Fritz, Jake and Sally, Rabbi Zimmerman, and Ida all connected to Jack, Apu and Alana and to all of the others simultaneously. They celebrated in the victory, knowing they had done their part, grateful for the opportunity.

Millions of people around the globe stopped in their tracks, looked up and smiled, reached out and hugged. They cried and laughed and touched. The keys were known by each and every one from rooftop to mountain top, from ocean side to riverside, from swampland to desert, from jungle to frozen tundra. They were understood in every language. *The quantum leap in consciousness united us.*

December 21st, 2012 was the end of duality's firm grip. It was the dawn of the Age of Unity, the Age of the Gods. It was forever known as the day we evolved into something new, something old, something timeless. Challenges still loomed ahead, but it was the dawn of a new day. *Our* new day. **Our new Age.**

AUTHOR'S NOTE

People have asked me what happens afterward. What does the new age look like? I think the answers already exist in our imaginations. I encourage you to find it in yours.

Investigation into the original research studies regarding The Hundredth Monkey, carried out in Japan, shows a more direct form of communication over time, between the individual monkeys using actions to translate the idea of washing potatoes.

It is this author's contention that this latter understanding does not cancel out the former (see Preface). Many believe that by debunking "the hundredth monkey phenomenon," they disprove any and all claims that would suggest a universal connection between each and every human on the planet or the suggestion that a quantum shift in human behavior is possible. Ken Keyes presented the story as a phenomenon. Dr. Rupert Sheldrake's theories regarding morphogenetic fields and critical mass are very authentic and the story serves to illustrate them.

Both ideas - a gradual change over time by direct contact, communication and interaction AND an immediate universal jump in behavior demonstrated by the majority of the whole, precipitated by a shift in a critical mass number - exist simultaneously and without conflict.

Never-the-less, each individual human can only take responsibility for their own actions and choices. Any paradigm shift that may take place in the human populace due to a critical mass in thinking and behaving is best left unto itself. Though it is my hope and dream that by introducing this idea to each of you individually, the awareness itself will create a positive change in your hearts and minds. Should this happen to enough people around the world, an evolutionary jump in consciousness is inevitable.

I hope you enjoyed the story and have realized that each and every one of us is, or can be *the 100th human*. This story grabbed hold of me and would not let me rest until it was written and offered to the public. The message of course, is hope and the knowing that every one of us can and do affect each other. Every decision we make can help change the consciousness of the whole, for the better. Real change comes at the individual level daily, and as enough of us choose the Keys set forth in this book, global change will happen. So YOU really are the 100th human. Embrace the keys to happiness, peace and new life. Share them. Live them. Evolve for yourself, for your children and for our planet.

JOIN THE EVOLUTION, ADOPT THE KEYS, AND BECOME THE 100TH HUMAN!

Continue the conversation at **www.the100thhuman.com**!

Namaste!

Chris Fenwick
January 2006

Chris Fenwick, a consummate optimist, artist and entrepreneur, has traveled the globe learning from societies, scientists and sages alike. Following the birth of her third child, she was captured by the story of the 100th human and not released until its successful publication in 2006, a year and a half later. She is a co-owner in three companies and lives in Central Pennsylvania with her partner and three children.

ORDER FORM

☐ Yes, I want _____ copies of **the 100th human**tm at $14.95 each, plus $3.00 shipping & handling per book (Pennsylvania residents please add .90¢ sales tax per book). Canadian orders must be accompanied by a postal money order in U.S. funds. Allow 15 days for delivery. Discounts are available for quantity purchases.

☐ My check or money order for $ _____ is enclosed. Please make checks payable to:
> **Sunbury Press, Inc.**
> P.O. Box 178
> New Kingstown, PA 17072-0178

☐ Please charge my: ☐ **VISA**   ☐ **MasterCard**   ☐ AMERICAN EXPRESS Cards

Name:
_____

Organization:
_____

Address:
_____

City/State/Zip:
_____

Phone: _____ Email: _____

Credit Card #: _____ Exp. Date: _____

Signature:
_____

You can also order online at: **www.sunburypress.com**. Or **call: (717) 422- 1494.**